Neil stared into the fire, and relived this day over and over. Could he have done anything differently? Could he really have ignored his feelings for Malise? He hadn't even realized he had feelings for her, till that night they sheltered from the rain together. At least she would have enough money; she wouldn't need to worry about that. And she had a position at the school. She was a pretty girl, someone would marry her. But it all came down to a single, harsh truth. Neil was no more in control of what he could do than she was. Than anyone was.

Diane Cosgrove was born and bred in Dundee; her grandmother was a weaver in the Dens Works, her father worked in Keiller's. Diane completed the '3Js' – jute, jam and journalism, for which the town is so famous – by becoming a journalist. She has also travelled Europe as a holiday rep and worked for a merchant bank in the City of London. When she isn't writing, Diane lives in Essex with her husband, two small children and a very large pile of ironing! *That Monroe Girl* is her first novel.

That Monroe Girl

DIANE COSGROVE

ORION

An Orion paperback

First published in Great Britain in 2003
by Orion
This paperback edition published in 2004
by Orion Books Ltd,
Orion House, 5 Upper St Martin's Lane,
London WC2H 9EA

A CIP catalogue record for this book
is available from the British Library.

ISBN 0 75284 285 4

Typeset at The Spartan Press Ltd,
Lymington, Hants

Printed and bound in Great Britain
by Clays Ltd, St Ives plc

For Daisy Donegan

Acknowledgements

The author would like to thank the following people for their contributions:

Staff of the Verdant Works in Dundee, and Dundee City Libraries for their research assistance and Angela, Helen, Nobby, Jeremy and John of the Havering Writers' Circle for their unflinching support.

Lastly, Elizabeth Wright, Kirsty Fowkes, Kate Mills and Nicky Jeanes for turning my dream into a book.

Chapter 1

'I don't think it's a good idea, Malise.' Gabriel Monroe scratched at the dark stubble on his chin as he walked out of his bedroom, his heavy working boots scraping over the bare floorboards. He yawned then took his seat at the worn table and waited for her to serve him with breakfast. 'You'll only get turned away. They'll love doing that to my daughter.' He looked around the darkened room that served as kitchen, living room and Malise's bedroom, courtesy of a bed that was pulled down from the wall every night. 'And where the hell's that draught coming from?'

'The window's sticking again and when I got the milk off the sill this morning, I couldn't get it closed,' Malise replied as she opened the tiny iron door of the range to throw another few sticks on the meagre fire. 'And maybe I want to be a clerk, Daddy, have you considered that?' She turned to her father, her petite face red from the sudden blast of heat.

'You'll be a schoolmistress, and then you'll be a councillor, me and Gordon Scott have it all worked out,' her father grumbled as he went over to the solitary window, opened the short faded curtains patterned with dog roses, and hauled down the lower portion of the pane till the rain-swollen wood slammed against the cracked frame. 'You're doing it to try and impress that suffragette woman and her cronies who won't even let you stand up on the bandstand with them. They're all firm believers in the rights for women, aren't they? As long as they speak posh and live in big houses.' The anger which bubbled from his dark-brown eyes and to the firm set of his high cheekbones gave him a

1

stern expression as he raised his foot and nudged her out of the way of the range, the sole heat in the house. 'Get your arse out of the way, you're sucking up all the warm!'

'I want to vote,' she replied. 'That way everyone, including the union, will have to listen to me. You'll have to do as I say.' She smiled cheekily as she raised her forefinger and pretended to scold him. Gabriel considered her; from the unruly brown hair and small, springy build, to her quick-silver temper and way with words, Malise was all his. And every day he felt a flush of pride at the way she was such a mirror of him.

'You might get your vote and be equal to me,' Gabriel said as he drank his tea, 'but you'll never be equal to a jute baron. And that's the fight you should be involved in. This is 1913, workers like you and me built this place from a wee market town to the richest city in Scotland and what do we have to show for it? A few families that own everything, a member of parliament who is English and a close personal friend of the King, and the rest of us living like rats, piled on top of each other without so much as a sink in the house!' Gabriel scraped his chair on the tiny, faded patch of rug as he reached for the bread that was sitting on the table, grey and speckled with the beginnings of furry mould. 'Any hough left?' He cut off a thick chunk of bread, pulling off the mould, before spreading it with dripping. 'And you want to give their wives and daughters even more.'

'That was for your dinner!' she said in resigned despair. 'And I just spent hours typing letters to the mills in Paisley asking what their wages were and how much rent they had to pay!' Malise rescued the crust Gabriel had discarded and, wiping off the fur, she spread some dripping on it. 'Didn't see any of your fellow unionists bothering to help you on that score.'

'I trust you to spell the word "rent" correctly.' Gabriel ran his fingers through his hair in a fruitless attempt to tidy it up. 'You and Gordon Scott are worth more than so many of those other bloody union men on the committee. They think it's all sitting in pubs talking revolution. Never occurred to them to fight with their brains.'

'That's why I'm going.' She chewed the hard piece of bread. 'So I won't get the job. Even though I'm the best.'

'I'm going to get into trouble from the brothers for this.' Gabriel gave a mock sigh. 'My wee lass trying to take a man's job from him.'

'Do you care?' Malise looked up at her father with softness in her eyes.

'Not really.' He began to brush down his jacket as Malise cleared the tiny wooden table, taking out a deep bowl from the small yellow press that held all their crockery and pouring the remaining hot water into it.

'But what I want to know, Malise,' her father stood and waited as she cut the last of the bread into two and spread the halves with the remaining hough, 'is what you're going to do if Blaine Hamilton offers you the job?'

'He isn't going to offer me the job.' She wrapped the sandwiches in brown paper before handing them to him. 'Firstly, I'm a wee lassie, remember, and secondly, I'm *your* wee lassie. That probably makes me the person least likely to end up slaving in that place.'

'It's a braw wee clerk's job, Malise,' Gabriel interrupted her. 'A decent job, better than what I'd ever have managed.'

'But you're a cart driver, and the convenor of the works, and no matter how many mathematical examinations I pass, I'll never get to be either of those,' she replied. 'Thought you ran that place, while Fraser sat in his office drinking whisky and making calls on his telephone machine.' A smile played about her father's fine cheekbones. 'Surely you, a fine upstanding member of the Independent Labour Party, and convenor of the Elizabeth Works to boot, wouldn't lie to his only child?'

'Like I'd get away with it.' He kissed her on the top of her head. 'Just remember to keep to your principles, and give Blaine Hamilton what for. That man thinks he's better than everyone else, just for wearing a tie to work.'

3

'Will you be in tonight, or are you seeing that Gertie Henderson again?' Malise asked as she snuggled into his woollen waistcoat, breathing in Gabriel's familiar smell of jute and tobacco.

'I don't know who you mean, Malise.'

'That fat, ginger-haired schoolteacher who keeps trying to get me to listen more and to talk less.' She put on a voice as she said it. 'The one you were walking through Lochee Park with the other night.'

'You're far too nosy for your own good, Malise Monroe. And don't worry, you'll not be seeing Gertie again. I was just seeing her home,' he chuckled.

'So I'll not be getting a new mammy?' She raised her eyebrows.

Gabriel laughed and shook his head. 'Me and you, we're fine just the way we are, aren't we?'

'Aye, Dad,' she returned. 'Even if Mrs Baker thinks that you are bringing me up as a lad and no a lass.'

'You'll be the death of me, Malise Monroe.' He grabbed his thick corduroy jacket and threw it over his frame.

'Only if they hang ye.' She waited for him to leave before sitting back down and pouring herself half a cup of tea from the dregs of the teapot and steeling herself for the day ahead.

Two hours later, she sat in the shipping office of the Elizabeth Works, one of the largest jute spinning and weaving factories in Dundee, up the stairs from where her father worked. She was wearing her Sunday dress and shoes, polished till she could see her face in them, and her best pair of lisle stockings, which had only a few darns in them. She had tied her curly brown hair into a schoolmistress's bun in order to make herself presentable. She looked so presentable, in fact, that she caught the attention of all the boys waiting to be seen.

'What are you here for?' One of them, a skinny youth not much taller than her own five feet and wearing a shirt and

4

tie he had obviously borrowed from his larger father, caught her gaze.

'For the clerk's job,' she replied confidently. He laughed.

'Lassies can't be clerks, it's a man's job,' he said loftily.

'If it's a man's job, then you're wasting your time an' all,' she returned. ' 'Cause I can't see any men here.'

'Like to see them wipe that smile off your face,' the boy retorted, discomfited.

Malise turned her head and examined the room, to take her mind off the interview ahead. It was impressive; heavy wood and expensive furniture surrounded her, and any one of the paintings on the wall could have heated her school for the winter ahead. She could feel the butterflies gathering in her stomach; suddenly, coming into the works and getting herself thrown out didn't seem like a good idea any more. She touched the polished mahogany panelling and left a fingerprint. Panicking, she grabbed her sleeve and tried to polish it away but it just smudged. Things were getting worse.

Malise tried to swallow but her mouth was dry. Then the door opened and an elderly man, knife-thin and sharp, with slick black hair and a drooping moustache, walked in. She presumed him to be Blaine Hamilton, the head clerk. The tall young man, with broad shoulders, piercing blue eyes and a gold watch that shone out of his waistcoat, she knew must be Neil Fraser himself.

'I'll see you later, Blaine.' The younger man looked dismissively round at the four young people sitting in the reception area as he brushed away a stray black hair that fell over his face with a large, confident hand, his signet ring gleaming on his little finger. 'Why is she here?'

'I've been invited to come for an interview as apprentice, mister, sir.' Malise could feel the familiar bubble of words tumbling out.

'Blaine, why have you invited a girl?'

'There are no females down on the list, Mr Fraser. John Hall, Edward Turton, Finbar Douglas and Malise Monroe.'

5

Blaine Hamilton turned to Malise. 'And which one are you, then?' he said curtly.

'I'm Malise.' She stood up and walked towards them, hand outstretched as she had practised. 'Pleased to meet you.' Her hand remained in mid-air as Hamilton stared at it disapprovingly.

'You can go home,' he said.

'But I scored top marks in the mathematics test you set last month for the schools, sir,' Malise replied politely, her hand still in mid-air. 'I'm sure that I could do the job.'

'You're a girl.' The head clerk stared at her pugnaciously.

Malise couldn't hide her surprise, then she looked down quickly. So she wasn't even going to get a hearing.

'It was the dress that gave it away, wasn't it?' She left her hand outstretched, although it was beginning to ache. 'But why do you need a boy to train? What's wrong with giving me the opportunity . . .'

'But your name – it's a boy's name.'

'My daddy was too busy celebrating my birth to ask what sex I was, sir.' She was emboldened by a few chuckles behind her. 'But why does it make a difference? Surely, if I'm clever enough to score one hundred per cent in the test . . . ?'

'Been listening to the Pankhursts, have we?'

Malise turned to see the younger man standing there with an amused expression. He had friendly eyes, but his bearing was such that she knew he was important. She hadn't needed to hear Blaine Hamilton call him Fraser. He even smelt like he owned the works.

'It's not illegal, sir.' She had to fight to keep her eyes on him. For some reason, he made her want to look at her feet.

The man bent down, till his head was at the same level as hers.

'Have you never heard that young ladies should be seen and not heard?'

'I'm not a lady, sir.' She tore her eyes away from his perfectly cut waistcoat and found his expression wasn't angry, he was looking at her curiously. 'But I have been

6

taught by my father that when you meet someone for the first time, you shake hands.'

'I don't shake hands with the workforce, even the ladies in it.' He laughed drily and stretched up again. 'You know where the door is, whatever your name is.'

'Won't you tell me why you won't employ a girl to do the work?' She heard her voice come out, higher than usual. 'I am clever, hard-working, clean and honest.' To her surprise, he just laughed again. She felt him take her arm and propel her gently towards the door.

'Run off back to school, wee girl. Or you can go and ask one of the foremen if you can start by sweeping the floor. In a few years you can do some typing, you seem like a bright enough girl.' His face was mild and friendly, as if he actually thought he was giving her good advice. Bridling with anger, Malise swallowed down the insult.

'Of course, Mr Fraser,' she returned. 'I think this place could certainly do with a good clean out.' There was silence as Neil Fraser took in her words.

'Quite a tongue in your head, girl,' he said warningly. 'Be careful, or it will get you into trouble.' He opened the door for her and gestured in the direction of the wooden stair-case.

'Get me those figures for this afternoon, Blaine.' With that Neil Fraser swept out of the office, following Malise as she walked loudly down the stairs to the factory floor where the spun jute was woven.

Strangely exhilarated and yet angry, Malise walked past the enormous machines, each of them rhythmically weaving, their shuttles going up and down, side to side with a hypnotically deafening clatter. The strong, oily smell of jute was in the air, she could see tiny hairs in front of her, like dust in twilight. The rough, heavy air caught in her throat and she coughed. All around her people were standing at their looms, careful fingers going in and out of each machine as the thread caught. Some were neighbours, who waved or nodded, but most just stared intently at the weave

7

and the waft. Not to concentrate could mean losing a finger, or even a hand.

'Malise!' Gabriel strode up to her through the misty air, carrying a large pile of sacks. 'How did you get on?'

'I didn't even get to make my speech!' she said with childish sulkiness. 'They just laughed at me as if it was all a joke. I was serious and they just laughed at me as if I was nothing!' She moved her shoulders uncomfortably. Down in the factory it was almost unbearably hot, and the air felt as if it had been scraped off the floor.

'Did you give Hamilton what for?' Her father grinned.

'Even better. Fraser's son, Neil, threw me out on my ear.'

'Shh, he's coming now.' Gabriel winked at Malise. 'You did yourself proud.' He kissed her quickly on the cheek. 'Now back to school or Mr Scott will be on the warpath.'

Neil Fraser stood at the foot of the stairs and watched the exchange. He should have realized. She was Gabriel Monroe's girl. It had been a set-up, by that bloody agitator who seemed to spend more time stirring up the workforce or standing in his office asking for more money, more breaks for the workers. Neil glowered at Gabriel, who blithely ignored him. Then, as he reached the man, Gabriel's expression changed.

'Mr Fraser?' Gabriel said confidently as he strode up to him. 'Have you thought any more about what we talked about? About a wage increase because they've put up the rents again?'

'Not now, Monroe,' Neil said dismissively. 'Talk to the works manager.' Neil wanted out of the factory. He hated the smell of jute, and the ever-present demands of the workforce. 'I have other things to do.' With that he pushed past the smaller man, and went out into the yard where his chauffeur was polishing his large black car.

'I need to go to the dock office,' he said shortly. 'Looks like we've just lost a whole shipment. Ship's been lost.' With that he got in and took a deep breath. Together with the

8

shipment, the profits for the next month were now at the bottom of the ocean.

'So, thrown ourselves on our sword, have we?' A few hours later, after Malise had reported to Miss Proctor, head of the local suffragettes, she had wandered back down the mud-caked cobbled streets to the little ramshackle school that served the nearby courts of the Overgate, one of the poorest areas in the town. 'Could have done with you earlier, what with the School Board visit coming up and hardly anything to show them.'

'Yes, Mr Scott.' Malise squirmed in the wooden chair that was fixed to the old, scratched desk in front of her. 'Got thrown out.'

'It was what you wanted, Malise,' Gordon Scott continued as he rapped on the desk with his fountain pen. 'To prove your point.'

'I know, Mr Scott.' She smiled wistfully at the elderly schoolteacher who was hunched in his wheelchair. 'It's just that I don't feel as right as I ought to . . .' she shrugged and looked round at the damp plaster on the walls, a cold draught from the broken window gently lifting up the cracks. It was so different from the room she had been waiting in at the factory. It was like comparing a cowshed to a palace.

'First time anyone's told you that you aren't good enough, Malise?' he said sympathetically. 'Get used to it. You're poor and you're female and there is nothing you can do to change that.' He looked down at the stumps where his legs used to be. 'No matter how hard you try, you just can't change it.' He patted her on the knee and wheeled himself out to the class, his chair rattling over the uneven, cracked floorboards.

Malise stared at her leg. Mr Scott, a man, had touched her knee!

All day she tried to concentrate on her work, but all she could think of was that a man had touched her, and

9

everyone knew what that meant. What would her father say, what would happen to her? Would she have to marry Mr Scott, what would happen if he denied it? She wouldn't be able to be a pupil teacher any more. Everything was ruined, because of Mr Scott. She had to speak to Jessie, but the hours had grown extra minutes and she found herself praying for the bell to ring.

'Malise, you can stay behind for some extra French if you want,' Mr Scott said as the rest of the class left at the end of the day.

'I have to go to the steamie,' Malise mumbled as she stood up and gathered her books together. 'Wash day.'

Gordon Scott laughed.

'Your father may profess to wanting you to make something of yourself, Malise,' he said almost fondly. 'But he's also turning you into the perfect wife.'

She rushed back towards Lochee, running up the stairs two at a time, till she reached her house on the third floor. She got out the wicker basket that lay under her bed, and piled up all the washing into Gabriel's bed sheet before tying it in a large knot to stop any escaping. Then she braced herself for the long walk to the wash house with the heavy basket. But as she got out into the road, she had an unexpected stroke of luck.

'Malise!' It was Tommy, one of her neighbours, a pale-faced boy with the sturdy legs of a pony. 'You want a hand with that?'

'Aye, Tommy,' she replied. 'Let's have a wee go of your cartie.'

The boy obliged, pushing his youngest brother off the cart, which was little more than an orange box on three wheels with a thick jute rope at the front. Together they lifted the basket on to the cart and Tommy put the rope over his shoulder.

'You need me to carry it back afterwards?' he asked as they walked amiably along a road full of men and women walking home after their long day in the works, their faces sallow with exhaustion and the remnants of jute.

'Please,' she said distractedly. What if Jessie wasn't there?

They reached the steamie and once Malise had unloaded the heavy basket, Tommy waved and wandered off in the direction of Lochee High Street, where his friends, who were also earning a penny transporting washing, were having a race. She paid her money to the red-faced attendant and went into the hot, humid wash room, looking for an empty stall. The floor was already running with soapy water, and children splashed past, dragging washing behind them. She found a stall with a bench and a copper. Pouring the water into the deep cauldron, Malise tried to forget her trouble for a moment as she got out her scrubbing brush and soap for her father's collars and cuffs, all the time looking out for Jessie, her best friend and confidante. Eventually the water was warm enough, and she loaded in the bed sheets and clothes, throwing in a handful of Persil soap flakes as she did so.

'Malise, I was looking everywhere for you.' Jessie Baker, a ginger-haired girl of sixteen pushed past the stream of children and stood on the pallet next to Malise, her face bright red from exertion and the heat. 'Ours are just steep-ing now.'

'Oh Jessie,' Malise squeaked. 'I think I've caught a baby.'

Jessie looked round, but the other women were too concerned in getting their washing done and the children were busy in a never-ending game of tig.

'What on earth have you done?' she asked, horrified. 'And who was it?'

'Mr Scott,' Malise wailed. 'We were talking and he put his hand on my knee.'

Jessie considered the statement for a moment.

'Malise, don't you know where babies come from?'

'Of course I do. They come from men touching you.' Malise chewed her lip. 'But he did it so quickly, I couldn't move away.'

'Malise, what have you been doing, letting Mr Scott touch you?' Jessie was agog.

Betweens sobs, Malise retold what had happened to her, handing her future over to the wisdom of a doctor's kitchen maid.

'You don't catch a baby by touching, Malise,' Jessie said sternly. 'A man has to make his thing get big then he wees inside you. And you have to kiss him first. And your curse stops.'

The look of disgust on Malise's face spoke volumes.

'You can't get a baby from his thing, can you? And how can he make it get big? Surely it's the size it is.'

'But when you kiss him, you inflame his carnal desires and it gets a foot long. And goes purple,' Jessie informed her. 'Imagine you not knowing that?' She giggled. 'Did Mr Scott's winkie grow big?'

'Don't be daft, Jessie, his legs aren't a foot long!' Malise retorted. 'You're scarlet, so you are.' She hesitated for a moment. 'So I'm definitely not having a baby?'

Jessie shook her head.

'My sister said you have to take your drawers off anyway, and you had them on, didn't you?'

'Never took them off!' Malise jumped up and down, splashing water over her skirt and whooping with glee.

'D'you want to come for your tea?' Jessie smiled at her friend's antics.

Malise shrugged.

'Dad's out at a union meeting, so I was only going to have bread and dripping . . .' She wiped the gathering sweat from her brow with a sleeve that clung to her in the wet air.

'Come on, then, I'll tell Ma.' Jessie giggled. 'Imagine you thinking you'd get a baby from Mr Scott putting his hand on your knee.'

'Come on, Jessie, I'll need help with the mangle,' Mrs Baker said heartily as she came up to them. 'No time for blethering.' She nodded at Malise. 'Tell you what, you help me with the mangle, then you can come back and help

Malise with getting her clothes rinsed.' She walked away to find someone to chat to.

'Leave me with all the work to do.' Jessie made a face at her mother's retreating back. 'Well, I'll come back and see you in a minute,' she said to Malise, then walked away, her eyes peeled for other friends.

After half an hour, the floor was swimming with water, but Malise had rinsed her clothes and dragged them over to the mangles, before loading them on to a wooden horse to dry. She could come back after tea to collect them, if she didn't fall asleep first. Luckily Jessie lived only a few streets away, in a tenement on Lochee High Street. As they walked up the street with Jessie's mother, they saw Cox's stack, the enormous chimney in the middle of the Camperdown Works, steaming away as usual.

'Must be the highest point in Dundee,' Jessie said as she looked up at the chimney.

'Except the Law Hill,' Malise returned. 'That was a volcano once, you know.'

'I mean the tallest building.' Jessie poked Malise in the ribs good-naturedly.

'Aye.' Mrs Baker, Jessie's mother, looked up at the stack. 'You cannae help but be proud when you see it. My spinning made that stack what it is. Good place to work, that.'

'Be even better if they increased your money to meet the new rents, Mrs Baker.' Malise looked up at the stack. Why was it so high?

'I'm a woman, can't expect to be paid a man's rate,' she said benignly.

'Why not?'

'Because men's work is harder. And if your father would stop filling your head with all that nonsense about workers' rights and letting you go to those suffragette meetings, you might be able to see it.' Mrs Baker looked up and down. 'Making you be a schoolteacher, indeed! You'll end up an old maid. No man wants a wife who knows more than him.'

13

They walked up the tenement and went in the door, only to be accosted by the smell of burning pea soup.

'Och, Keith, did you not notice the smell?' But there was no reply. 'He'll be down at the pub again,' she said despairingly. 'Well, we'll have the wee bit that's not too burned.'

Malise sat down to eat with Jessie and her mother. Jessie's father worked shifts in the shipyard with her brother and so it was just the women of the family. Mrs Baker talked incessantly about Sheila, her eldest daughter, who was now married and having her third child.

'Just think, Malise, you're getting on for sixteen now,' she said with a smile. 'Soon be your turn.'

'Isn't it Jessie's first?' Malise made a face at her friend.

'What I meant was that our Keith's looking for a young lady, and we know you're a clean-living girl. You should go out together, you'd have a lot in common. Keep you away from the Monkey Parade. All those young lads and lasses, parading up and down. Getting up to all sorts of business.' She pursed her lips.

Malise shrugged. Keith had a good job repairing trawlers, unlike many of his peers who were unemployed kettle boilers, but at only twenty he had already lost what ginger hair he had, and smelt permanently of fish.

'I've got my eye on someone.' She tried an innocent stare.

'She means Johnnie Turpin,' Jessie interrupted as Malise blushed.

'I do not, you fancy him, yourself. You told me!' Malise cried.

'You two will stay away from that family!' Mrs Baker said indignantly. 'That Turpin family are a bad lot, and especially that Johnnie. He's got a wandering eye for a pretty girl and you'll ruin your chances if you go anywhere near him, Malise. And I mean it!'

After dinner, the two girls washed up, and Jessie and Malise returned to the steamie to collect their laundry. Tommy was there with his cart, eager for the penny he would earn for this job.

'Come back round after you've hung those up,' Jessie said amiably. 'I've got the stairs to wash, but after that we can go for a turn round the park if you want.'

Malise shook her head.

'Got to clean out the lavvie, then go to the library, I've got things to look up. I'm giving my first speech on Sunday in Magdalen Green.'

'You, a speech?' Jessie's eyes opened wide.

Malise nodded.

'You know how I went for that job, well, Miss Proctor is giving a speech and I have to stand up and tell everyone what happened.'

'In front of people?'

'Only if they turn up.'

'Everyone turns up for the suffragettes.'

'Everyone turns up for the punch-up afterwards,' Malise wiped away the sweat that had formed on her forehead after only a few minutes in the wash house, 'to see if any posh women get dragged away by the police and show their drawers.' She tucked a stray sleeve back into the basket. 'So are you coming?'

'Of course,' Jessie replied. 'I wouldn't miss your first speech for the world. Wait till I tell Mammy and Sheila. They'll be made up.'

Together, Tommy and Malise pulled the cart back to her home. She gave him a penny, then wrestled the snow-white washing up the stairs, hanging it neatly on the horse that was suspended from the ceiling of the kitchen and filling the house with a damp, clean smell.

But there was no time to admire her handiwork, it was her turn to clean the communal lavatory in the stairwell. Sighing, she took out the bowl and cleaning powder, and her large scrubbing brush. 'And Mr Johnson,' she called loudly, 'if you've been getting drunk and weeing on the floor again, I'll kill you.'

She cleaned the communal lavatory as quickly as she could, then returned to her house to pick up her papers. As she did so she looked at her hands – they were red and sore from constant immersion in water and the soap and vinegar mixture she had used for her chores. Perhaps, at the weekend, she would go down to the arcade and get some hand cream, if she could manage to save a few pennies from the housekeeping before her father took it all for his Friday-night drinking. But for the moment, she would have to make do with a bit of margarine. She rubbed some into her hands, the oily substance unpleasant against her fingers, however it made little difference to the chapped skin.

Malise then gathered some paper and a pencil, which she put into her bag before steeling herself to go out again. She walked down the Logie Road towards the centre of town, and then through the back of the Wellgate till she came to Ward Road. There stood the library, an enormous dark building, the heavy Victorian decoration gloomy and full of secrets. She pulled out a piece of paper on which she had written the two names Gordon Scott had told her. Mary Wollstonecraft and John Stuart Mill. They would give her the background she needed, the words that she wanted to use. She was going to show the ladies in the League that she was no silly little working-class girl. She could hold her own with the richest and most educated of them. She'd been one of Miss Proctor's foot soldiers long enough. Now she was going to be an officer.

'Get what you wanted?' Gabriel was home and sitting looking over the *Courier* in the light from the gas mantle.

'I did, but I don't know if it is the right thing to say.' Malise took off her coat and beret and hung them up on the peg.

'Never mind, first speech is always just a practice,' Gabriel said consolingly. 'You'll write a better one tomorrow.'

'Do you want to hear it?' She took off her leaking shoes,

careful not to place them too close to the fire, so that they wouldn't crack as they dried.

'Go on then,' Gabriel said as he sat back. 'Impress me.'

'It's good, Malise, really good,' Gabriel said, considering her words. 'Do that again and you'll have the crowd in the palm of your hand.'

Malise looked at her father.

'Do you mean that? I mean, I don't want to let you down. Everyone knows you are a good speaker.'

Gabriel took his daughter in his arms, holding her small body against his.

'You couldn't let me down, Malise,' he said fondly. 'You can't let anyone down if you try your hardest. You can fail, but if you did all you could do, then you haven't let them down.'

'I know you think this is a waste of time,' she replied.

'You're right, you know, Malise.' He stopped as she moved his feet off the range and put the kettle on the black lead top. 'If you want to be someone, you need to be able to influence who talks in parliament.'

'But it doesn't always make a difference though, does it, Daddy?' She said as she got out two cups. 'Doesn't give us water in our houses, or put clothes on our backs.'

'When you're on the council, Malise, you'll tear down every slum in Dundee.'

'Why don't you do it yourself?' Malise carefully unwrapped the small screw of tea.

'After eight years in the Elizabeth I have a reputation, mind you I've earned it, but people are wary of me. They've no inkling of what it was like with Old Man Fraser. He thought his workers were the scum of the earth. At least the new Fraser's a wee bit more modern. In the year he's been there, he's given us more than his father did in ten. But he's just like the others, really – at the end o' the day he'd close that place and move to India if he thought there was a penny more profit in it.' Her father exhaled deeply. 'He doesn't know what it's like to be poor and do a job that can rip off your fingers, or to have a cough which turns into consumption while you can't afford the medication to keep you alive. He walked into that job not because he's clever, but because Old Man Fraser is a lazy bastard. And when he talks about everyone having to tighten their belts, he'll never know what it's like to have to take your clothes to Uncle, just to feed your bairns. If only I could make him see that, if only someone could make him understand, he would be a good man. You can see it in his eyes. He just needs an education.'

Malise sat down with her tea and looked at her father, who had returned to his reading. He believed in Neil Fraser. But he hadn't seen the way he had laughed at her, as if the whole idea was ridiculous. Just because he'd not been dismissed, he couldn't understand how she had been. She would prove herself to him. And she'd make him proud.

Chapter 2

That Sunday, Malise was up early, ready for the weekly suffragette demonstration. She hadn't slept much the night before and had practised her speech so many times that she didn't need her crib notes.

'Dad?' She said as she went through to his tiny window-less bedroom, holding a cup of tea. 'Are you awake?'

But her only reply was a grunt. Gabriel had been out the night before, she had heard him come in less than one hour ago. He wouldn't be attending her first ever speech. In a way it was a relief; she wanted her father to hear her, but only if he could be proud of her. She didn't want him to be disappointed.

'I'll be away now,' she said softly as she put on her hat and thin coat, lacing up her second-best pair of shoes. But her father had already turned over and gone back to sleep.

The walk to Magdalen Green took her past churches, their congregations spilling out of them, friends meeting up. Malise looked longingly at the families, mothers and daughters, grandmothers and little children, preparing to go home for a Sunday lunch together. Her father had a real hatred for the church, but she could remember going to it when she had lived with the Bakers. They were Catholics and Mrs Baker marshalled everyone, even Mr Baker, still full of his Saturday-night drinking, to the church for mass every Sunday. Even if her father had allowed her to go when she had gone back to live with him, it still wouldn't have given her brothers and sisters, aunts and uncles. Her father said they were fine as they were, so Malise did her best to believe him.

She crossed the road and went past the entrance of the Elizabeth Works, where the heavy gates were closed, and only a little smoke came from the watch-room chimney. When she reached the top of the road, she could see the River Tay glistening in the sharp sunlight, as if the waves themselves were dipped in silver. She headed down past the clean, posh tenements and villas that led to the Perth Road. The clerks, solicitors and doctors lived here, those with wives who had no need to work and who instead raised children with clean faces in houses which had sinks and taps and windows.

Eventually she got to the park, where Miss Proctor was waiting by the bandstand, looking out at the Tay Bridge as she paced up and down with her usual nervous vigour.

'Not much of a crowd,' Miss Proctor said pensively. 'Let's hope the sun keeps shining. People don't want to stand in the rain.'

Malise studied her shoes. She never knew whether Miss Proctor was asking her a question or making a statement.

'I've practised my speech,' Malise said nervously.

'It's not a speech, you are simply to say a few words about what happened when you went to the works. I am the one who will be making the speech.' Miss Proctor drew herself up to her full height. She was a tall woman, and had a sharp mind.

The crowd was gathering now, people who had come straight from church, weavers wearing hats and gloves, spinners wearing neither, and the unemployed in the uniform of parish clothing. Malise watched them promenade along the wide green gardens that surrounded the bandstand and swept up to a copse of thick trees and bushes; they were a group of people who lived in small, tied houses, leading small, tied lives. There were a few visitors from out of town, mostly university students. It was easy in Dundee to tell who were visitors. They were tall, and could breathe all day without coughing. Finally, Miss Proctor was satisfied with the attendance of her middle-class officers, who joined her on the bandstand, and the working-class foot soldiers, who were allowed to stand round it, clap and do the heavy lifting.

'Get the drum.' Miss Proctor scanned the crowd for notable faces. 'Oh good, over by those trees. The Frasers and the Dorans are here.' She turned and ostentatiously waved to the foot soldiers at the back and, on cue, Bessie Templeton, who worked in a coal yard and had the arms of an ox, began to bang her drum. Malise listened with half an ear as Miss Proctor began to lecture the crowd. Because that was what she did. She talked *at* them, not *to* them.

'Even our illustrious Member of Parliament, Winston Churchill, has finally realized that women, for so long the backbone of the parties, can be of more use than simply an amusing distraction from politics, and that women can give honest, well-informed opinions. We understand about international trade, because so many of us work. We understand about budgets, since we have to stretch our housekeeping in so many ways, and we understand the need for a strong moral backbone for the country since we are the home-makers, the providers . . .'

'How many times have you heard that dried-up old spinster haver on with the same old speech?' Bessie said in a whisper. 'You'd think, since she doesn't work, she'd have the time to write a new one.'

'Hang on,' Malise said quietly. 'Just wait and see what I've got to say.'

'. . . and still we aren't given a chance to prove ourselves,' Miss Proctor continued. 'Now here we have a young girl, cruelly denied the chance to serve Dundee. Simply because she was born into the so-called gentler sex.'

Malise elbowed her way past the ladies on the bandstand till she stood in front of the crowd of about two hundred people. Don't fix your eye on any one person, unless they are causing trouble, her father had told her. So she looked at some of the people on the fringes of the crowd.

'All my life I have been good at mathematics,' she began.

'In fact my teachers thought me so good as to allow me to sit the mathematics test that is held every year for apprentice clerks. And I scored so highly in it that I was invited to attend an interview with no fewer than three works.' She held her hands up. 'Of course, they didn't know I wore a dress. But, as soon as I arrived at the Elizabeth Works, that little mistake was put to rights. I thought the owner's son would drop dead on the spot. All I wanted was a chance. A chance to work for them, a chance to help the very trade that has put food on my table. But I was being a fool. Because, according to Mr Neil Fraser, all I was fit for was sweeping the floor. I had scored one hundred per cent in the test, but I wasn't good enough for the Elizabeth.' She stopped and looked around at the crowd, she had certainly caught their attention.

'And why was I refused even a hearing?' Malise's voice rose clear and loud above the crowd. 'Not because I was incompetent, not because I couldn't answer questions, not because I wasn't clever enough.' She paused for effect. 'Simply because I wear a dress.' She smiled around at the rapt expressions of the women present. 'And then I was thrown out of the factory by the owner's son. Down the stairs, head first. He didn't think I was so much a woman he couldn't manhandle me.'

Horrified silence reigned, and Malise felt a shot of exhilaration.

'Why can't I do a job I am obviously capable of doing?' she called to the women present. 'I'm not taking the job from anyone else, I just want the right to be considered as an equal. If I'm no good, then I shouldn't get it. But if a girl is the best candidate for the job, then who can say that she shouldn't be the person who gets the position?'

'Thank you, Miss Monroe.' Miss Proctor had appeared at her shoulder and gripped Malise's arm with iron-tight fingers. 'Leave them to me,' she hissed.

'But—' Malise began.

'Ladies, this is another example of how we are not treated

as equals,' Miss Proctor shouted. And Malise headed back, rubbing her arm.

'How dare she?' Neil Fraser, walking back from the Green with his father, tried to vent his frustration, without drawing attention to himself.

'Is it true?' Richard Fraser looked at his son, as his heavy brogues crunched over the path.

'I was so stupid!' He thumped his gloved hands together. 'It was all staged for this, she's her father's daughter, all right. That bloody Monroe girl is up there telling all sorts of lies in order to help her father.' He tightened his lips. 'And to think I offered her a job as a secretary!'

'It's your own fault, Neil.' Richard acknowledged a greeting from an acquaintance. 'You are getting yourself a reputation as a soft owner. The young one straight from university who gives in to everything the union asks for.'

'Or perhaps I have simply been bringing conditions in the Elizabeth up to those enjoyed by workers in other factories,' Neil returned defensively.

'There's a fight going on, and the union have scented your weakness. I told you that improving both the rates and the hours at the same time wouldn't give you an ounce of goodwill, but no, you ignored me. And now Gabriel Monroe and his daughter can malign you in front of Dundee and you can't do a damn thing about it. You're a fool, Neil, and it's about time you learned that when you want the likes of these donkeys down there to work, a stick works better than a carrot every time!'

Neil stared at his father. He was clearly enjoying this, living proof that Neil and his ideas had come to nothing, and that the factory should have remained as it was – one of the lowest-paying in Dundee, with a workforce who worked out of fear.

'What should I do?' Neil said quietly. 'I suppose that this means I shouldn't consider Monroe's request for a rate increase to meet the new rent rises?'

'Exactly,' Richard replied implacably. 'If you did, then the

23

whole city would know the Frasers have lost control of their own works.'

'I was only trying to make life better for them,' his son said slowly.

'Why didn't I send you to India and keep Dick here!' Richard said in mock despair. 'But you'd only end up paying them Scottish rates too.' He shook his head and walked away, clicking his fingers as if he were ordering a dog to follow him. Neil sighed and obediently followed. That Monroe girl had forced him into a corner, now he had no way to give the workers a rate increase without losing his dignity, his status. There was no way his father would let him.

They walked back to their house, a large, pale-granite mansion set in leafy, secluded grounds not far from Magdalen Green. Richard continued his rant about Neil's inadequacies as the butler took their coats and hats in the mahogany-panelled hallway which was littered with imposing oil paintings of stern-faced men. He stopped only when they reached the conservatory at the end of the passage. Inside, Neil's mother Elizabeth, his brother Dick and his new wife Madeleine were chatting – Dick was explaining how vanilla was extracted from the orchids that his mother grew there.

'Hello, Mother,' Neil said, as he bent to kiss her on the cheek, the soft scent of violets coming up to greet him. 'And hello, Madeleine. I can't look at you without wondering how a lovely lady such as yourself should want to take up with a ruffian such as my brother.'

'Simply because he has even more charm than his younger brother.' Madeleine turned, the silk of her elegant day dress rustling as she did so. 'Although you would deny having so much as an ounce of charisma, with your usual shameless false modesty.' She walked over to him, and tucked her arm through his. 'Dick has told me that you fall in love on a regular basis, but as yet, no one lady has managed to make this situation permanent.' She raised mischievous eyebrows at her brother-in-law before returning to her husband with her slow, straight-backed walk, that seemed designed to draw attention to her.

Everyone laughed politely, as a maid came round with glasses of sherry.

As Dick told Madeleine about the curious lilac flowers in the corner, Neil watched them. Dick certainly seemed happy in a marriage which had been more or less arranged by his parents. But how would Madeleine take to life in India? Dick would have to return there in a few short weeks. She was a pretty girl, with dark hair and pale skin, but she was a hothouse flower, like his mother, more at home in a conservatory than in the heat of the Indian summer. But the Frasers' future was in India. It was only a matter of time before Neil closed the Dundee works and joined them in Calcutta, as his parents retired to raise new varieties of flowers and undertake appropriate good works.

'I thought that Agnes might be joining us,' Madeleine said as they walked into the dining room, where the beautiful silverware on the table glinted in the bright sunlight.

'Well, Neil?' Richard said pointedly.

Neil swallowed. Agnes was a constant source of conversation with Madeleine. A friend of hers, Agnes was the only daughter of Thomas Briar, shipyard owner and kirk elder. Despite the fact that Neil patently had nothing in common with Agnes except a large inheritance, fate had conspired that they were a good match. So every week he played bridge with her, and escorted her to social functions where she was remarkable for her ability to fade into the background. And unless he could find someone equally well-connected, Neil had the sinking feeling that Agnes, like Madeleine, would be changing her surname to Fraser. And he would acquire a quiet, obedient little wife, like so many of his friends had recently. How long would any of them last in a jute factory, he wondered?

'Finding something amusing, Neil?' Richard Fraser asked sharply.

'Just thinking of something,' he returned smoothly as they were seated at the table.

'How was your walk after church, Neil?' Madeleine asked politely. 'Agnes was most upset that you weren't able to join us for a chat.'

'There were suffragettes in Magdalen Green whose screeching rather spoilt the mood,' Richard returned, in his usual habit of answering for his sons when the fancy took him.

'Oh, them.' Madeleine grimaced.

'I take it you are not a follower of Mrs Pankhurst's cause?' Neil commented, as he played with the heavy damask napkin.

'I have a maiden aunt who insists on going to meetings', Madeleine looked round almost shamefully, 'with working-class women. I mean, why would anyone want to converse with them?'

'Perhaps they wish to vote. They do pay taxation, after all. And our workforce is overwhelmingly female.' Neil ignored the grumpy snort from his father.

'I don't think ladies should work,' Madeleine replied hastily. 'Their duties are to keep a nice home for their husbands. A peaceful, relaxing place where they can escape the stresses of business life.'

'We aren't talking about ladies, my dear,' Richard returned. 'I agree with you completely. A woman's place is in the home.'

'But don't you want to vote?' Neil persisted as his fingers traced the pattern on his silver napkin ring.

Madeleine shook her head, her earrings glinting in the autumn sunlight.

'I trust Dick.' She smiled adoringly at her husband. 'I have no knowledge of politics. And no desire to learn.'

'A hat shop,' Mrs Fraser announced suddenly. 'If I had to work, I should like to have a little hat shop.'

'And spend all day chatting to your friends?' Richard Fraser said gruffly.

Elizabeth Fraser laughed and put a soft lily-white hand on her husband's.

'Darling, if I were to take a position in trade, I shouldn't have a friend left in the world.'

'But Mother, we *are* in trade,' Neil replied in surprise. 'The jute trade.'

'No, we aren't,' Richard replied quickly. 'I do apologize, Madeleine, Neil has lost an argument with a sixteen-year-old slum girl and is attempting to take his ill humour out on the rest of us.'

Everyone laughed, and Neil brushed his feelings aside, trying hard to hide his hurt.

There was no rest for the wicked, or those unjustly accused of being so, however, and on Monday Neil went back to the grimy factory, as his mother took her daughter-in-law to a dress shop then lunch, and his father and brother played golf together. It was easy for his father to criticize when he didn't have to run the place, didn't have to care about the conditions of his workers' lives. Not that he ever had, he had shut his eyes to it. But times were changing. Neil didn't want to be his father, to rule by fear; he wanted his workers to respect him, to see him as a fair employer. Dick didn't seem to care, he appeared content with his life in Calcutta, which seemed to be nothing more than an endless round of drinks and croquet, and polo played on elephants, when the fancy took them. He hadn't noticed their workers were people either.

'Aye, that was where . . .' The man's voice tailed off as he saw Neil walk from the machine floor to push past him. As Neil walked up the stairs, he could hear the muttering following him. As it had all that day.

'That bloody Monroe girl!' he said as he walked in to see Archie Taylor, the chubby, self-satisfied works manager, who was looking out of the window as he scratched idly at his sweaty face. 'I just don't understand what she thinks she can achieve by blackening my name like this.'

'I wouldn't bother trying to understand troublesome pieces like that, Mr Fraser,' the man replied as he moved to sit back in a chair that strained under the weight of him. 'They are best ignored, they're just like rats. Nothing more than a pest, but impossible to get rid of.'

'Why can't they see just how much we give them?' he asked despairingly. 'Why are they so damn ungrateful?'

Archie Taylor said nothing, his thoughts folded under his face like his chins.

'Sometimes they need showing the error of their ways, Mr Fraser,' he said with respect. 'You've got to strike back, show them what you're made of.'

'I've given them a break in the afternoon and I'm fighting to keep the business going when others have closed down!' He looked over at Archie, whose lardy face betrayed nothing. 'I've spent money on the machinery and there're less injuries now than ever before.'

'They think you're soft,' Archie replied. 'And that'll be a hard reputation to break.'

'Very good, Malise.' Mr Scott handed her the jotter and the copy of *The Merchant of Venice* that she had been studying. 'Although I think you over-defended Shylock.'

'What right have they to insist he change his religion? And if there was a problem with the contract it should have been checked at the time of signing.'

Gordon Scott laughed.

'Do you argue just to be contrary, Malise? You're taking the rich man's side.'

Malise raised her hands, a habit she had inherited from her father.

'I argue to practise, Mr Scott.' She sat back in her chair. 'And if you don't mind, I will go back to the class. I've got to get the sums on the board, ready for the visit tomorrow.'

'Take care, Malise.' Gordon Scott moved his chair to let her pass. 'I heard your speech on Sunday. Very good.' He looked her straight in the eye. 'But you ought to be careful about the way you say things. You made it sound as if Fraser threw you down the stairs.'

'No I didn't,' she protested. 'I said he threw me out.'

'A rather sophisticated difference, don't you think? For a very unsophisticated audience.'

'It made it more dramatic, Mr Scott,' Malise excused herself. 'You should have seen their faces.'

'What about Neil Fraser's face?' Mr Scott persisted. 'He was there, you know.'

'Och, I'm not important enough for him to give a mind to,' she replied with a confidence she didn't feel. 'It was nothing personal.'

'Stand up straight, everyone.' As she cast an expert eye over the forty-three small, undernourished children, Malise felt the nervousness rise up in her again. 'Our visitors will be here in a minute and we want to show them that we know our money. Willie, wipe your nose, it looks like half the Tay's running out of it.'

Willie, a grey-hued seven-year-old, wiped the green matter from his upper lip on to his ragged woollen sleeve, then sniffed loudly. There was a clatter as a gust of wind blew the cardboard covering a small broken window into the classroom, landing on the floor in front of Malise's feet.

'Don't anyone move,' she warned, as she grabbed the cardboard and clambered up on the nearest desk, then on to the high window sill, and attempted to wedge the cardboard back into the space.

'And this is our primary three class.' Gordon Scott's voice came up behind her.

Malise turned to see the headmaster and two members of the Board – Neil and Richard Fraser – entering the class-room.

'Surely it can't be that bad, Mr Scott,' Neil Fraser said amiably. 'Looks like your teacher is about to jump!' He hesitated, then let out an indignant snort. 'And look who it is! The girl who wouldn't know the truth if it fell down the stairs in front of her!'

Malise flushed.

'I'm trying to fix the window. Sir.' She hesitated noticeably before adding the 'sir'.

Neil Fraser walked over to where she stood and put his arm out to her. Malise looked at it for a moment, then jumped off the sill, holding his arm for support, landing heavily on his foot.

'Sorry,' she said, as she felt the ground swallow her up. 'Sir.'

'Wouldn't want you to hurt yourself.' Neil nodded to her, then walked along the line of children. 'So what have you been learning?' he asked thoughtfully as he looked at the ragged band of children standing to attention in the bare draughty classroom, the cold walls decorated with damp, furred plaster and a fading portrait of George V.

'Money,' Willie said with another loud sniff.

'And what do you know about money?' Neil continued.

'That it is the root of all evil.' Willie shrugged. 'Miss Monroe gives us a bit of apple if we get it right.'

'Monroe, I thought it was you.' Richard Fraser gazed at her from beneath his bushy eyebrows. 'What are you doing here?'

'I'm a pupil teacher,' she said with nervous defiance. 'Sir.'

'And you are bribing the children into learning with apples?' Richard Fraser looked over the children as if he were afraid some insect would jump off them and on to him.

'I use apples to illustrate fractions,' Malise added. 'You'll find that they remember quarters if they've actually split an apple into four.'

'Children learn better without bribery,' Richard Fraser snapped. 'Or is that a mortal sin you are prepared to overlook in order to meet your own ends?'

'They learn best with something in their bellies. Hardly a single one of them has a hot meal every day.' She forced her eyes to the older man for a moment, then, after catching sight of the barely concealed anger on Gordon Scott's face, she dropped her gaze.

'Shall we have a look at primary four?' Gordon said hastily.

Richard nodded and turned, walking out of the classroom, Gordon wheeling himself behind him. Neil walked towards the door.

'My class have been preparing to meet you. For days,' she said pointedly. 'They want to show you what they can do.'

'We don't have time for them,' Neil said stiffly. 'We've seen four classes already and there are others.'

'Please, they really want to show you their work.' She looked straight at him and Neil was taken aback by the warmth of her deep-brown eyes. He saw the earnest look, as she fought against herself to ask him the favour. 'No one really cares what they do.'

'Maybe next time,' he murmured, mollified by the expression on her face. It had humility, without being humble. He continued down the bare corridor, towards the classroom where he could hear the twelve times table being recited.

Neil sat with his father and Gordon Scott in the little school office as the headmaster pressed tea and excuses for the poor performance of the pupils on them. He listened to his father as he criticized the lack of knowledge of some of the students, wondering how his father was unable to hear what the schoolmaster was saying. Of course, children without food couldn't concentrate enough to learn, and some were forced into work whilst still of school age. There were more important things to know than the line of succession or the countries of the empire.

'We have to get back to our other duties, Gordon,' Richard said quickly. 'So thank you, and we'll see you again for the Christmas service.' He stood up and put his teacup and saucer on the headmaster's desk. 'And one last thing. Get rid of that Monroe girl. She's a pernicious influence on that class.'

'But Mr Fraser, Miss Monroe is a very good teacher. By far the best of the crop and her class are doing remarkably well considering . . .'

'Considering they are being taught by a girl whose only desire is to insult my family and to make mischief. I want her out. And I want her out by the end of the week.' He stood up. 'Are you going back to the works, Neil?'

'Yes, Father, but I'll walk,' Neil replied as his father left.

'But I've no one to teach the class,' Gordon insisted. 'She—' But he was talking to Richard's back. 'Her father is Gabriel Monroe,' Gordon hissed to Neil. 'A vendetta will serve no one and harm every one of us.'

'I wish to speak to her. Might I do it here?' Neil sat back in the chair and Gordon fought the feeling that he was the visitor in his own office.

Malise was cleaning the sums off the faded blackboard when Mr Scott wheeled himself back into her class, as the children enjoyed a well-earned playtime.

'You've really rattled them,' he said pensively.

'I can't stand the way we dress up for them, all please and thank you and they just don't see what's wrong.' She walked over to a window and opened it, slamming the blackboard rubber against the wall with vigour. 'These bairns have no food, no clean water to drink, they breathe in the air that is full of smoke and damp, and the likes of the Frasers have not an ounce of guilt that it is *their* wages that won't give the families enough to eat, *their* houses that they have to live in, *their* lives, slaving in a factory when they get older.'

'Malise, I know more than most.' He wheeled himself over to her. 'But you're in danger of going too far. Now is the time to let them forget about you. Your time will come.'

'I don't want to wait.' She gave the rubber one last slam and walked away.

32

'You've no choice. You know we've got plans for you. But you've got to get your teaching certificate first. A real profession, and then, when you talk, people will listen. You'll have a seat on the council, Malise, but you have to be careful. For Gabriel's sake as much as your own.' He cleared his throat. 'Mr Fraser is in my office. He wants to talk to you.'

'Why?' Malise suddenly felt sick, there could be only one reason.

'It might not be good news.' He grabbed her hand and stared at her fingers. 'But remember that you are a Monroe. Remember to conduct yourself with dignity. And don't let that tongue of yours get the better of you.'

Malise nodded uncertainly and pulled her fingers from Mr Scott's grip. Then she walked along the high, cold corridor until she came to the cosy little office, lined with Mr Scott's own books. Inside she could see Neil Fraser, deep in thought.

'You wanted to see me?' She didn't bother with the 'sir'.

Neil Fraser nodded and offered her a seat.

'I'd prefer to stand, thank you,' she said as she closed the door behind her, holding on to the brass door knob for moral support. He wasn't much older than she was, she noted.

'How are you?' he asked politely.

'Very well, thank you,' she returned. 'How are you?'

'Troubled,' he answered. Then he took a deep breath. 'Gordon tells me you are a good teacher, and your class certainly seem happy with you.'

Malise flushed with pride at the unaccustomed compliment.

'I like teaching.' He was a fair man, after all, she thought.

'It is good to have an occupation that satisfies you,' Neil said. 'My own I enjoy, but these are difficult times. For all of us.' He waited for Malise to answer, but she didn't. 'What would you do if you weren't a teacher? I seem to recall you had an interest in working with us. As an apprentice clerk.'

33

'Actually, Mr Fraser, I wanted to be an apprentice clerkess,' she replied almost shyly. He was being nice to her. Polite. Treating her like a lady. And he had a face she could look at all day and not tire of it. A strong jaw and white teeth, a face that always seemed to want to smile. And those twinkling blue eyes, she really liked those twinkling blue eyes.

'No, you didn't. You wanted to manufacture a scene. For political gain.' He saw the colour drain from her face.

'I'm sorry,' she said quickly. 'I never meant it to happen. But it did, and Miss Proctor—' She stopped, aware that neither of them believed her feeble excuse.

'Oh no, Miss Monroe.' He stared at her. 'In fact, you manufactured such a scene that the Board wishes you to be removed from the school forthwith.'

'You can't sack me!' she said incredulously.

'Yes, I can,' he replied smoothly. 'I can do anything I want to.' He held her gaze. 'You are a good teacher, but a bad influence.'

'But you can't.' She took one step, then another, over to him. 'You can't just sack me, I have to become a teacher. If I don't—'

'If you don't, what?' He cocked his head to one side. 'What could you do to help the situation?'

'But what does it matter what I do outside this school?'

'You slandered me in front of the whole of Dundee. You are a liar, and that makes you a bad influence.'

'But I didn't say that you pushed me down the stairs.' She grabbed his arm, heedless of anything except the words he had said. 'I can provide you with copies of the speech. People just got the wrong impression. I can't help that.'

'You planted the idea in people's minds, and because of that my reputation has suffered.' He gently but firmly removed her fingers from his sleeve, but she clung on to him again, desperately.

'Please, you c-c-can't just . . .' Malise stopped as her lip began to tremble.

'Of course, if you could persuade me that you can be a good influence, then I might be able to persuade the Board to reconsider its decision.' He pushed her fingers away, somehow surprised they were so rough.

'Of course,' she returned with relief. 'I can show you how the class is ahead of—'

'I'm not interested in the class, Miss Monroe,' Neil said gently. 'I want you to prove to the people of Dundee that you are a good influence.'

'How?'

He hesitated. Every part of him wanted to accept her apology and go, but he had to strike back. She had used him and now he was going to use her. Fight fire with fire, as Archie and his father kept telling him. He swallowed the bile that was gathering in his mouth.

'Persuade your father to call off the work-to-rule.' Neil watched, as her pretty face almost crumbled before him.

'I can't do that,' she said softly. She didn't sound like a threat to his position now, she sounded like a frightened girl.

'You can try. And if you succeed, you can keep your position here. And if you fail, don't come looking for a job in any of my works, or anyone else's. You're a troublemaker, Malise Monroe, and I'm putting a stop to it. Now.' He turned his head from her, so he couldn't see what he had done.

Malise pressed her hands to her mouth, to stop the sob that was gathering in her throat, and forced herself to breathe. She was Gabriel Monroe's girl, and she didn't cry.

'I can't, Mr Fraser,' she said hopelessly. 'I can't do that.'

'But you'll never be a teacher. What will be left to you? Housemaid? You've far too much spirit in you for that. You'll never be able to amount to anything.'

'I'm nothing in your eyes anyway,' she returned bitterly as her anger gained momentum. 'You know, Mr Fraser, you might as well give me my cards now. Because those people need my father to be honest and I'll not betray them for a crumb off your table. So sack me for thinking I was good

35

enough for a decent job in your works, and for a few badly chosen words in a speech, because your workers need more money to live.' Tears were in her throat now, threatening to take away what was left of her voice. Tears of anger, frustration and, most of all, disappointment. Because he was serious. And she knew it.

'You don't want to think about it?' he said with some surprise.

She shook her head.

'Good God, you're Gabriel's daughter, all right!'

'I'll tell my father one thing,' she said quickly. 'I'll tell him he was wrong about you. Because you are definitely Richard Fraser's son!'

'You have till the end of the week, Miss Monroe,' he said wearily. She nodded and fled from the room. 'Then God knows what I'll do,' he ended quietly.

The week couldn't have passed more slowly. Every moment that Malise was awake, whether she was at the steamie, doing the ironing, cooking or cleaning or teaching, or whether she was studying, all she could think about was that it was her last few days as a teacher. But she never said a word to her father, for she knew she had brought it on herself. And it wouldn't be fair to make him pay for it.

When Friday came, she felt her stomach sink when Gordon Scott appeared at the door of her classroom, beckoning her over.

'Fraser's come back. He's in the office and wants to speak to you.'

'Mr Scott—' Malise began.

'I don't want to know, Malise,' he said curtly. 'I don't want to judge you and your father if the work-to-rule is called off without any concessions on Fraser's part.'

'I didn't think this would happen,' she said quietly. 'But I can't . . .'

'I know, lass,' he murmured. 'Sometimes you start a fire, and find you're the one who gets burned. Off you go.'

Malise walked along the corridor till she came to the office. Without knocking, she walked in, and saw Fraser, looking out of the window.

'Since you obviously had no intention of coming to me . . .' he began.

'I've nothing to say to you,' she returned coldly. 'I told you my decision. And I didn't tell my father you had threatened me. Or all your works would have walked.'

'So this is the end of your teaching career,' he said, without taking his eyes off the playground where the children were enjoying their break.

'If I gave in this once, then the next time, the same thing would have happened. And from then on you would have used me, as a way to get to my father.' She wiped her hands together, then smelt the chalk dust that was on them. She knew it could be the last time she smelt it.

'The children are so very small. And thin,' he said pensively.

Malise said nothing.

'What could be done to help them?'

'Hot food, clean water and a decent home would be a good start,' she returned. 'Jobs for the parents.'

'Yet you sit in relative luxury, your father earns a decent wage and you can afford to be a pupil teacher.' He turned to look at her. 'Who are you to lecture me?'

'My mother died when my father was in prison, for leading a strike of handcart drivers,' she said slowly. 'I was four. It took months for anyone to realize that we were living under the arches in the Fishgate. I had been eating earth and anything that I could pick off the ground at the market.' She willed herself not to break down. 'Then a man walking home from the pub found me and took me home. It was Mr Baker.' She halted at the memory. 'When I told them who my daddy was, they didn't tell the parish, who'd have put me in an orphanage. But they told the union, so that when he got out, two years later, he came and got me.'

'You're lying,' he said in disbelief. 'No one has to live that way nowadays. We have charities, the parish . . .'

Malise shook her head.

'Why would I lie to you?' Their eyes met and for once Malise was not going to drop her gaze respectfully. Because she was right.

'I want to arrange for the children to be given breakfast when they arrive each morning. Children learn better with something in their bellies.' Neil's voice was low.

'And in return you want me to talk to my father?' she said disappointedly. 'You can't threaten me, so you'll bribe me instead?'

'No, I can afford to feed your children. So I will.'

'Why not give their parents jobs, so they can earn money to buy bread, instead of living off charity?'

'I want to give them breakfast.' Neil's voice held a note of finality. He looked back at the children, running about in the shabby, uneven playground as Malise went to the door. 'Why didn't you tell anyone, when you were alone and starving?'

Malise laughed bitterly.

'Who'd have wanted to know? I wasn't alone, there were plenty more in the same situation. And there still are.'

'You said you would tell your father he was wrong about me.' Neil wanted to turn his mind from the thought of her as a starving child. It didn't sit well with his opinion of her as a mischief-maker.

'I know,' she said grimly.

'What did he say about me?' Neil looked at her, his gaze clear and true.

'Fishing for compliments, Mr Fraser?' she returned tartly. 'Why should his opinion of you matter?'

'I doubt that your father would have anything complimentary to say.'

She laughed unexpectedly. Relief had just bubbled up inside her.

'My father thinks you are a good man. Thinks you could

be good for the folk of Dundee. But you need an education.'
She stopped as she saw the smile flit across Neil Fraser's
face.

'And what does the schoolteacher think?' he asked
suddenly.

Malise stared in surprise. He was almost conspiratorial.

'I don't know you well enough to have an informed
opinion of you, sir.' As she said the words, she could feel her
cheeks redden. 'But I hope my father is right about you. For
all our sakes.'

'Looks as if there will be a walkout,' Neil said as the family
drank sherry before dinner that night. 'The union won't
move on the rate increase. Monroe thinks he has my measure. He's been holding meetings outside the gates every
night this week.'

'Monroe always was a law unto himself,' Richard said
gruffly. 'He needs to be taught a lesson in who really runs
this town. Get Archie to have a word with him.'

'Monroe won't listen to reason, he's blind to the fact that
we can't afford to have a good price for our jute if we pay
the workers more. Both the spun and woven jute coming
out of India is much cheaper, and of the same quality.' Neil
looked out the window at the Firth of Tay which was
sweeping relentlessly down towards the sea.

'Well, it is made in our works there.' Richard smiled.
'But I'll be happier when Dick and Madeleine have left for
Calcutta. I don't trust some of the factory managers there.
Not one inch.'

'Has he told her yet?' Neil asked as they took their seats.

'Told her what, dear?' Elizabeth said as she walked into
the dining room.

'Told Madeleine that she'll be living in India.' He picked
up his napkin.

'Madeleine will do whatever Dick tells her to,' Elizabeth
replied. 'It's her duty.'

'Monroe is just testing you,' Richard interrupted. 'He

thinks that, because you are only twenty-one and just out of
university, you don't have the nerve to fight fire with fire.'

'And Archie does?' Neil looked at his father.

Richard nodded knowingly.

'Archie knows how to keep him in line,' he said eventually. 'He knows ways to make Monroe listen.' Richard stared
at his glass. 'Monroe has forced your hand, now you can't
back down. Or you will be known for ever as a man in fear
of his workers.'

Neil looked at his father, the disgust on his face was
palpable. He had made some concessions, but the union just
kept on asking.

'All right, Dad,' he said resignedly. 'Whatever you say.'

Neil sat in his office the next morning and wondered what
he could do. Why was his father so insistent that Archie
could solve their problem? If it was up to him, he'd give
them the rate, but they couldn't afford to push the price of
Dundee jute up another penny, it would only serve to make
Indian jute more attractive. He twirled his pen through his
fingers. He had no choice, he'd have to admit to the works
manager that he couldn't do it. And get into debt with
Archie.

'You wanted to see me, Mr Fraser?' Archie said as he
walked in, his innocent tone at odds with his knowing,
guilty face.

'Monroe is pressing for a rate increase,' Neil said calmly.
'A rate increase that we cannot sustain. But I can't afford a
walkout, either. My father suggested that you might have an
answer.'

'Well, what do you want?' Archie said thoughtfully. 'Do
you want to stop the walkout, or to stop Monroe pressing
for one?'

'He needs to understand that we cannot pay more money
in wages,' Neil said to Archie. 'I don't care what it takes, I
want you to show him who runs this place. And it's me, not
him.'

'There are ways to show that,' Archie replied casually. 'But it does take a certain amount of money.' He looked up at the man.

So that was it, thought Neil. Archie was going to buy off Monroe.

'Would it work?' he asked doubtfully. 'He doesn't seem the type.'

'Everyone has their price, one that is just too dear to ignore,' Archie returned blithely. 'Worked on others.'

'Very well, Archie,' Neil said. 'Do whatever you have to. I'll cover you.'

Archie nodded his squat head as he headed out of Neil's mahogany-panelled office and into his own considerably smaller one.

'If you want me to show him, Mr Fraser,' he said with quiet bitterness. 'I'll make him rue the day he took the pair of us on.'

'Where is he?'

Malise was sitting in the living room when she heard the door open later that night. She turned to see three heavy-set men walk in.

'What are you doing here?' Her voice was high. The three men filled the room, she couldn't see the door. But they were looking round the house, as if they were pricing it. Looking for what to break. She backed away from them, towards the wall where her narrow bed was hung on thick jute ropes. These men had their orders, and Mr Scott's story came crashing into her mind.

But in response to her, they simply took out a chair leg and began to crush the crockery that was laid on the table.

'No!' screamed Malise at the top of her voice as she rushed over.

'Just stay out of this, lass.' One of them pushed her aside and she fell on the floor, watching as they threw the crockery press on the ground, the cheap china smashing as it fell out of the cabinet and on to the heavy wood floor.

But Malise was having none of it. She launched herself at the first man, scratching and tearing at his face in an all too female fashion. She heard his laugh, then a fist grabbed at her hair and threw her against the wall.

'Our quarrel's not with you, lass, don't start,' the second man warned, but Malise grabbed at the first thing that came to hand. The poker for the fire. She brought it down as hard as she could on the man's arm, before she felt a punch at the side of her head, which brought her down against the fragile gas mantle, breaking it. Barely conscious, she sensed a red-hot pain sear through her as he brought his boot again and again into her stomach.

'She's broke my fucking arm!'

'Malise!' It was one of the neighbours, shouting through the wall. Through the mist of pain she heard the men run out the door, then they were gone.

'Malise, Malise.'

She realized that she had been carried out on to the stairwell by Mr Johnson.

'I want my dad.' She didn't want to fight the pain, it hurt too much in too many places. Dad had always said you couldn't hurt in two places at once. But Malise now knew how wrong he was.

'A couple of days in bed and she'll be right as rain.' The doctor, an expensive luxury that had cost Gabriel Monroe the money he had saved for his winter coat, turned to him. 'Nothing broken, except your furniture.'

Gabriel reached out a work-worn hand and stroked Malise's forehead.

'How are you feeling?' He looked down with such compassion that it made Malise want to cry again.

'I'm all right, Dad.' She tried to open her eyes, but found she couldn't. 'You should see the others.'

Gabriel brushed her hair from her face.

'Did you recognize any of them?'

She tried to shake her head, wincing as she did so.

'Sorry, they were looking for you. Fraser's men, probably.'

'You just rest now, Malise.' Gabriel kissed her gently on her battered, swollen cheek. 'Get better.'

'I just got angry when they broke the teapot,' she said suddenly. 'I liked that teapot.'

'I should have been there for you,' he said sorrowfully. 'Those men, they could have done anything they wanted to you.' He looked away for a moment. 'And I was too busy trying to cure the ills of Dundee, while some bastards were beating the living daylights out of my daughter.'

'Daddy.' She reached for his hand. 'Don't upset yourself. Not on my account.'

'You're the most important thing in the world to me, Malise.' He stroked her fingers. 'All I've left of your mammy.' He stopped for a moment to pull himself together. 'My job was to protect the both of you, and all I've ever done is let you down.'

'Daddy, no,' she struggled to get the words out, 'I'm proud of what you do. I wouldn't change you for the world.'

As the doctor left, Gabriel gave her a hot toddy, sitting with her as she fell asleep. Then he put on his jacket and walked out of the door. Outside, his expression changed. Three men were waiting patiently for him, standing next to the lavatory.

'I don't mind being in a fight with him, but I'm damned if he'll take it out on my Malise.'

'It's Wednesday night,' one of the others said. 'He goes to play tennis every Wednesday night.'

Chapter 3

The four men made their way to the tennis courts, and waited outside the club itself, mindful of having the watch called on. Eventually, they saw a figure make for the car they were watching. The car they had already tampered with, so that it wouldn't start.

'Mr Fraser?' Gabriel said the words quickly and quietly. 'Had a busy night, between playing games and attacking lassies?'

'What?' Neil looked up, but there were four men around him, four angry, violent working-class men.

'What you did to my house, Mr Fraser . . . not clever at all.' Gabriel put his fist up to Neil's throat, pinning him to the side of the car with effortless anger. 'And what you did to my Malise was unforgivable.'

'What have I done to her?' he blustered. 'I've paid for her students to have breakfast every morning. I hardly thought that was a crime, Monroe.'

'Thought you'd set your men on her, because I wasn't there? Thought that would show the world what a powerful man you were?' He looked at him. 'Even your father wouldn't have stooped so low.' He let him go for a second. 'You tell your men that I'm coming for them, and you tell them they will pay for everything they did to her, and once that is finished, Mr Fraser, then I'll deal with you.' Gabriel spat in his face and walked off, leaving Neil silent and shaken, leaning against the car for comfort and support. So this was how Archie handled things? Then the awful realization hit him. His father must have known it would end this way. Because he had insisted on Archie taking over.

'I want to know what the hell happened, Archie.' Neil faced the works manager angrily the next morning. 'You told me you'd make sure Monroe understood who was in charge of this place and nothing more, I'm not in the business of harming people.' He looked down. 'I've no intention of turning this into a feud, it's a simple labour dispute.'

'Tam got a bit upset when she broke his arm.' Archie Taylor shrugged. 'And things got a bit out of hand.' He looked at his boss. 'But you wanted some muscle, not the Temperance League.'

'But she's a girl. And I can imagine exactly what he did to her. How would you feel if your family were threatened like that?'

'Like I said, Mr Fraser,' Archie scratched at his greasy moustache. 'You wanted me to talk to him in a language he would understand, and I did.'

Neil Fraser walked back to his own office. He shouldn't have got Archie involved. And he had hurt someone who had the courage of her convictions. A girl he wanted to show the real Neil Fraser to. And now, it seemed, he had.

'Are you sure you want to do this?' Miss Proctor said, as they stood next to the bandstand, waiting for the crowd to gather while Bessie banged the drum.

'Of course she does.' Gabriel Monroe's dark eyes bored into Miss Proctor and she took a step away instinctively. 'The speech has been written and the whole town will know what Fraser did to her.' He put a hand round Malise's shoulder in a comforting, yet forceful, gesture. Malise nodded shakily, this was what her father wanted and therefore she had to do it. Even though it seemed very wrong.

'Off you go,' he said as the drum stopped, and he pushed her on to the platform. 'Go and ruin Fraser. Tell the world how he used an innocent wee lass.'

There was an appalled hush as Malise walked on to the platform. She shivered in the crisp October air, and she looked behind her. Gabriel was standing there, a glowering general. She had to do it, or Miss Proctor and her father would never forgive her.

'A few weeks ago I told you of my treatment at the hands of Mr Neil Fraser.' She hesitated as the crowd quietened. 'And low and behold I had some visitors into my home this week. A warning, they told me . . .'

Neil stood on the green, next to a dew covered tree, and listened in horrified silence as Malise told the world what had been done in his name. Part of him wanted to run up to the bandstand, to announce to the world that he hadn't meant for her to be hurt, he had been told by his father to use Archie's expertise. But he couldn't. So he stood there, together with his father, who had sat next to him in church and said his prayers only one hour previously. There was no stain on his conscience, because it was business. Nothing personal. It was immaterial who got hurt in the process. Neil crushed the branch he was holding, under his grasp. How on earth would he salvage his family's name after this?

'Neil?' Richard shook his head as he began to walk, gesturing for the rest of the family to do the same. 'You fool! I'd have expected a damn sight better from you. She might be just a wee slum lass, but she's beaten you at your own game.' He shot a harsh look at his younger son.

'I didn't send anyone after her!' Neil saw a few accusing looks from the modestly dressed women around him as they reached the path leading out of the park. 'She just got in the way. It was unfortunate, but unavoidable, since I had taken your advice and asked Taylor to handle things for me,' he hissed at his father.

'I'm beginning to wonder if you are suited to running the Elizabeth.' Richard glared at a few walkers who had the temerity to intrude on his line of vision. 'We must keep some of our reputation intact.' They stopped and got back in the car. 'And I've invited Agnes over, with her parents, for a late lunch.'

Neil groaned.

'Not Agnes, Dad. She's a mouse.'

'A mouse with money. And connections.' Richard chuckled to himself. 'You've got to get married eventually. You've wasted enough time already!'

'You told me to sew my wild oats.'

'And now I'm telling you to plant them. In Agnes. Do something right for a change.' Richard stamped his foot and that was the end of the conversation.

And so, that night, as Malise and her father played cards in the bare little living room with hardly any furniture left, Neil Fraser asked Mr Briar for consent to marry his pallid, withdrawn daughter, and assured him that rumours of discontent among his workers were nothing more than a simple labour dispute.

Malise finished chalking the ten commandments on the blackboard and stood back to look at her handiwork. She was tired, but had to go to the library before getting home, because her father was talking at the Pillars at the weekend and wanted some quotations on freedom which the Americans talked about. Her dad liked the Americans; every so often he would talk about emigrating, the way his brother had. But he was too busy with union business to look up the quotations himself. Malise knew it was a lie, her father wasn't very good at reading, even when he read the paper, she could see his mouth working, helping his brain to understand the words. But he was a good speaker.

She had all but left the school when she saw Neil Fraser draw up in his motor car. She ignored him even when she saw him alight and begin to walk behind her.

'Are you following me?' she called.

'Yes. Are you going to stop?' He caught her up, and she stopped.

47

'What do you want, Mr Fraser?' she said uneasily, looking around. It would serve neither of them to be seen together.

'I think you and I should have a little talk, but not here.' He led her towards the car.

Malise sat in silence as they drove a short distance.

'Never been in a motor car before,' she said softly as she ran her hands over the thick leather seat. 'What do you want to say?' She looked down at her hands, at the books on her lap.

'I'm sorry. I never meant for it to happen,' Neil said slowly.

'You did, the men had come for Dad. And you're the person who sent them to give him a warning.'

'I did no such thing.'

'Daddy said no one else had the money to pay for them.' She looked up at him. 'They work for Archie Taylor, sometimes. He's well known in Dundee for that kind of behaviour. That's how your works have got away with paying less for so long. Because they're run by a thug.' She glanced out of the window. 'They used to be run by two.'

Neil was silent as he drove through the town, wishing he could find a way to defend his father's actions. 'Is there somewhere you want to go?'

'The library, please. I'm writing a speech for Daddy.'

'I would imagine that your father has a different opinion of me by now,' Neil said as they neared the library.

'What difference does it make what the people of Dundee think of you?' She turned to him. 'You're rich enough to buy yourself a good name. Give us a park and we'll love you for ever. We can walk round it and wonder where our next meal's coming from.'

Neil stopped his car outside the library.

'I'm sorry,' he said eventually. 'I think you've got my measure now.'

Malise exhaled loudly.

'I know, Mr Fraser. You probably told Archie Taylor to sort it out, and you didn't want to know the details.' She turned round further, so he could see all her bruises. 'Well, now you can. In black and blue. Just like so many other respectable owners, aren't you?'

'Is this a normal occurrence?' he replied, horrified.

'Mr Scott . . . you know, the headmaster?' She raised her cut eyebrow at him. 'He led a demonstration over twenty years ago, in Edinburgh. Afterwards, men were sent to his home. They burned it, but only his wife and baby son were inside. But they didn't stop there, they were getting paid to teach Mr Scott a lesson. They smashed his legs into so many pieces he had to have them cut off.' She laughed quietly. 'Now, are you telling me that the man who paid for it to happen actually thought about the fire, that an innocent woman and child would die? Or that the warning Mr Scott would receive would turn him into a cripple?'

Neil shook his head. 'It could have been . . .'

'Mr Fraser, these people hurt others for money. It's their job. Just be thankful that my father doesn't have enough for them.'

Neil drummed his fingers on the walnut dashboard.

'You need to understand, Malise,' he put a hand on her arm, 'I never meant for you or your father to be hurt. I was given bad advice. I made a mistake.'

Malise could hardly believe her ears. Here was Mr Neil Fraser, apologizing to her.

'People like you don't apologize to people like me,' she said, unnerved by his words.

'Do you forgive me?' He looked her straight in the eye and Malise could see his sincerity. This man had admitted he had made a mistake.

'Promise you won't hurt me again?' she ventured finally. Neil smiled with relief.

'I promise.' He squeezed her arm.

Malise coughed uncomfortably.

'Well, there is something I ought to say to you.' She could feel her throat constricting, as if she were about to do something terrible, but the words were forcing themselves

49

out. 'I purposely went to your factory to be turned away. So that I could be on the platform at the meeting and make a speech. And so that Miss Proctor and the other posh ladies would see I was fit for more than carrying a banner or banging a drum. And I couldn't help myself, telling them about the staircase. It made people listen, remember me, and not just dismiss me as another silly wee mill lass moaning about not being able to get a good job.' She forced her eyes to his. 'And then after the men came, Daddy said it would be the best way to teach you that you can't frighten people into giving up. By making it sound as if you came after me. He even wrote the speech for me. But I didn't want to give it, after all you've just given my pupils money for food, but no one's going to know about that. I'm sorry too.' She sniffed, as Neil handed her his handkerchief.

Both of them, their burdens lifted, sat in contemplative silence.

'You're an excellent speaker, Malise,' Neil said thoughtfully. 'But a true politician would have been sufficiently ruthless to put such an experience behind her. Casualties of war.'

'You're not the enemy,' she replied. 'You're the prize. Your vote, your influence, is what we need if we are to make a real difference.'

Neil nodded, and, as he watched her get out of the car and disappear into the library, he began to wonder. Just how little separated was his life, in fact, from Malise Monroe's?

'I saw Neil Fraser the other day. Came to school to find me.'

Malise and Jessie were sitting in Malise's house, unravelling one of her father's old jumpers to knit into a new one for herself.

'He's not threatened you again, has he?' Jessie chewed her lip anxiously.

'No, Jessie, he apologized. To me.' Malise set Jessie's hands apart as she began to wind the wool around them.

'He was so nice to me, as if I was a lady.' She stopped and stared at the knots in the wool. 'He gave me a lift. In his motor car. All the way to the library.'

'Malise, are you sure it was the ride in the motor car you liked?' Jessie braced her shoulders against the long job. 'That Mr Fraser seems to be in every other sentence you say.'

'He listened to me.' Malise pulled on the curly wool to get rid of a knot. 'When he was talking about the breakfasts, he actually repeated the words I'd said to him. Jessie, I convinced him. Me! We start serving breakfasts next week.'

'Well, you always could talk the hind legs off a donkey, Malise!' Jessie said in horrified excitement. 'You haven't caught his eye, have you?'

'Of course not!' she retorted. 'He's polite, and interested in what I have to say. Not because I'm Gabriel Monroe's girl, but because he thinks I have something to say.' She relived the car ride in her head for a long, delicious moment. 'I think that he could really help the people of Dundee, and I think he wants me to help him. I've caught his ear, that's all.' She considered carefully, suddenly conscious that she had said more than she meant to.

'You sound like you're sweet on him, Malise,' Jessie said warningly. 'After all, he is the man who had you beaten. And who broke your teapot and chair.'

'Don't be daft, Jessie,' Malise returned. 'I'm not sweet on him. And he said he was sorry in the car. It was an accident. He gave Daddy a pound to pay for the damage. It was in his wage packet.' But as she said the words, she could tell she was blushing. 'What's the point being sweet on him,' Malise added wistfully. 'He's a nob and we're us, and anyway, I never had a conversation with him that didn't end up in an argument.'

'That's a sure sign,' Jessie returned. 'And anyway, Malise, you argue with everyone. Except people like me who have known you long enough just to let you haver on about whatever it is.' She laughed. 'Imagine Malise Monroe being sweet on a jute baron's son! What would everyone say?'

'Same as they would say about you being sweet on Johnnie Turpin, Jessie Baker.' Malise raised her eyebrows at her friend. 'If my daddy heard I was setting my cap at Johnnie, he'd have his guts for garters.'

'Aye,' Jessie nodded. 'I don't think your dad is going to help you find a husband, Malise. No man's going to be good enough for you. Not even a jute baron's son.'

Malise said nothing, but she patted her pocket where Neil Fraser's handkerchief, freshly laundered and bearing his monogram, was neatly folded.

That night, however, as Malise did her homework, her hand returned to the fine linen handkerchief again and again. She ought to thank Neil for the money he had provided for the children. A personal thanks, so that he understood. She wanted to talk to him again. But she had no idea what she wanted to say. She went over to the dresser and took out her best writing paper, then took a deep breath.

'And the correspondence, Mr Fraser.' Blaine Hamilton handed over the correspondence which had come into the works. Neil Fraser scanned the envelopes as Blaine hovered, trying as always to be taken into a confidence.

'That will be all, Mr Hamilton,' Neil said as he opened the first.

'Mr Dick must be well on his way to India now,' Hamilton continued.

'It will take some time,' Neil answered automatically. 'That will be all.'

'It's just that there are so many rumours, sir, and we all have families,' Hamilton continued. 'Since we lost the shipment and cannot get another in time . . .'

'I hope you have not been using your privileged position in order to spread malicious gossip, Mr Hamilton.' Neil Fraser looked up. 'Tell Monroe to come in.'

Obviously humiliated by his curt dismissal, Hamilton went out to the reception area, where he saw Gabriel

Monroe standing in a sweat-stained shirt, his sleeves rolled up.

'Mr Fraser will see you now.' He looked at the man as if he had just crawled out of the sewer. 'And for goodness sake, can you not tidy yourself up?'

'It's what working men look like, Mr Hamilton,' Gabriel replied calmly. 'Just so you'll know in the future.' He walked past him and opened the door.

'Mr Fraser.'

Neil looked up, seeing the man framed in the doorway. How alike the father and daughter were. It was something in the eyes, the anger behind the fearful respect.

'There will be no rate increase, Monroe. That is all.' He turned back to his desk.

'But, Mr Fraser, our workers need it. You aren't supposed to get poorer every year. We have that big order coming up, you'll need the extra time to complete it.'

'The jute shipment has been lost at sea, Monroe. So we have nothing to make the order with. We don't need any extra work.' He kept his eyes firmly on his ink blotter as he said it.

'Will you be putting us on short time, then?'

Neil shook his head.

'Not for the moment. You may return to your work.'

'Mr Fraser—'

'I told you to return to your work,' he repeated, this time a little louder. 'As I have to return to mine.'

'Aye, Mr Fraser.' Shoulders slumped, Gabriel turned to go.

'How long were you in prison, Monroe?' Neil said quickly. The look on Gabriel's face stunned him. Because the man actually looked guilty.

'Two years, sir,' he said slowly. 'But they knew that when they took me on here.'

'I'm not trying to have you sacked, man,' Neil replied. 'I just wondered if it was worth it. For your family.'

Gabriel's head dropped and he stared at his feet.

'I lost my wife, and my wee lass almost starved,' he said shamefully. 'It wasn't worth it for them.'

Neil nodded, then once the heavy oak door was safely closed, he put his head in his hands.

'So what's happening, Gabriel?' Billy Turpin, the bullish deputy convener, came up to him as he reached the hot and dusty factory floor.

'It's the beginning of the end,' Gabriel said grimly. 'And he knows it.'

Neil stared at the pile of letters on his desk. One, written on cheap paper, caught his attention, mainly for the beautiful copperplate hand it had been written in. He slit it open with his knife.

My children are learning better. He read. *Thank you.* And it was signed simply *Malise*. For the first time that day, Neil smiled. Someone actually thought he was doing a good job. For some reason, Malise Monroe's opinion of him mattered.

'Your mum would kill you if she knew you were here,' Malise said as she and Jessie reached the Overgate. 'I told my dad I was going to visit your Sheila.'

'We're just here for a look,' Jessie returned, scanning the people who were promenading along the street, the girls all walking in one direction, the men in the other.

'You know what she thinks about the Monkey Parade,' Malise returned.

'Aye, but that's how my Sheila got her man, and I'm seventeen next year.' Jessie waved her arm about. 'What do you think of the perfume?' The overwhelming smell of violets accosted Malise's nose.

'That's lovely, Jessie, really posh.' Malise tucked her arm through her friend's and began to walk.

'Thank you.' Neil accepted the whisky from the white-liveried waiter and set it down on the high table next to his heavy leather-studded armchair. This was his father's club, a club for the families who owned the jute works in Dundee, and a few select others. Where they would sit in the half-light of the gas lamps and talk about how their Indian-produced jute was undercutting their Scottish-produced jute, and boast about their good works, the parks and gardens they were building. And ways in which they could crush the unions. He looked up at the oil paintings on walls that were stained with the fug of cigar smoke. Stags roamed through lush green glens and Highlanders fought glorious battles. He stretched his legs out, the carpet thick and soft under his feet, and looked at his companions, men he had been to school with, who, like himself, were being dragged along in their fathers' footsteps. They had to listen to their elders telling them how to run their works more efficiently, how each improvement they made to the lot of their work-force was disastrous for the city's trade, and how it was better in the old days. Gilded memories, like the gilded staircase that swept down from their mansion and into the Town Square.

Weary of the conversation, Neil drained his glass of whisky and stood up. He'd had enough of jute for the week. Ignoring the loud voices, he slipped away from the fading Victorian splendour, which, like the people in it, was so much a sign of a grander past, and went down the ornate staircase till he was outside beside the Pillars. No doubt Gabriel Monroe or someone like him would be standing under them that Sunday, telling the world what an ogre he was. And there were other factory owners in the club, owners who were feted for their kindness to their workers. Owners who were planning to leave Dundee for Calcutta, and to take their factories with them.

Aimlessly, he wandered through the town. It was busy, but it was a Friday night. Young men and women were stopping, chatting happily to each other. Neil saw more than a few curious glances at him from shop girls dressed in cheap coats and smart hats, but he thought nothing of it. He had more important things to consider. How Dick and Madeleine were in India. And when he would be joining them.

He leaned against the door of G. L. Wilsons department store, and watched the people, most of whom were around his own age. They were standing in little groups, the men uncomfortable in collars and ties, and the girls coy and preoccupied with their gloves or handbags. How lucky they were, he thought, to have no worries, to be able to enjoy themselves; not to be weighed down with the futures of so many people the way he was.

Then he saw her, laughing with a ginger-haired girl and a young man he was sure worked in his factory.

'Right, Johnnie,' Malise said cheekily. 'Like they'll ever get a motorized van, never mind let you drive it.' She tucked a stray curl behind her ear.

Johnnie Turpin smiled, his handsome young face lighting up as he put a hand up to the wall.

'When I do, Malise, I'll take you for a ride in it.' His eyes raked over her.

'What about me?' asked Jessie indignantly.

'Aye.' He smiled lazily at Jessie. 'You an' all.'

Malise turned. She could feel someone looking at her. She saw a young man, dressed in a suit and wearing a fine overcoat against the autumn sea breeze.

'Just a minute,' she murmured as she began to walk towards him. But Jessie was too busy mooning over Johnnie Turpin, and Johnnie was too busy basking in the attention, to notice she had gone.

'What are you doing here, Mr Fraser?' she said as she reached him.

Neil shrugged.

'Just watching life,' he replied, trying a smile that she returned without realizing.

'Why not watch your own life?' She cocked her head to one side as she reached the doorway.

'I know what happens in mine,' he answered. 'What is everyone doing here?'

Malise chuckled.

'It's the Monkey Parade. How to catch yourself a lad.'

'So you are looking for a young man?' He raised his eyebrows.

'My friend is.' She leaned against the doorway, unconsciously mirroring him. 'But you can't come down here alone.'

'Why, aren't you looking for someone too?' he persisted.

'I'm not interested in a kettle boiler,' she replied hotly. 'Most of the lads just want a quick cuddle and someone to keep them in ale for life. Because they don't have jobs. Because you won't pay a man's rate in the works,' she ended pointedly.

'Now don't try and blame me for your inability to find a suitable boy, Malise Monroe. Perhaps they are just all frightened of you and your politics,' he said lightly. 'And it would appear that your friend has abandoned you.' He moved her shoulder till she could see Jessie's ginger head disappearing up the street.

'I'd better go and find her.' Malise made as if to go, but Neil touched her arm.

'Stay and talk to me. She doesn't want a chaperone.' He looked her up and down. Her bruises had faded, and he found himself appraising her face and her blossoming figure.

'She needs one with him. And I can't stand and talk to you in the street. People will see us.' But she couldn't ignore the warmth she felt from Neil Fraser actually seeking her out, wanting to talk to her.

'Then come for a stroll with me.' Neil Fraser considered the options. 'I know. Take me to the place you lived, the Fishgate, wasn't it?'

'No.' Malise shook her head. 'I can't take you there.'

'I want to see it.'

'But maybe I don't want you to see it,' she said almost desperately.

'Ashamed of where you come from?' he said teasingly.

'No, it isn't that,' she replied. How could she tell him that she didn't want to go back to the Fishgate? That she was frightened of it? But if she didn't, she'd have to find Jessie and Johnnie. And she didn't want to leave. 'It's rather rough,' she said. 'I don't think your father would approve.'

'I can guarantee that, Malise,' he tried her first name cautiously. 'But if I am to continue my education in the poor of Dundee, then I have to be prepared for the worst.'

'So that's what you want, is it?' she asked angrily. 'A Cook's tour of the slums?'

Neil looked at her face, and realized that he had made a genuine interest seem like an idle bit of fun.

'I have a duty to Dundee, as you seem to be at pains to remind me,' he replied gently. 'And I can go there and look at it. But you can help me understand what it is like to live there.'

Malise stared at him in amazement. Here was a man, a rich man, who wanted to do more than throw a coin at a beggar then retreat to his private road. But he wanted to go to the one place she dreaded. She looked up at the clock on the Steeple. It was barely nine o'clock and a mild drizzle was starting to fall. They should be safe.

'Come on then,' she said shortly. 'And don't blame me if you get robbed.'

The Fishgate was a maze of back streets winding down from the town proper to the docks, filled with the bonded warehouses where whisky was kept before being sent abroad. But as they walked through the dark cobbled alleys, the gas lighting providing them little comfort, Neil began to rue his decision. He could feel his shoes, handstitched leather, splashing into puddles which had grown out of the overflowing drains, and the smell of rancid fish permeated everything. There was little to see except some public houses and high tenements. But there were people, mainly women, standing out on street corners or under the gas lights, turning to each man as he weaved drunkenly past.

'Are they what I think they are?' he said in a murmur.

'All the women who live here come out and do that,' Malise said innocently. 'It's how they meet their friends. Since we aren't allowed in pubs in case we start a fight.'

'You are joking, aren't you?' Neil replied.

'No, when we lived here, my mum used to leave me in the room and come here for a blether. Stay out all night, she would.'

'I think you'll find she'd been doing something else,' he returned, slightly embarrassed.

'What?' Malise shrugged and stared at him. Neil looked at her, at her sweet face. She obviously had no idea that the women were selling themselves.

'Nothing.' He bit back his tongue and continued to walk.

'Hey, you!' A large, thick-set man walked up to them. 'What are you doing here? This is my patch.' He said threateningly to Malise.

'Nothing!' Neil squared up to the man. 'She is not what you think she is.'

The man took in Neil, his broad shoulders, the bearing that commanded respect.

'Then make sure I don't see her again,' he muttered.

'Come on, my dear.' Neil put his arm behind Malise's back and ushered her from the man who walked over to the nearest woman and put out his hand.

'See, told you it was rough down here. Near the docks.' Malise's head was filled with the scent of her old home, the sound of her old home. 'Just down here,' she said as she headed towards a dark corner.

Neil and Malise stumbled through the detritus of broken stones and old jute sacking which lay against the high stone walls of the buildings. He could hear the scuttle and squeak of rats, but since there were no lights, he was unable to see any. For which he was thankful.

'Here it is.' At the end of the alley was a set of what looked like derelict sheds, inside some arches. 'We lived in

59

the end one.' There was a crack of thunder as the heavens opened and it began to rain heavily.

Neil flexed his hands inside his gloves then pulled open the splintered black wooden door. Inside was a tiny room, smaller than the garage where his car was parked every night. He stooped down and stepped inside, finding himself unable to stand up straight. And his foot immediately went into a puddle of thick water.

'It flooded every time it rained,' she said softly. 'We had a straw mattress, but between the rats and the damp . . .'

'You slept on the floor?' Neil said, appalled.

'There was nowhere else.'

'But there isn't even a tap for water!'

'We don't have one of those in our new house.' She stepped inside, seemingly unaware of the flood and, unlike Neil, she could stand up straight. 'We slept over there, next to the wall, because it meant the water didn't reach my part of the bed as quickly.' She went over. 'Mammy slept there.' She put her head down for a moment. 'Then when she died I went to live in the one next door.'

'Why?' Neil doubted that the next cellar would be any more salubrious.

'The rats came.' Her voice broke. 'The rats came and I couldn't stop them and there were two girls next door, big girls. They must have been nine or ten and . . .'

'Malise?' Neil went over to her and put a comforting hand on her arm.

'The rats were too big, I couldn't stop them.' Unable to keep it back any longer she turned into his shoulder, burrowing her face in his overcoat. 'I couldn't stop them,' she repeated, over and over again through her tears.

Neil held her, but his mind was shocked to the core to think of a four-year-old girl, living here with her mother's body. And of what the rats had done to it.

'I shouldn't have made you come here,' he said as he stroked the tears from her cheek. 'I shouldn't have.' He held

60

her to him, somehow it was as comforting to him as it was to her. 'Don't worry, Malise, you're safe now.'

'Take me away, please,' she whispered. 'It's dark and I'm frightened.'

Holding her tightly to him, Neil ushered her out of the cellar and up the alley, ignoring the casually curious glances from the women in their badly fitting clothes and the beer-stained men who were fleeing the driving, ice-cold rain. They were reaching the bottom of Commercial Street now, and stopped for shelter in a doorway.

'It was terribly thoughtless of me,' he said, his arm still at her back. 'I shouldn't have made you go there.'

'It's all right,' she said as she wiped her eyes. 'I'm sorry, Neil, I'm not usually like this.' She turned round. 'I just never thought I'd have to go back there.'

'You called me Neil,' he said curiously.

'Sorry, Mr Fraser.'

He felt her move backwards, away from him. As if she was about to run.

'No.' He pulled her back towards him. 'I liked it.' He felt her shiver. 'I think we ought to stay here for a moment, don't you?'

Malise felt her throat close completely. She knew what she wanted to do. Stay here for ever, safe, and away from everyone else except for him. She felt his fingers trace the lines of the tears, now mingling with the rain on her face. She saw his shadow bend towards her in the darkness and then he kissed her. Over and over again, holding her as if she was something precious which he might break if he wasn't careful. And she kissed him back.

'I've thought about you so much.' Neil broke away from her with real reluctance.

'I'd better get back to Jessie,' Malise said awkwardly. 'And you'd better get home. You smell now. It's your shoes.'

Neil looked down, the leather shoes were stained, and he didn't want to think what the mud-like substance they were covered in actually was.

'I can always get new ones,' he replied. 'Monday night. Tell them you're going to the library. I'll meet you outside.'

Malise nodded, all thoughts of her Monday washing duties forgotten. 'And don't forget to go to Churchill's speech on Saturday at the Green.'

'I know. I'm having lunch with him.'

'And I'll be giving him an appetite.' She reached up and kissed him swiftly. 'We've a little something for him.' Unable to think of anything more to say, she took to her heels and ran off into the night.

Neil watched her retreating figure. Then turned up his collar and returned to his world. Smiling with satisfaction.

Chapter 4

'Now, who has ropes and chains?'

At Miss Proctor's request Malise and a few others raised their hands. Miss Proctor gave a grim smile as she surveyed the dozen or so women who were sheltering under the thick trees and bushes of the copse above Magdalen Green. Malise could feel the butterflies gathering in her stomach, she hadn't been able to eat that morning.

'You will go out into the crowd and watch politely, like the ladies you are.' Miss Proctor tightened her lips as her cold eyes rested on Malise. 'On my signal, you will run to the bandstand and fix yourselves to it. I will lead the talking. I want no shouting unless I order it.'

Malise fingered her rope, unlike the others, it was old and rather oily. Most of them had brought stringy cord, or what looked like thin chain.

'Now I don't want you all bunching up like grapes, spread out round the bandstand, I will be in front of Mr Churchill and you must imagine yourselves like clock numerals. Miss Smith, you will be one, Miss Beaker number two . . .' she went on, and Malise waited for her name. 'You, Miss Monroe, will be six.'

Six, that was at the back, no one would see her. Malise crossed her arms, trust Miss Proctor to give her friends the good numbers. It was always the same.

'Now leave one at a time. We don't want to draw attention to ourselves.'

Malise waited as, one at a time, the ladies walked down the steep bank and made their way along the neat path that circled the green. The grass was slightly damp under her feet, but she couldn't help but notice there had to be at least two hundred people there. And there were some policemen walking about. Suddenly it seemed less like fun and much more serious. To take her mind off it, Malise stared at a train steaming over the Tay Bridge, crossing by the pillars that marked where the bridge had collapsed into the sea, a few short years after it had been built. The crowd was gathering near the white wrought-iron bandstand. And they were different from the usual crowd, these were clerks and men who wore hats, not caps. Women and children, wearing Sunday-best, despite it only being Saturday. That was why the workers weren't there. They were working. Today, her audience would be the professional classes, and even some of the gentry. They weren't laughing and talking, the children weren't running around. Everyone was on their best behaviour. And that unnerved Malise. She saw Miss Proctor, walking briskly as if she were a general marshalling troops. Malise scurried away, she didn't want anyone to see Miss Proctor signalling to her. She was giving the game away before they'd even started.

Malise glanced around at the women who were standing with studied casualness, under trees or beside bushes. None of them looked like they'd be any good in a fight, but it wasn't as though they were going to do any fighting. And, despite Miss Proctor's attempts to take the fun out of the demonstration, Malise began to feel that she was going to enjoy herself.

'Nice to see Winston back in his constituency,' Richard murmured to his son.

'Surprised to see he still knows the way here,' Neil remarked, as they took their places at the side of the bandstand. 'He's been vocal enough of his dislike of the place.'

'He truly is an excellent public speaker,' Richard said, as Winston Churchill took the stand and began to address the assembled crowd. But as soon as the MP began to speak, Miss Proctor interrupted.

'Votes for women!' she shouted in her strident voice and, at the rallying call, the women streamed out from their places, clambering unceremoniously on to the elegant bandstand as an obviously furious Member of Parliament tried to be heard above the mêlée. Neil and Richard smirked at the slightly ludicrous sight of a group of women tying themselves to the ornate railings, as various assorted Liberal Party organizers attempted to remove the cleaner, better-class ones. Malise took her place at the back, tying her rope the best she could, but it kept slipping. This wasn't going well at all, and she couldn't see anything, she could only hear a lot of posh, raised voices.

'Police!'

As the cry went up, Malise pulled herself from the rope and peeked out from her place to see two lines of policemen running towards them. What should she do? Wait and get arrested, or try to slip away? But then she felt a man grab her by the hair, it was one of the organizers.

'Might have known Monroe's girl'd be here!' The man shook her head like he would a dog. Struggling desperately, she pulled away from him and ran away, straight into the path of the other Liberal Party members.

'I suggest you do not treat the young lady like that!' Neil had reached her before the others had time to gather their anger. There was a scream as one of the demonstrators was arrested and Neil took advantage of the distraction. Swiftly, he ushered her away from the people.

'I think you ought to leave,' he said as they weaved their way past the tall men. They'll only hand you over to the police and you don't want to end up in Bell Street.' They dodged through the confused, curious crowd, losing themselves in the commotion. 'So this is what you meant last night,' he continued as they reached safety in the little copse, high up on the hill and away from the scattering crowd, both of them laughing with nervous exhilaration.

'I don't believe you, Malise Monroe,' he said as he rubbed the stitch in his side. 'I can't believe that you actually tied yourself to that bandstand. What were you going to do?'

'It wasn't my idea,' Malise protested. 'But Miss Proctor said it would make a good photograph, and that means you get in the newspaper. Which is good for the cause.' She shrugged. 'Glad your rope is so useless.'

'Hey!' He grabbed her by the arm, still grinning wildly. 'So that's all the thanks I get for saving you from the local constabulary?'

'I saved myself.'

'You show me absolutely no respect,' he complained mockingly. 'One day, young lady, you'll learn.'

'I've told you before, I'm no lady.' His eyes were such a beautiful blue, she thought absently.

'No, you're Malise Monroe, people's champion, scourge of perfectly innocent parliamentarians, and you've got really rough hands,' he said drolly.

'I'm a really rough person.'

Neil shook his head slowly.

'No, Malise. Scratch off your veneer, and you're a completely different person.'

'What kind of person am I?' she asked softly.

'Unselfish. What you do, you do for other people. Not for yourself. You'd give up everything for those people down there. Without them even asking you. And you're not afraid of a fight.'

'I don't want to fight,' she confessed. 'It's just that when you need to make people look, you have to do something exciting. Dangerous. Different. So people remember it.'

'Well, I certainly remember all my encounters with you,' he said as he drew her to him. And then he kissed her, gently at first, then, as she kissed him back eagerly, he found himself moving till they were against a tree.

'You intrigue me, Malise,' he murmured into her cheek. 'I've never met anyone like you before.' He rubbed his face against her soft skin.

Malise looked into his eyes. They sparkled like the Tay on a sunny day. She'd never had anyone look at her that way before. As if she were the only person in the world.

'Malise,' he repeated as he kissed her once more. She felt his hands moving over her body, and she felt herself move and stretch, wanting him to touch her, to hold her. She felt them both slide down till they were at the foot of the old oak tree, sunlight dappling through the leaves, warming the lush green grass.

'I want you, Malise.'

'I want you,' she repeated. And she did. She wanted him to talk to her, to hold her as if she were the most precious thing in his life. And it seemed so natural that it was him. She felt his hands moving over her legs, she could feel his body, heavy yet gentle on hers, then it was becoming uncomfortable. He was too heavy for her, he was crushing her. Then she felt the pain.

'Ah!' She opened her eyes and saw his face, his dark hair falling over it. She saw his clothes, his heavy overcoat brushing against the wild yellow flowers that lay next to her. But he wasn't looking at her. His eyes were closed, and a vein was bulging in his forehead as he moved heavily, rhythmically, jolting her body. This wasn't what she wanted. She wanted to talk to him, to kiss him, for him to seek her out from the others. She didn't want him to do this, like an animal in the woods on the damp ground. His face was growing red and then he groaned and she felt him spill inside her.

Neil opened his eyes, and smiled with triumphant laziness. He moved to kiss her, but she turned her head.

'Malise, you should have said,' he murmured tenderly as he touched her cheek. 'The first time . . .'

'I didn't want there to be a first time, Mr Fraser,' she returned despairingly. 'What have you done to me?' She watched the smile on Neil's face droop, like his hair.

'I thought you wanted me.' He was confused, and less sure of himself now.

'I didn't want that.' Kicking out at him, she pushed herself up into a sitting position. 'You've ruined me! Get away, I tell you, get away!' Her voice was loud in the silent wood. Neil stood up and buttoned himself up, brushing down his clothes.

'Malise.' He crouched down and tried to touch her hand. 'We haven't done anything wrong. It's just a way to show feelings for another person. Next time . . .'

'Just go away, Mr Fraser,' she replied bitterly. 'You've had what you wanted.' She turned her face to the tree and she heard him go. Then she looked down. All around her were crushed wild flowers. For ever broken by Neil Fraser.

'Where on earth did you get to?' Richard said as Neil arrived in the club a short time later. 'I thought you'd been kidnapped by the suffragettes.'

Neil flushed with embarrassment.

'No, Father, I just saw someone whom I knew.' He cleared his throat. 'Got rather carried away chatting with them.' He hesitated for a moment, for some reason he wanted to confess, he wanted his father to reassure him. 'Actually, it was a lady friend.'

'Well, you'll need to be a mite more discreet, Neil, since you are going to be wed soon.' He laughed gruffly and slapped him heartily on the back. 'You sly dog, got more of your father in you than I thought. Come and have a drink.'

But as the waiter handed him a sherry on a silver platter and the talk turned to ridiculing the suffragettes, Neil tried not to think of Malise's words. Of her face. And the knowledge that he had done something she hadn't wanted. That he had wanted. He remembered her face, her anger, her disappointment in him. He'd never be able to face her again. Running away was so much easier than facing up to humiliation.

Malise went back to her house and stripped off her clothing. Then she washed herself, scrubbing at her skin. All the time cursing herself. Neil Fraser was no different from the lads in her street. How could he want to do something like that with her? That was something you did in your marriage bed, with someone you had promised yourself to. Why couldn't he have contented himself with kisses and cuddles, with talks and walks? But he hadn't wanted that, he hadn't wanted to talk to her at all. He was just the same as Johnnie Turpin. She recalled how shocked she had been when Mr Scott had touched her leg. Well now she knew how to catch a baby, and she didn't like it at all.

Every day she lingered at school after lessons, hoping that he would be there, to tell her that it had been a misunderstanding, that his carnal desires has got the better of him. But he never came. He didn't even attend the Christmas service. She found herself walking past the Elizabeth, hoping that he would come out in his motor car. But he didn't. And as the weeks stretched into months, Malise realized she had another problem. Her curse hadn't come since that day, either.

As she woke up early on Boxing Day morning, Malise felt her stomach gurgling in a way that had become all too familiar over the past few weeks. She rushed out of the house to the lavatory, ignoring the stench from Mr Johnson's inability to urinate into the bowl, and began to retch.

'Come on,' she heard wee Jimmy Johnson knocking on the door, 'hurry up. I'm bursting.'

She wiped her mouth with her hand, then stood up, pulling on the chain to flush the lavatory.

'There you go,' she said shakily.

'Are you being sick again?' Jimmy said as he squeezed past her. 'You're in there every morning.'

'I've got the flu,' she mumbled. 'You get in there.' With that she clamped her jaws tightly shut, waiting for the boy to come out. She must have the flu, what else could she have? But that afternoon, when she was feeling as right as rain, darning her father's socks as she waited for him to come home, her hand slipped over her stomach. Hadn't Jessie said her Sheila was sick with her bairns? Malise jumped up and grabbed her coat. There was someone she had to talk to.

'Please, Jessie, you have to help me.' They were sitting on the wall behind Jessie's house, watching the brown slushy snow freezing into lumps of dirty ice.

'But who's the father, Malise?' Jessie was agog. 'Is it that Johnnie Turpin? He was friendly enough when we went to the Monkey Parade.' She drew her name in the frosted snow on the wall. 'Your daddy'll make him marry you, you lucky thing.'

Malise hesitated for a moment.

'Malise, I did it with Johnnie too. It was awful messy, and I thought his head was going to explode, he went so red. And he didn't want to know me afterwards.'

'If I tell you, do you promise not to tell?'

Jessie nodded solemnly.

'It was Johnnie,' Malise said slowly. 'Oh Jessie, he just used me and now I'm in trouble.'

'There are ways to get rid of bairns, Doctor McPherson's always going on about the women who do it. Most of them used to be midwives.' She flicked a bit of ice with her finger. 'But he doesn't say anything nice about them.'

'Jessie, I'm desperate,' Malise returned. 'I need you to help me.'

'I'll see if I can find out for you.' Jessie shook her head. 'But Malise, you should just tell your daddy. He'd sort it all out for you.'

Two weeks later, Malise was walking through the Overgate looking for a particular tenement. She had a woman's name and address from Jessie, and a list of what she had to bring. But what did she need a bottle of gin for, she wondered? At last she found the tenement and turned into the steps. They were filthy, and running with mud. The cold wind howled in the roof, and as Malise walked up the stairs, she could see the walls were covered in tiny, dirty handprints. Children's handprints. She put a hand to her mouth, sickened at the sight. She struggled past a pool of vomit on the stairwell, fighting the desire to run away, back home, to tell her father the truth. She knocked on a heavy black door and recoiled as an old woman, wizened from drink, answered it, wearing a slimy, torn pinny.

She handed over the money and the bottle of gin and went into a room that looked surprisingly like her own, except that she swept out her own every morning, and her range wasn't rusted and caked in old, rancid grease, and her crockery wasn't sitting on a crumb-encrusted table, next to an empty bottle of whisky and a smelly half-eaten fish supper. So this was where she would be getting rid of the final remnants of Neil Fraser.

'What do I do now?' Malise looked at the woman – she was grimy, with dirt-encrusted fingernails, and the few teeth she had in her head were little more than rotten yellow stumps.

'Take off your drawers and squat over that.' She pointed to an old trough that stank of stale urine. Malise shuddered then did as she was told.

'You're only a wee lass.' The woman bade her to hold up her skirts as she eased her fingers between Malise's legs. Malise held her breath as she felt a cold metal rod inside her and then there was a popping sound and liquid poured out from her.

'Go home.' The old woman turned away. 'It'll start soon.'

'Can't I have it here?' she said desperately.

'No!' The woman became agitated. 'They'll throw both of us in prison, you know, if they find you here with a dead baby.' She hauled her up from the trough and pushed her towards the door of the tenement. 'You're leaving a trail behind you all over my floor!' The woman gave another push and left her outside the door, her drawers still down by her knees.

Wrapping her handkerchief between her legs, Malise began the walk home. She could feel a pain in her stomach and the handkerchief was sodden, but there was nothing like the labour she had heard about.

That night, though, she could feel her body sweating. She lay in her tiny bed, alone and scared, waiting for the moment. But morning came and still there was no child.

'Malise, look at the time.' Gabriel shuffled out of the bedroom, scratching his head. 'The fire isn't lit.' He stopped as he saw her, grey and sweating. 'Oh my God, what's wrong with you?'

Malise just looked up at him with feverish eyes.

'You should have told me you were unwell.' He stooped at her bedside. 'Where does it hurt?'

'Down below, Dad,' she murmured. 'Please, Dad,' she grabbed his hand, 'I don't feel well.'

'It's this bad weather, and you staying out with Jessie,' he said. 'Those shoes of yours aren't good enough. I told you to get some galoshes.'

'We used the money to send those letters out. The ones to the docks in Liverpool and London,' she replied.

'You should have told me, I'd have found the money somewhere else.' He took out his handkerchief and wiped her brow. 'I work you too hard, and you have all that studying. You've run out of energy, wee lass, and I've kept pushing you.'

'Oh Dad, it's not that at all,' she replied. 'I'll be fine in a wee minute.'

'I'm sending a note for the nurse,' he said resolutely. 'The factory can wait.'

Nurse Baxter took one look at Malise and a suspicious look flitted over her features.

'How are you, my dear?' she asked briskly.

'I don't know,' Malise replied uncertainly.

'Let's get these blankets off you.' She lifted the covers from Malise's little pull-down bed. Then she put her hand on Malise's stomach and felt her distended womb.

'Pregnant.' She looked at the girl. 'You could have killed yourself, you know. Who was it?'

'Who was what?' Gabriel said from the background where he was hovering anxiously.

'Your daughter has been to an abortionist, Mr Monroe.' Nurse Baxter looked grimly at the man. 'A woman who has probably torn your daughter's bladder, and given her an infection. The baby is still in her womb.'

'She can't, she's . . .' Gabriel looked lost for words.

'Your daughter is pregnant.' Nurse Baxter held out her hand for her payment. 'From the feel of her belly, I'd say about four months gone.'

Gabriel's face grew pale. Malise could see him, it was as if he had heard the nurse, but couldn't remember what the words meant.

'But how could my wee lass be expecting?' he said dumbly.

'That's something you ought to ask her.' The nurse began to pack away her bag. 'Look, it's the age she's at. Some get away with it, but I see a fair number of girls in her situation every week. Couldn't she marry the father?'

Gabriel handed over the two-shilling fee, still staring at Malise, as the nurse made her way out.

'But who was it? How can you be?' He gave up attempting to say the words.

'I'm so sorry, Daddy,' Malise whispered. 'I didn't want to do it. But he did.' Fat tears began to roll down her cheeks. 'I was so stupid. I should have known.'

'Who made you, Malise?' Gabriel said tightly. 'Tell me, did someone attack you?' He went to hold her, then stopped himself.

'No.' She screwed her eyes up like a child and scrubbed her hand across her face. 'It was when the police came to the demonstration. I should have known, Daddy, but he was nice to me and he said he liked me. That I was special.'

'Who on earth said he liked you, Malise?' Gabriel said incredulously.

'Mr Fraser. Young Mr Fraser.' Malise looked over at her father. 'He was there and took me off up the hill. I didn't realize what he wanted, then all of a sudden it was too late and he was doing it . . .' She bit her lip.

'Mr Fraser forced himself on you?' Gabriel had gone pale under his mop of gypsy-brown hair.

'He kept telling me how special I was, and he wanted me to help him. He said he wanted to help the workers too.' She looked up. 'I never thought for a moment that he wanted anything else.'

'He wanted to use you to hurt me.' Gabriel turned, furious, to his daughter who shrank away instinctively. 'I'm going to see that the bastard pays for doing this!' Gabriel grabbed his coat and cap.

'Daddy!' she shouted after him. 'Daddy, please.'

But Gabriel had gone. Malise lay back. All she wanted him to do was give her a cuddle, tell her he still loved her, that she hadn't let him down. But Gabriel was too lost in his own thoughts to notice.

'Fraser!' Gabriel's voice had never been louder, more strident, more fearsome.

'What on earth . . . ?' Archie Taylor came out of his office as he saw the union leader march up the stairs as if he were about to beat the living daylights out of someone.

'Fraser!' Gabriel ran at Neil Fraser's office and almost ripped the door from its hinges. 'You slimy underhand bastard!'

Neil Fraser lifted his head from the ledger he had been reading. 'Can I help you?' he asked nervously. He'd never seen the man this furious. Gabriel roared and punched Neil clean out of his seat, dragging him up by the collar and smacking his body against the wall, every muscle in his lean body primed with hatred.

'Enjoy having my daughter, did you, Fraser? Did you enjoy it, with a fifteen-year-old child? She's pregnant now, you bastard, and, as the devil is my witness, you'll pay for

74

this!' His hand tightened, forcing Neil further against the wall.

'I thought she was older.' Neil struggled to get the words out.

'She told me what you did to her, forcing yourself on her.' Gabriel slammed him against the wall again. 'An innocent wee lass! You used her, and now you'll pay!'

'What the hell are you doing, Monroe?' Archie, followed by three of the draftsmen, came running in, grabbing Gabriel who kicked out wildly as he was wrestled to the ground.

'Look, Gabriel,' Neil began. 'I don't know what she's told you.'

'Go home, Monroe, before you get yourself sacked.' Archie kicked him hard in the stomach to stop his words.

With an anguished cry, Gabriel ripped himself from the men's arms and sprang at Neil. The two men rolled like drunks on the floor as Archie and the others tried to extricate them, Gabriel landing punches and kicks, till Archie separated them.

'Get out, Monroe,' Archie said in a ragged breath, 'before I get fifty men to stand up and say that they've had the wee whore an' all.'

The men manhandled Gabriel to the stairway, but he slipped his jacket and made one last lunge at Neil. Archie punched out at Gabriel, a lucky punch that hit him on the side of the face. Neil watched as the man, roaring like an animal, arms flailing, fell backwards down the steep staircase, till he landed heavily on his back with a sickening crunch.

Neil ran down the stairs, closely followed by the clerks.

'Monroe?' Neil said, but Gabriel's eyes were open, unseeing, his face contorted in shock, his body broken like a discarded puppet, his arms under him.

'Shall I call for the ambulance wagon?' asked one of the clerks as Neil knelt and put his hand to Gabriel's neck. Neil shook his head. There was no pulse.

'He'll not be needing an ambulance.' He looked up at Archie, standing at the top of the stairs. 'He's broken his neck. He's dead.'

Neil looked at the union leader, there was no peace in his death. He could still see the hatred on Gabriel's face, etching itself on his memory. Then he walked back up the stairs.

'We'll need to call the police, Mr Fraser,' Archie said quietly as they went back to the office. 'But you'll need to sort your clothes and I'll need to speak to the boys before we do anything.'

'But what will we tell them?' Neil looked helplessly at the man who had taken charge of the situation.

'Minor argument, then fell down the stairs.' He looked at Neil – his face was swelling and there was a cut above his eyebrow. His fine clothes were badly torn and it would be obvious to anyone that this had been no minor altercation. 'I think it would be better if you went home. I'll handle things here.'

'No, I . . .'

'Mr Fraser, there is no need for your laundry to be aired this way,' Archie said commandingly. 'I know what has to be done.'

'That was Taylor,' Richard Fraser said as he put down the telephone receiver and picked up his teacup. 'The police have their statement from him and there will be no further action taken. Monroe was well known for his temper. He'd been in prison.'

'Dad,' Neil said helplessly. 'I've no idea how it happened. He just fell, I saw him, it took such a long time for him to hit the bottom.' He looked up at the elegant carriage clock that sat on the mantelpiece calmly ticking away the minutes. 'If only—'

'He attacked you, and you defended yourself, and remember that you didn't strike the blow that felled him. Someone else did.' Richard's face clouded over and he sat down on an elegantly upholstered armchair, his large body seeming too large for it's spindly, carved legs. 'And I think the words "if only" are rather pointless in this situation.'

'Monroe didn't attack me over a labour dispute,' Neil said as he fingered his black eye.

'Archie told me,' Richard's fingers clenched around the claw-like arm of the chair. 'In such circumstances it is usual to give the woman a sum of money, to recompense for any inconvenience. Ten pounds will suffice. Archie will take it to her, to avoid any speculation.'

'I should at least go and talk to her, to apologize for my conduct.' He looked out the French windows to his mother's rose garden, the bushes now simply leaves and thorns.

'You will do nothing of the sort, Neil,' Richard forcefully put down his teacup on the side table. 'You have embarrassed your family enough simply by lying with the girl. You will gain nothing by prostrating yourself and asking for forgiveness. Except harming our family name even further. Good God, man, you'll be married soon enough, we all have these little adventures. You were unlucky, you should have stuck to dancers like everyone else. But you didn't. You had to have that Monroe girl. Well, you've had her, so now you leave her alone!' And with that he walked out, leaving Neil alone in front of the large, blazing fire.

Neil stared into the fire, and relived his day over and over. Could he have done anything differently? Could he really have ignored his feelings for Malise? He hadn't even realized he had feelings for her, till that night they sheltered from the rain together. At least she would have enough money; she wouldn't need to worry about that. And she had a position at the school. She was a pretty girl, someone would marry her. But it all came down to a single, harsh truth. Neil was no more in control of what he could do than she was. Than anyone was.

Malise was unusually silent as the men from the co-operative funeral parlour brought her father home, even when Mrs Baker put her arm around her, she didn't say a word. She just looked at her father, and she remained dry-eyed and seemingly emotionless.

'Comes to us all, Malise,' Mrs Baker said softly. 'And at least he didn't suffer.'

'He was right,' Malise whispered shakily. 'Always said I'd be the death of him.'

Theresa Baker cuddled Malise's small, still body, thinking back to the time when Mr Baker had brought her home. At the way she would retreat inside herself when she was scared. And Mrs Baker could tell now. Malise was terrified.

'You'll come back and live with us, won't you?' Mrs Baker said comfortingly. 'Can't have a young girl like you alone in the world. It'll be like old times, you and Jessie together.' She brushed Malise's curls from her pale, strained face, her brown eyes enormous in her head. 'You'll always be welcome at ours, Malise. You know that, don't you?'

Malise nodded absently. But what would Mrs Baker say when the truth began to show? No one in the world would want to know her then.

She was barely aware of Mrs Baker leaving, or of some of Gabriel's friends, coming to pay their respects. It was as if she were watching a moving picture show. This didn't feel like her life, she didn't fit in at all. As the last one left, she heard the door knock again. Archie Taylor stood there, in his working suit, its high collar straining against his heavy chin.

'Just come to pay my respects, Miss Monroe.'

Wordlessly, she let the works manager into the room that was dwarfed by the cheap, roughly made coffin.

'The union'll miss him,' Archie said softly. 'Especially now with the wage negotiations coming up.'

Malise looked up curiously. Her father had hated Taylor. What was he doing?

'Billy Turpin will manage.' She shrugged her thin shoulders.

'But Monroe always knew he was different. He always

knew that the Frasers were more than slightly feared of what he could do.' He stood there deep in thought. 'Of course, that was before everyone found out he had a dirty little slut of a daughter.' He stared into the air. 'When Fraser told him exactly what you did with him, in front of a good twenty men, I thought he would die of shame. Which he did.'

Malise stood frozen to the spot. Here he was, Archie Taylor, telling her he knew everything. Now the whole world knew of her shame.

'Oh, he told us all about you, Malise,' Archie continued to whisper. 'Made your father stand there and listen.' He put a hand on her arm. 'And now you've a taste for it . . .' His hand moved over to her breast, as he squeezed it hard. 'You socialists. Didn't take Mr Fraser long to turn you, but I remember hearing that your mother was anyone's for a shilling.'

Malise stood stock-still, too frozen with horror to slap away his soft, bloated hand.

'And now you owe Mr Fraser money, Malise. Five pounds for the banister Monroe broke when he fell down the stairs, running away from Mr Fraser and the truth. But he told everyone else. We all know what you are like, Malise. And we'd all like a go.'

'Get off me!' She pushed away from him, throwing herself at the wall.

'There are twenty men willing to stand up in court and say that they've had you,' Archie continued, 'if you try and take it any further.' He smiled. 'And I'll be right at the front of the queue.'

Malise stared at him in horror, this was his true face, the face of a man who had already had her beaten. And now she was alone.

'I won't take it any further, Mr Taylor,' she said quickly. 'I won't say a word.'

'You remember that, Malise.' He licked his lips. 'Because if you do, I'll make sure you can never hold your head up in Dundee again. Just like him.' He tossed his head in the direction of Gabriel's body. 'And one last thing. Mr Fraser wants recompense from you, for the damage you've caused to his reputation by bringing all this out into the open.'

'I've no money to give him,' she exclaimed.

'I've your father's wages here, and you have to find the rest. Five pounds for the banister, and the rest will go to Mr Fraser.'

'But he has enough money, I'll need mine!' she exclaimed.

'You don't get rich by giving it away, girl,' Archie returned. 'Now get me the money.' He bent down till his head was next to her ear. 'You don't want me to send the boys round again, do you?'

Afraid, Malise hastily went to the bed and took out a sock from under the mattress. In it was almost eight pounds. Their life savings.

'Thank you.' Archie counted it carefully before putting it into his pocket. 'And sign here, just so that everything is in order.' He took out a thick roll of paper and a pen.

Malise picked up the pen and signed at the bottom without looking at it. She just wanted Archie Taylor to leave, to go away and never come back.

'Thank you.' Archie blew on the signature to dry it, then put the paper back in his pocket. 'And remember, Malise, if you want to earn a penny or two, you come and see me.' With that he walked out of the door, slamming it before he went down to the street trying not to whistle.

'So then what happened?' Each of the clerks was three sheets to the wind, courtesy of Archie and a few bottles of cheap whisky.

'Mr Fraser, I'll do anything for the job.' Archie put on a high effeminate voice. 'Walked in on them. She was on her knees and he was smiling, trousers around his ankles.'

'The dirty wee besom,' Charlie, the clerk who had managed to land a punch, laughed.

'Aye, but at least it had shut her up. Can't complain when she's got a gob full now, can she?'

'But he said she was having his bastard,' Charlie persisted.

'Aye, well, you'll see whatever works she ends up in . . .' Archie laughed lasciviously. 'Let's face it, pretty wee thing like her, if she wants a bit of money, she could go round all the works, then come back nine months later and just how many would pay up?' The men all laughed. 'And I'll tell you something, though, when I went over with her father's wages, she offered it to me. Can't fall again, she said.'

'And did you?' Charlie asked excitedly.

'What? You never know what you could catch off someone like that. Let her have a wee fiddle with it, though.'

'And did you fiddle with hers?'

'Certainly did,' Archie said triumphantly. 'Certainly did.'

Malise paced round and round her father's coffin, where it lay on the rough, wooden table. Then she stopped. Tenderly, she went through his pockets, taking out his wallet, which contained only a few shillings and a photograph, the only photograph of her mother they possessed. And then she found it: her father's whistle. The whistle he had used when he was calling out his workers. It was dull, the shine worn off it where his rough fingers had rubbed it for luck when speaking to the likes of Archie Taylor.

'He'll pay for this, Daddy,' she said in a whisper. 'As God is my witness, Neil Fraser will pay for your death. But I'll pay more. Because I'm the one to blame.'

'Lovely piece of ham, this.' Billy Turpin, the new convener of the Elizabeth, stuffed his face into another sandwich as he chatted with some others back at the house. Malise looked at him, holding court at her father's funeral. As though he were in charge or something. 'And I'll need to see you next week, Malise. I'm giving a talk at the Pillars and you're good with facts and figures.'

'Why?' Malise looked at the man, the brutishly handsome elder brother of Johnnie.

'Of course Malise will be happy to do it.' Gordon Scott came over to them.

'Sorry, Gordon, didn't see you down there!' Billy made as if to put a pint on top of the headmaster's balding head. 'You can write me a wee speech, and if it's good enough, I'll give it a go.'

Malise was about to reply that she had no intention of helping Billy Turpin, but Gordon grabbed her arm and gestured for her to wheel him to one side.

'I think we know who your father's successor is going to be,' his cultured voice said, once they were safely away from the raucous Billy.

'I know, Mr Scott, I was just thinking that myself,' Malise replied in a whisper. 'My dad always said Billy would melt down his granny for glue, if he could gain out of it.'

'I'm sorry I couldn't come to the graveside.' He shrugged helplessly at the chair. 'What are you going to do?' he continued. 'If you go to teacher training college, you'll need to work till then, but you'll manage it.'

'I'll not have time to study,' she walked away from the teacher.

'Malise,' Gordon said urgently as he wheeled after her, 'he wouldn't want you to give up like this, you've a great future ahead of you.'

She looked at the teacher, sitting in his chair. And felt sick.

'Och aye, a future that you and my dad had planned for me.' She laughed drily as she walked out the front door. 'I'm not going to be a teacher.'

'You are easily capable of teaching, Malise.' He wheeled after her. 'And don't forget it was Gabriel's dream that you would be on the council.'

'Dreams aren't real, Mr Scott. That's why they're dreams.' She began to hurry down the steep winding street.

'Malise!' Gordon Scott hurried after her, easing his chair through the doorway and down the step. But the wheels slipped on some of the mud brought in by the mourners and he spilled out on to the dirty, wet street, to the accompaniment of children's laughter as they ran away from the scene.

Malise turned then went back to Mr Scott and offered her hand.

'Put the brake on the chair, please.'

She did as she was bid, then watched as Mr Scott hauled himself up into his seat.

'See, Malise?' he said quietly. 'Even I know that sometimes I need help.'

'Mr Scott, I can't.' She screwed up her face like the child she still was. 'It was all my fault he died and now I can't do anything to get rid of it.' Big gulping sobs were coming from her now, in the deserted street, in the cold rain.

'What do you mean?' Mr Scott said gently.

'He died defending me, and for what? I got what I deserved, for being stupid, for not knowing my place; for being me.' She bit down hard on her lip.

'Malise?' Gordon Scott gripped her hand, and she looked at him as if for the first time. He understood, she didn't know why, but he understood.

'I'm waiting for a baby, Mr Scott,' she said bitterly. 'That's why I'll never be one of your precious teachers!' She stormed off down the hill and around the bend past the rows of tiny houses, all huddled together on the side of the hill, until she came to the elegant opulence of the Perth Road. And there it was, his mansion, the home of the man who had ruined her life. There was a high stone wall surrounding gardens as large as a park, which were full of oak trees. Feeling small, Malise walked round the wall till she came to the ornate wrought-iron gates, painted black and gold. Instinctively, she curled her hands around them, the freezing, driving rain running down her reddened knuckles. The house was like a palace, with lights twinkling in all the windows, the occasional figure passing across them. Malise could just imagine the family sitting down to dinner at a table groaning with cooked hams and vegetables. Neil's castle – a house so large that there was a whole park around it and gates to keep intruders away. This was where he belonged. This was his world.

'You said you'd never hurt me again,' she whispered as her fingers were battered by the icy rain. 'You promised. But you were lying. All the time, you lied.'

Chapter 5

The next morning, Malise returned to the school. The children, after three days of being taught by Mr Scott, were lively, playing up and checking her. Eventually, she got through the morning, and as she settled down to her work that afternoon, her mind wouldn't let her study. What was the point, anyway?

'Malise!' Gordon Scott was at the door, watching her with a strange, distant look on his face. Malise looked up, then shrank away. She had told him her deepest, darkest secret, and she didn't want to face his disgust. 'Are you sure about your health?' he asked pointedly.

She nodded.

'There are women you can go to,' he began as he wheeled himself over to her desk.

'Tried that. Didn't work,' she cut him off rather cruelly.

'You can go to an unmarried mother's home and have it adopted,' he said calmly.

'My father died for this bastard.' She stroked the pencil in her hands, then broke it in two. 'I think God is trying to tell me something, don't you?'

'Bearing an illegitimate child is something that will ruin you, Malise,' he persisted. 'And it is such a waste of your brains, your talents.' He slammed his fist down on the desk. 'My God, girl, if you were just another silly wee sweeper I could have understood, but you could have made it to the corporation!'

'Why are you so annoyed about it? It's my life I've ruined,' she snapped at him. 'No one else's.'

'You need to marry the father of your child, and I'll help you study. It'll be difficult.'

'He won't marry me, Mr Scott,' she interrupted him.

'Why not?'

'Because he's a Fraser.' She stared at the pages of mathematical problems, the numbers and letters swimming in front of her. 'One of those Frasers.'

Gordon Scott composed himself for a moment.

'Did no one ever tell you to be careful of men like him?' He said in a tired voice.

'So you think I should march up to his big house and demand that he makes an honest woman of me?' she goaded bitterly. 'Everyone knows what Dundee is like. Half the women here have bastards, and now I'm just another.'

'Can't you find someone else to marry?' he said desperately. 'You're an attractive enough girl. Get some waste-of-time kettle boiler like the rest of the women in this town.'

'I'm almost five months gone! Who could I fool into that?' She stopped. 'And anyway, it would hardly be fair now, would it?'

'Malise,' Mr Scott said eventually. 'Would you not marry someone you didn't love, so that your child could have a father and you could continue to do your work for the party and the union?'

'Who would want to marry me, knowing what I had done? Who would want to take on me and . . .' her hand went to her stomach.

'That's settled, then.' He hesitated. 'We can marry.'

'What?' Malise's shock showed on her face. Mr Scott patted her hand.

'I'm offering for you.'

She grabbed her hands away.

'Mr Scott, but you're . . .'

'Your only chance of keeping at least one of your dreams.' He stared at her. 'With me, you can have your child, and I've the contacts in the party, you know that.' He looked down. 'You are someone who can go somewhere, Malise, and I won't let you ruin your life.'

'But . . .'

'I can't have children, Malise, and I'm under no illusion about that side of marriage.' His hands went automatically to his thighs. 'That you would have to give up, but you'd have one child and I can help you. This is about you doing your duty.'

'To my father, you mean?'

'To yourself. In ten years' time you could be a councillor, with the right guidance. You're a born politician, Malise. You understand that sometimes you have to give up one thing to gain another. I lost my chance with my legs, your father lost his because he didn't have the education, but you can still have your chance. But only if you are respectable.'

'I don't want to marry you, Mr Scott,' she whispered.

'I know, Malise, and I don't particularly want to be married. I've got used to my own company over the last few years.' He nodded in an almost resigned fashion. 'I don't expect you to agree immediately, but I would say that you might want to consider marrying before you start to really show, and that won't be long now, will it?'

'Would I have to, you know . . .' She nodded her head towards his lap.

'No, Malise, I can't have that kind of relationship with a woman.' He licked his lips awkwardly. 'And I'll not marry you in a church, it would be a civil ceremony only.' He began to turn his wheelchair to go.

Malise looked at him, she could feel her stomach churning. Mr Scott actually wanted to be her husband! An old man with no legs and no sense of humour. The only man she had never seen laugh, she had never seen going into a pub. A man with nothing. Except a name he would give her. A name she needed. A name that would help her to be the person everyone thought she could be. A person who stood at the front of the crowd.

'Well, Malise?' His voice was more uncertain this time.

'I'm not a bad man, clean-living and I have a house with two rooms. And a kitchen. And you would be a respectable headmaster's wife, rather than a slattern with a bastard.'

'All right,' she said softly. Gordon took her hand, smiling grimly.

'I'll need your birth lines, when are you sixteen?'

'August.' She let out a sigh. 'Not for almost four months.'

'Can't be helped.' He shook his head. 'I'll book it this week.'

'Thank you, Mr Scott,' she said timidly.

'It's all right, Malise,' he said wearily. 'And from now on, try to call me Gordon. And I'll still need that maths homework in on Monday. If you're to sit your higher a year early, you'll need to get it all done.'

'Yes, Mr Scott.' For some reason, she was finding it difficult to talk.

'I know it's not what you want, Malise,' he said softly. 'But trust me, I have your best interests at heart.'

'So you're engaged to be married now?' Jessie said as they sat on the wall of Lochee Park. 'You didn't actually do it with Mr Scott, did you?' she added in a horrified whisper.

Malise shuddered with revulsion.

'Of course not. I need to get married, and he offered. He was a friend of my dad, and he will help me do things.' She smiled tightly. 'It'll not be like being married, we're just going to be friends,' she added in a whisper.

'Did he say that?' Jessie looked at her incredulously.

Malise swallowed and looked away.

'We have an understanding, Jessie, it's all about other things. Love doesn't matter. It doesn't last.' She could feel the tears begin to come and she blinked them away fiercely.

Jessie laughed shortly.

'You might have an understanding,' she said knowingly. 'But does he?'

Malise looked out over the park. In the distance, she

could see the road, the dray horses plodding up and down with their loads. Just plodding, never getting any further. This was where she belonged, this was who she was. How could she ever have dreamed differently?

'Let's go.' They jumped off the wall, Malise rather clumsily, because of her swollen stomach, and they began to walk over the grass. In the distance, a black car traversed the narrow road. 'You can tell me about this Arthur you've met.'

'Briar has reservations about this,' Richard said as he looked at his disconsolate son.

'He isn't the only one,' Neil retorted as he fingered the box in his pocket.

'Neil, please,' his mother remonstrated gently. 'Agnes is a lovely, quiet girl. Perfect for you.'

'He thinks you're a radical, you've made too many changes in the Elizabeth recently. Good God, what has it come to when even the Briars have heard about your troubles?'

'It's all changed now, Father,' Neil replied listlessly. 'Now I'm doing as I'm told.' He looked over at the park, there were people walking through it. How free they were, to do as they pleased, to marry whomever they wanted. He took the box out and opened it. Then snapped it shut again.

It was late the following afternoon when Neil drove over to Lochee, a part of town he rarely had cause to visit.

He took a deep breath as he got out of the car, and he began to walk down the wynd. He would offer his condolences first, then, when they were inside, he would talk to her, ascertain that he actually was the father. And then . . . he didn't know what he would do then. But he wanted to talk to her, needed to see her, so that in some way he could convince himself that she didn't hate him, that he hadn't ruined her life. Even though he knew he had.

Neil felt his shoes slipping on the worn cobbles, and a

smell of cooking cabbages and rancid fat seemed to fill the air. What an awful place to live. He went up the steps and inside the tenement till he saw the door and knocked on it. There was no answer.

'Are you from the parish?' An elderly woman's head appeared from the house next door.

'Is Miss Monroe in?' he enquired politely.

The woman laughed.

'Thought you were from them. Some of your other folk were round earlier, told her to pack and sent her off. She's fallen, you know. Back to the docks where she belongs. That Gabriel, God rest his soul, had women coming and going like there was no tomorrow.'

Neil walked away, leaving the woman to ramble on. So Malise had been taken into the care of the parish. That was fine, then. She'd get cared for there. He got back into his car and headed towards his comfortable home. He had bridge that night with Agnes and her parents, but his meeting with Billy Turpin had gone on longer than expected; and it had been a bloody battle; they'd got nowhere on paying the spinners, carders and checkers for a day's work lost when they had walked out over the young woman who had been injured when she was caught in a belt and thrown from a great height. Gabriel Monroe would have helped him work out a payment for the girl. But Gabriel wasn't there any more, and so there'd been a strike instead.

The following day, his name, along with that of the lovely Agnes, was to be in the paper. Under his father's instructions, they had decided on a short engagement. Because his father wished it, and, of all the things that he and his brother had done in their lives, defying their fearsome father was not one of them.

Malise was bored. She had been forced to leave the school when her condition became obvious, and since then she had been stuck inside the little house with Mrs Baker. Even Jessie was reluctant to go out for a walk to Lochee park with her, or to sit on the wall and chat. She didn't want to be tarred with the same brush.

'I need to go again,' Malise said as she got up from the sofa. 'This wee monster has me running up and down that stairwell all day and night.'

'Same with all mine,' Mrs Baker laughed. 'Little beggars sat on my bladder for the full nine months.'

Malise went to the stack of newspaper that had been cut up and placed on the table and took a few sheets. Then she went out and up the stairs to the stinking lavatory that was shared by the six families on their landing. She opened the door. Someone had urinated in the stall and the stench hit her like a needle. Gingerly, she pulled up her dress and went to sit down. As she did, water gushed from her, but it wasn't urine. No one could hold that much water.

'Mrs Baker!' Running as best as she could with the fluid still coming from her, Malise staggered back into the house.

'My goodness.' Mrs Baker grabbed that day's *Courier* and put it on the floor. 'You're early, aren't you?'

'It can't be coming,' Malise whimpered. 'I'm not married yet.'

'Sit down on the *Courier*, or it'll end up all over the place.' Mrs Baker put her arm around her and helped her over to the paper. 'By the looks of you, you'll be a mother soon.'

'I don't want to be someone's mammy or somebody's wife. It's horrible,' she wailed.

Mrs Baker pursed her lips. 'Should have thought of that before you had your fun, young lady.' She settled her on the floor. 'You'll just have to put up with it. I'll get a cloth.'

Malise felt the wave of pain sweep through her. She felt as if every muscle in her body was tearing in two.

'Don't push yet, you'll need your strength,' Mrs Baker warned. 'Babies take their time about things.'

'Get it out!'

'Always were the impatient one, weren't you?' Mrs Baker said despairingly. 'I've birthed all my Sheila's bairns and my sister's four and it's never taken less than a day.'

But Malise couldn't think about anything, not that it was a baby, not that it was the end of life as she knew it. All she could think about was how much it hurt.

As day turned into night, the men arrived home and were promptly dispatched to the pub to wait in peace. Then, when Jessie arrived, she took one look at her friend, sweating and red-faced, and making a din that could wake the dead, and turned to her mother.

'I'm never doing this, Ma,' she said, horrified.

'It's just Malise, Jessie,' Mrs Baker said consolingly. 'She's never believed in doing anything quietly.' She bent down to check between Malise's legs.

'Not long now, my dear.'

Malise looked at her in horror.

'You've been saying that all day!'

But within three hours, Malise had screamed and grunted and eventually given birth to a baby boy.

'Oh Malise, just look at him,' Mrs Baker said fondly. 'Don't you just want to eat him all up?'

Malise looked up, wanting to hate him. But the tiny child was absolutely perfect, from his tiny fingernails to the shock of dark hair on his head. And his beautiful Fraser blue eyes. She watched as Mrs Baker washed him down, hearing him cry like a frightened animal.

'Time for a feed now.' Mrs Baker put him into the crook of her arm. 'Just offer it to him, he'll know what to do.'

The baby started suckling almost immediately. Malise looked at him, her perfect son. And somehow all that she had gone through, all that she had lost, didn't seem that important, because he was here.

'You're all mine,' she said softly to the baby. 'All mine and I'll love you for ever. And so will everyone else.'

Neil Fraser's eyes looked up at her, as if she was the world.

'Looks like him,' Gordon said when he came the next morning. 'And I don't know why you couldn't wait till we were wed.' He tickled the child.

'Looks like himself.' Malise smiled down at the small figure lying next to her, his tiny fists clenched. 'I'm going to call him Alexander Gabriel.' She faced Gordon.

'A leader of men, eh?' Gordon raised an eyebrow as he wheeled himself round to where they were lying. He stroked the baby's face, lost in thought.

'That's what he'll be,' she said proudly. 'One day he'll be our Prime Minister.'

Gordon laughed drily and wheeled himself out, leaving Malise with Jessie and Mrs Baker, as Keith carried him down the stairs.

Ten days later, Malise went down to Commercial Street, to the Registrar, housed in some tiny offices high up, looking over the Library and the High School, the school for the children of the first families of the town.

'One day you'll go there,' she whispered to the baby who slept in her arms. 'One day you'll be head boy.'

'Next!'

At the sound of the young man's voice, Malise walked in.

'Name?' There was no please in his words or manner.

'Malise Gabriel Monroe,' she said quietly as she put her birth lines on the desk.

The young man looked up, his moustache quivering slightly.

'I know. It's a man's name.' She was about to say something else, then stopped as the man looked down at her finger. 'I'm not married.' She could tell it wasn't a surprise.

Slowly she walked down the stairs, clutching the piece of paper that would mark out Alexander as a bastard.

'I'm sorry I couldn't hold on to you for a while longer,' she whispered to him as she hitched the child into her light coat and headed back towards Lochee. 'I'll make it up to you, I promise.'

On her sixteenth birthday, she stood in her best Sunday dress, the buttons strained over her chest, swollen with milk for Alexander. This wasn't the wedding she had dreamed about, and as she looked down at Mr Scott, sitting in his chair, his neatly brushed grey hair thinning with age, she felt a spasm of disgust at the way the man had dressed up for the wedding in his good suit, his pocket-watch glinting in the sunlight. Why was he bothering to pretend? She didn't want him, he didn't want her. It would be like living with an uncle, nothing more. Jessie stood next to her with a posy of flowers, and Malise could tell by the look on her face that, for once, the bridesmaid was not coveting the place of the bride.

'Well, that's it all settled now,' Mr Scott said cheerfully as Malise signed her name at the bottom. 'Now back to my house for the party.'

But there was no party with dancing and laughter and saucy jokes about the wedding night. Instead, Jessie and her family drank a small sherry and ate two cheese sandwiches as Mr Scott chatted to an awkward Mr Baker about what he was doing at the docks, and Mr Baker escaped gladly when a man came to the door with a handcart carrying the few bits and pieces that Malise had kept from her home.

The two rooms were surprisingly well kept for the home of a man who could not walk. The rooms were spotlessly clean and tidy, one side of the living room filled with books and periodicals that sat on a bookcase which reached from floor to ceiling. There was a kitchen, too, a narrow galley with a proper stove and cold store and sink. There was even rhubarb growing next to the privy on the green outside.

Malise made them some dinner, and they ate it in silence, after which Mr Scott wheeled himself over to the bookshelf and picked out a book to read. Malise stood in the tiny kitchen, her breasts were heavy now and she felt tired. She wanted to go to bed and sleep. She wanted to go back to being Malise the rebel, Malise the terrible, Malise the conqueror – not to being Mrs Scott.

'You're dropping on your feet,' Mr Scott said eventually. 'Feed the baby then away you go to bed.' He turned back to his book.

'Where will I be sleeping?' she said hesitantly.

'The bedroom is the other door.' He didn't look up. 'I won't join you for a while.'

'But . . .'

'Where did you think you would be sleeping? We're married now.' He looked up curiously. 'Stop staring at me like that.'

'Yes, Mr Scott.' She walked into the bedroom and sat down on the wide bed. She could see the empty chamber pot peeking out from under the bed; somehow it made her feel sick. Carefully she undressed and put her clothes in the drawer of the tall dark wooden chest of drawers, then put on her nightdress, an old one – she hadn't bothered getting a new one, she hadn't thought she would be having a wedding night. But now she had a suspicion that Mr Scott's idea of being married was very different from hers.

She fed Alexander, then put him in his little cot beside her, wrapped up in a warm knitted shawl. She closed her eyes as she cuddled herself between the cold sheets, convinced that she would never be able to sleep. But eventually sleep overtook her.

She woke when she felt Mr Scott's hand on her shoulder, shaking her gently.

'You might as well see it now,' he said as he began to open his cardigan. Malise squinted through her sleep as she watched Mr Scott take off his clothes, revealing enormous muscular arms, testament to his years in a wheelchair. 'Come here.' He grabbed her hand and dragged her over to him.

Malise watched horrified as he took off his trousers, revealing for the first time the stumps that ended almost where his knees would have been.

'Don't pretend you aren't disgusted, girl,' he said calmly. 'Look at them.' He pulled her hand over to the end of his leg where the skin was smooth and she could feel the end of the bone beneath the red scar. 'Touch them. Because you have to get used to them.' He looked at her, seeing the horrified

95

disgust in her eyes. 'Gets worse.' Still looking her in the eye, he moved her hand up to his lap. To the tiny stump of a penis. 'Can just about get three fingers round it, can't you?' he continued. 'That's why I'll not be having intercourse with you. Rotted, you know. Something to do with blood not getting into it.' He forced her fingers over the top.

Malise bit her lip to prevent herself from retching. This was Mr Scott, the boring old teacher that talked about her as if she were someone special. How could he possibly want to do something like that with her? How could he possibly think she would want to do anything like that with someone like him?

'Still, we can enjoy ourselves in other ways,' he muttered as his hand moved from hers and went to the neckline of her nightdress. 'No, don't let go, keep playing with it.'

As he opened her nightdress, Malise rubbed the soft damp skin between her fingers, unsure what she was supposed to do.

'Big teats for a lass your size.'

She stopped breathing as she felt Mr Scott take a hold of her, pinching her hard.

'You got rid of your milk?'

She nodded her head in a terrified manner.

'Good.' As he bent his head towards her, Malise felt a freezing water drip into her veins. This was what she would have to do now. To please him.

She lay as he touched her everywhere, almost clinically, although occasionally he would mutter a few words about how she was a pretty girl, then, once his curiosity was satisfied, he turned over and went to sleep.

Malise lay in the dark, feeling far dirtier and more violated than she had after Fraser had touched her. Mr Scott, for she couldn't think of him as anything else, had made marriage sound like she would be back living with her father. But in reality it wasn't. She was married to a man who repelled and disgusted her. And he could do anything he wanted to her. She turned away, so she couldn't see his shadow. If only Daddy were here, none of this would have happened. But he wasn't, and she'd just have to learn to live with it.

Less than one month later, the country was at war.

'It's just a parade!' Malise said, as she put on her coat.

'It's a line of young men being sent away to be slaughtered. And for what! Does anyone actually know?'

'Archduke Ferdinand,' Malise returned as she fixed her beret on her head.

Gordon laughed bitterly.

'You can't be so foolish as to think that is the reason we are fighting. It's because other governments are coveting the colonies.'

'Oh, for crying out loud, Gordon, it's just a parade!' She stamped her foot and held her breath as Gordon's schoolmaster expression came over his face.

'Off you go,' he said slowly. 'Enjoy the parade.'

Leaving Gordon and his bad mood behind her, Malise tucked Alexander into her arms and joined the hordes of people walking down to the train station at the Tay Bridge. As she walked past the churches, she saw the people walking out. But they seemed less happy than they had been before. It was a long walk to the station, and as she got to the Steeple, someone pressed a flag into Alexander's chubby fist.

'They're coming now!' a man shouted, and she heard the pipes and drums – a loud, glorious sound that lifted the crowd. It was deafening now, and she could only just make out the top of the pipes over the others standing watching in the bright Sunday sunlight.

'Hurrah!' Everyone began to cheer and Malise, using a skill she had learned from a hundred demonstrations, ducked under arms and elbows, till she got to the front. And there they were, line upon line of young men, some smiling broadly, but most of them concentrating as they marched, attempting to keep their arms straight and true.

'Keith, Keith!' she shouted as she saw Jessie's brother. But

97

he was in the middle of a line, and couldn't hear her. Girls jumped out of line to kiss men goodbye, not caring that it was shockingly public. On and on, the rows of men never seemed to stop.

'Hurrah for the Black Watch!' a man cried and Malise shouted as hard as the rest. 'Hear that, Alexander!' she said, but he was intent on chewing the paper flag. 'That could be . . .' and then she stopped. The noise was quietening now, as the marchers headed down towards the train station. Malise watched the others, gone was the jubilation, gone was the excitement, gone was the colour in their lives. Now all she could see were women, old women, young women, women with children. And old men. For there was no one else.

'To Neil and Agnes!' As the assembled company raised their glasses in a toast to the couple, Neil smiled nervously. He wasn't in control of his life any more. He couldn't even choose the clothes he wore. Automatically, his hand went to the stiff, heavy dress uniform he was wearing. Agnes was wearing a beautiful white dress, with a long veil that trailed over each side of her face. She looked more like a ghost than ever before.

'Won't have her for very long, will you?' Bertie, his mother's cousin from the Ministry of War, toasted them again with his glass.

'No, I start my training on Friday,' Neil returned.

'Very admirable of you, volunteering to go and fight,' Bertie said casually as he savoured the wine he was drinking. 'You know that I will do all I can to help you.'

'To avoid unfortunate postings?' Neil raised an eyebrow.

'With your skills, a job working in the Ministry would be more appropriate.' Bertie drained his glass. 'Leave the fighting to those better disposed to that. You know there was no need for you to sign up, anyway.'

Neil considered the man, he was offering him a way out, a way to be seen doing his duty without actually serving. To work in an office in Glasgow. And be away from the thick of it.

'No, Bertie.' Neil looked ahead of him. 'I have a duty to do.'

Evening came, and as he walked through the garden of his home, he could see the sun setting up the Firth of Tay towards Perthshire, in beautiful, soft, peach and pink. Warm, nurturing colours. He looked back at his bride in her cold white.

'Strange to see you going off to war,' Elizabeth said as she walked up to her son and put her arm through his. 'But at least you're married now.'

'Mother.'

'No, Neil,' she chided gently. 'Duty takes many forms, you know. And you will warm to her. She needs gentle care. Like an orchid.'

'I don't know if I can do it,' he answered.

'You'll find things to talk about,' she replied. 'You won't recognize her when you see her next. She'll be a bright and happy wife to you. Wait and see.'

Neil nodded. And steeled himself for the night to come.

'I don't see why you have to go.' Gordon supped his porridge as Malise fed the baby and drank a cup of tea.

'It's my duty.' She unlatched the child from her breast. 'I'll come over to the school to feed him at lunchtime and you can bring him home at night. Plenty of people to mind him.'

'You don't have to.'

'They need people to work now. So many of the men have signed up.' She stood up and picked up her coat. 'This way I get in as a weaver, and don't need to start by sweeping the floor or spinning.'

'It's manual labour.'

'Time I learned what hard work feels like.' She kissed Alexander on the top of his head. 'You sure you'll be all right with him on your knee?'

'He's got a grip like a vice.' Gordon looked down with a certain detached pride. 'Youngest member of my school, at least the office is dry this time of year.'

'Then I'll see you both at lunchtime.' She patted Alexander's dark head before hastening out the door.

Ian Smith, an old colleague of her father's, showed her how to operate the machines.

'It's not difficult, just complicated. The problems happen when the thread breaks, be careful of your fingers, as you don't want to stop the machines unless you really have to. Costs us all money, you know.'

Malise nodded, fighting to hear him over the noise of the machines. Despite the cool summer weather, it was extremely hot in the factory and the whole place stank of a mixture of jute, oil and sweat. Ian hovered around her for most of the morning; it was difficult to chat, but his hands were always there, covering hers as he showed her how to make adjustments to the enormous mechanical looms. Malise felt his arms around her; Ian would stand behind her, his body hard up against her back. It wasn't like Ian at all.

'I can hardly breathe,' she complained as she looked up at him, smiling tightly.

'All part of the fun of being here, Malise.' He winked at her.

Malise took a step back, resting the full weight of her small frame on one shoe, which ground relentlessly into his foot.

'I've never been one for that kind of fun,' she said innocently. 'Mr Scott wouldn't approve.' Her smile froze into a set expression.

'I'd better go and see how the others are getting on,' he muttered and walked away.

Malise continued to watch her looms, then rushed over to the school at lunch, to feed Alexander, before returning to her station.

She stood for a while, fighting the tiredness which was threatening to overtake her.

'What do you think you're doing?' She heard one of the gaffers, a thickset man with a florid complexion jutting out of his frayed shirt collar, shout.

'I don't know,' a young girl stuttered. 'It just went wrong.'

'Daft besom,' he said as he grabbed the girl and slapped her hard in the face, knocking her down, before walking away.

'Ignoring her looms, Malise rushed over to the girl.

'Are you all right?' She held out a hand to her. 'He shouldn't have done that.'

'How can I stop it?' The girl, older than her, but needing her comfort, leaned on Malise as she pulled herself up. 'What can anyone do, he's the gaffer.'

'Have you spoken to the union?' Malise said quietly.

The girl shrugged.

'They don't want to know, and besides, half of them would do it themselves if they could. They're all men, and most of them gaffers too.'

'What if there was a woman you could go to?' Malise could hardly believe what she was hearing.

'Well, that would be different. But what woman has time to do union work?'

Malise held out her hand.

'My name is Mrs Scott. And I work for the union.'

'Billy,' Malise said that evening, as she walked into the pub round the corner from the Elizabeth, known as Billy Turpin's domain. 'I'd like to talk to you.'

'Of course,' he looked round. 'You'd better sit down. Though you know women are banned from coming in here. Man's world.'

'It's a man's world in that factory too,' she replied. 'A while ago, I did some work for you.'

'Aye.' Billy looked her up and down. 'Never used the letters you gave me. Too busy to send them off.'

'What if I did a wee bit more work for you?' Malise inhaled deeply.

'Always welcome, Malise.' He smiled. 'Union work's not easy.'

'But it will be difficult to do without anyone knowing who I am.'

'You're well known in that place, lass,' he said mockingly. 'Heard a lot about you.'

'It'd look better if I was a steward.' Her smile was set.

'I don't need a woman shop steward,' Billy retorted. 'They are nothing but trouble.'

'Excuse me, Billy, but I think I've been nothing but help to you,' Malise kept her voice light, she didn't want Billy to suspect what she really wanted. 'What I'm saying is that with the new workers coming in, there'll be new problems. All those women together, Billy, can you imagine what it'll be like? And do you really want to have to deal with their problems? Women's problems?'

Billy was silent, but she had crossed a corner now, she had moved from a definite 'no' to a thoughtful silence. 'What's the matter, Billy,' she said, almost suggestively. 'Wouldn't you like me to work for you?'

She watched as a lazy, avaricious smile crossed Billy's face.

'Aye,' he said eventually. 'I'll have you working for me. On women's matters.'

Chapter 6

'So what does he look like in his uniform?' Malise teased as Jessie strode purposefully ahead of her towards the railway station.

'Handsome,' Jessie turned and grinned through the crowds. 'Lovely, actually.' She rubbed her hand as, under her glove, she could feel the tiny diamond chip in its setting.

'Who'd have thought that I'd be married with a bairn and you'd be engaged,' Malise remarked as she struggled to keep up with the girl. 'Hold on, I've Alexander to carry!' But Jessie had disappeared into the throng of people at the station platform, standing round soldiers and puddles of kitbags. Sighing, Malise hoisted Alexander on to her shoulder and slid through the people in the direction of Jessie.

'Malise!' Arthur, Jessie's handsome soldier who had used his shilling to buy her a ring, shouted with all his might. More than one person looked round.

'Arthur!' Malise took a look at his red hair and freckled face. God only knows what his and Jessie's children would look like, she thought as she pushed towards him.

'You take care now, Arthur,' Malise said fondly and reached up to kiss him on the cheek. Arthur grinned and planted a clumsy wet kiss on Malise's lips.

'Arthur!' Jessie and Malise said simultaneously. Arthur just kept on smiling.

'I'll let you say your goodbyes,' Malise said, and squeezed Jessie's arm. 'I'll meet you outside.' She pushed her way through the crowd and began to head towards the stairs.

*

'Well, good luck, son.' Richard Fraser shook hands with Neil. 'Write to us, and keep yourself safe.' He patted him awkwardly on the shoulder and walked away.

Neil nodded, feeling a crushing disappointment that Agnes had declined to wave him off, because of the crowds. He knew it wasn't true. They had been married for a week and it had been an unmitigated disaster. All his memories were of Agnes avoiding him, turning away from him, her face shutting down, and of the distaste in her eyes when he touched her. He watched the soldiers who had arrived, everyone seemed to be embracing someone, everyone had someone who loved them. Everyone except him. His eyes followed his father's retreating figure, and caught sight of someone else, making their way from the crowd at the other end of the train.

'Malise!'

Malise, a few stairs up, turned and saw him standing there, his face earnest and almost scared. She wished with all her heart that she could hate him. The man who had ruined her, the man who had contributed to her father's death. The man who hadn't looked at her since that fateful day. But it was all that she could do, not to run into his arms and beg him to keep himself safe. To hold him one last time.

'What are you doing here?' she said coldly to hide her weakness. 'This is a send-off for heros. No room for the likes of you.'

Neil stared at the child on her shoulder.

'What's his name?' he said shakily.

'Alexander Gabriel.' Malise could feel her chest tighten, this shouldn't be happening, she hated Neil Fraser. 'Don't worry, no one knows.'

The child moved and Neil saw his face. The Fraser eyes, framed by Malise's face. Her hand came up to comfort him and he saw the shiny gold band.

'You're married.'

'He knows, and he's bringing him up as his own.' Her voice became husky.

'I'm going to do my officer training.' Neil made no attempt to move.

'You can't lead men. Or will they be happy with you staying at the back, getting others to do the dirty work? You excel at that,' she said bitterly.

'Malise,' Neil said desperately. 'If there had been any other way . . .'

'No, your way is always best. Because it's the one that matters. The rich man's way.' But she couldn't move away, her feet were firmly planted.

'Goodbye, Malise,' he said sorrowfully. 'Take care.' He looked at the condemnation on her face and forced his feet to move. Go back, a voice said in his mind. Go back and kiss her, hold her, breathe in her smell. He pursed his lips together. He couldn't do what he wanted. There were far too many people. He put his hand to his mouth as if to blow a kiss to her, but stopped. She would wait for him, with Alexander. And somehow, when this was all over, he would make her happy. He turned and took one last look at her. She was standing in a crowd, but, for Neil, she was the only one there.

'Come on, old chap,' a voice said behind him. And Neil found himself in the carriage with six other officer cadets.

'Leaving anyone special?' one asked.

'Wife and son,' he replied unthinkingly.

'Me too,' the other replied. 'They're who I'm doing it for.'

Neil hesitated and nodded. Then sat down and fell silent. Thinking about Malise and Alexander.

Malise waited till she saw him get on the train, then bit down hard on her lip.

'Come back, Neil.' Then, wiping the tears from her eyes, she walked out of the station. 'Come back and save me.'

'I don't know how my father managed it,' she said to Jessie as they sat one night, six months later, both knitting socks for soldiers and wrapped up against the cold as there was little coal to burn any more. 'I've no idea what I'm supposed to do, half the time. The women never stop asking, and the gaffers don't want to know, and when you manage to work out a compromise, then everyone thinks you're useless because they didn't get their own way.

'And that Billy Turpin! He spends hours with Archie Taylor in pubs having meetings! He's even been to lunch with him. In a restaurant of all places! Who's ever heard of folk like us going into restaurants?'

'But what's the union supposed to do?' Jessie said curiously. 'Your father was always at the Pillars or on the Green making speeches.'

'A union is for everyone who works there to get together so that they can't be picked on,' Malise interrupted. 'But the machinery isn't what it used to be, there aren't any spare parts as all the iron works are making guns now, and things break. But we shouldn't be penalized for that. The work is getting more dangerous, but it isn't just that. There are a couple of gaffers who approach the women, they tell them if they produce sub-standard kitbags they'll be sacked, unless they go round the back with them.' She raised her eyebrows. 'And the union should be able to put a stop to all that too.'

'But the gaffers won't be there for that much longer, I heard they're going to start calling up all the men,' Jessie returned.

'No, there is such a thing as a reserved profession, people who are too important for the country to lose,' Malise replied. 'And I know that Fraser has put in for some of his gaffers to be given that stamp.'

'And what about Billy?' Jessie stopped as she dropped a stitch.

'He's signing up.' Malise paused thoughtfully. 'All the men are worried that they will be getting a reputation as a coward.'

'So where will that leave the union?' Jessie asked curiously. 'Who else is left?'

Malise took a deep breath.

'All the unionists are going,' she said quietly. 'All the

stewards are joining up. Because they seem to think they will be getting conscripted. All of them except me.'

'But Malise, you've been there less than a year,' Jessie faltered. 'And you don't have the time as it is to do your cleaning and your cooking. How many times this month have you eaten cheese sandwiches or bread and dripping?'

'There's no one else,' Malise responded. 'So it looks as if I'm in charge of the union come the end of the month. Whether I like it or not.'

'Gordon will help, won't he?' Jessie asked as she stood up to make a cup of tea.

'Yes, but—'

'Is he still . . .' Jessie turned her face to the range to avoid Malise's expression.

'Aye, not as often, but . . .' Malise pulled hard at her wool and it broke. 'He makes my skin crawl, Jessie, I should never have married the man!'

'Why didn't you marry Johnnie Turpin?' Jessie asked sympathetically. 'I mean, I know what happened to your dad, but—'

'Johnnie's not the father.' The words tumbled out of Malise's exhaustion and unhappiness.

Jessie sat down and gently took the knitting from Malise. Then held her hand.

'It was Neil Fraser,' she said as she burst into tears. 'That's why I couldn't get married to him. Because a Fraser would never marry someone like me. But even when I saw him at the station, when you were seeing your Arthur off, all I could think of was how much I wanted to touch him, for him to tell me that he loved me.'

'And?'

'And he was so nice to me, Jessie.' She cuddled into Jessie's shoulder. 'I try and I try to hate him, but I can't. I just can't forget him.'

That Sunday, Malise took Alexander down to the Pillars, in the remnants of the winter snow. A few people were there,

107

though not many, since most of the men had left and the women had better things to do than to listen to a political speech.

There were three men from Glasgow. And they were talking to the crowd about the cost of the war. About the cost for ordinary families. She stopped to listen to one of them. He was talking heresy, because he was doing the unthinkable – speaking out loud the words Malise could only feel inside. She couldn't help but be glad that the reception they got was lukewarm. No mother who had lost her son, no wife who had lost her husband, would want to stand and listen to a tall, thin, educated Glaswegian telling her it had been for nothing.

At the end of the speech, however, she lingered. She wanted to talk to the man, to tell him that she understood, that he hadn't wasted his time and his fare coming to Dundee.

She watched the man's face as everyone drifted off. Then he began to walk towards her, rubbing his long slim hands together as he did so.

'Your husband is serving, I presume?' he said as he reached her.

'My husband is an invalid. And I agree with you. What you said. But I think some things are too dangerous to speak out about.' She raised her eyebrows.

'You are no ordinary housewife, are you?' He looked at her keenly with pale-green eyes. 'Do I know you? Ought I to know you?'

'I'm Gabriel Monroe's daughter, Gordon Scott's wife.' Would he know those names?

'I want to know who you are, not who your family is, although their names are familiar,' he persisted gently.

'Malise Scott, I'm a steward at the Elizabeth.' She held out her hand.

'Jack Buchanan.' He shook her hand. 'And I'm freezing cold. Might I invite you for a coffee at our offices?'

'Yes.' She gathered the sleepy Alexander from her hip and

together they began to walk from the Pillars to the Independent Labour Party offices not far away in the Fishgate.

'Your father was a party member, and I know Gordon from old, he has corresponded with our offices in Glasgow on many an occasion,' Jack said conversationally. 'And I've seen your name on many letters, requesting information. I'm one of their solicitors. But you aren't a member, are you?'

'I haven't got round to it, and, just now, when all the socialists are preaching pacifism . . .' She shook her head.

'Might not be politic, I know.' Jack steered her up the stairs. 'But still, you are a steward.'

'The women needed someone.' She shrugged her shoulders as Jack opened the door for her and led her into the damp office. The rooms were filled from floor to ceiling with papers, boxes and books. As he found two chairs and a box for the now sleeping Alexander, Malise looked at him. He had breeding, it shone out of the way he held himself, the way his sandy hair flopped over his face.

'Here.' He handed her a Camp coffee, the warm smell lush and inviting.

'You made me a coffee?' she said in amazement.

'What kind of socialist would I be if I didn't stick to my own rules on something like that?' He laughed and sat down. 'So tell me, what is happening with the Elizabeth?'

'It's difficult, and will get even more so, when the rest of the stewards go. Then there'll just be me.'

'Oh, they'd call you up if they thought they could get away with it,' Jack replied. 'Don't tell me, they've cut the time for training people to do the work, they've made the shifts longer and the wages less and, if anyone complains, they are accused of hampering the war effort?' He looked at her. 'We hear tales of this every day. Everyone in the country is being told to pull together, but the people who own the factories and who are enriching themselves in this war seem to be doing substantially less pulling than others.'

'We've fought tooth and nail for concessions, for a lunch

break, and now they are threatening to take it away,' Malise returned. 'And without Billy . . .'

'You don't need Billy Turpin, that man is a good worker for the union, but he's too argumentative; he cannot see another point of view.' Jack sipped his coffee.

'But there isn't anyone else,' Malise returned. 'He's the convener.'

'But you'll still be there, and you know I can always give you any support that you need. Even if you aren't a party member.' Jack smiled supportively.

'But Billy just lets these things happen,' Malise persisted.

'He's probably too busy thinking about his own future to worry about anyone else's,' Jack ruminated. 'That's one thing you don't have to worry about, being sent off to fight.' He hesitated for a moment. 'Why don't you try asking if instead of everyone going for lunch at the same time, the women can have staggered breaks during the day? That will give them a chance to shop for food. It's being done in Glasgow.'

'You know, that just might work. It would mean that there would be no loss of production, and it would help the women. It's very difficult trying to do a day's work and look after a family as well.' She nodded to herself as she worked out the possibilities.

Jack handed her a card.

'If you want any help, Malise, you just contact me.' He smiled. 'There are plenty of women in your position, women who want to help, but are worried about how to do it. I can help you, but you need to tell me all the facts. Don't try and hide uncomfortable truths.'

'Everyone tells me that I can do it, but I just don't know how I'll cope. I'm scared I'll let them all down.' For some reason, she felt Jack was an ally, he understood.

'Just do your best, that way you won't let anyone down.'

Malise looked up in surprise.

'My father always said that,' she said.

'And he was absolutely right.'

*

110

The following day at work, the whole place was abuzz with rumours.

'What is it?' Malise asked as she took her place by the pile that needed finishing.

'It's Billy Turpin,' the weaver next to her said quickly. 'Apparently he's gone. All the shop stewards signed up for the navy. To save being called up for the Watch.'

Malise felt the blood drain from her face. It had happened already.

'Come in, Mrs Scott,' Archie Taylor said as she walked into the mahogany-panelled office that once had been Neil Fraser's. 'And what can I do for you?' He looked her up and down, as if he were imagining her in her undergarments.

'Since Mr Turpin is not here, I am in control of the union,' she said in her most businesslike manner, ignoring the butterflies that were gathering in her stomach. This was Archie Taylor, the man people feared. And for good reason. But Malise knew she couldn't let that affect her. Her women depended on her. She reached into her pocket and rubbed the old tin whistle. 'It's about the lunch break.'

'Aye, well, we all have to pull together,' Archie Taylor said thoughtfully. 'There's a war on.'

'But the women still need to feed their families. So what I am suggesting is that we stagger the lunch breaks instead of getting rid of them, so that they can still get out and shop if they need to.'

'And who will mind their machines?' Archie said quietly.

'I suggest we take on extra workers, workers who will provide a pool of people able to do more than one job. This will mean you are better able to cope with busy periods and you will also be able to cover sickness and absence.'

'Absence?' Archie Taylor looked at her with his little piggy eyes.

'People will have to buy food, and surely it is better that they don't slip out when no one is looking but do so instead when you give them a specified time, and provide someone

111

who can keep an eye on their machines. It works in Glasgow.'

'Are you saying that my workers leave their posts during the day?' he asked angrily.

'That is exactly what I'm saying,' she returned. 'And I am giving you a chance to nip it in the bud, without causing bad feeling. You need all the workers you can get. Anyone could walk out of this place and get a place in Cox's or Den's and leave you with trouble. Word gets around, you know, Mr Taylor.'

Archie Taylor walked out from behind the desk till he was up close to her.

'Don't you remember me, girl?' he said menacingly. 'I know all about you.'

'And what, precisely, would you do with that information?' She raised her eyebrows at him, holding her breath as she did. What could he do?

'I could let it be known that you were nothing but a wee slut, and that your son is not your husband's,' he replied.

'Oh, everyone knows that,' she gave a short laugh. 'And everyone thinks that he is Johnnie Turpin's. So who's going to believe that a jute baron looked my way? Because everyone knows that Johnnie Turpin's had half the girls in Lochee. And he isn't here to deny it.'

Archie's complexion grew florid with barely concealed rage.

'I'm not the one who gets into trouble if you don't reach your quota, Mr Taylor,' she said innocently. 'And I doubt that Mr Fraser would understand why you couldn't keep your workers at work.' She raised her hands despairingly. 'Think about it.'

'All right,' Taylor said angrily. 'But don't think you'll get away with this much longer.'

'And the Fraser Works?'

'You've not bloody taken them over too, have you?'

'Makes sense to offer the same in each of your works, Mr

Taylor.' She turned and looked at him. 'They do it in Glasgow.'

'How old are you?' he asked suddenly.

'I'll be seventeen next birthday. And my name is Mrs Scott. Good day, sir.' She inclined her head and walked out and down the stairs. At the bottom, when she had reached the factory floor, she opened her hand. Inside it was the old tin whistle.

'You were right, Daddy,' she said softly. 'I can do this.'

That night, after work, she loaded her basket full of clothes and headed off to the steamie to do her washing. She was just waiting for her water to heat up when she heard two women talking.

'So you'll never guess what the gaffer told us?' the first said. 'We are keeping the lunch breaks, but we are getting them during the day, at different times, and someone will cover for us, so that we can go out to get some messages if we need to.'

'Wish we got that in ours,' the second returned. 'I never seem to get a moment to myself any more.'

'Should come and work in the Elizabeth,' the first replied. 'It's a braw place, and the union is a good one. Run by that Monroe girl, you know, the one who married the crippled schoolteacher.'

Only the bubbling of the copper stopped Malise from basking in the glory, because there was still the washing to be done.

When she got home, Gordon was asleep, with Alexander in his crib next to him. On the plate beside him were some crusts of the hough sandwich she had made. Sighing, she went into the kitchen. She had to make Gordon a decent meal, his health was not all it could be. It was 2 a.m. before she finally crawled into bed, having hung up the washing, cleaned the front step, and set out a pot of lentil soup ready for the next day, but the smile still hadn't left her face.

*

Archie Taylor was different after the lunch incident. He no longer tried to threaten her, but he would still make comments every time she turned up at his door, to ask about people losing rates for broken machinery, or to complain when one of the few remaining male gaffers tried to coerce women into having sex with them. As the spring drifted into summer and then to winter again, she saw less and less of him; he was having to split his time between the Elizabeth and the Fraser Works.

'It's no use, Malise,' one of the spinners who had come with a small group to see her said. 'We cannot manage to get our bairns to and from the nursery in time. Not with these shift times.'

Malise thought for a moment, pushing her thoughts about the things that needed to be done at home to the back of her mind.

'I can see if he can move the shift,' she said slowly. 'But I doubt we'll hear another word about it.'

All that day she wondered what she could do. Archie Taylor would march her out of his office if she as much as suggested it to him. So that night, when she had finally finished her housework and Alexander was asleep, she took out her writing paper and the card that Jack had given to her. Within three days she had a reply.

'What are you doing here, Mrs Scott?' Eddie the watchman said as she walked around the back rooms, to where the old stockrooms had been situated.

'Just looking, Eddie,' she said thoughtfully. 'Just looking.' And she had found it. The answer to their problems.

'I would like to see Mr Taylor,' Malise announced as she went upstairs to the offices after work a few days later.

'Mr Taylor isn't here,' the clerk replied courteously. 'One moment.' He walked into Archie Taylor's office then came out again. 'Mr Fraser will see you.'

'Neil?' Malise said automatically. For some reason he always came to mind.

'Mr Richard Fraser,' he answered. 'Senior.'

Malise went in and there was the old man, the head of the company, sitting at the desk. How like his son he was, she thought, as she felt a stab of remembrance. Although his hair had turned white and he had a neatly trimmed beard, it was something about the eyes. About the way they could look into you.

'Mrs Scott?' Mr Fraser said slowly. 'You have been keeping your workers in check. And yourself. I presume that this is all about to change?'

'We are all pulling together for the good of the country,' she returned. 'We are all doing our bit.'

'So what do you want?' His eyes narrowed.

'The government is introducing a scheme of setting up crèches and nurseries where women can put their bairns while they work. They provide a nurse and food for them and this allows the women to work without worrying who is looking after their weans, and enables them to serve their country the way their husbands have.'

Richard Fraser looked at her, his curiosity roused.

'And . . . ?'

'And I think it might be a good idea for you to ask the government for money to set one up here, sir, in the old stables. It would mean that the women won't have to run all over town first thing in the morning, and, because their children will be here, if they have to stay late to finish an order, then they can.' She stopped, waiting for him to say something.

'How do you know all this?' he said thoughtfully.

'It's my job to know all this, sir,' she replied. 'There is no point going to a busy man if all you have is another problem to give him. So you try to find the solutions too. Save him having to do it.'

'So you are hoping that my innate laziness will enable you to get your own way?' he said cuttingly.

Malise stared at him. She could back down, or she could face him. Did he really want to know?

'Works a charm with Mr Taylor, sir.' She saw his face tighten.

'I don't doubt that it does.' Richard considered her, the small slip of a girl who knew so much. 'And how would I find out if I can get this done by the government?'

'This is the address you apply to, sir.' She handed him a piece of paper. 'And this is where you can find a suitable nurse for the children.' She then took out a drawing which had been made by a friend of Gordon's the night before. 'That is basically a plan of what could be done with the stables, and a pricing next to it.'

'You did all this?' he asked curiously as he studied the plans.

'I wouldn't come to you unprepared, sir.' Malise felt a glow of pride.

'You can go now.'

But as Malise walked out she smiled. She had caught his attention, caught his interest. She was halfway there.

'Gordon,' she cried as she walked through the door, her face smirking with triumph, 'you'll never guess what happened today!' She opened the door to see Gordon slumped in his wheelchair. 'What's wrong?'

'There's been a battle at Loos,' he said quietly. 'They had a push to try and take over the lines. The Germans used poisoned gas. Half the Watch has been wiped out, it's not official, but there've been telegraph boys going up and down the streets all day. Our battalion, Malise, our Dundee lads. They're as good as gone.'

Malise sat down, with her hands covering her face, thinking of all the women who talked proudly about their husbands, sons and brothers. All the men in Dundee were gone. Jessie's Arthur and Keith. Every one of the lads she had cheered off in their uniforms. Wiped out in a single stroke. She walked over to Alexander, sleeping contentedly by the fire, and stroked his face. She hoped that his father was the coward she had accused him of being. Because that would mean he would still be alive.

Captain Neil Fraser walked up and down the almost deserted trenches with his commanding officer and stared at the grey faces of the men who were left, the men who had been sent to the trenches to replace the battalion that had been gassed. Gas – the one thing which they had thought the Germans would never actually use. And they had. Wiping out hundreds of his fellow Dundonians in a single night.

'Reinforcements are due in a few days,' Major Harris said carefully. 'In the meantime, we'll have to stay put.'

'Hear that, men?' he said with an enthusiasm he couldn't feel. 'You'll just have to hold on for a few more days.'

'But what if they gas us again, sir?' a young boy said quietly.

'You've your mask,' Neil returned sharply. 'Use it.' He ducked down as he reached the covered tent where the commanding officer had been. 'Oh my God!' Ten greasy rats, the size of small cats, were on a body, feasting on it with their sharp claws and teeth. He took out his pistol and fired at them. Two were blown apart, their fat bodies flung against the bed with the force of the blast, but the others remained, intent on their task.

'No point, Neil,' Major Harris said quietly. 'The men club them, but those bloody rats don't know the meaning of fear.' He gestured for Neil to leave. They walked through the low communication trench until they were safely back to their base far behind the front lines. But as they squelched through the earth, the mud knee-deep in places, Neil could feel an old memory coming back. Of a young girl in a cellar, frightened when the rats had come for her mother.

'Heard you had a call back to Blighty,' Major Harris said conversationally. 'You deserve it, after six months here. Strange time, though, since there is a push on.'

'Yes, I'm about to become a father.' Neil held open the door to what served as the officers' mess. 'And since they are prepared to give me leave, could it mean a respite for those left behind?' He raised his shoulders quizzically. 'Or will they spend all summer here?'

'Congratulations.' Major Harris shook his head. 'And not just about the baby.'

So it was his family's doing, Neil thought. Bertie had secured him leave to get him out of the trenches.

'Oh, I'll be back here,' Neil replied. 'Can't escape that easily.' But all he could think about was the rats. And how fat they were.

At last Malise had drawn up a list of circumstances of when women would be eligible for a place at the works nursery. They were painting the building now, and every day Malise would walk round it. But there was no feeling of triumph in what she was doing. The fact that there were one hundred new widows in the Elizabeth alone had put paid to that. One hundred women she had visited in their cramped, noisy homes. One hundred evenings when she had sat with Alexander on one shoulder, and a weeping woman on another. And one hundred promises that had been made. To help whenever they needed it.

'Mr Fraser,' she said as she walked into his office. 'I've done a few notices to go up, about the nursery and . . .'

But Fraser was standing, looking out of the window.

'Mr Fraser,' she repeated quietly.

Fraser continued to stare out of the window.

'I'll put the notice up then, the builder says it'll be ready next week. Have you got some women to work there?' she pressed. Still he looked out of the window.

'Would you like me to do that too?' she ended, almost impatiently.

'What?' he said absently.

'Do you want me to organize the nurses for the children?'

she repeated. 'If you do, you'll have to tell me how much you'll pay.'

'Whatever you wish, Mrs Scott.' He waved her away.

Malise tightened her lips. Trust Fraser to get bored with good works already.

It was late when Richard arrived home.

'Neil is here, Richard,' said Elizabeth, but her face was pale. 'And the doctor has been again.'

Richard nodded and went through to the conservatory, to where Neil, thin from months of living on a soldier's rations, was drinking his way through a bottle of whisky.

'Son,' he said quietly.

Neil ignored him, intent on filling his glass.

'It's early days,' Richard said softly.

'There is something wrong with him, Dad,' Neil said in a strained voice.

'He'll grow out of it,' Richard returned. 'It's a bloody battle, coming into the world. He's only a week old.'

'The doctor says that he shouldn't be so floppy, not after a week. He doesn't move his legs, Dad, he just twitches them occasionally.'

'It's early days, son. And everyone in our family is normal.' He looked over at his son. 'How is Agnes?'

'Silent. She hasn't even touched him. She doesn't want to know, Mother's had to get in a nurse. To feed him.'

'That woman is too delicate,' Richard replied. 'Far too delicate. There's no life in her.'

'No, but she's got half a bloody great shipyard,' Neil said harshly. Then he stood up. 'I didn't mean that, Dad, it's just . . .' He put his hand over his face.

'Come on, lad,' Richard said awkwardly. 'This is a time to be strong, not weak.'

'Why am I being punished like this?' Neil said despairingly. 'Why has this happened to me? I'm a good man, I try to help others, I've always attended church. What the hell have I done to deserve this?'

'You can have more children,' Richard began.

'I could get killed as soon as I go back,' Neil returned furiously. 'You've no idea, Dad, what it's like over there.'

'I served my country in Africa,' Richard replied defensively.

'No, Dad, you didn't fight in a trench, in freezing-cold mud, watching rats eat parts of bodies. You didn't have to stand to every evening, wondering if this was the night when the Germans were going to gas you. I was in Loos for six months, and the most strenuous activity I had to undertake was to check that my men's hair was the regulation length. Then, just when the men needed us to provide them with real leadership, the bloody Hun gassed them all while we let it happen.' He stared at his father uncomprehendingly. 'You had a chance of fighting like a gentleman.'

'You know that it would only take a phone call to your mother's cousin,' his father began. 'Dick has got his place in the Royal Flying Corps now. As soon as we realized what had happened, it only took one phone call from him, and you were granted leave. At a fortuitous time for you. He is of the opinion that the campaign in Loos will be long and difficult.'

Neil shook his head and stared out of the window at the beautiful gardens, the trees, and the tennis court at the bottom. And, for the first time, he felt the emptiness of his life.

'It isn't fair, Dad,' he exploded. 'It's not supposed to happen to people like us!' He threw his glass against the wall with such vigour that it shattered, some of the glass embedding itself in the elegant panelling. 'All the time while I was there, I thought about coming home to my family, and look at it!'

'We just have to wait and hope, Neil,' his father said gently. 'Perhaps tomorrow . . .'

'I'm going back, Dad,' Neil said with finality. 'There's no point in my being here any more.' He gazed out of the window. 'No point at all.'

*

120

It was the first day of the nursery. Malise was there early, watching as the mothers waved a cheery goodbye to their small children. The room was bare, there were a few toys, but nothing much.

'Is this it?' Richard Fraser asked as he came up behind her.

'We didn't get much money,' Malise replied defensively.

'And where is your son?' he said curtly.

'Alexander goes to school with his father,' Malise returned calmly. 'It wouldn't have been fair to have taken a place that could be used by someone else.'

'Nonsense, he's just a small child,' Richard Fraser said. 'An infant in a school! Whoever heard the like?'

'He's very forward for his age,' Malise replied.

'Like his mother.' Richard Fraser took a deep breath. 'Send him here.'

Malise stared at him. Did he know?

'Mr Fraser—' she began.

'Of course, I trust there would be no unpleasantness.' His eyes, so like Alexander's, bored into hers. 'No accusations, favouritism, or anything else.'

'Why would I do something I wouldn't gain from?' Malise said cautiously.

'Such pragmatism. You understand the situation well, Mrs Scott.' He walked away from her, back to his office.

'Aye, I understand all right, Mr Fraser,' she muttered. 'Give me a little and we'll all pretend that it didn't happen. Just the way you like it.'

Three months later, she had a place for her son. A new nurse had been donated by Richard Fraser, and there were more toys, a wooden train set and some chalks. Malise was entranced as she watched Alexander play with the trains, fascinated by them, his little fingers forever moving them round the track.

'Better get to work,' she said sorrowfully to one of the nurses. 'Though I could stay here all day.' As she left, she looked up at the office block, and saw Richard Fraser looking out of the window, a thoughtful expression on his face.

But there was no end in sight to the war, and while it meant the factory had work, the days and nights seemed to drift into a round of work and sleep, the household chores fitted into any spare moments. The weeks slipped by, and the months. Even the telegrams were getting less frequent now, like the autumn leaves which had mostly fallen.

'Mr Fraser,' she said as she walked into the office. 'It's about the overtime.'

Richard Fraser looked up. He was holding a brown telegram.

'Mr Fraser, I'm so sorry,' she said as she took a step closer.

'It's Dick. They call them the twenty-minuters for a reason, you know.' He pinched his nose between his thumb and forefinger for a moment. 'And we all have to make sacrifices.'

'I don't have a family to lose,' Malise murmured.

'I have precious little myself,' Richard turned, visibly pulling himself together. 'And about the overtime?'

'It can wait, sir,' she said gently. 'Another time.'

'Nonsense,' Richard said with a false heartiness. 'Just because Dick has gone, it doesn't mean life stops for everyone else.' He was struggling to keep his composure, clinging on to anything that would stop him from thinking about his son.

'Well, you pay for overtime, but I was thinking that if instead we took on more people and had a half-shift, then you wouldn't be putting such a strain on the workers. There would be less money for them, but, to be quite frank, money isn't a lot of use when there's nothing in the shops, and you would have a pool of people you could call upon when needed. To work in any of your works.'

'A half-shift?' Richard said curiously.

'Yes, no one can work fourteen- and fifteen-hour days for ever, and you know that there is far more sickness now.'

'Very well,' Richard said. 'You put it in writing for me, and I will talk to Archie.' He watched as she yawned. 'And it is seven o'clock. Both you and I ought to be with our families. While we still have them.'

'I'm just off to collect Alexander, then home to do the cleaning.' Her voice was soft, she could see that the man was barely holding himself together. 'But the nursery is a success, Mr Fraser. Thank you for agreeing to it.'

Richard Fraser walked over to the door.

'I wonder if those improvements have taken,' he said wistfully. Then, much to Malise's surprise, he walked out of his office together with her, and over to the old stables.

'Mummy!' Alexander cried and ran over to her. 'I'm a busy boy.'

Richard stared at the small child, a misty look on his face.

'Doesn't take much after you, Mrs Scott,' he said thoughtfully. 'Favours his father's side.'

Malise's head shot round and their eyes met in a momentary acknowledgement of the truth. But Fraser said nothing more. As Alexander ran towards her, she picked him up with tired arms, and saw the man's harsh profile soften, as if he were looking at one of his own.

As she walked out of the nursery with Alexander in her arms, Richard watched her. The child favoured his father's side, all right. Tall, and with a face that was a mirror of Neil's at his age. The same dark, straight hair. And the eyes. The piercing, blue Fraser eyes. Richard stared till she was no longer in his line of vision. Then he walked away.

When the paper was ready, Malise took it to the office.

'I've a paper for Mr Fraser,' Malise said to his clerk.

'You'll have to give it to Mr Taylor,' the clerk replied. 'Mr Fraser is out at the moment.'

Malise walked in to see Archie Taylor, back in his old office, glaring at her as he sat at his plain dark wooden desk.

'You're trying to take my job from me, Scott,' he said menacingly. 'And I don't like it.'

'Whatever you think, Mr Taylor,' Malise replied politely. 'But this is what he wants.' She put the papers on the desk and went to walk out. As soon as she did, Archie threw them in the waste-paper basket. She was a damn sight too friendly with the old man.

'Getting the same treatment she gave your son, Fraser?' he said loudly with avaricious malice. Then he thought for a moment. And picked the papers up out of the basket.

Richard stood in the nursery, looking at Alexander. What a perfect little boy he was. What a tragedy that Neil's and Agnes's son Euan was now in a nursing home, with no visitors apart from himself and his wife.

'Why couldn't it have been you?' he said now. 'It wouldn't have mattered then.'

Alexander, sensing the attention, walked over to the man.

'Block,' he said holding out a wooden block. 'Red block.' He gazed up at the giant in front of him. And, for the first time since his eldest son had died, Richard Fraser smiled back.

'Thank you,' he said carefully. 'Do you like playing with blocks?'

Alexander nodded.

'Play with me, please.' Alexander held out his hand.

'I'm not very used to playing,' Richard said gruffly.

'Play with me, please.'

Richard nervously took the child's hand, and let Alexander lead him to the piece of jute matting on the floor where six offcuts of timber, roughly painted as blocks, sat.

'Make a factory.' Alexander squatted on the floor and Richard bent down on arthritic knees. 'Look.' Carefully, he put one block on top of the other. Then when it was complete he stared up at the man.

'And what do you do now?' Richard said to the child.

'Knock it down.' He laughed with glee as he swiped at the blocks and they tumbled to the ground. Richard found himself laughing too as he knocked the last brick away.

'Mr Fraser,' Nurse Downie came rushing over, 'I'm sorry. Has Alexander been bothering you?'

'Not at all. He's been teaching me how to play.' Holding on to the nurse for support, Richard got up from the floor. 'I'll have some more toys sent over. Six bricks aren't enough for a decent tower.'

'Thank you, Mr Fraser,' Nurse Downie said politely. 'And please come to see us whenever you can.'

'I will,' Richard said as he shared a smile with Alexander. 'I'll do just that.'

'You're late, again,' Gordon said as she walked into the house. 'What did he think of the paper?'

'Gave it to Taylor, so that's the last we'll hear of it,' Malise yawned as she walked into the kitchen. 'You've made dinner!'

'I spent all those years looking after myself, Malise,' Gordon replied mildly. 'And I find your staple fare of sandwiches rather insubstantial.'

'I'm sorry, Gordon,' she said quickly. 'It's just– '

'I know, Malise, I know.' He patted her on the knee. 'I'm not much of a husband to you and you aren't that much of a wife.'

'It'll get better,' she replied.

'What, your cooking? Or lack of it?' he said mockingly. 'I somehow doubt that.'

'No,' Malise said shyly. 'I mean being married to me.'

'I knew what I was letting myself in for when I wed you, my dear,' Gordon said good-humouredly. 'Though I doubt you did. And we will be like this for ever. It won't change, but I can live with that. At least you get to see more of Alexander, you missed his first step and his first word.' He held his hands out to Alexander. 'Come on then, lad, let's see if you can read that book yet!'

'He's only eighteen months, Gordon.'

'Watch this.'

Gordon took out a little cloth book he had made.

'Dog,' said Alexander. 'The dog.'

'He's just memorized it,' Malise said quickly.

'That's how you start reading, Malise,' Gordon replied. 'This child is extremely clever.'

'Clever,' repeated Alexander. 'I am clever.'

Gordon patted her gently on the bottom and Malise, too tired to squirm away, let him. She had learned how to switch her mind to another problem.

As the winter of 1915 came, Malise found Richard to be even less concerned with the factory. Whatever she asked him, he would acquiesce to, as if he trusted her implicitly not to take advantage of him. But as spring arrived, and melted into a chill watery summer, things took a turn for the worse.

Life just seemed to be a round of people asking for her. It seemed that each woman in the Elizabeth had a tale to tell. And she wanted to tell it to Malise. Whether she was at work, shopping in the market at the Overgate, washing her clothes or scrubbing her step, there was always someone there. What had started as a challenge was in danger of becoming a crushing responsibility. And as the food available in the shops began to diminish into a round of potatoes, cabbage and the occasional sausage, Gordon's health began to suffer. He caught a cold which lodged in his chest and brought on a bout of bronchitis, which developed into consumption. It meant that he was unable to work, and Malise became the sole breadwinner. She now had a kettle boiler for a husband.

'Sorry, Malise,' he said weakly. 'It's hardly what you need at this time.'

Malise drew a hand down his face, wiping away the now white hair.

'You didn't do it on purpose, Gordon.'

'I've had bouts before, Malise. It'll go. Perhaps I'll be able to go back to work. If not, when I recover I'll have to find a job. They always need teachers, even cripples like me.'

But it didn't go. It stayed and he had good days and bad

days. Most of the time, he simply sat, weakly trying to write letters on her behalf – letters in handwriting that was failing.

It was late, her shift had ended but Malise was still there, wrestling with the problems of the women. There were so many of them who owed enormous amounts to money-lenders, or to the black marketeers who could get anything, if the price was right. But her most pressing problem was Edna O'Neill, a spinner who had brought up four sons, three of whom had died in the trenches. And the forth, Barry, was in prison. She had received a letter from one of his comrades, telling her that he had been caught trying to run away, and was awaiting a court martial. Edna desper-ately wanted to hear from him.

Malise looked at it, she knew that conscientious-objectors were being imprisoned, although some of them went to the front, to serve as ambulance men and medics. What was going to happen to Barry? A prison sentence? Of how long? As she tried to think who could help her, one name came to mind.

'What on earth?' Richard Fraser looked up from his correspondence as she knocked on his door and came in.

'Mr Fraser, sir,' Malise said nervously. 'I wonder if you would be able to help me?'

Quickly she outlined the problem.

'He's only a young boy, he was in the year above me at school,' she ended. 'His mother is so worried, but she can't find out anything. She just needs to know that he is safe.'

Richard Fraser stared at her. Didn't she realize?

'The penalty for cowardice is execution, Mrs Scott,' he said slowly.

'But conscies are sent to prison, sir,' she interrupted. 'Surely . . .'

'There is a world of difference between what they do and a soldier deserting his post in the heat of battle.' Richard's voice was harsh. 'Cowardice is a disease that cannot be allowed to spread.'

'Then please just help me find him,' Malise said desperately. 'So his mother can at least say goodbye.'

'I cannot promise anything.' For a moment he debated telling her that the execution was often summary, but his natural caution took over. 'But I will make a few enquiries.'

'Thank you, sir,' Malise said gratefully.

'Please don't make this known, Mrs Scott,' he warned. 'I am not about to lobby for a change to his sentence.'

'Thank you, sir,' she repeated. 'And goodnight.'

Richard Fraser went back to the large family house that was home to himself, his wife and the silent Agnes.

'Mrs Fraser is in the drawing room, sir,' Adams, the butler, said as he took Richard's overcoat. Richard walked through the sterile grandeur of his house, till he came to the small drawing room where Elizabeth liked to sit with her sewing. Inside it was warm and peaceful, the only sounds the ticking of the large carriage clock that sat on the mantelpiece beside the family photographs and the comforting crackle of the apple logs in the fireplace beneath. Elizabeth sat in a chair, her embroidery on a frame next to her. But she had fallen asleep, her head to one side, a portrait of her husband and sons in her hands.

'Drink, darling?' Richard murmured as he walked over to the table of decanters. 'I must look at your address book. I need to contact Bertie.' He poured both of them a generous sherry and walked over to her.

'Sleeping in a chair, Elizabeth?' He smiled fondly at the woman. 'It's a sign you are getting old, you know.' He put down her drink and took her hand. Her cold, lifeless hand.

'No!' Richard fell to his knees. 'Please, Elizabeth, wake up.' But he knew the words would not be heard. 'No!' He put his head in her lap. And his tears began to fall.

He didn't return to work for three days, three days in which Malise haunted his office relentlessly. But no one seemed to know where he was.

'I need to speak to him,' she said to the clerk. 'It's a matter of life or death.'

'Come inside my office,' Richard Fraser's voice floated on the air behind her. She turned. He looked as if he was ill; he hardly seemed to know where he was. She followed him as the clerk bustled away.

'Barry O'Neill was executed for cowardice two days after the event,' he said in a flat voice. 'Almost one month ago.'

'Thank you, sir,' she said quietly. 'I will tell his mother.'

'What will you tell his mother?' he said bitterly.

'That her last son is dead, along with all the rest.'

'And the circumstance?' He looked at her for a moment.

'It won't matter to the woman,' she replied. 'The fact that she has lost all her sons is enough, don't you think?' Then she nodded and left the room.

Richard walked down to the nursery for the first time in weeks. He had forced himself to stop, to ration his sight of the boy, the boy who was so much a part of himself. How Elizabeth would have enjoyed looking at him. Then he chided himself. Elizabeth would have died of shame at the thought that she was looking at Neil's bastard child. Or perhaps she would just have enjoyed the guilty pleasure of gazing at a child who was the image of her own sons at his age.

'Hello,' Alexander said as he walked over holding the cloth book.

'Mr Fraser.' Nurse Downie hastened over to Alexander.

'He's a handful, isn't he?' Richard said fondly. 'And so bright.'

'Aye, could be doing with a nurse just for him,' Nurse Downie agreed. 'He can read, Mr Fraser, and he is only two and a half years old.'

'Must come from good stock.' Richard Fraser bent down to the child. 'So read your book for me, boy.'

'Shiny.' Alexander touched the gold watch in his waistcoat. Richard took it out and opened it, so Alexander could see the face.

'Not ticking,' he said curiously. Then his fingers traced over the inscription. 'Till . . .' He looked up innocently.

'Till time stands still.' Richard took Alexander's fingers and ran them over the engraving. 'My wife gave that to me on my wedding day. And there is her name: Elizabeth.'

'Pretty name. Elizabeth,' Alexander repeated. 'Not ticking. You need to wind it.'

'Yes,' Richard agreed. 'I think I do.' He carefully wound the watch as Alexander watched, fascinated.

'It works now.' Alexander smiled at the old man.

'Yes, time isn't standing still any more,' Richard agreed. 'And this is only the beginning of it.'

Chapter 7

Neil felt a burst of excitement as the train rounded the bend and began its approach to the Tay Bridge, the city stretching round the coast and the Law. Since he'd left for his training, he had returned only twice, for the birth of Euan and the funeral of his mother. But as the Dundee shoreline came into view, he found himself looking east, to the beaches of Broughty Ferry, where his son now lived. Surely Euan would be better now, although his father hadn't seen fit to mention the child in a single letter and Agnes simply hadn't written. But he would make a fresh start with Agnes. They would have more children, and fill the house with laughter. He would rebuild the family in a way that would make his father proud. And let them all forget their mistakes.

Neil alighted at Tay Bridge station, jostled out of his carriage by other officers, eager to meet their loved ones. The platform was packed, with wives looking for their first glimpse of their husbands, children who had never met their fathers, and parents, clucking round sons they had sent off as boys, and who had returned as men. Fathers threw propriety to the winds and hugged their sons, or awkwardly patted shoulders, in silent and profound relief. So many had left, so few were returning. He could hear women sobbing, but it was a happy sound, a heartfelt sound. The soldiers melted into the sea of coats and hats, as each was borne off. He scanned the crowd, looking for his family, but he saw no one. Gradually he pushed his way through the smoke and the people, the tears and happiness, until he got to Calum, the family retainer.

'Mr Neil!' The old man smiled respectfully. 'Good to have you home in one piece.'

'At least one of us.' Neil nodded mechanically. As he did so, he felt a small boy run past him, tripping over the kitbag he had dropped at his feet.

'No harm done.' He smiled at the child.

'Daddy?' The little boy looked up at Neil, eyes gleaming with excitement and innocence.

'That's not your daddy, Will.' A young woman walked up to the child and took his hand. 'I'm terribly sorry. It's just he's never seen his daddy before.' She looked up and her face brightened as if sunlight had glinted on it. 'There he is, Will!' They ran past, leaving Neil in their wake.

'Miss Agnes is feeling rather delicate, sir,' Calum apologized needlessly.

'How is Euan?' Neil asked wistfully, already knowing the answer.

'Still the same, sir. Happy and content.' Calum bent to pick up the kitbag, but Neil stopped him.

'I'll take it.' As he swung the bag over his shoulder, Neil felt a pang of jealousy at the other man, Will's father. Neil would have given the world to have his son running to meet him, holding his arms out, shouting at the top of his voice.

The drive back was quiet, despite the time spent away, Dundee hadn't changed dramatically. The streets were still busy with horse-drawn carts clattering over the old cobbled streets under the watchful eye of the Steeple. But soon they were out of the town and moving along the Perth Road. There were a few more cars now, as the owners of the large houses could afford them. As Neil walked into the house, everything looked so normal, almost as if he had left only a few weeks ago. The tiles on the floor still shone with constant polishing, the wide, sweeping staircase still gleamed as if it had never been used. Almost nervously, Neil walked through to his father's study, where a light was burning and the smell of cigar smoke was drifting on the late afternoon breeze. Richard was sitting at his wide mahogany desk, smiling with quiet satisfaction as he puffed on an enormous cigar and gazed unseeing at the heavy wooden bookcases that filled the room from floor to ceiling.

'Hello, Father,' he said quietly.

'Hello, Neil.' Richard looked up at his younger son, now his only son. 'Welcome home.' He reached over to the mother-of-pearl inlaid humidor and offered it to him.

'Seems so quiet,' Neil murmured.

'Aye,' Richard nodded in agreement. 'It's strange how when you are with people you need to get away, then when you have some silence, it seems to haunt you.' He turned away, leaving his aged profile facing towards Neil.

'How are things?' Neil began.

'There are things we need to discuss, but they can wait. First, I think you ought to reacquaint yourself with your wife. She's up the stairs, I expect.' He shook his head. 'That's where she always seems to be. Not much for talking, your wife.'

Neil declined a cigar, then, feeling oddly dismissed, walked back to the beautiful staircase and climbed to the second-floor suite of rooms he shared with his wife.

Agnes was sitting looking out of the window, a few skeins of embroidery silk in her fingers. She was thinner and paler than before, almost as if the very life had been taken from her.

'Agnes,' he tried nervously. She turned to him, smiled vaguely and turned back to the window. Neil put down the kitbag and walked over to her.

'It's our second chance, darling,' he said softly to the inert, doll-like figure. He kissed the top of her head and stroked a finger down her cheek. But she remained aloof and motionless. 'We can begin again. Have another child.'

'They say I can't have any more children,' she said coldly, as if she were complaining a waiter had removed her drink too soon. 'When it happened, the doctors told me I would die if it happened again.'

133

'I don't understand.' He tried to get in her line of sight, but her eyes remained fixed on something else, far away, out of the window.

'I am not fit to have children,' she faltered, 'I'm just too delicate.'

'I'm sorry, Agnes,' he nuzzled into her hair, 'why didn't you tell me?'

But she just kept looking out of the window.

Neil stood and watched her, still unable to ascertain what he felt. All his resolutions of a new start were fast fading. He wanted to love Agnes, but all he felt was a strange sense of duty. A duty neither of them wanted to fulfil. And now there was this unexpected news. There would be no son to hand the family name to. Agnes had done all she was going to. And they had no other need for each other.

At a loss as to what to do, Neil wandered back down to the study. His father was there, but this time he had a more thoughtful expression on his face.

'So you've seen her?' he asked quietly.

'How long has she been so withdrawn?' Neil took a seat in the armchair by the fire as Richard walked over to him.

'Since Euan.' He shook his head. 'Your mother tried, she explained so many times that it happens, but it was no use. We gave her time, but it's been three years now. Agnes should have pulled herself together.'

Pull yourself together. They were words that Neil had heard others use so many times in the last few years. He had uttered them himself, when some of his men, or even his fellow officers, had put into words the fears that haunted them all.

'Well, I'm back now,' Neil nodded a thank-you for the drink his father offered him.

'Aye, give her a few children, that'll give her something to occupy herself with.'

'She says she can't have any more children, Father, there will be no more children.'

134

'Nonsense,' Richard returned. 'It's the only duty she has to undertake.'

'The doctors have told her,' Neil cut short Richard's opinion. 'She is too delicate.'

Richard sat down in a heavy armchair and stared into the fire.

'We need someone to carry on our family name,' he said slowly. 'Our family has been torn apart by this war. By God, what are we to do? We cannot leave our fortune to a useless cripple.'

Neil felt a wave of shame sweep over him.

'Good God,' Richard said bitterly. 'If you could only see the other boy. I've been keeping an eye on him. Tall, strong, extraordinarily bright. Everything you could wish for in a son.'

'Who do you mean?' Neil trawled his memory, but nothing was forthcoming.

'Alexander Scott. That Monroe girl's bastard son.' He sighed and shook his head. 'Then there's nothing for it. You'll have to adopt your bastard.'

'Dad, I've been here for about three hours!' Neil said incredulously.

'Aye, son,' Richard returned almost cagily. 'But I've had to live with that woman up there for the last three years while every day I have seen Alexander Scott grow into a fine young boy. He can read and write, the schoolmaster has been teaching him. She's taken him out of the nursery and sent him to school so all I've got of him for the past year is what she tells me.' He stood up and banged his fist against the heavy marble mantelpiece. 'Neil, that child is the kind of child our family deserves, that we need. And that child needs us even more.'

'Dad, what on earth would happen when people found out who he was?' Neil's breath was taken away.

'Trust me, Neil. The Scotts will keep quiet, they don't want anyone to know that the child is yours. Not with the girl being so important with the unions. She's committed treason in their eyes. Sleeping with the enemy.'

'They might not want to give him up, either,' Neil returned. 'He's her son too.'

'If you could just see him, Neil, it'll be worth the risk.' Richard looked away. 'When first Dick, then Elizabeth died, I realized that everything I had worked for, and my father before me, and everything you were fighting for, would crumble to dust without someone to take it over. But then I met the boy. And I would wait every day, till he was in the nursery, till she was away. And I would go and see him. He knows, somehow, he knows that he belongs with us. He even seemed to recognize my watch.'

'She's told him!' Neil was horrified.

'No, no,' Richard returned emphatically. 'But he feels it. The blood. Our blood.' He walked over to his son. 'I thought at the time that Elizabeth had sent him to me to keep my mind off what had happened. Foolish, I know, but I thought that. But now I know. Elizabeth sent him to me because he is our future. And we have to get him back!'

Neil looked at his father in horror. He was suggesting the unthinkable. To claim his bastard son. To have a family with Agnes.

'Dundee's a small place, Dad,' he began.

'But you won't be in Dundee, lad,' he returned. 'Someone will have to go to India. The jute industry's on its last legs here. We can't rely on your cousin to look after the factories there for ever.'

'You've planned this all out, haven't you?' Neil looked at his father; he seemed like a stranger, a man who had decided his life for him. But this was the way it had always been.

'I'll not deny I'd wondered about the boy, and as for the works, you knew you would end up in India, Dick's death has only brought it forward.'

'But I don't want to go to India!' he shouted back. 'I want to stay here. I want to run things my way.'

'You can't,' Richard replied implacably. 'You have your duty.'

Neil closed his eyes, rubbing his rough hands over his eyebrows. Nothing had changed after all.

'Mr Fraser!' Archie Taylor, older but no wiser for it, greeted Neil with enthusiasm as he saw him walk into the office the next morning. 'Good to see you.' He shook his hand. 'Now that we're getting the men back, we'll have trouble.' He laughed. 'But you'll find out about that sooner or later. Cup of tea?'

Over tea and oatcakes, Neil found out what had been happening at the works in his absence.

'Well, we got the women to cover for the male jobs, and that made a real difference to our profits. They've never given a damn about unions, just work hard and for a lot less. Shame they have to go, but . . .' He shrugged his shoulders.

'No unionist deserves to lose his job simply for serving his country.' Neil raised his eyebrows.

'We've had a female convener here the past few years. And trust me, Mrs Scott has an opinion on that matter. No woman who served her country in a factory deserves to lose her job either, but, get this, they should be paid the same as men.'

'God preserve us, they're back again!' Neil put his hand to his head in mock despair. 'Just when you thought it was safe to go back to the park on Sundays, the suffragettes strike again.' He looked at Archie. 'But surely she's got no real backing. They gave up that fight years ago.'

'Not official, but she actually carries more sway in this place than she ought to.' Archie drank the last of his tea. 'Used to stand in my office, hands on my desk, whinging about overtime payments. Could see right down her shirt. Like two puppies fighting under a blanket it was. But she'll be out soon too, and back to her family. Not as if she needs to work, husband's got a good job.' Archie stopped, and Neil saw he was trying to avoid saying something.

'What is it?' he asked.

'Nothing, Mr Fraser,' he said respectfully. 'Nothing at all.'

That evening Neil got in his car, old and slow with ill use over the last four years, and drove to Broughty Ferry, where the quiet little sanatorium was.

He waited for a few moments, before a nurse took him up the stairs to a little nursery with one solitary cot in it. A boy of almost three lay, dribbling on to his sheets, his head tossed back, his eyes vague, his body thin and wasted. His hair had been cut, but with functionality rather than care. Neil looked at his son, lying on the mattress, bars stopping him from moving his useless limbs.

'Does he have many visitors?' he said quietly.

'Your father comes to visit every month,' the nurse replied in a matter-of-fact tone.

'My wife?'

The nurse's hesitation said more than her words ever could.

'She came once, there was an incident,' she said eventually. 'She never came back.'

'What do you mean, an incident?'

The nurse sighed.

'I think your wife didn't realize how fragile children can be.' She backed away, unwilling to give out any more details.

'Tell me,' Neil said harshly.

'Your wife came to visit him, and the nurse went to put away some clothes he had vomited on. Your wife was holding him, but she was unaware that the way she did it meant that the child was unable to breathe. Luckily, the nurse came back in time.' The nurse looked at her shoes for a moment.

Neil looked down at his child once more. There he was, little Euan, a child whose mother had tried to suffocate him, because of the shame of having him. The lingering hope that he might reconcile himself with Agnes disappeared like a wave on a beach. She had tried to kill her son. The future of the family, the only heir. Except for one other.

Malise put on her clothes in the dark, trying not to yawn. Gordon had been up half the night coughing, and it was only now, when she was getting up, that he finally had achieved some rest. She rubbed her gritty eyes as she looked at the clock; there was no time for breakfast again. Grabbing her mask, scarf and hat, she bundled herself up as best she could, before setting off for work.

Everyone she passed was wearing their masks, but strangely enough they were as easy to recognize as before. But people were less inclined to speak, less inclined to stop with someone in case they were carrying the influenza. She reached the gates of the factory and went in. At least no one had died from it. Yet. But she needed to speak to Taylor about it. Keep the half-shift on a little longer, to cover for the illness.

'We need to keep the women on, Mr Taylor,' Malise said urgently as she stood in Archie Taylor's office. 'You know only too well what this flu has done to your workforce. Thirty people today, and it'll get worse before it gets better. We need them to cover the illness. We're not out of the woods yet, you know.'

Archie Taylor snorted.

'I can't help feeling that your conviction comes from as much of a desire to keep your own job as it would be to save the other workers,' Neil said as he walked into the room.

'You're back,' she said as she gazed at him with undisguised pleasure.

'Yes.' He drank in the sight of her, unable to take his eyes from hers.

Archie cleared his throat and Malise, the spell Neil had cast broken, forced herself to look at the works manager, and pushed her mind to think of the problem.

'My conviction comes from watching your workforce kill themselves by working here all the hours of the day and night, then go home to nurse their families who all have this flu!' She rounded on him. 'And unless you do something to help, you may find yourself with no one to work your half-broken machinery, Mr Taylor. This situation has been getting steadily worse since the men brought it back with them.' She felt herself stumble as the words tailed off into awkward silence in front of Neil Fraser.

'There really is nothing I can do,' Neil said, then stopped. For some reason, his eyes were roaming shamelessly over her face and body. Even Archie hesitated as he watched the man appraise Malise. So that was how it was to be, was it? Might rein her in a bit, he mused.

'Mr Fraser?' Malise's voice was less sure of itself. She could feel his eyes, they were sliding under her clothes. Treating her as if she were a fancy woman who enjoyed that kind of attention. And she was enjoying it.

'What?'

'Stop that, please,' she sounded nervous.

'Stop what?' He appeared to shake himself out of his preoccupation.

'Looking at me.' She crossed her arms over her chest.

Archie Taylor smirked.

'You've grown up a lot, Malise,' Neil replied. 'I'd hardly recognize you.' But from the look on his face, he liked what he had seen.

'As I was saying, Mr Fraser . . .'

Archie could see that for once Malise Scott was almost lost for words. As if she had forgotten what she was saying. Typical woman.

'Your people will get overtime. I thought that was what they wanted.' Neil tapped his lips with a long slim forefinger.

'We need more people to work here, not more overtime.' Her eyes flashed with anger as Malise remembered what she'd been saying. 'This influenza is ripping right through the place.'

'I can't afford any more people,' Neil replied simply.

'Then why not keep the second shift on, it's only a half-shift anyway?'

'Because we don't need to supply the army with half of what we did, Mrs Scott,' Archie Taylor interrupted.

'But since this flu hit, the half-shift have spent all their time making up the numbers the day shift can't complete,' Malise returned. 'We won't have any members left, the way you and Mr Fraser are killing them off.' She looked at each of them in turn. 'I will ensure that we have a smooth transition, if you can keep on the second shift for the duration of the epidemic.' She swept out.

'Bloody hell, if she thinks she can handle Billy Turpin for us,' Archie Taylor practically whooped with glee.

'Has she been a good worker?' Neil asked, far too casually.

Archie Taylor's piggy eyes narrowed.

'Well, she was close to your father. Very close.' He raised his eyebrows meaningfully.

'I hope you are not inferring there was any impropriety, Archie?' Neil said sharply.

'Mr Fraser,' Archie responded. 'I hardly think a member of your family would dally with a union besom like that!' He chortled at his own clumsy joke and left the room.

Neil and Richard took their places in the family pew at the church. Neil tried to pretend it was to be seen there, doing his duty, but he knew it wasn't, he just wanted the company of others, of strangers. He wasn't used to being so alone, so quiet.

As he listened to the organ play, he allowed himself a wry smile at how his tastes in evening entertainment had changed. But the boy he had once been had died, some-where in a trench, terrified and with the sudden realization that his name hadn't blessed him with good sense, with leadership qualities, only with influence.

He knew now he could make bad decisions as easily as he could make good ones.

'She's taking too much of that laudanum,' Richard said in an undertone. 'People notice that she's never here.'

'Who?' Then Neil remembered he was married to a wife who was unconscious by the time he retired every night. Or who stayed up until he had fallen asleep.

The hymns lifted his heart somewhat. He remembered singing them, the year before, in a little church not far from the front. The voices belonged to men, weary and desperately lonely, who, for a brief moment, had been able to forget what their lives were like. And who had been able instead to think of what their lives could be like.

As the minister began his sermon, he looked at the people gathered before him. He could see Archie Taylor, and Gordon Scott, the crippled schoolmaster, sitting at the edge of a pew. And nearer the front were the Lindsays, Balliols and the Gordons, other mill owners, all with families. Everyone was still wearing their masks, careful that they shouldn't sit near someone who had fallen victim to the curse of the 'Spanish lady' which was killing people all over the world.

Eventually the sermon ended and when Neil left the church, his heart growing heavy at the prospect of another silent evening, he could see the other families and friends gathering, but he had only his father. Even that miserable old schoolmaster who was coughing so alarmingly had a small child who was holding a blood-stained handkerchief. Neil smiled, the child looked so much the way he had, with his unruly black hair and cheeky eyes above the muslin mask. Neil enjoyed watching the boy for a second until Gordon Scott called him back over to him. And then he saw a familiar figure walk over and ruffle the child's hair.

'Neil!' The minister, Reverend Horatio Samson, walked over to him as Neil saw Malise lift her head and look directly at him. Neil watched as the blood paled from her attractive features and she pulled the boy behind her, as if to hide him.

'No, Mummy.' A surprisingly educated voice sounded

over the hubbub as Neil dropped his Bible. He suddenly realized exactly whom he was looking at.

'Reverend Samson, fascinating sermon,' Neil said politely, his mind somewhere else.

'Yes, I always think St Paul is neglected this time of year.'

'Who is that boy?' He gestured to the schoolmaster and his son.

'That's Alexander Scott, he's not quite five. Gordon is very proud of him.'

'Why is that?' Neil looked at the boy who was being rewarded with a particularly sticky toffee by his mother.

'He's the youngest child in school. In a class full of eight-year-olds. There's talk of him being a genius, but of course you can't tell till they're much older.'

'His parents?'

'Gordon Scott and his wife Malise. Do you remember that union agitator, Gabriel Monroe? She's his daughter. Quite a May-to-December pairing they make.'

Neil nodded his thanks without thought. That child was his son, the one his father talked of incessantly. He was walking towards them, he knew he was, but he couldn't stop himself. But Neil saw the family disappear into the crowd, like grains of sand on a beach.

'Was that why you wanted me to come?' he said quietly to his father.

'Aye.' Richard looked keenly at him. 'Let's get away. There're too many here for my liking.' He tapped his mask.

Neil sat in the car as they drove home, trying to think of something other than the fact that he did have a healthy child. A beautiful child. A genius child. The perfect heir.

That night he lay awake in his bed, Agnes deep in her poppy-laced sleep next to him, and thought of his perfect child, a genius. It was only too clear to Neil why his father wanted to adopt him. He was a son a man could only be proud of. Malise would see sense, he thought. She would understand that his son deserved the life that only a Fraser could give. He'd make her understand. He had to.

Monday morning brought yet more problems.

'Can you go and see what's happened in the carding room over at the mill?' A woman rushed over to Malise as she walked into the factory. 'Apparently there's a right stramash.'

Outside the carding room, Malise found Betty Christie, a young woman of about the same age as herself, in tears.

'It's not fair,' the girl wept. 'They've given me my cards.'

'How come?'

The girl wiped her nose on her sleeve.

'You know Johnnie Turpin, him that drives the van?'

Malise nodded. Johnnie had newly returned from the navy, and was back driving the new motorized van.

'Me and him were,' she shrugged, 'you know what I mean. In the back of the van. It was cold and—'

'Johnnie Turpin's wed!' Malise said, shocked.

'I know, but he was so nice to me, and since Jamie fell, I haven't had anyone look sideways at me.' She tailed off.

'And?' Malise prompted her gingerly.

'And I just got the sack for doing it on company time in the company van!'

Malise thought for a second.

'You leave it with me.' She patted the girl gently on the shoulder. 'But I can't make any promises. You are here to earn money, not for a bit of slap and tickle.'

She hastened out to the yard, where Johnnie Turpin was smoking a roll-up. He looked her up and down and smiled lazily.

'Johnnie, have you been sacked?' she asked him. 'For – you know.' She gestured with her head towards the back of the van.

He laughed and shook his head.

'Got a bit of a telling off, though.'

144

'And nothing more?' She cocked her head flirtatiously, automatically registering what kind of woman Johnnie Turpin would talk to.

'Of course not.' His eyes rested on her chest. 'Archie Taylor himself told me that I should think myself lucky.'

'On a break, were you?'

Johnnie shook his head.

'When do we ever get breaks around here?' His eyes registered lazy interest. 'You've grown up a bit since I last saw you.'

'Thanks, Johnnie.' She winked at him and walked away, ready to tackle Archie Taylor.

'I need to talk to Mr Taylor,' she said to the clerk who sat outside the office.

'Of course, Mrs Scott,' the clerk replied. 'I'll see if he's in for you.' He disappeared, coming back a few minutes later. 'He'll see you now.'

Malise marched in, a displeased expression set on her face. But it wasn't just Archie that she saw.

'Malise!' Neil Fraser smiled broadly at her. 'How nice to see you. Have a seat.' He looked over at Archie Taylor. 'Is there another cup for Malise, or should we get some more?' He looked over at the young woman, whose mouth had fallen open in disbelief. 'You'll catch a fly, if you're not careful.'

She looked at him, then turned to Archie Taylor.

'Mr Taylor, about Johnnie Turpin. Apparently he was celebrating his return from the navy with Betty Christie in the back of his van. And she's been sacked.'

'Of course, the wee tart deserves what she got, Mrs Scott, you know that.'

'But Johnnie Turpin gets away with a talking to?' She arched her eyebrows.

'You're not stupid; you know why,' Archie returned defensively.

'I know. But you can't punish one person for a two-man

145

job.' She cocked her head to one side. 'My comrades won't stand for such treatment.'

Archie Taylor looked at Neil.

'If a woman chooses to behave in such a way, then she has to take the consequences,' Neil said evenly.

'I'm not disputing that. But if you will not punish Johnnie Turpin, then is it fair for Betty Christie to carry the can?' Malise turned to him.

'No, it isn't. But she doesn't have his influence with your union now, Malise, does she?' Neil sat back, enjoying the exchange.

'Please call me Mrs Scott. Since I afford you the respect of your name, perhaps you can afford me the respect of mine.' She didn't want to talk to Neil Fraser, she wanted to have it out with Archie Taylor. 'And as for Betty Christie, if you sack her, my comrades will not take this lying down.'

'Betty Christie did!' Archie remarked. Malise glared at him.

'This is not a laughing matter, Mr Taylor. A young widow's livelihood is at stake. She has a child to keep and no money coming in. Her husband died for his country, you know. Her son will never know his father. And now, you will throw them on the mercy of the parish, rather than simply remind her of her duty?'

'What would you have us do, Mrs Scott?' Neil asked quietly. 'You understand that we cannot have our workers doing as they please. Certainly not in this manner.'

'I understand that. Why not suspend both of them without pay for a day? Enough to teach them that their lack of attention to their duty doesn't go unpunished, and then you haven't had to sack Johnnie Turpin.'

'Do that, Archie.' Neil nodded to his manager, who looked meaningfully at Malise. 'And now, will you have that cup of tea?'

'I don't have time to drink tea while my fellow workers—'

'For crying out loud, woman, just sit down.'

146

Malise looked strangely at him.

'You want me to sit down in your office?'

He nodded.

'But he never lets us sit down. I've stood here—'

'I know, you could talk the hind legs off a donkey, Malise.' Neil gestured to a chair, as he took his own behind his desk. 'Archie, could you sort out some fresh tea, please?' He watched as Malise looked around.

The tea arrived and Malise poured them both fresh cups. Neil watched her as she sat elegantly and drank it. If she hadn't been in working clothes, she could have been sitting in his house. She was pretty, and had grown up considerably in the last four years. But then again, hadn't they all?

Neil sat and considered how he could begin the conversation. He knew she would be pleased he wanted to take an interest in his own son, that went without saying, but how could he start it?

'Must be four years old now,' he mused. 'We made a fine son, you and I.'

Malise hesitated for a second. So that was why he was seeking her out. Not because he wanted her, he just wanted to talk about their son. Disappointment mingled with relief.

'Alexander is a wonderful boy, Mr Fraser,' she said softly. 'I just wish I could—' she stopped.

'What do you wish you could do, Malise?' he prompted gently.

'Give him all the things he deserves, all the things he needs.' She looked up at Neil Fraser, her eyes shining. 'He's the most wonderful child in the world, and I'm not saying that just because I'm biased. He is so clever, he was reading when he was just eighteen months old, and now he's working on his mathematics. If only—'

'Perhaps I can help, Malise.' Neil put his cup down. 'Perhaps I can give him all the things that you can't.'

'But how would you do that?'

'I want to acknowledge him.' He cleared his throat. 'Malise, you have taken care of my son for almost five years.

Now perhaps it's time for me to take responsibility for Alexander. I want to adopt him, bring him up as my own. Give him his birthright.'

'No!' Malise jumped out of her seat, the contents of her cup spilling over the floor. 'You can't just take him from me.'

'But you said yourself, you can't give him what he needs, and I can.' Neil walked over to her. 'As my son, I can give him everything he wants.'

'You can't give him a mother.'

'I have a wife,' he said quickly.

'I won't let you steal my son from me.' She backed against the wall.

'He's my son too, Malise.' Neil put an arm out to her, but she brushed it away. 'And you said yourself, he deserves more than you can give him.'

'And what about me? He's my son.'

'You know that wouldn't be possible.' He took a deep breath. 'But you're young, you can have more. What can it be like for your husband, bringing up another man's child?'

'You can have your own child, you have a son already.' She struggled to get the words out, her breathing short and shallow.

'Alexander is my son. He deserves the life of a Fraser.'

'You cannot seriously be wanting to take my son. Not my Alexander.' She looked at him in horror. 'Even you couldn't be so cruel.'

'It's the best solution for all concerned,' Neil tried to placate her.

'It's the best solution as far as you're concerned,' she shouted back at him. 'Alexander has a mother and a father. He doesn't need anyone else. He doesn't need you, and he doesn't want you. And he isn't your son!' She ran out of the room and hurtled down the wooden stairs to the safety of the machine floor.

Neil watched her go. He hadn't expected her to behave like this. Surely a woman like her would have been happy her son would be given the chance to grow up in a good house? But he knew he should have handled it more delicately. He'd give her time to calm down, time to see reason. He didn't want to fight her for the child, that would serve none of them. But Alexander was his son, the only son he would ever have. And if that meant a court battle, then so be it. It would be a fight worth the casualty.

Alexander was his heir. His future. His salvation.

Chapter 8

'So what exactly did he say?' Gordon asked as he watched Malise peel potatoes ready to put in the bubbling pot on the stove to boil as she made the dinner that night.

'He knows.' Malise shuddered despite the warmth of the tiny kitchen. 'And he wants him.'

'Why?' Gordon stifled an ever-present cough.

'Says we can't give him what he needs.' She threw the potatoes into the steaming water. 'Says Alexander deserves the Fraser life.'

'But what does he want to do?' Gordon persisted.

'He says he'll adopt him and make his wife Alexander's new mammy.' She looked over at Gordon. 'He can't, can he?'

'He can't force you to give up your child.' Gordon stated vehemently. 'And Alexander's birth certificate names me as the father.' He stopped. 'Oh my God, I never reregistered him!' He wheeled himself over to the press and took out the old biscuit tin that held all their papers. 'No name in the father's space.'

'But I married you just afterwards.' She looked away. 'Surely that must count for something.'

'If he is willing to fight, he must think he has a case. What exactly did he say?'

'I can't remember.' She brought the knife down sharply on a small turnip, cutting into the hardened flesh of her fingers. 'But I admitted that Alexander was his. I never thought for a moment he would want him.'

'If you have admitted it, and it goes to court, he will

get Alexander, you know that. He's one of the first families in the city.' Gordon shook his head. 'And the scandal of a court case would finish your career in politics.'

'I don't give a damn about the council. I want my son.' She spat out the words.

'Then you'll do what you do best, lass,' he said finally. 'Negotiate.'

Malise walked to work in the darkness, after a long night when sleep had deserted her. Fraser had no case, this was just the whim of a rich man with nothing to do. If it came to it, she would simply name Johnnie Turpin again, he had so many bastards that he wouldn't remember whether or not he had fathered one with her. Even if he denied it, she could just deny she had ever been near Fraser. There had been no witnesses. But deep in her mind she continued to think. Would what happened with her father count against her? Neil Fraser, how could he do this to her? He was a decent man, she knew that. Yet everything he did seemed to hurt her. Just as she managed one step forward, someone pushed her back again. Neil Fraser had dragged her back down again.

'In my office now, Mrs Scott,' Archie Taylor said as he walked over to her bench with the other finishers. Malise grimaced at the others, then followed him.

'We now have over eighty of your members off sick,' he said shortly. 'We need everyone to work the full shift-and-a-half.'

'Mr Taylor!' she returned indignantly. 'D'you want the others to fall ill, too?'

'Tell you what then, Scott,' Archie sneered. 'Why don't we just send the work over to India? They haven't gone off with the flu there.'

'If you're bringing in casuals, Mr Taylor, why don't you just tell me?' She deliberately walked up and stood right next to him, tilting her head up to stare into his eyes.

'What on earth is going on?' Neil said as he walked into

the office, carrying his beautifully monogrammed brief-case.

'Put your handbag down, Mr Fraser.' Malise didn't take her eyes off Archie. 'Because Mr Taylor is about to shut your works and move to Calcutta.'

'What are you talking about?' Neil said cagily.

'If I don't accept casual workers, who Mr Taylor seems to think have miraculously escaped any trace of the flu, then he is threatening to close the works down. Which is odd, considering your Fraser Works is about to go on short time.' She raised an eyebrow. 'But they can't help out, can they?'

'Well I can't see a problem in the Fraser helping,' Neil returned with a shrug. 'But I will want it to be known that the union made no complaint about us removing work from the Elizabeth. I'm not having you manoeuvre this situation into a strike.'

Malise turned as Archie moved away from her, scowling fiercely.

'My workers are too busy nursing their families to strike, Mr Fraser. At the moment.'

'Aye, Mr Fraser,' Archie's voice floated over them. 'This flu is getting worse. There's talk of them closing the schools down.' He nodded and walked out.

'Alexander,' he said quietly. 'Is he still attending?'

'Mr Fraser,' she said slowly.

'I want him to move to the Ferry with my household, till this is over.'

'I'd have to ask his father.' She held her hand up to stop him talking. 'Mr Fraser, when I found out I had fallen, I told my father it was yours, because we had – ' She couldn't bring herself to say the words. 'But the truth is, he wasn't yours, you can't fall the first time.' She cleared her throat. 'Alexander is Johnnie Turpin's son.'

Neil gave a dry snort of disdain.

'I couldn't tell my father, because he would have started a feud with the Turpins.' She looked up pleadingly. 'It's really kind of you to want to take Alexander, but it wouldn't be fair of me. To go along with it, then when I'd got all that I could out of you, to tell you the truth.'

Neil considered what she was saying. It was a lie, he knew that as surely as he knew that Alexander was absolutely identical to himself as a child.

'Malise, if you are sure of what you are telling me . . .' he began gently.

She nodded, the way a child does when trying to believe in a lie.

'I'm sorry. I should have told your father, he was becoming so attached to Alexander that the nurses were getting suspicious. At least when Gordon had to give up work, Alexander was able to stay at home with him, and then he began school when he was four. Straight into Primary Two class, as he was so advanced.'

Neil nodded and gestured for her to leave. Then he turned back to his desk. He had other things to think about. But nothing that he cared about so desperately.

The days passed, and with them the numbers of people stricken with influenza increased steadily. People started to die. Gordon read the paper, grim-faced, as Malise darned her stockings by the light of a single gas lamp.

'Alexander will be staying at home from now on,' Gordon said firmly. 'I'm not risking him any more.' He looked at Malise the way he had done when she hadn't done her homework.

'But people think we know more than others,' she replied. 'If we do this—'

'Sometimes you have to be selfish, Malise,' he replied. 'And you have to put his health before anything.'

'I know, Gordon.' She took hold of his hand. 'I know.' She rubbed her tired, aching eyes. 'It's just that I don't know what to do for the best. We can keep him in and hide him away, but I go out every day, I mix with three thousand people in that works.'

'You wear your mask, though,' he said sharply.

'Of course.'

Gordon thought for a second.

'No,' he said resolutely. 'I will not have my son risking himself like that. And anyone who wants to complain about it can complain to me!'

Malise nodded gratefully, it would be easier for her if she told everyone that Alexander was with his father. No one dared question what Gordon Scott said.

The flu had taken hold with a vengeance, and even the baths and steamies were becoming quieter as no one wanted to risk the chance of catching something. People were now dying within a week or two of catching it. The hospitals were full, and even those lucky enough to get a bed had few people to nurse them. For the hospital staff were down with it too.

'God, I'll be glad when this is all over,' Maisie Nicholl said to Malise as they checked the latest batch of jute, snipping away loose fibres and sewing up open hems. 'These fourteen-hour shifts are killing me. Look at this, those machines are no good any more.' She held up a small patch of the jute she was checking, the hard weave was half frayed, from the old machinery rubbing against it.

'Well, now the factories are moving back from making guns, perhaps they'll make a few new parts for us,' Malise said mechanically. She closed her eyes. Suddenly she felt so tired, and hot – even hotter than usual. Then she coughed. Maisie looked over cautiously.

'Are you all right?' she said as Malise fought to get a breath between her coughing.

But Malise slumped to the floor.

'Malise, Malise!'

Malise was woken as Maisie shook her as hard as she could.

'What happened?'

'You were coughing and then you fainted.' Maisie instinctively moved away as Malise spoke. 'Thought you were gone.'

'Takes more than a cough to finish me off,' Malise returned weakly, then pulled herself up by the heavy oak table leg.

'Mr Taylor wants to talk to you.' A young clerk, holding his hand over his mask, looked fearfully at the women. Malise nodded almost vacantly and followed him, weaving drunkenly as she did so. The climb up the stairs to the offices seemed to take for ever. Every step was becoming a mountain, but eventually she made it.

'Mr Taylor?' she said breathlessly as she walked in. She looked around, but the room was spinning and framed in a thickening band of black.

'One hundred and fifty people didn't turn up for work today,' Neil said as he checked the figures with his works manager who was standing behind him. 'We cannot keep production going with the amount we have. We'll have to send them all home.'

'What?' Malise was only half aware of where she was. 'I don't—' But the floor was rising up to meet her and all she could feel was the warmth of sleep.

'Jesus, Mary and Joseph!' Archie and Neil watched as she collapsed on the floor in front of them.

'Malise!' Neil made as though to go to her, but Archie grabbed his arm.

'No, Mr Fraser,' he said firmly. 'No point in you catching it from her.'

'Send for an ambulance wagon,' he ordered, and as Archie left, Neil fastened his mask and went over to her.

'Not you,' he said as he cradled her head in his arm. 'Please God, not you.'

'What on earth!' Gordon said as the door was hammered on as though the rent collector had come to throw them out.

Neil Fraser walked in, a mask over his face.

'Your wife is ill, Mr Scott,' he said gravely. 'She has contracted influenza.'

Gordon closed his eyes.

'Not my Malise.' He put his hand to his mouth. 'How is she?'

'How is Alexander?' Neil looked around for the child. 'I will take him with me. Mrs Scott will be home as soon as she is well enough.'

'You can't take Alexander,' Gordon said incredulously.

'I can't risk him being exposed to it,' Neil replied.

'Aye, and then you'll not return him in case he gets diphtheria, or bronchitis, or head lice.' Gordon stared back at the man.

'I am simply trying to save his life.' Neil cleared his throat. 'I have a home in Broughty Ferry and my family are moving to it until this epidemic has run its course. Alexander will be welcome to a place there. Afterwards, we will talk about what is to be done.'

Gordon was silent for a moment.

'And I have your word that you will return him,' he said slowly, 'as a gentleman?'

'Of course.'

'I want it in writing, she'd want it that way,' Gordon added.

Neil nodded.

Gordon turned his chair and went back to the tiny living room, crammed with books, papers and pamphlets. He took out a writing sheet. Neil bent and wrote on it.

'That ought to suffice,' Neil murmured as he stood up. Gordon looked at it, at the promise to return the child. And the bold signature that proclaimed his name.

'He isn't your son, you know,' he said quietly as Alexander came through from the kitchen and looked curiously at the man.

'Get packed, young man,' Neil smiled as he bent down to him. 'You are going on a little holiday to the seaside.'

'Are Mammy and Daddy coming too?' he asked curiously.

'Mammy is ill, Alexander, and Daddy has to nurse her.' Gordon gestured for him to come closer. 'So Mr Fraser here is going to take you in. So you have to be a good boy, and practise your sums and reading. And say your prayers every night. Now get your clothes and your good Sunday ones as well.'

As Alexander scampered off, Gordon wheeled himself over to the lowest shelf and picked up a sheaf of books.

'He'll need these.' His voice was gruff.

Alexander came back in with a pair of shoes, and a few clothes.

'Get the brown paper,' Gordon said almost harshly.

Neil watched silently as the child collected up a piece of brown paper and string and held out his thumb as Gordon tied up first the clothes, then the books.

'There you go, wee man.' He smiled tightly as he ruffled Alexander's hair. 'You be a good boy, and we'll see each other very soon.'

'Bye, Daddy,' Alexander reached over and kissed the man. Then he looked up. 'I know a Mr Fraser. He's very old. He has a watch.'

'He's my father, Alexander.' Neil looked down at the child, it was his own face – younger, but definitely his own face – staring back curiously at him.

'I have to say cheerio to Mammy,' Alexander said happily.

'Mammy is ill, Alexander,' Gordon took his hand. 'So she cannot see you in case she gives it to you.'

'But I want to see my mammy!' Alexander's bottom lip began to tremble.

'You'll see her as soon as she's better.' Gordon took the small child into his clumsy embrace. Neil was silent. 'Come along now, be a brave boy.' He patted his back.

Alexander, a purposeful expression on his face, picked up the two parcels as Gordon put on his mask. Then he followed Neil Fraser out of the door.

Gordon watched as the door closed.

'I know, Malise,' he said softly to himself. 'I know this is the worst thing to do, but it's better that he is alive and with him than buried in a grave next to you.' He wiped away the tear that had formed on his eyelid. 'I'm sorry, Malise,' he said as his voice began to break. 'But I had no choice.'

'I've never been in a motor car before,' Alexander said as he climbed in the back with Neil. 'But I saw an aeroplane once, really high up. I waved, but I don't know if he waved back. Do you have an aeroplane too?'

'No, but my brother used to fly an aeroplane.' Neil had to stop himself from touching the child, from stroking his hair, from holding him tight.

'Did he let you have a go?' Alexander persisted.

'It was in the war. It wasn't his aeroplane.' He smiled at the child.

Alexander was silent for a moment.

'Is your brother dead, then?' He chewed his lip, a mannerism that immediately reminded Neil of Malise.

Neil nodded.

'Mammy used to take me to see the lists at the Pillars every week.' He thought for a moment. 'She said that she didn't know why we had to go to war. And then it stopped. Did we win?'

Neil looked at the child. What could he say? Had they won the war?

'Of course we did, Alexander,' he said hesitantly.

'Mammy said we didn't. Just that everyone agreed to stop shooting for the time being. So there would be some folk left for the next one.' He smiled. 'I want to be a soldier, and have a big gun, but don't tell Mammy. She says I should be a doctor, to help people that are hurt. But—'

'I was a soldier,' Neil said thoughtfully. 'And I think that your mother is right. Be a doctor, Alexander.'

'But you get to sing songs and march if you're a soldier. Uncle Keith was in the Watch. He said that he got to sing

158

songs, and people sent him socks to wear.' He nodded carefully. 'He's only got one arm now. He pins his sleeve up.'

'Uncle Keith?'

'He's my Auntie Jessie's brother. We don't see her much because she's live-in now, and Mammy says the doctor makes her slave night and day.' He yawned under his mask. 'Will there be someone to read me my story book?'

'Yes, I will.' But Neil couldn't think of what else to say. Except the one thing he couldn't tell him.

Richard was standing at the door when Neil arrived.

'I've got the doctor coming,' he announced as Neil walked up. 'Just to check him. For all our sakes.' Then he bent down. 'Hello, Alexander. So you're coming here to live with us?'

Alexander looked around. At the wide pale drive that swept over surprisingly lush green bushes, and at the enormous oak tree that stood in the centre of the garden. But most of all he looked at the house, the large, imposing house that stretched round the garden and out of his view, its pale granite frontage seeming to touch the sky. He looked at the carvings, the beautiful stone statues that proclaimed the house to be that of a very rich man indeed.

'Do you live in a cathedral?' His lip began to quiver.

'No, Alexander.' Richard reached out and touched him gently, behind his ear.

Alexander just stared.

'He was fine on the drive over here,' Neil said hastily.

'Well, he's only ever lived in poverty before. Got to get used to it.' Richard stood up and ushered the boy into the marbled front entrance. 'Miss Emmerson here will take you up to your room.' He gestured for a plump, amiable woman dressed in black to come forward.

'Come along now, Alexander,' she said in a matter-of-fact tone. 'Bath time, then up the stairs to Bedfordshire.' She held out her hand. Alexander took it, and as his small skinny legs followed her automatically, he turned and looked at Neil, his eyes full of fear.

'Perhaps I ought to go with him.' Neil began, but Richard dismissed his offer.

'That's not the work of the man of the house,' he replied. 'Agnes can supervise his bath time when she has been made aware of the situation, but men don't look after children. We have far more important things to do.' He looked keenly at his son. 'I've told her we have a boy who will be staying with us, a child who is a genius and whom, if he proves suitable, we may adopt.'

'How can he not prove suitable?' Neil said defensively.

'Well, you can hardly inform her that he is your bastard, Neil,' his father replied sharply. 'She can count, after all.'

Both men walked out into the marbled hallway, and Neil saw his wife, holding her mask to her face. He went to her, but she moved quickly into the drawing room.

'You shouldn't have brought him,' she said quickly. 'He may have any number of infections. I am very delicate, you know.'

'Agnes,' Neil said, but he could see the expression in her eyes.

'Do you think I am a fool, Neil?' she replied as she turned her head away. 'Did you really think anyone would believe you had taken pity on some poor orphan out of the slums? Did you think that anyone seeing you both together wouldn't know?'

'I don't know what you mean,' he answered.

She walked over to the piano, to the photograph that stood on it. Of Dick, Neil and their father.

'How old is he?' she asked fiercely.

'Nearly five.' Neil looked at his shoes.

Agnes looked at the photograph almost tenderly, then she slammed her hand into it as hard as she could, the glass gouging her palm.

'Agnes!' Neil rushed over to her, but she stared at him

with an almost calm, triumphant expression. Then she slipped past him and disappeared as silently as a ghost.

Neil picked up the photograph. The family portrait was now in shreds, and for ever stained with Agnes's blood.

Doctor Patrick had rushed to the scene, and Neil accompanied him upstairs to where Alexander was sitting in his pyjamas, eyeing Miss Emmerson rather warily.

'Alexander, this is Dr Patrick,' Neil said as he walked over to the little boy, who looked so tiny next to the large, almost clinically white bed. 'He wants to check you over.'

'Is this hospital?' Alexander said carefully. 'Am I here because I'm going to die?'

'No,' Neil replied as he took the child's hand.

'Will you read my book to me?' Alexander gripped hold of Neil's hand tightly.

Neil fought back his pride that the child wanted him, trusted him.

'Of course, Alexander,' he said happily. 'I wouldn't go back on a promise, would I?'

He sat on the bed as the doctor examined Alexander's chest and listened to his heartbeat.

'He seems fine,' Dr Patrick said thoughtfully. 'Bit of a rattle in the chest, but that is common for children from those backgrounds.' He took a small jar from his briefcase. 'But I'll take a sputum sample, just in case.'

'I know what to do,' Alexander said as soon as he saw the bottle. 'My daddy has to do that. He has consumption.'

'Does he, indeed?' Dr Patrick took the words calmly. 'And is he still well?'

'He sicks up blood,' Alexander shrugged. 'But apart from that, he's happy. Apart from him not having any legs,' he ended helpfully.

'Perhaps not the best environment for a young child to live in?' Neil asked the doctor, willing the result in his favour.

'Actually, it makes little difference living with someone

who has consumption,' the doctor returned unhelpfully. 'You see, we all have the capacity to develop it. Whether you do or not depends on your health.'

But Neil still looked troubled.

After the examination was finished, Neil settled Alexander in the large, soft bed and opened the book of Bible stories. As he told his son the story of Noah's ark, he saw Alexander's eyes begin to close, then listened as his breathing became heavier, till at last he was asleep.

'Home at last, Alexander,' he said as he held the boy's small hand. 'And I'm never letting you go.'

For a week, Malise lay in the little bed, incoherent with pain, while Gordon washed down her body. Every day Jessie or Mrs Baker came with food, or just to sit with her to give Gordon a chance to sleep. And every time he awoke, the first word he uttered was his wife's name.

'Gordon?' Malise opened her eyes through the blinding red pain almost ten days later.

'Shh, Malise,' he said fondly. 'You just rest and get better.'

'Alexander?' She tried to move but it was pointless, she didn't have an ounce of strength in her body.

'He's safe, Malise,' he returned. 'Safe and staying with someone.' He brushed the hair away from her forehead. 'Don't you worry yourself about him.'

It was a few days before Malise was on the road to recovery.

'Hello, Malise,' Mrs Baker came in carrying a pot of soup. 'Just give this a warm-through. You look better, love,' she said as she took off her coat. 'Jessie was asking for you. She can't get away for a visit, that doctor's rushed off his feet and she's up day and night getting the house ready for him. Honestly, that man needs to sort himself out, his cook's gone off and left him and he's got Jessie cooking dinners! That girl could burn water—'

'How is Alexander?' Malise croaked.

'Alexander?' Mrs Baker looked puzzled. 'He's staying with a friend of Gordon's. Till all this flu blows over. Curse of the Spanish lady, indeed! Curse of the pletties of Dundee, more like . . .'

'Who?' Malise persisted.

'Who what?' Mrs Baker returned.

'Who is Alexander with?'

Mrs Baker thought for a moment; an unusual activity for the woman.

'Some pal of Gordon's.' She straightened the blanket that lay on the top of the bed. 'Now I've to be away early tonight, my Sheila is down with it too, but she's on the mend, like you.' She stood up, her wiry grey hair falling obediently back into place. 'You take care, Malise, and I'll pop in tomorrow if I can.'

As Mrs Baker buttoned up her heavy woollen coat, Gordon arrived back at the door.

'Can you move your chair for me, Mr Scott?' she said cheerfully. 'My hips won't fit in that wee gap there.'

Malise watched as Gordon and Mrs Baker did a rather complicated little dance that at one point had Gordon's arm disappearing into Mrs Baker's wobbly behind. Then, as they heard the door shut behind her, Gordon squeezed his chair up to Malise's pillow.

'You're looking a lot better, my dear,' he said quietly.

'Where is Alexander?' she responded. She wasn't interested in the fondness in Gordon's eyes, or in the way he was stroking the hair from her forehead.

'You just rest.' He tried to reach over to kiss her cheek, but he couldn't. So instead he took her little work-reddened hand in his and pressed his lips to the palm.

'Where is he, Gordon?' she said urgently.

Gordon sighed.

'Fraser came and offered to look after him. Till this flu has run its course. It was the only solution, Malise, people are dying of this . . .'

'Rich people an' all,' she replied.

'But his family are all living out in the Ferry, the air's better there.'

'Gordon, how could you do it?' She struggled up from her pillow. 'How could you give my son to that man? You know he'll not let him go.'

'Just because you've recovered doesn't mean that the whole town has,' Gordon remonstrated. 'Bring him back here so he can fall ill next week, next month?'

'I can't be without him.' She closed her eyes against the blinding pain in her forehead. 'You just don't understand.'

'I do, my dear.' Gordon took her hand again. 'I've buried a son, remember? A son murdered because of something I did.' He stroked her fingers softly. 'And I've no intention of burying another one. You get better and then we'll go and collect him.' Gordon flinched as she pulled her hand away.

'Collect him from where? Do we know where he lives?'

'When he told me you were ill, I was out of my mind with worry. All I could think of was that I could lose you.' He reached for her hand once more, but she didn't want him to touch her. 'I couldn't look after both you and Alexander, and you needed me more.'

Knowing he was right, Malise slumped back down on to the pillow. What Gordon had said made sense. Perfect sense. People were dying from influenza, men, women and children. But she was terrified that she might never see her son again.

Neil took off his mask as he sat in the car. He watched the crowds of people thin out as the motor car drove westwards, to the clean sea air of Broughty Ferry. Even though the works had fewer orders than before for their sacking and rope, it was still proving to be a struggle to get them fulfilled in time. So many people were ill. What a bitter pill for some of them, to survive the trenches and then fall victim to influenza. Bruce, his driver, expertly steered the car up the steep hill, then turned sharply as he reached the driveway, the house hidden by the trees and bushes. He was home at last. Neil, abandoning his briefcase, overcoat and hat, leapt out of the car before Bruce had a chance to open the door for him, and hurried up the stairs to the bright, clean nursery room.

'Alexander!' he called, but it was deserted, save for Miss Emmerson, darning a stocking as she sat by the fire.

'He's downstairs with Mr Richard, sir,' she said with a smile. 'They had tea together.'

Neil turned and headed down to the study, where he found his father and Alexander, sitting in the heavy leather armchairs by the fire, both huddled over a carved wooden table.

'And this is?' Richard's voice was unusually playful.

'A knight.' Alexander took the ivory chess piece from his grandfather. 'And it moves in threes.'

'Clever boy,' Neil said as he walked over to his son. 'Teaching him chess, Father?' He crouched down beside the boy. 'I remember you doing that with me.'

'My daddy taught me to play chess,' Alexander announced. 'Said Alexander with the elephants played chess. It made him clever.'

'You run off back to the nursery now, Alexander,' Richard said fondly. 'Miss Emmerson will be wondering where you have disappeared to.'

'But I want to stay with the books,' Alexander pouted. He looked round at the shelves, all lined with large, leather-bound editions.

'Now.'

Much to Neil's regret, Alexander walked slowly past both men and left the room.

'How are the works?' Richard said as Neil sat down.

'Struggling.' Neil sat back in the chair. 'Every day there are less people to work the machines and the looms are in a terrible condition; there've been no spare parts available for years.'

'Well, you'll be off to India with Agnes and the boy soon,' Richard replied.

'I don't have legal guardianship of him,' Neil returned. 'And I doubt that Malise will ever sign him over to me.'

Richard went over to the desk and took some papers from it.

'I had Mackenzie put in the papers today,' he replied. 'Legal guardianship.'

'Father, we agreed . . .' Neil started angrily.

'She has no case. This is Alexander's birth certificate.' He passed it to Neil. He scanned it, trying to work out what he ought to be seeing.

'No father. Legally, Alexander is a bastard.'

'This is not a fight, Father,' he turned away from his father's gloating, 'I simply want what is best for my son.' He took another look at the certificate. 'Why on earth didn't she marry Gordon Scott in time?'

'From what Mackenzie told me, Miss Monroe gave birth at fifteen. He has ways of finding things out. And getting certificates like these.'

'She was so young.' Neil felt a wave of guilt crash over him.

'Must admit, surprised me too, she is so good at organizing the women.' Richard chuckled to himself. 'If she'd been a man, I'd have offered her a job running the works in India.' Then he took a look at his son. 'I'll take a turn round the gardens before dinner.'

Neil sat in the chair, only moments ago he had wanted to go to Alexander, to talk to him. To be his father. But now all he could think of was the terrible wrong he had done to a young innocent girl. And knew he was too dirty to sully his son.

'You should stay off for another day,' Gordon said later that week. 'You're not well enough.'

'I have to get back,' Malise said resolutely. 'We need the money.' She turned away, as she always did, when she was dressing. 'And I need to talk to Fraser.'

'He won't be there,' Gordon replied. 'He'll be hiding in the Ferry till the influenza's gone.'

166

'For your sake, Gordon, he'd better not be.' She picked up her coat and hat and walked out.

She walked purposefully, ignoring the lingering effects of her illness. She would not feel the aching of her limbs, she would not feel the slight headache that she still had. She was better. And she needed to talk to Neil Fraser.

Enjoying the freedom of not having to wear her mask any more, Malise walked through the brown slushy snow at the gate. But she knew that there were many others who were sick. There were hardly enough people to run the factory. Fraser had been right to protect Alexander, she knew that. But it also meant he didn't believe that he was not the father.

Malise walked into the factory, it was quiet, with only the hum of half the looms, the rest standing as idle as tombstones. They were old, many of them were broken. She walked over to the checking benches, smiled at Maisie, and picked up the first batch of jute sacking.

'Well, let's get this lot checked and packed,' she said grimly.

The day flew past in a hot haze of jute-infested air. Malise worked solidly, her fear keeping her going. What would she do if Fraser refused to return him? And what might happen to Alexander if he did?

At half past six, Neil walked into the still factory, his thick leather-soled shoes making a crisp sound that echoed through the high-roofed building.

'Malise.'

Malise turned from the bench to see him standing there, masked and wary. Then she looked around, checking that there was no one to see or hear them, to know their secret.

'Alexander,' she began.

'You look well.' He went over and stood beside her, and she could smell him, so different from the other smells in the factory. The scent of jute and sweat was nowhere to be found on him, just lemon and liquorice. And power.

'Sorry, Mr Fraser.' She lifted her eyes from the table. 'Didn't die. Can't get it again, you know. So I'm back.'

'I can't let Alexander come to you, not with the disease still rampant,' he said calmly.

'And after it has run its course?' She searched his face for a clue.

Neil took a deep breath.

'Since you claim someone else is his father, then I have no choice but to take your word for it.' He knew he couldn't antagonize her, one word from her and she could set the police after him. 'But whatever happens, I would like to pay for his schooling.'

'He doesn't need your charity, Mr Fraser,' she replied. 'If he needs to go to the High School, then he can fight for a bursary.'

'I hope he is mine, Malise.' Neil looked at her face, it was a face he saw every day now. 'I hope he is. Because he is such a special boy, he's brought life back to the house again. My father—'

'He's Johnnie Turpin's. Billy's his uncle.' Malise's face twisted in worry. 'What do you think he would say, if he knew a member of his family was living with the Frasers?'

Neil opened his jacket and took out a photograph. He handed it to her.

'Oh my goodness.' Malise put a hand to her mouth. 'He looks so handsome there.' Alexander was standing on the patio. 'Hello, my wee man. I miss you.'

Neil watched her purse her lips together to stop herself from weeping.

'I want to see him,' she said suddenly.

'I'm afraid that is difficult,' Neil murmured. 'You may still be infectious.'

'Then can I write to him?'

'He beat me at chess today.' He grimaced slightly.

'And is he eating his vegetables, and practising his sums, and his reading? And is he saying his prayers?'

'I've been reading his book to him every night.' Neil's face shone with pleasure.

'Tell him I love him, and his father sends him his love too.' Her voice broke.

'He knows that.' Neil put a hand on her shoulder. 'You are so lucky, Malise, to have a son like Alexander. It's ironic, you have a son that would benefit from everything I could give him, and I have no one, except the family in India.' He looked around him. 'And all this will be theirs.' He walked away from her.

The following day she was at the door of his office when he arrived, holding a letter in her hand.

'Did he sleep well?' she said as soon as he opened the door.

Neil swallowed. It felt wrong; he wanted to separate Malise from Alexander, but she was turning a knife in his guilt. There's no other way, he reminded himself.

'Very well, thank you,' he said stiffly.

Malise handed him the letter.

'That will be all,' he mumbled. He could see Malise wanted to talk about Alexander, but he didn't want to discuss him with her. To remind himself that his son had another family. A family Neil was attempting to wrest him from. As she reluctantly left, Neil looked at the letter. Then he opened his desk and put it in a drawer.

'I'm sorry, Malise,' he said softly. 'But it's best if he forgets you.'

As December progressed, the influenza continued to rage. Neil sat in his office and looked at the orders he had yet to fill; one of them was for a company which made money bags for the Bank of England, but he had delayed it twice now, and if it wasn't on the train first thing tomorrow morning, then the contract would be lost for ever.

'How many people haven't turned up today?' he asked, as Archie walked in for his morning meeting.

'Don't know,' he replied dumbly, and Neil looked up quickly. Archie was red-faced, but not his usual high colouring, he was full of fever.

'Good God, man, you've got it.' Neil stared at his works manager. 'Get off home with you and don't come back till you're better.'

As the shift continued, it became obvious that the few hundred workers they had were never going to finish the order and have it packed up in time. Neil walked up and down looking at the looms, and the checkers busy pulling at threads before nodding their agreement and the bales being loaded on to the vans. Through the heat and the dusty air, he saw the small checkers and drivers, lifting and packing, running from one place to another, as the weavers went from one loom to another, checking thread, replacing spindles, all of them praying that the loom would work for another day, that somehow the old worn parts would struggle on till the order was finished. Neil could feel the panic in the air, it was as tangible as the jute. Everyone knew that things were not going well, despite the fact that he hadn't told anyone.

'Malise!' He stopped at her bench and gestured over to her. He saw her look up and an expression of annoyance cross her face. Then she put down the bale she was examining and walked over to him.

'Yes, Neil,' she returned as she greeted him. Neil looked at her, he hadn't heard her use his Christian name in years. And it was inappropriate, she was one of his menial employees. Even if he liked the way she said it.

'My name is Mr Fraser,' he hissed. Malise sighed.

'Sorry, sir,' she returned innocently. 'Since you decided to call me by my first name without asking permission, I thought you wanted to be friends. Or were you simply being over-familiar?'

Neil bridled, and he was aware of the other women covertly watching them.

'Miss Monroe,' he began.

'It's Mrs Scott, now. I got married. To Mr Scott. You know, the old schoolmaster who's in a wheelchair, and has consumption—'

'Mrs Scott, I do not have time to listen to you try to score petty points!' he shouted at her. Malise stared at him wordlessly, her face so like Alexander's, that he actually felt a twinge of guilt that he had shouted at her.

'We'll need the people to work late tonight,' he began. 'But—'

'But?' Malise replied archly.

'We won't be able to pay them till next month.' He took a deep breath.

'Are you going bankrupt?' She looked at the man incredulously. Neil shook his head vehemently.

'Of course not, it's just that I have had to buy a substantial amount of jute—'

'You've just bought ground for another factory in India,' she replied. 'And you've taken the money from this place to do it.'

Neil gazed at her. How on earth did she know?

'We have friends in sunny climes too, or rather, you have enemies.'

'So I presume that you will not help me persuade your members to stay on for the next shift?' he said.

'Since you're intent on sending our jobs to India, we might as well make hay while the sun shines.' She laughed drily. 'I will talk to them, but only if you can arrange for the canteen to stay open; maybe it can offer soup. How long do they have to work?'

'If the spun jute isn't out of here by four in the morning, then we've lost the order. And we won't get another one.'

'Leave it to me.' She stopped for a moment, wiping the sweat from her brow. 'What are you doing?'

'Going home for dinner.' He stared at her, trying to understand.

'Not staying to help yourself?' She cocked her head to one side. 'Who's going to run the place?'

'I was under the impression that you thought you already did,' he answered quickly.

'Well, Mr Fraser, if I ran the place I'd be leading from the front. I'd stay late, help pack the vans, just do things, so people could see that I was trying my best and that I understood the sacrifice they were making. Because I was doing it too.' She smiled patiently.

'There's nothing here I can do,' he muttered.

'Then organize the canteen, for the free soup.' She looked at him. 'You can do that.' She looked over at the people. 'You leave them to me.' She walked away from him, over to the central gangway of the factory, and took out her old tin whistle. Neil watched as she blew it hard, three times. The factory stopped as if by magic. Everyone turned to her, and then began to walk over.

'Times are hard, hard for all of us,' she began. 'And we need to fight for every order. Unless we get this one finished tonight, we've as good as lost a chance of keeping this place open. Fraser doesn't even have the money to pay the overtime, but, listen – ' she put her hand out to stop the grumbling ' – if we work till four, he will pay us for a whole extra shift and provide free soup to keep us all awake. And he has guaranteed that he will get us the money by the New Year.' She turned so she could see everyone individually. 'Give us some money for when the snow comes.'

'Aye, but then what'll happen?' a woman shouted from the back.

'Then we'll have proved that nothing can beat a Dundee worker! Will we let them take our jobs away, or will we stay and fight for them?' Her voice rang out over the sound of the looms. 'Will we prove that we won't win the war and then lose the peace?'

Neil stood in amazement as he saw the women, hesitant at first, each begin to nod.

'Will we do it for our lads, prove to them that we don't give up when it gets hard?'

'Aye!' It rang out in the factory, as the people clapped and cheered at her words. They then returned to work, energized for the long night ahead of them.

As the second shift arrived, Malise stood and personally organized the weavers, spinners, checkers and sweepers. Now the factory was at full strength and there was a feeling of excitement in the air.

'You have a full workforce, Mr Fraser,' she said as she walked into his office. 'Every job is filled. You'll need to stagger the breaks though.'

'You've done it all yourself?' Neil asked with real admiration.

'Someone had to.' She shrugged and turned to go. Then she fished in her pocket. 'I've a letter. For Alexander.' She put it on his desk. 'Ask him if he can write back, or draw a picture. Or something.'

'He is very busy, you know, with lessons. We've engaged a tutor for him,' Neil said awkwardly.

'The influenza is beginning to go now,' she added. 'Tell him he'll be home soon.'

Neil watched her go. Then he picked up the letter and put it in his desk with the others. One day he would explain to Alexander. But he couldn't. Not now. Not now that the child had begun to like him.

Neil watched as the last of the jute was loaded on to the carts, ready to be taken to the railway and transported to the factory. They'd made it, by the skin of their teeth, but they had made it.

He went to the front of the factory, to where the women were streaming out. Malise was standing on the wall, hanging on to the gates, her face glowing with vitality.

'We showed them, Malise!' one voice shouted.

'Aye!' she shouted back. 'Wha's like us?'

'Gang few, and they're a' deid!' A chorus of jubilantly tired voices replied. Neil watched as she stood there, perched precariously on the pillars. And then he realized what she was doing. She was thanking them for their work. A personal thanks, from the union. A thanks he should have been making. As the last person left the gates, he walked over to her, sliding on the icy cobbles.

'Get down, woman.' He held his hand up to her. She took it as he helped her on to solid ground again. 'And come with me. You're freezing cold. Let me get you something to warm you up.' He ushered Malise towards the office stairs.

'A drink to celebrate?' He was rather taken aback by the feelings inside him. They had done it together. And she had been magnificent.

'I'd love a cup of tea,' she said hesitantly.

'There isn't anyone here to make it,' he returned with a grimace. 'I am afraid it will have to be whisky or brandy.' He smiled at her. 'What's your poison?'

'I'm in the Temperance League,' Malise replied stiffly.

'Are you trying to tell me, Malise Monroe, that you actually have decided on a lifetime of moderation?' He laughed as he leaned back against his desk. 'You know, you never fail to amaze me.'

Malise tried and failed to hide her smile. He was being so friendly, so normal, not at all like Mr Fraser, the man who owned the works. He was like the Neil from before, when he liked her and she liked him.

'What does brandy taste like?' she said shyly.

'Warm and smooth.' Neil picked up two large round glasses.

'Sounds like tea,' she returned with slightly more confidence.

'Oh, I think you'll like it.' He poured two generous measures into the balloon glasses. Then he handed one to her. 'Cup your—' he stopped as he saw her filthy, work-worn hand reach towards him. 'Would you like to wash your hands?'

Humiliated, Malise nodded. Neil ushered her over to his bathroom, which lay off his office.

'Oh my goodness!' Malise said as she opened the door. 'It's enormous.' She went over to the sink and tried one of the taps. Water gushed out immediately. 'Hot water!' she said incredulously.

Neil leaned against the door jamb as he watched Malise wash her hands. She was enjoying it, he could see by the way she was taking her time, lathering the soft soap into bubbles. And seeing her do that, something so intimate, stirred him in a way that he thought his body had forgotten. He saw her catch sight of her face in the ornate mirror. And then lift up the water in her hands, so that she could wash her smudged cheeks.

'Here.' He handed her a soft white towel. Their eyes met as she took it from him, and Neil could see she knew what he was feeling. That she could feel the pull of him as much as he felt the pull of her.

Malise gazed at him, she couldn't have taken her eyes away if someone had dragged her from the room. He wanted her, she could see it in his eyes, and she wanted him too. But she couldn't. He was the enemy, and she wasn't a pupil teacher any more. If he touched her now, she wouldn't be able to stop herself. Even now, even before anything had happened, she could feel the guilt and disgust prowling round her. The gurgle of the basin emptying broke the spell of the silence. Malise turned, there was a thick tidemark on the porcelain.

'I've left a mark,' she said unnecessarily.

'Yes.' Neil forced his eyes from her and walked back to the office.

'I ought to go,' she said when she emerged from the bathroom to see Neil sitting in one of the two armchairs next to a fire which was burning down to the embers.

'Stay, please. Talk to me.'

Malise looked at him. His time in the trenches had changed him, made a man of him. In the same way that her time in the war had changed her. They both understood why the other was here. Because it was how they wanted it. The fire crackled, spitting small pieces of coal on to the guard.

'No, Mr Fraser,' she returned. 'Unlike you, I'm back here at eight o'clock. Better get some sleep tonight. Kiss Alexander for me.' She pulled herself away from the room and almost scurried up the hill back to Lochee, all the time wishing she'd been reckless enough to have accepted a drink from the enemy.

Gordon was asleep in bed when she got home. Exhausted, Malise climbed in beside him, but as Gordon's arm automatically crept out to hold her to him, she felt the twinge of disgust that always came over her when he tried to touch her. As she closed her eyes, however, another man came to mind. The way he'd looked at her when he offered her his hand. And the way she knew she'd looked back at him.

A few short hours later, she was back at work. After the previous night, the workers were subdued, there was no excitement in the air. It was just drudgery again. Malise went through the motions of checking the jute sacking, her thick needle sewing up any loose seams. But her mind was full of one thing. Neil Fraser. Did he still want her, and did she still want him?

'Christmas next week,' Maisie said as they walked out towards the gates together. 'Wonder if there'll be anything in the shops this year?'

Malise felt her heart stop. Surely Fraser couldn't be intending to keep Alexander at Christmas? He belonged with her. If Alexander stayed with the Frasers, they would turn him, with presents, with money.

'Mrs Scott!' Archie Taylor strode over to her, pushing the others out of the way.

'What is it now?' she said wearily.

'We'll not be needing you any more,' he said gleefully. 'Here are your wages.' He handed her a brown packet. 'Your checker has come back.'

Malise stared at the wage packet. This was it, their thanks for her work.

'Here's your coat.'

'What's your hurry,' she murmured.

'Surely you're not wanting special treatment, just because you're in the union,' he said in a low voice.

'No, I never said that,' she replied numbly. 'Thank you.'

Still in a daze, she walked home, took off her coat and hat and put on the kettle.

'How was your day?' Gordon said as he wheeled himself up to her.

'They don't need me any more,' she said in a whisper. 'So they've sacked me.'

'Well, it is within the terms of the Act, Malise,' Gordon said in a matter-of-fact voice. 'You couldn't expect to be there for ever.'

'But what will I do?' she said incredulously. 'We've no money coming in.'

'Something will come up.' Gordon patted her hand. 'I'll write to the union and tell them.' His face darkened. 'Meanwhile, I think it's about time that we got Alexander back, don't you?'

Archie sat with Neil as he went over the day's production figures.

'You'll need to do better,' Neil said warningly.

Archie bridled, then a thoughtful expression came over his face.

'Do you remember that bit of unpleasantness with the Monroe girl, which has recently raised its head again?' he said innocently.

Neil's eyes narrowed.

'I've a wee insurance policy. With her signature on it.' His face was inscrutable.

'What do you mean?' Neil persisted.

'She signed a declaration that you are the father of her child,' Archie said casually. 'Been witnessed by a notary and everything. Legal and binding. Thought I ought to do it, under the circumstances.'

The grin of relief almost broke Neil's face in two.

That night, Neil was at home when Adams, the butler, came to the study where he was working.

'There is a policeman at the door, sir,' he said respectfully. 'About the boy.'

'Show him in.' Neil felt his stomach churn.

The police inspector was a tall, thin man, with a heavy ginger moustache. He looked around the study, at the mahogany furniture inlaid with intricate carvings, at the walls of books and the ivory-and-jet chess set that sat on a table so smooth it could have been glass.

'How can I help you?' Neil said as he rose from his seat behind the table.

'We have received a complaint from a Mr Gordon Scott,' the inspector began. 'A most unusual complaint.'

'What of?' Neil said smoothly.

'Kidnap of Alexander Gabriel Scott.' The inspector looked more than a little worried at facing a man from one of the town's first families with such a serious accusation.

'His name is Alexander Gabriel Monroe. I have his birth certificate here.' Neil took it out of a drawer. 'I trust I have your discretion in this matter.'

'So why is Gordon Scott wishing the child returned?' Inspector Harris checked the certificate thoroughly and handed it back.

'I have no idea, but I am awaiting an affidavit that confirms I am the child's father.' Neil looked down for a moment. The inspector nodded understandingly.

'It might be better, in the circumstances, if the child were returned to the family, the other family, till we have proof that you have a claim on the child.'

'With all this influenza . . .' Neil shook his head. 'He's been here since his mother contracted it, five weeks ago.'

'Mr Fraser, if you have no legally binding arrangement to keep the child, then I will be forced to arrest you. This needs to be sorted out in a civil court, but for the moment, unless you have the mother's permission, then you are committing a criminal offence.' Harris cleared his throat. 'Bide your time.'

'I can't risk his life,' Neil returned.

'You are risking your own liberty,' the inspector warned. 'Even a man such as yourself cannot live above the law, however unjust it may seem. The mother has the right to the child and Mrs Scott is the mother, even if there is no mention of Gordon Scott on the certificate.'

'Please,' Neil tried. 'Alexander means the world to me.'

'It would seem that his mother feels the same way.'

'Let me talk to him for a moment.' Neil left the room, running up the stairs two at a time till he reached the nursery.

'Alexander!' he called. Alexander was sitting on the window seat, looking at the snow that was beginning to fall gently but resolutely on the wrought-iron patio table.

'Hello.' Alexander smiled cheekily at him. 'Have you come to play with me? We can play with the trains. I like the train set.'

'No, Alexander, there is a policeman downstairs. Your mother wants you back.'

Alexander pouted as he looked around the bright, clean nursery, toys neatly piled into the large toy chest in the corner, the train set going round it.

'I want to stay here,' he said glumly.

'You will be coming back, it's just that your mother wants to see you one last time.' Neil's heart leapt as his son said the words he had always wanted to hear.

'Can't Mammy come and live here?' Alexander asked quizzically.

'Your mother has her own house, but I want you to tell her every day that you want to come back here and live with me.' He squeezed Alexander's little shoulder.

'But I want Mammy to live here too,' he protested.

'You can't have both of us, I'm afraid,' Neil replied. 'Where would you rather live? With your mother, or here with me?'

'With Mammy,' Alexander answered slowly, and Neil felt his stomach sink. He shouldn't have pushed the child, it was too soon. 'But can I take some of my toys, please?'

'What would you like to take?' Neil said sadly.

'The train set, please.'

Neil took Alexander's hand and together they went over to the train set. It was old, it had been his and Dick's when they were boys, and now it was Alexander's. Then he had an idea.

'There isn't room in your house for a train set,' he said quickly. 'But why don't I send for you every week and you can come and play with it here? The two of us together?' He smiled at the boy, who nodded back enthusiastically.

'Can I take my farm set, then?' He looked up for a moment. Neil nodded.

'Of course you can, Alexander.' He bent down and embraced the child. 'I'll miss you so much.' He closed his eyes as he inhaled Alexander's smell. 'I'll write to you.'

'I'll miss you too.' Alexander kissed him gently on the cheek as he wrapped his skinny arms around Neil's neck.

'So you just let him go?' Richard was saying as Neil explained to his father what had happened as they sat at the dinner table that night.

'Father, legally, I had kidnapped him. But Archie Taylor has assured me that he can find the affidavit that she signed after her father's death.'

'Say what you like about that brute, he has a way about him of getting you into his debt,' he said admiringly. 'Will we have the child for Christmas?'

'No, I spoke to Mackenzie; the hearing has been set for the fourteenth of February. But he's confident that the affidavit will strengthen our case considerably.'

'We need the boy home, and with his real surname,' Richard laughed to himself. 'I don't suppose Mrs Scott would do the honours again and provide us with another bastard.' He laughed at his own joke. 'Where is Agnes now, the food's getting cold?'

Malise waited at the door as Alexander walked up with Inspector Harris, who was carrying a large suitcase. Then she could wait no longer. Hurtling down the stairs, she ran with all her might towards the little boy, who, catching sight of his mother, ran to her.

'Mammy!' he shouted as she caught him, enveloping him in the largest hug he had ever experienced.

As Alexander slept in his little bed in the kitchen, warmed by the heat from the range, Neil found himself in the car, driving around. He reached the street, lined with high tenements, and saw the one where Alexander lived, the two wooden boards that lay over the steps for Gordon to get down in his wheelchair. Without thinking, Neil got out of the car and walked into the block till he reached the black door with the polished nameplate. He reached up with his hand, then dropped it as his shoulders slumped in defeat. He got in his car and drove away slowly.

Agnes was in bed when he returned. Neil undressed in the dark, then reached for his wife's inert body. But Agnes was deeply asleep, her pale, sharp body providing him little comfort as it relaxed in the comfort of laudanum. She was delicate, yet unyielding in her rejection of him. For she never turned away from him, she was just never there. Agnes had run away from him, to somewhere else, and even if he had wanted her, he wouldn't have been able to reach her. Neil closed his eyes, but as soon as he did, he saw someone else, and felt the shame. He wouldn't think about her, he tried to put her out of his mind. But all he could see was that Monroe girl. Smiling, happy and alive.

Malise stood in the kitchen, watching Alexander sleep. Now she had no job, and no money. But she had Alexander and nothing else mattered. She would find something else to do, somewhere else. Whatever it took, she would provide for her son. And keep him safe from Fraser. Yawning, she went into the bedroom, Gordon was already there, sitting on the bed as he took off his clothes.

'It's good to have the wee man back,' he said quietly. Malise nodded as she began to undress, trying to ignore the fact that Gordon had stopped to stare at her. She undid her blouse and folded it neatly on the chair, then began to remove her liberty bodice.

'Don't put on a nightdress,' Gordon said huskily. 'I'll keep you warm.'

Malise nodded resignedly, then once she had removed the rest of her clothes, slipped into the cold bed.

'Glad to have a smile on your face again,' Gordon's hands began to move over her. 'Now we can get back to normal.'

As his head bent to kiss her collarbone, then move downwards, Malise closed her eyes. And tried to pretend that she was anywhere else. And that the hands and lips on her body belonged to someone else.

'How many people are off today?' Neil said as Archie Taylor walked into his office.

'I don't know,' Archie blustered. 'I've spoken to the gaffers and they are going to have a count. Make a list.'

'Send for Mrs Scott, at least she knows what's going on here,' he said sharply.

'She doesn't work here any more,' Archie returned. 'I had to let her go. The Act.'

So that was why she had done it, revenge because she had been sacked. Neil felt a stab of anger. Why hadn't Archie consulted him first? 'Who's in charge of the union now?'

Archie shrugged.

'Then I suggest you find out,' Neil replied. 'Since we are going on short-time after New Year. And I don't want a walkout.'

Archie laughed.

'There's no one to fight you now, Mr Fraser.' Archie stifled a belch. 'So there's no one to organize a walkout.'

'Talking of that person,' Neil began, 'you said that you had an affidavit?'

Archie's smile spread all over his face. He reached inside his pocket and took it out, placing it down on the table.

'Glad to be of service, Mr Fraser,' he said in an oily tone. But Neil was too busy opening it. And there it was, a legally witnessed affidavit, signed by Malise Monroe. Stating that Neil Fraser was the father of her child.

'When did she sign it?' he asked curiously.

'What matters is that she signed it, Mr Fraser.' Archie's tone brooked no argument.

Neil stared at him. Something had happened, and he didn't want to find out what.

'Thank you, Archie,' Neil said as he looked at it again. 'You have no idea how useful you are.'

Archie just smiled.

Chapter 9

Malise arrived home from the steamie, her heavy basket of washing in her arms. Taking off her hat and coat, she smoothed down her work-worn skirt and walked into the tiny living room to warm herself by the fire. There was a tall rangy man, sitting at the table. A man she recognized, but couldn't remember where from.

'Jack, this is Malise.' Gordon pushed her towards the table. 'Malise, this is Jack Buchanan, from the Independent Labour Party in Glasgow. He is responsible for the party here and helping out the union; bringing all of us together.'

'Hello, Mr Buchanan,' she said carefully. 'I think I heard you speak, and I've had some good advice from you over the years.'

'It's a pleasure to see you again, Mrs Scott,' Jack stood up to shake her hand. His lean frame seemed to fill up the whole room in its tweed jacket and workmanlike corduroy trousers. 'And I would like to apologize for those speeches. I'm not a particularly gifted demagogue. My talents lie in other areas.'

'Have you heard Malise speak?' Gordon said eagerly. 'She certainly has the gift.'

'I haven't had the pleasure, but one day I am sure I shall.' Jack smiled and Malise reddened at the compliment. 'Am I taking your seat?' he said quickly.

'I can sit in the armchair.' Malise helped herself to a cup of weak tea, adding a touch of condensed milk to it, and sat down next to the fire.

'You should have informed me when you were sacked,'

Jack said cautiously. 'I came here as soon as I received Gordon's letter.'

'I was sacked because of the Act, an act your party supported,' she said calmly.

'But the women there now have no representation.'

'I have other things to think about!' Malise retorted.

'Malise!' Gordon rebuked. 'I'm sorry, Jack, Malise has had a difficult time recently. Personal matters.'

'The party is opening a full-time office in Dundee, now is the time to expand, and I need someone to run it for me.'

'I'm not a party member.' Malise chewed her lip pensively.

'You can join now. As you can imagine, I won't be able to have someone who isn't committed to socialism.' He sipped his tea for a moment, as he let the words sink in. 'We need you to help bring the union and the party together. To advise the union leaders. Help them.'

'Work for Billy Turpin, you mean?' She looked glumly at both men.

Gordon nodded.

'He's gonna love that.' She rolled her eyes. 'I know what he's like.'

'And you will study part time for a degree in law, you've the highers, I checked.'

'I can't afford the fees,' she returned, amazed.

'They will be paid for you.' He laughed. 'And you will be expected to sing for your supper, you know.'

'Me, a solicitor!' She put her hands to her face. 'I never imagined—'

'The party is putting a lot of time and money into you, Malise,' Gordon said quietly. 'They think you are worth it.'

'And there can be nothing that will compromise it. No lovers, I'm sorry to be blunt, no scandal. We want you because when women become fully enfranchised, we will have a number of women who will be ready to serve.'

'You mean take the seat from Churchill? But he's a Cabinet Minister!'

'He hates Dundee, and the town is rapidly losing its infatuation with having a member of the Cabinet as its elected member. He's English aristocracy in working-class Scotland.' Jack looked at her keenly. 'We are doing this in all the major towns, and you will have a fight on your hands, with the likes of Billy Turpin, and these men know how to fight.' He stopped. 'So if there are any skeletons in your press, I would urge you to tell me now, so I can find someone else.'

Malise and Gordon stared at each other for a long moment.

'I can't think of any, can you, Malise?' Gordon said quietly.

'Why would there be any skeletons?' she said carefully.

'Good. You know, for all Dundee's reputation as being full of rough women, those weavers of yours are remarkably easy to shock. And we can't waste money on someone that will prove to be unsuitable for their palate.'

'Thank you, Mr Buchanan.' She smiled again, this time to herself, unaware of the picture she presented to the young man.

'Call me Jack.' He stood up and shook her hand. 'You're destined to make something of yourself, Mrs Scott. It'll be hard, but you're made of the right stuff. And I'll see you on 3 January at the offices in the Fishgate.' He handed her a card with an address written on it, before shaking hands with Gordon and leaving the house.

'Gordon,' Malise said as she put her hands to her mouth. 'I'm going to be a solicitor.'

'Oh no, my dear,' Gordon laughed. 'You're going to be a member of parliament.' He grabbed her round the waist and buried his head in her lap. 'You're going to London to make your mark!'

Malise closed her eyes and drank in the moment. This was it. She was going to show the Turpins, the Taylors and the Frasers of this world that there was nothing that could keep the Monroe girl back. Then she opened her eyes and saw Gordon looking at her. He deserved what he wanted. She bent down and kissed him, moulding herself into his hands, her eyes and mind tightly closed.

'Happy Christmas, Alexander,' Malise said as she handed him the little package that she had wrapped only a few hours ago.

Alexander squatted down next to the fire and opened the brown paper.

'I have a train set at my other house,' he announced as he looked at the little tin engine.

'I thought you would like to have one to play with here.' Malise smiled nervously at him.

Alexander looked doubtfully at the engine and two carriages.

'The other one's better.' He reached up and kissed his mother.

Gordon and Malise smiled tightly at each other.

'This is for you.' Malise handed Gordon a sweater that she had knitted. He held it up against him and grinned.

'Splendid,' he said as he leaned over to kiss Malise on the cheek. 'If you look over there, you'll see what I got you.' He gestured to the table. Malise stood up and went over to the table. On it was a box. She opened it. There was a black fountain pen sitting in the box. 'Useful for your new job.'

'Thank you, Gordon.' Malise traced her finger over it. 'It's really lovely. I shall write all my speeches with it.' She bent and picked up the brown paper that Alexander's train set had been wrapped in.

'Now it's time to get your stocking,' Gordon teased Alexander as he reached for the sock that was hanging from the mantelpiece. 'What have you got?'

'An orange, and some chocolate and – ' Alexander smiled triumphantly, ' – some monkey nuts!'

As Malise went off to make the tea, she couldn't help but wonder what the other, better train set looked like.

'It doesn't matter,' she muttered to herself. But it did.

Despite the fact that she knew she could never buy Alexander the things he could get from Fraser, she couldn't help the disappointment she felt knowing that Alexander preferred the train set he had played with at Fraser's home. Sighing, she added a small portion of salt to the grey sludgy porridge that was cooking on the stove. Slowly, the porridge began to bubble, and she began to stir with her wooden spoon, round and round as the oats that had soaked in the water all night finally began to turn into a warming, rib-sticking breakfast. She poured it into three bowls, and put them on a tray with the tea things.

'Breakfast,' she said to Alexander, who was busy playing with his second-best train set. She laid the table and they sat down.

'At least the Spanish lady's leaving us,' Gordon said as he wheeled himself over to the table. 'Outstayed her welcome.'

'Aye, just bronchitis and the rest to kill us now,' Malise said as she poured milk on the three bowls, which settled around the rim of the porridge. 'Alexander, it's getting cold.'

'It's been good having you at home,' Gordon said. 'Just one more week, then you'll be starting your new position.'

'Aye, be good to have a bit of money coming in.' She passed him a cup of tea.

'Still, we'd managed to . . .' Gordon gestured towards Alexander.

'Aye.' Malise smiled, a genuine smile that lit up her pretty features. 'Who on earth is that?' She added as there was a knock on the door. 'Jessie must have got up early.'

'Well, no one gets a whole day off, just for Christmas,' Gordon replied.

Wrapping the edge of her cardigan around her nightgown, Malise went to the door and opened it.

But it wasn't Jessie. It was Neil Fraser. Holding a package in his hands.

'May I come in?' he said cautiously.

Malise hesitated, suddenly aware that she was standing in

her nightgown, her nut-brown hair curling loose about her shoulders.

'You are not welcome in my home, Mr Fraser,' she said coldly.

'I have something for Alexander.' He looked round her, and saw Alexander running down the hallway to him.

'Hello, have you come to take me to your house?' he said excitedly.

'No,' Malise said quickly. 'Mr Fraser has come uninvited. To show us all how rich he is and how poor we are.' She glared at him.

'This is for you, Alexander.' Neil Fraser drank in the sight of the child. 'Please Malise, just for a moment.'

Malise stood aside as Neil walked into the living room.

'I'm sorry, I didn't realize you were having your breakfast,' he said as he took in the sight.

'Well, you just turned up on the doorstep. I wouldn't have expected you to consider what anyone else would be doing. You're too used to people doing whatever you want them to, whenever you want them to.'

'Would you like a cup of tea, Mr Fraser?' Gordon said quickly.

Neil glanced at Malise, who glared back at him.

'I don't think I could risk it,' he returned. 'Open your package, then, Alexander.'

The child ripped open the paper. Inside was a set of model cars, including a Crossley, the one that Neil owned.

'Mammy, look!' Alexander said loudly. 'There are four motor cars.' He held them up for Malise's examination.

'Very nice, Alexander,' Malise hissed. 'Now say thank you to Mr Fraser.'

'Thank you, Mr Fraser,' Alexander's eyes gleamed with pleasure.

'And this is for you.' He handed Malise an envelope.

'I don't want your money,' she returned angrily.

'It isn't money.' He stood, still in his cashmere overcoat and hat. 'It's official notification that I wish to have guardianship of Alexander and formally acknowledge him as my own. The court hearing is in February.'

Malise stood stock-still, the envelope in her hand.

'You come into my home, under the pretence of bribing my son, to do this?' She stared at him, hurt and confusion in her eyes. 'How can you be so cruel?'

'He is the last member of my family. If you will not give him to me, then you have left me with no choice.' He reached for her arm, but she snatched it away.

'You're blaming me for this?' She looked at him incredulously.

'I have no choice, I don't want to have to do this, but there is nothing else that can be done under the circumstances.'

Malise stood there, frozen.

'Get out, Fraser!' Gordon said as he wheeled himself over to him. 'Alexander, give me those motor cars.'

'Daddy, no.'

'Take your bribe with you, Fraser, and we'll see you in court!' Gordon grabbed the cars from Alexander's hands and threw them at him. Then he began to cough, again and again, purple streams of phlegm shooting from his mouth.

'Gordon!' Malise turned to him.

Neil began to back away, but it was the sight of Alexander that wouldn't let him leave the room. He watched as Alexander ran out of the room and returned with a bowl and a cloth.

'Here, Daddy,' he said helpfully. But Gordon was caught in the vicious circle of struggling to breathe through his congested lungs. He heard the awful rattle as Gordon tried to force himself to inhale, saw Alexander and Malise trying to lift him.

'I'll fetch a doctor,' Neil said quickly.

'Just get out!' Malise screamed. 'Just get out of our house and our lives!'

Neil went to speak, but mother and son were busy with

Gordon. He took a deep breath and walked out of the house.

The rest of the week passed quietly, and even New Year was subdued as so many families were suffering from the lingering effects of influenza. But on the third of January, Malise put on her best hat and carefully placed the new fountain pen in her bag, before walking out of the door. Despite all that had happened, she felt confident and happy. She had a job that paid enough to keep them all, a future at university, and she had Alexander. There was nothing that could go wrong. And she was not going to give up any of it.

She caught the number 10 tram, and as it wound its way down to the town, she gazed at the people already gathering outside the Poor Relief office in Barrack Street, waiting to see someone, to ask for clothes for their children, or shoes that squeaked. As she continued past the Overgate, she could see the market setting up, but it was winter, and there was little or nothing to sell apart from cabbage and potatoes. She got off the tram and checked the time on the Steeple clock – it was a quarter to nine, she was in plenty of time to cross down the maze of alleys that was the Fishgate.

The office was up two flights of stairs, in a dark, gloomy tenement block, the glass in the few windows broken and, in one, a tattered lace curtain blew in the harsh wind that came off the Tay and pushed its way up the roads. She climbed the stairs till she reached the door. On it was a shiny brass plate with the words INDEPENDENT LABOUR PARTY written on it. Taking a deep breath, Malise walked in.

'Hello,' said Jack as he looked up from the pile of boxes that were lying in the circular hallway. 'Not getting very far sorting these out, so I'll be glad of your help.'

Malise smiled.

'Where do you want me to start?'

Jack gestured to her. Following him, she walked into a small room. It had a table, a grate, and a few chairs in it.

'This is where we make the tea.' He grimaced. 'Crockery

in that box over there. Tea still in the grocers, but I did bring a pint of milk which is on the sill.'

'It'll be ice cream soon,' Malise said.

Jack took some coins from his pocket. 'Get some tea and sugar, I don't care if you like condensed milk though, I think it's abhorrent.'

'That's because you're posh!' Malise retorted. Jack warmed his hands for a moment by the grate.

'I'll put the kettle on; it should be ready by the time you get back.'

'See that, Jack Buchanan?' she joked as she put down her bag. 'Five minutes in Dundee, and you've become a kettle boiler like the rest of the men here.'

'But I have my secret weapon,' Jack replied conspiratorially. 'I have you!'

By the time Malise returned with the tea, the water had boiled and she made them both a cup.

'Billy Turpin's started work today,' Jack said casually as he lit a cigarette. 'Which is ironic, since the Elizabeth's gone on short-time.'

'No!' The colour drained from Malise's face. 'I swear they've been trying to do that for years.'

'Well, I'm going to give you my black book, Malise,' Jack said seriously. 'It has all the names of our friends, some known, some more covert in their support. This will enable us to get a good picture of what is going on in India. How much is going over.'

'But now it isn't just weaving out there, they spin it too, and we don't have the army contracts any more,' Malise replied.

'I know, but what we need to do is to link the local knowledge, much of which is based on supposition and rumour, often true but still rumour, and then we can tackle it.'

'But what can we do if they are taking their money away?' Malise looked at Jack's face – it was long, the way a racehorse's was long, and thin, but not sharp. Patrician, she decided. He looked like one of those Roman busts which you saw in museums.

'If that is the case, we can look at what we can do legally: we have trade treaties, as there are rules about what money can be moved, even within the empire.'

'You mean take them to court?' Malise said, amazed.

'Well, I doubt we can do that, but we can put pressure on the government to stop awarding them contracts. Jute is still needed for every carpet in Britain, for every rope that is used on every docks here. And now the people are becoming more organized, we can break the stranglehold that the owners have to do what they want. They want to make their goods as cheap as possible, but the people who give them their wealth, whether by making or buying their goods, still live in appalling circumstances on low wages. Dundonians have some of the worst housing in Britain, yet we are one of the richest cities. Did you know that most men who apply for the Black Watch get turned down because they aren't fit enough? Because their lungs have grown up in some of the worst air in Scotland? It's a place full of the shortest people I know. And that is because of the way you have to live. Your wages are lower than other mills, sometimes by as much as twenty per cent. But we need to get everyone working together, which is my job. And I want you to help me do it.'

They were interrupted by a knock on the door.

'That'll be Billy,' Jack said slowly. 'I sent a note round to his house, telling him to come here. We can't afford to lose the Elizabeth, simply because we aren't ready. I've arranged for a march on Sunday. To tell the people exactly what is happening.'

He got up and went to the door.

'Billy, good to have you back,' he said as he shook the man's hand. 'You know Malise Scott, don't you?'

'Aye, Malise.' He nodded to her as he looked her up and down with his rough, heavy eyes. 'Have you written ma speech yet?'

'You're making the speech?' she said incredulously.

'Of course. After all, who else would they rather hear? The returning convener, just back from his service.' He smiled smugly, his lined face aged from his service. And alcohol.

'Speaking of which, shouldn't you be at work?' she replied sharply.

'A man in my position is too busy on union business to work, specially since I've now joined the party. And we aren't working the day till two.' He looked at her with amusement. 'Don't tell me you've spent the last four years actually working there?'

'Of course. That's what I was getting paid for.' Malise bridled.

'Kept my lasses in line, or so I heard, till you got sacked. And you'll have prepared a speech.' He sat down in the chair and Malise could smell the alcohol upon him. 'No one writes them like you do.'

'How would you know, Billy?' she returned. 'You never wrote any.'

'You don't have a dog and bark yourself, hen,' he answered cheerfully. 'Any tea in that pot? I've a terrible head on me.'

'Then shouldn't you be having a hair of the dog that bit you?' Malise went over and picked another plain white cup and saucer out of the box, pouring tea into it and handing it to Billy.

'No connie onnie?'

'Milk and sugar?' She pushed the bottle and packet towards him.

'I want you to give me something good, Malise, something to show that I'm back in charge and that there'll be no more shilly shallying about any more.'

'There was nothing wrong in the way I ran that union, Billy,' she replied indignantly. 'I had every single worker in the Elizabeth in it, more than anyone else has ever managed.'

'Aye, but now I'm back. You were far too pally with Richard Fraser. Heard all sorts of talk about you and him.'

'Aye, I was never off my back for him. Like an old man, me.' She smiled sarcastically. 'And got more out of him than any convener has ever managed.'

'Could I remind you that the fight is with the owners,' Jack interrupted them. 'Malise will write you a speech, but first she has to go through the fact and figures we need to put in it.'

'Nice to know I've you under me, Malise.' Billy leered at her chest.

'I'm working with you, Billy, since you're too busy toiling in that works to string a few sentences together.' Malise squared up to Billy; she knew it was a mistake, but she couldn't help herself. He was walking into her job.

'Just do a speech, something that will get them out. Show the owners that I'm back in business.'

'I will not!' Malise returned indignantly. 'The workforce in Dundee doesn't have the money to strike. Or the will. Things have changed, Billy, women are looking to others now, Edwin Scrymgeour and his Temperance League and the like.'

'The man's useless.'

'The man's got more influence than you think, Billy. You've been away a long time.' She looked from one man to the other.

'I think you can continue with the unpacking now, Malise.' Jack stopped the increasingly bitter argument. 'Just get everything on the bookshelves in the two offices and I will sort out anything else later.'

Aware she was being dismissed, Malise nodded and walked out, bristling with humiliation. She should have been the one discussing policy with the party solicitor, not a brute like Billy Turpin, who thought that threats and no surrender were the only way to get anything done.

It was almost an hour later when Jack came into the office.

'Malise,' he said simply.

'I know I shouldn't rise to his bait, but he is so useless. I could do a much better job.' She tightened her fingers into a frustrated fist.

'I know, but Billy can't see the benefit in a workplace crèche, in having an extra half-shift instead of overtime. You can't expect a man to understand a woman's point of view. We think differently.' He patted her hand, gently straightening her fingers. 'Over there are the letters that have come back about the short-time working. We've some good stuff from the dockers. At a push, we can get them to black Fraser's ships.'

'I'll make another cup of tea first, shall I?' she grimaced shamefacedly.

'Then?' Jack prompted.

'Write that damn speech. The best one he's ever given!'

When Malise and Alexander arrived at Magdalen Green on the Sunday morning, she was taken aback. People were milling around like ants, thousands of them. There were miners, the handcart drivers, and the stevedores. And there was Billy, holding court under the banner of the Independent Labour Party. She couldn't remember him being a member in the past and he'd never so much as been to a meeting. But now here he was, and as a piper roused the people into an obedient line, Billy was there, at the front.

'Come along now, Alexander,' Malise said as she strode past the crowd, pushing her way towards the front. 'We lead the marches round here.' But by the time they reached where the Labour Party had been, the men under the banner were halfway along the road.

'Excuse me!' As she unceremoniously dragged her son through the crowd of men, she could feel her anger burning inside her. Didn't they know who she was? Didn't they know what she had done for them?

'Take your time, hen!' one said, as she elbowed past him, her navy-blue felt hat coming off and being trampled underfoot. She put her hand up to her head, then turned.

'Alexander!' she shouted, but he was lost, lost in a sea of men who were marching mechanically towards the town.

'Mammy!'

A man hoisted Alexander on to his shoulders.

'You lot are at the back, hen!' he said helpfully.

'I don't march at the back of anything!' she retorted, as she put her hands up and took the child from his shoulders. 'Try to keep up, Alexander!' But try as she might, she couldn't get any nearer the front of the march. She was stuck, stuck in the middle of everyone. Just as though she were a common demonstrator.

They were marching along the Nethergate now, under the watchful eye of the Steeple clock, and Malise, holding a tired Alexander in her arms, had reached the upper fringes of the crowd, by moving to the side, always a dangerous place to be, because that was where the police were.

Neil Fraser sat in the club, overlooking the Pillars, waiting for the fun to start. He put down his Bible and picked up his malt.

'Nothing ever really changes, does it?' Mackenzie, his solicitor, walked in straight from church and headed for the armchairs.

'At least they can march better.' Neil peered out at the marchers beginning to congregate below. 'What's it about?'

'It's the march for work, apparently.' Mackenzie sat down and was handed a whisky by the elderly valet. 'They want people like you to conjure work out of thin air. Think the whole world owes them a living.'

'Well, they do deserve something. They fought hard enough, after all.' He looked down at the ragged columns of men and women. 'Perhaps they deserve some kind of work. Digging roads, building houses . . .'

'You sound like you ought to be down there,' Mackenzie said wryly.

'I've changed my outlook, somewhat.' Neil stopped then peered out of the window. 'I don't believe it!' He stood up and left the room.

The police were waiting opposite, by Samuel's Corner, standing warily. Waiting.

'We want work! We want work!' The men under the beautifully sewn banners shouted in unison, as Malise and Alexander headed down past the Pillars. Malise knew that if in the very least she wasn't allowed a say, she would be at the front, with Billy and Sime and the others.

The Labour Party banner stopped under the shadow of the Corporation as Billy stood up on the large crate that had been thoughtfully provided by the handcart drivers.

'What need have we for this place then, brothers?' He swept his hand over the square. 'What need have we for these people, when we have no food in our bellies, shoes on our feet?'

It was wrong. He had started the speech in the middle. It sounded like anarchy. They were her words, but they were in the wrong order. What on earth was he doing?

And then she saw them. Bloody agitators, no doubt paid off by Billy and his beer money. With a sinking heart, Malise realized what Billy wanted to do. To announce he was back in charge by causing a riot.

The scuffles started by someone throwing a bottle at the policemen. Immediately, they moved in. There was a roar and suddenly everyone was running, throwing, shouting.

'Alexander!' She snatched him and pushed him under her crouched body, as Billy continued to stir up the crowd, hurling his words at them like stones.

'Let's go.' She grabbed Alexander's hand and was about to head away into the arcade when she saw a burly police-man heading towards them, his truncheon outstretched.

'Where do you think you're going?' he growled. As she tried to run past him, he raised his truncheon.

'Malise!'

She turned, and as she did so, the truncheon caught her full on the side of the head, felling her with one blow.

'Mammy!'

Neil rushed over to her as the policeman disappeared into the mêlée.

'Are you all right?' He pulled her into his arms, as they were jostled by the crowds running past them.

'You shouted at the wrong time. They just hit you on the arm or the back, usually.' She had to shout over the noise of the crowd, the police and the crunch of boots.

'I saved you from a beating!' he said incredulously.

'I got a worse slap than I would have. You just make things worse.' She brushed at her clothes.

'You've no business bringing Alexander to these things.' He helped her to her feet, holding his arm out to her when she swayed.

'He has to learn.' She stared at him. 'This is his blood, you know.'

'Is it right that he watches his mother fight? Your head's bleeding.' He handed her his handkerchief.

'Fighting's what our family does, Mr Fraser. Look out!' she cried as a bottle flew out of the crowd towards them. It smashed, sending a plume of smoke and flame. Then another came, towards the police who were standing not far from them.

Neil grabbed Malise and Alexander, hustling them into a shop doorway in the corner.

'What is going on?' She tried to peer round his shoulder.

'Someone's throwing bombs. Sugar bombs, so they stick to you.' Neil pushed Malise and Alexander into the corner, protecting them all with his back. He closed his eyes, the noise, the fighting, it brought back so many memories, memories he wanted to push away. He buried his face in her hair, and he could smell her blood, warm and sweet. He tightened his grip around her and Alexander. 'You'll be fine, don't worry. It'll be all over in a minute,' he murmured, for himself as much for Malise.

'Who is throwing them?' she said as she craned over his broad shoulders, encased in mohair. 'I need to see what's going on.'

'This isn't a time for curiosity, Malise,' Neil said sharply.

'I organized this march. And I want to know who's doing what. I bet it's Billy's bloody Bolsheviks,' she said angrily, as a bottle landed with a crash in front of the doorway, sending up a searing curtain of flame. 'No!' She held herself and Alexander to Neil's thick overcoat.

Neil pushed her into him. 'Stay low.' He closed his eyes and willed his memories to remain at bay as they sheltered, so close that he could feel every inch of her body against him. Malise could hear the screams, the noises, scuffles and cursing.

Eventually, the fighting began to decrease, as the people moved away. Reluctantly, Neil let her go, and stood and looked at her.

'Thank you,' she said as he picked up Alexander in his arms. 'Thank you.'

Taking her arm, Neil steered her past the remains of the bottle, and out into the arcade, past empty shops, windows smashed or stained with debris.

'Mr Fraser!' A policeman hailed him and he stopped. 'Are you all right, sir?'

'Thank you.' He nodded to the constable, then walked past the others, and outside to the air, stained with the smell of sugar, oil and anger. Malise shook off his arm, she couldn't be seen with him, not like that. As she walked past the police, she saw them looking curiously at her, and she glared back angrily. Let them try to touch her now, now she was with a jute baron. They wouldn't dare. Only the powerless got a hiding.

'I can't believe this happened. We didn't plan this,' she said over and over again. 'Why are they doing this? We all know that this is not the way it's to be done.'

Neil looked at her. She was confused, lost, and somehow

ashamed. 'Let me take you both home.' He ushered her towards the car.

'You don't want to take us home,' she returned. 'You only want him.'

Neil stopped. She saw him hold back a retort, then look back at the wreckage of the banners, the broken bottles, the stones, and the blood of a few unlucky demonstrators who had been caught by police batons. And somehow it frightened her.

'This was a demonstration about the Elizabeth, you know. People want to know why they fought, sent their husbands, sons and brothers out to die, and then have been rewarded by losing their jobs.' She grabbed Alexander. 'See that man, Alexander, that friendly man?' She pointed to Neil. 'He is a liar, a coward and he has betrayed the people of Dundee. Never believe a single thing he says. It's his fault that the policeman hit Mammy, and it's his fault that there is blood on the ground.'

'Don't you speak to my son like that!' Neil shouted at her. 'Don't you dare try to poison him against me!'

'But you can try to buy him with train sets and car rides. Throw him the money you've stolen from the workers of Dundee.' She turned to Alexander. 'Do you know what he wants to do? He wants to take you away from me so I'll never see you again, so you'll never see me, or Auntie Jessie, or anyone again. So you and his son can play in that house and you'll never be allowed to talk to me, or cuddle me . . .'

Alexander began to sob, enormous tears running down his face.

'Satisfied?' Neil said, but Malise was on her knees, holding Alexander.

'I'm sorry, I'm sorry,' she kept saying. 'I won't let him take you away, I promise.'

Alexander looked over his shoulder, his eyes so like Malise's. Full of anger and fear.

'I hate you,' he said to Neil. 'You're a bad man. Go away!'

Neil hesitated for a moment, in the deserted detritus of the Pillars. Then walked away.

By the time Malise reached home, Gordon was waiting for her.

'Jack sent a note round,' he said quickly. 'You've to go to the office. Thirty people were arrested today.'

'But I've the dinner to get on,' Malise said as she warmed her hands by the fire.

'You said you would read my book for me,' Alexander added.

'Mammy has to go to work,' Gordon said, but he never took his eyes from Malise.

'I don't know when I'll be back,' she said miserably.

'Come on, Alexander, get your book,' Gordon said to the boy.

'Cheerio, Mammy.' Alexander smiled grimly.

When Malise arrived at the office, Jack was rummaging in a large cardboard box full of files.

'What are you trying to do?' she said quickly.

'You were there, weren't you?' Jack returned. 'I was concerned that you might have been arrested. My God,' Jack exclaimed as he saw her hair. 'What happened to you?'

'I ran into a police stick.' She fell silent as Jack examined the bloody hairline. 'It's nothing,' she murmured.

'So you're saying that the police have the right to hit you?' Jack guided her slowly to the sink.

'What I'm saying is that it goes with the job.' She winced as he touched the raw scalp. 'So what are we going to do?'

'Go to the police station, I've already sent someone down. I will be doing my duty as a practising solicitor, and you will be taking statements from each of the men.'

'But most of them were Billy's thugs, Jack,' she said warningly. 'They were doing that to advertise that Billy Turpin's home again. Time for a celebratory pitched battle.'

'What do you mean?'

'He has a little band of men, you know the type, they'd

turn up anywhere so that they can have a fight. It was the same before they all left for the war.' She stared up at him. 'Billy's boys. Bullies and thugs. He takes union subs to pay them.'

Jack looked puzzled for a second, as if he couldn't quite bring himself to believe it.

'I think it's time we got to the police station,' he said eventually. 'And I doubt you'll be home much before dawn.'

Malise undressed as she stood in the dark room, waiting for the kettle to heat up on the tiny stove. After seven hours of sitting in the saloon of the public bar nearest the police station, she could smell the smoke and hops on her. She didn't want to wear them the next day, but she had few clothes left after four years of war with nothing in the shops and no time to make anything, even if she could have got material. Wearily, she hung her clothes on the back of the chair, ready to be worn tomorrow, and slipped into her thick nightgown. She could see the blouse already beginning to tear at the seams, and her skirt had given up trying to keep its shape and was now little more than a sack. But, since Gordon wasn't working and they now had to purchase medication to alleviate his increasingly worse symptoms, they just didn't have the money. She bent down and looked at her shoes – they were almost worn through. Was this the life she wanted for her son?

The next morning, Malise was sitting quietly filing all the statements from the men, when she heard the door open and close.

'So this is where you work?'

Malise turned to see Neil Fraser. He seemed to tower over everything in the office as he scanned the acres of files which were sitting there on naked wooden shelves, held together with a few nails and the goodwill of the cheap wood.

'What are you doing here?' she said slowly. Neil walked towards her. He stopped at the other side of the old scarred desk that was covered with newspapers.

'Newspaper cuttings?' He picked up the first. 'My goodness!' He picked up a newspaper he had never read before. 'Your reading has changed somewhat.' He waved the paper at her.

'It's not a crime, reading Indian papers,' she replied as she walked over and took it from his hands. 'Now if there is nothing you want, I must ask you to leave.' She folded the paper carefully and put it back on the pile.

'How is your head?' he said cautiously as he reached out to touch it. She flinched.

'None of your business,' she cut him short. 'As is what we do here. Get out, Fraser. You're not welcome here.'

'I want you to understand why I need Alexander so much,' he said as he let his hand fall to his side.

'You want him because you believe he is yours. Avarice,' she said bitterly.

'No, it isn't that at all,' Neil replied. He drummed his fingers on the table for a moment. 'If I tell you this, then I must be assured of your discretion.'

'No.' Malise clamped her jaws together, to stop herself from railing at him, despite her suspicions that he wouldn't listen to her anyway.

'Well, I'll tell you anyway.' He rubbed his fingers together, as if he were plucking up the courage to tell her something awful. 'Perhaps it's time for me to be honest.'

'Tell me what?' Suddenly Malise was curious; she didn't know what he was going to say, and he seemed less sure of himself than he ever had been previously.

'My wife is unable to have any more children. She is too delicate.' He looked at her with shyness in his eyes. 'But you can, you're only young.'

'And you are what, thirty?' Malise replied quickly. 'Throw your wife away and get a new one. Easy for you to do, there're no men left, they all died at Loos.'

'I'm twenty-seven, actually,' he stumbled over the words. 'My son Euan will be unable to carry on the family business; he is ill.'

'You have money, you can afford doctors and hospitals,' Malise answered. She didn't want to understand why he was doing it.

'All the doctors in the world can't cure Euan,' Neil said softly.

'What's wrong with him?' Malise persisted.

Neil restarted his drumming on the table.

'I can't explain,' he said briskly. 'But I can show you.' He went over and picked up her coat and hat from the stand in the corner. 'Come with me.'

Malise checked the clock, it was almost lunchtime. She took her clothes from him, unwilling to give him the knowledge that he had helped her the way a gentleman would a lady, and grabbed the office keys.

'Where are we going?' she asked as his driver opened the door for them both.

'Broughty Ferry. Where Euan lives.' They drove past the Harbour and the Arch, following the sea as it wound its way from the heavy, dirty air of Dundee to the salty sea breezes of the Ferry.

'Here we are.' They drove into the grounds of a light-grey building. But it wasn't a family home, there were nurses in uniforms, pushing two young men in wheelchairs.

'He doesn't live with you?' she asked as they got out.

'No,' Neil replied. 'He doesn't.' He ushered her up the clean steps till they came to a hallway with a nurse sitting in attendance. Malise looked around. Footsteps echoed in the marble building. It was more like a mausoleum than a place for a child.

'Is he dying?' Malise asked as they walked up the stairs, conscious of her cheap, squeaking shoes.

'Perhaps you will understand now.' He opened the door and they walked into a bare white room which shone with sterile cleanliness. There was no carpet on the floor, just linoleum. No pictures on the wall, just a small chart. No toys. Just a small press and a cot.

'This is Euan, my son.'

Malise looked inside the cot, at the frail little body that lay still. He wasn't asleep, she could see by the way his eyes were staring vacantly into space.

'Hello, little man.' She ruffled his hair. 'What are you doing?' She ran a finger down Euan's cheek and found that he moved, to look at her.

'He can't talk,' Neil said shortly. 'He can't do anything. The sole heir to our fortune and he is a—'

'Don't say that.' Ignoring the bars, she bent down and picked up the child. 'He's a little boy, not something to be put in a box.' The child waved his arms about clumsily and he dribbled as she settled him against her chest. 'Strong little lad, aren't you?'

'You shouldn't pick him up,' Neil said in panic.

'Why, will he break?' She set him down on the floor and knelt beside him, putting a hand in the small of his back. 'Hello.' She grinned in the exaggerated fashion that people did with children, and the child gurgled back at her. Slowly she took her hand away, but Euan swayed for a moment, wobbled, then fell over. But Malise's hand was already behind his head.

'Bit wobbly, aren't you?' She rubbed her nose gently against Euan's. 'Do you pay a lot for this place?' She looked around the room.

'A fortune.'

'Would it kill them to put up a few pictures, something for him to look at?'

'What would be the point?' Neil was finding it difficult to understand. She wasn't recoiling in horror from Euan. She was taking it in her stride.

'Well, if he stays here all day, on his own, it would give him something to look at.' She looked keenly at Neil. 'Or have you just thrown him away, as something not well enough made?'

'They look after him,' he repeated.

'A child would be bored senseless in this place,' she stated with a mother's practicality. 'Wouldn't you?'

'What do you suggest I do?' He walked over to Euan and crouched down, shying away when she went to put him into his arms.

'Why don't you speak to some doctors about what they can do for him? Look at his eyes, they're bright. He's crippled, but he's not daft,' she returned.

'This is the best place for him.' Neil was taken aback. He had brought her here so she would understand, not so that she could criticize the way he was looked after.

'Bet they tried to drown you in a bucket,' she cooed to the child.

'What?'

'It's what midwives do to crippled children, they drown them in buckets and say they were stillborn.' She turned her piercing gaze to him.

'They don't.' He didn't want Euan to hear this.

'Surprised that he is still here.' Her voice tailed off as she said it.

'Well, now you know,' Neil swallowed nervously, 'why I need my heir.'

'Tell me, Mr Fraser,' she wiped the hair from her face, 'if Alexander had been born like Euan, would you have wanted him?'

Neil looked at his shoes.

'I need an heir.'

'You have Euan. If you really want another son, then why not marry someone else?'

'It isn't that simple.' He put a hand out to her arm. 'She's not like you. She isn't healthy and she had no other interests apart from her place as my wife. You have so much that she doesn't, so much that for all the money and influence we have, I would trade in a moment . . .'

'So now I'm supposed to feel sorry for you?' Malise couldn't conceal her outrage.

'No, just to understand the difficult position I am in. If I could, I would just settle some money on you and Alexander and watch from a discreet distance. But since Euan was born, all my father has worried about is the future of my family.' He gazed deeply into her eyes. 'My family needs him, and Dundee needs him, because without the Frasers there will be no works.'

'And I should sacrifice my son for the good of the town?' she said in disbelief. 'Who do you think I am, Joan of Bloody Arc?' She walked over to the window and raised Euan's head so he could see out. 'See the birdies?'

Euan gurgled happily and raised his hand. Malise laughed and pretended to blow bubbles at the child.

'You ought to have been a nurse,' Neil said gently.

'I'm a mother. You can't see a wean and not want to love him.' She stroked Euan's hair.

'My wife doesn't love him.' He watched as Malise instinctively held the child closer, to protect him from the truth.

'Perhaps that's the difference between your kind and mine,' she returned. 'We don't have the money to pay someone else to love our bairns, so we just have to do it ourselves. However they turn out.'

Neil gazed at her; she wasn't seeing a cripple, she just saw a small boy.

'He has your eyes,' she said softly. 'And the set of your chin.' She laughed slightly as she wiped away the child's saliva from her coat with her hand. 'How could you lock him away here? He belongs with his mammy and daddy.'

'Malise, you must understand. In my position such a child . . .' He felt ashamed of himself, but she had to understand.

'I can't understand,' she said gently. 'I can't understand how you can be ashamed of your child. It isn't his fault, it's just the way God made him. And you're punishing him. You're punishing a three-year-old child for something he didn't do.' She put Euan back in the cot and turned away.

'I'll make my own way back. I don't want to listen to your excuses. Goodbye, Euan.' With that she fled from the room, suddenly desperate to get away from the feelings that were welling up inside her. And the knowledge that Neil Fraser had good reason to want his bastard child. Because his legitimate one was in a prison.

Alexander was sitting doing his English homework, learning the kind of words that made up a sentence. She stared at the child as he bent over his work, his soft dark hair falling over his face. What if Alexander had been the one that was crippled? She'd have made the best of it, taught him as much as he could learn. But knowing that Neil had thrown away his child preyed on her mind. He had disappointed her.

Neil sat with Mackenzie, the solicitor and his father, going over the salient points of the case as they sat in Mackenzie's rooms in Reform Street.

'So she went to a solicitor and signed this affidavit in front of him?' Mackenzie asked as he examined the document.

'I presume so,' Neil replied unsteadily, as he put down his teacup.

'Yet now she denies that you are the father?' He looked keenly over his half-moon spectacles at the young man in front of him.

'That would appear to be the case.'

Mackenzie sighed, and then wetted his thin lips with a sip from the Crown Derby cup.

'Are you sure it is genuine?' he said slowly. 'It does seem rather strange that a young woman would go to a solicitor and swear an affidavit on the Bible that you were the father, take recompense for the child, then deny you had anything to do with it.' He stared at the paper again.

'The girl is a Bolshevik, I doubt that she knows what a Bible is!' Richard returned. 'When she worked for me, I heard her talking against the war.'

Neil glanced over at his father.

'What did she say?' Mackenzie said curiously.

'She had asked me to find out if a young man had been put in prison. His mother had received word that he was on trial. For cowardice, I mean, and you know what that meant!' Richard tightened his lips for a moment. 'Well, I spoke to Bertie and found out that he had been executed as was right and proper. And so I told her.'

'And what did she say?' Neil said quickly.

'Only that she would tell his mother he was dead. Apparently how he died didn't matter. I put her right on that, of course, but she couldn't see the shame of it. All she could see was that she would have to tell the woman that her son was dead.'

Neil studied the patterned rug in front of him.

'Perhaps she was thinking of the woman. That she had lost her son. Did Mother ever know that Dick never flew against the enemy, that he died during training?'

Richard glared at his son.

'Your brother was a brave man,' he returned.

Mackenzie waited for a moment, for the humours to settle, then he cleared his throat.

'The way I see it is that this document is genuine. The judge, however, may take it at face value, or may question its validity. But it is our best chance. Without it, we have no hope of regaining the child.' He looked at Neil.

'You know the situation we are in.'

Mackenzie nodded carefully.

'Then we go to court, gentlemen. On Valentine's Day, rather ironic, don't you think?' He gave his nearest approximation of a smile and stood up, shaking both their hands.

'We ought to consult a solicitor,' Malise said as she sat with a pallid, sickly Gordon a week before the trial. 'They will have one and I don't know what to say.'

'We can't let anyone know what is happening,' Gordon

replied through laboured breaths. 'If the party found out, you would lose your chance, and they have nothing but hearsay. Just go in and stick to your story.' He began to cough again, and Malise went over to the kitchen cabinet and reached for the laudanum. It was the only thing that would ease his lungs now. Nothing else worked. And the price of it was steadily eating away at her salary. She couldn't afford a solicitor, even if she had thrown her future to the winds. No, she thought grimly, she'd just have to trust in justice.

Malise woke early on the day of the hearing. She had slept fitfully the night before, her head full of fears about Alexander. And even when sheer exhaustion had won, Gordon's constant coughing meant that there was no possibility of having a rest.

'Just let me get a few decent breaths, and then I'll get up,' Gordon said hoarsely, as he lay in the darkness of the bedroom.

'There's no point,' Malise replied. 'You're not fit to get out of bed, Gordon, you just stay there and have a rest.'

'I can't let you face this on your own,' he insisted, but his voice was as weak as his body.

Despite his obvious illness, Malise felt a stab of anger that he wouldn't be there to support her. He was deserting her to face them all on her own, because he didn't want to be there, to have to support her in any way but privately.

Leaving Alexander in Gordon's semi-conscious care, Malise walked down the Lochee Road to the courthouse. As she did, she could see the men and women who were standing around waiting for the courts to open, so that they could have a day's entertainment in the warmth, at the expense of another. Surely no one would be there to hear this, she thought. Surely it was as shaming for the Frasers as it was for her.

She pushed her way through the bustling court corridors

until she came to a small court, away from the main ones. There on the door was one word: FRASER.

For a full thirty minutes, she stood outside the courtroom, as the clerk called her name again and again. This was it. Eventually, she walked in. Fraser wasn't there. Just a man sitting at the desk. They rose for the judge and then the other man, who she presumed was the solicitor, handed over some documents.

'Mrs Scott?' The clerk, a small man, came over to her. 'Do you have any documents pertaining to the case?'

'Documents?' she asked dumbly.

'Affidavits, statements of income,' he murmured helpfully.

'No.' She looked over at the man.

'Then I think we can rest.' The judge looked at each partner in turn. 'You will be informed of my judgement in due time.'

Malise obediently rose as the judge walked out, and the others left the courtroom. And then she realized. The fight for Alexander was over.

'But I haven't said anything!' she protested to the other man.

Mackenzie stared at her.

'You signed an affidavit stating Mr Fraser was your child's father. In front of Archibald Taylor. And you accepted money from him. Both these lend credence to Mr Fraser's assertion that he is the father of your child.' He nodded to her politely. 'Good afternoon.' With that he walked out.

Malise looked at his back. She had been tricked. By a forgery. But one she couldn't expose. But she was Alexander's mother, no one could take that away from her. Not even Neil Fraser and all his money.

It was less than a week later, a week of long days at the office and endless, sleepless nights where she would go into the little bed under the table in the kitchen and cuddle Alexander. But then the letter came.

'What?' Gordon said as he struggled through his breathlessness and watched her open the letter from the court at breakfast time.

But Malise just stared at the letter, the words all jumbling up in front of her eyes.

'Custody of Alexander Gabriel Monroe, known as Scott, has been awarded to Neil Fraser,' she said dumbly.

'No.' Gordon tried to move over to her, but then he began to cough, his breath forcing up a tidal wave of blood that began to pour from his mouth.

Malise still looked at the letter.

'Mammy!' Alexander rushed to her and pulled at her elbow. 'Daddy.'

'Run and get the doctor, Alexander,' she said slowly. 'Run along now.'

The ambulance wagon arrived almost at the same time as the doctor. Gordon, still dripping blood from his mouth, was taken away in it, Malise and Alexander travelling with him, holding on to each other as the wagon bumped and jolted its way to the Royal Infirmary. For the rest of the day, they sat in the corridor as Gordon was examined, and re-examined. As night began to fall, however, she saw three figures coming along the corridor towards them.

'Mrs Malise Scott?' a man said. 'You have been instructed by the court to relinquish custody of the child Alexander Gabriel Monroe to his lawful father, Neil Fraser.'

'No!' She gripped Alexander to her and as Neil Fraser and his father looked on, the court official grabbed her hands, twisting them down sharply, attempting to get Alexander from her grip. 'Don't take him away!'

'No, Mammy, don't let them.' Alexander grabbed her back, but Richard Fraser was too quick. With swift movements, he wrested the child from her grip and passed him to Neil.

'Take the boy,' he said grimly.

'No, Mammy!' Alexander screamed. 'No!'

'Alexander, no!' Malise shrieked with all her might, but the man was holding her, seemingly oblivious to her kicking and scratching.

'Mammy!'

'Alexander!'

The child fought desperately in Neil's arms, but Neil held him tight.

'I'm sorry, Malise,' he tried, but she was deaf to him. All she could hear was Alexander's heart, tearing in two.

'Alexander, no!' She lunged forward desperately, landing flat on the heavy floor, with the court official putting his boot between her shoulder blades to stop her from moving.

'No!' Neil shouted, but as he moved, Richard took the hysterically struggling boy from him.

'I'll take him to the car, we don't want a repeat of this scene.' He put his hand over Alexander's mouth and almost ran to the door.

'Mrs Scott!' A doctor walked in. 'Your husband.'

'I don't give a damn about my husband. This is all his fault,' she babbled frantically. 'If he hadn't given him to them . . .'

'Mrs Scott, your husband is dying.' The doctor, glaring at the heavy-set man on top of her, helped her to her feet and pushed her into the tiny room.

'Ma . . .' Gordon was struggling with the last remnants of life. 'No . . .' he closed his eyes.

'This is all your fault, Gordon,' she said bitterly. 'You gave Alexander to them and now they have him for ever. God damn you to hell!' she shouted at the tiny, frail figure on the bed. 'God damn you for ruining my life!'

'Love you.' Suddenly it was as if a damn had broken inside him. Thick dark blood poured from his mouth and Neil, who had followed Malise into the room, stood horrified as he watched the man drowning on it.

Then Gordon was still.

'Malise?' Neil said softly. 'I'm so sorry . . .'

'Please, Neil,' she said as she turned into his arms, her face white with panic. 'Don't take Alexander. I'm begging you. Don't take my son from me. He's the only thing in my world!'

Neil bit down hard on his lip. Every fibre of his body was telling him to let Malise keep the child. Every inch of him wanted to tell her that she could live in a house he would buy for her and he would visit them. But he couldn't. Alexander was part of him, and the Frasers lived in another world. A world Malise couldn't be a part of.

'He's mine too, Malise, if there was any other way . . .' Ashamed at the paucity of his words, he patted her shoulder. 'I promise you he will be cared for.'

'How could you care for him?' she said distantly. 'You don't know what love is.'

With that, she pushed past him and walked out the door.

'Malise, whatever's wrong!' Jessie said as Malise stood at her door, soaking wet and with a strange, distant look on her face.

'Gordon and Alexander,' she said in a light sing-song voice. 'They've been taken.'

Over one of Mr Baker's stiffest whiskies, Jessie heard what had happened.

'How could he do it, Malise?' she said as she held the frozen girl to her. 'How could he take a child from its mother?'

'He had a paper, that he said I'd signed,' she said hesitantly. 'He was just taken. I tried my best, but I couldn't save him.'

Jessie held her tight through her own tears. 'No one deserves to have your life.'

Malise stayed the night, then she went back to her own home, shut the blinds and put salt down at the front step to stop Gordon's ghost from returning. She didn't know what she was supposed to do; she didn't want Gordon back in the house, to have to face his body. To face what she had said to him. But she couldn't face the knowledge that although Gordon had let her down when she needed him, she had also betrayed him.

'Malise?' Jack Buchanan was standing at the doorway of the living room. 'The door was open. I hope you don't mind.'

Malise shook her head.

'I believe that Gordon was taken,' he said slowly.

'And Alexander.' She looked up. 'He was taken too.'

Jack sat down next to her and took her hand.

'I am so sorry that this has happened to you,' he said gently. 'To lose a husband is terrible, but to lose a child is a wound that you can never heal.'

'I'd sell my soul to get him back,' she said absently.

Jack looked at her, but saw only a bereaved mother, half-crazed with grief.

'You just rest up, and I'll see you for the funeral. Gordon deserves all of the party to be there, and wee Alexander too.'

'Not for Alexander,' she returned.

'But Gordon,' Jack replied.

'None of them bothered to cross his step to see him when he was alive, so what use are friends now? He doesn't need them any more.' She stood up. 'Thank you for coming, but I want to be alone now.'

'He still won't eat anything,' Edith Emmerson, Alexander's nanny, said a few nights later. 'He says he is on hunger strike till he sees her again.'

Neil sighed. 'I am sorry, Miss Emmerson, I would have thought Alexander would have settled in by now.' Then he looked over at Agnes, but she was sitting staring into space as if she were alone in the world. 'I'll go and speak to him,' he said slowly.

As they walked up the wide staircase, Neil was aware of his footsteps. When had his home become so silent? It was almost as if the life was slowly being drained from the grand

216

building with every day that passed. But they had reached the nursery. Neil opened the door, Alexander was there, sitting in a corner, trying to make himself as tiny as possible. The toys were in the toy box, he had made no attempt to take them out and play with them. He was just sitting.

'Will you come downstairs and have some crumpets, Alexander?' Neil said as he walked over.

'No.' The boy turned his head to the wall.

'Will I have Emmerson bring some up, and we can eat them together?'

'I want my mammy,' he stated boldly.

'Your mammy and I talked, and we agreed that this was the best place for you to live. Because I'm your daddy.'

'Liar!' Alexander rounded on him. 'My mammy told me you were a bad man, that you were trying to steal me. And you took me away and you kicked her, I saw you.'

'Alexander, please.' Neil reached out his hand, but Alexander flinched away. As he did so, Miss Emmerson came up with some toasted crumpets, dripping with butter and some hot milk.

'I'll leave you with Emmerson,' he said regretfully. 'And just eat something, Alexander. It isn't healthy not to.'

Instead of going back to the drawing room, Neil went over and put on his hat and coat.

'Tell Bruce to get the car ready,' he said to Adams.

Malise was sitting looking into the fire, reliving her last moments with Alexander and Gordon, the words, the screams echoing round and round in her mind. Then somewhere in the distance she heard a knocking at her door. She made no attempt to move, there was no one she wanted to see, no one who would make a difference to the way she felt. But it persisted, and was getting louder. Eventually, she stood up and shuffled, like an old woman, to the door.

'I need your help,' Neil said quickly. 'Alexander won't eat; he's had hardly anything since he's been there.' Neil took in Malise, the dark circles round her eyes, the confused expression. She seemed broken; a part of her seemed missing.

'You have to help me, Malise,' he said urgently. 'I can't make him eat.' He walked into the house and closed the door behind him.

'If he was in a grave I could visit him, talk to him. Tell him that I tried to keep him, that I tried so hard to fight for him, but that his father was stronger. That he lied and cheated and won him.'

'I know, Malise, but none of us wants that to happen. What kind of mother would just leave her child to die?'

Malise stroked the sleeve of her sweater.

'What kind of person would steal a child from his mother?' She stared at him.

'Just tell me what I ought to do,' he continued.

'You have money, that's all that matters in this world,' she replied. 'Buy his love.'

'He has every toy that a child could want,' Neil said. 'He's like you, Malise, Alexander can't be bought. He hates me.'

'Now you know how I feel, Fraser,' she said as she looked at the door. 'All the love in the world couldn't keep him, could it? Money won, and now all the money in the world can't make him happy.' She looked down at her bitten fingernails. 'How many times have I had to come to the likes of you, and ask for help, only to be refused?'

'If Alexander doesn't eat something, he will have to go to hospital.'

'Throwing away another child because he isn't what you thought he would be?' She shook her head. 'Not much of a family, are you?'

'What does he need, Malise?' Neil grabbed her hands. 'Just tell me.'

'Love, Fraser,' she said coldly. 'A child needs love. And that's the one thing you can't give him.' She walked away from him. 'You forged my signature on a document and you won him.'

'Forged?' Neil hesitated. 'What do you mean?'

'The only thing I ever signed was when Archie Taylor

gave me a bill for the staircase my father broke when he fell down it. He took his wages and our life savings in recompense.' She looked up at him, the ice in her face hardening into hatred. 'You left me the option of going to an abortionist or marrying Gordon Scott. You ruined every one of my dreams and walked back behind those big gates to your house.'

'No!' Neil came after her, rushing into the tiny galley kitchen. 'I won't let you kill my son.'

'I will give you this.' She opened the cupboard and took out a tin. 'They're just oatcakes, but he'll know that they've come from me.' She opened a drawer and took out a brown paper bag, wrapping them in it. 'And some jam, he loves my jam.' She handed them to him. 'You have to tell him that I love him, and that I am still here, and that you bought him, and there is nothing you can do about it. Then he'll know. That I'm still here, that'll stop him from starving himself.'

'He'll hate me,' Neil replied.

'The whole of Dundee hates you. Alexander will just be doing the same as everyone else.'

'Thank you,' he said, curiously humbled. He went to the door, then turned. 'I'm not a cruel man, Malise. Really, I am just trying to do the best I can.'

'Who'd miss you if you died, Fraser?' she said insidiously. 'Who would really miss you if you just died?'

Neil was silent.

'You'd miss me, Malise,' he said softly. 'Because your life would be so much easier.' And nodding to her, he walked away.

It was dark by the time he got back to his home. He went straight up the stairs, to where Emmerson was sitting with Alexander. One half-eaten crumpet was sitting on the plate.

'I tried, but . . .' Miss Emmerson shrugged her shoulders apologetically.

'Look what I have, Alexander.' He handed him the brown bag.

Alexander flicked a small finger at the bag, then looked up at his father.

'Mammy?' he said in wonder.

Neil nodded.

'I thought you had killed her to death.'

'Why?' Neil crouched down next to him.

'You were hurting her. I saw you.'

'Your mother is fine.'

'Is she in jail?' Alexander was fingering the oatcakes.

'No.' Neil carefully tore open the bag. 'It was just my turn to look after you for a few years. She got you when you were a baby. And now it's my turn. Because I'm your father.'

'So I'll see her again?' Alexander broke off a tiny piece of oatcake.

'Of course you will.' Neil smiled. 'But it'll be our secret.' He winked at the child. And Alexander winked back.

She buried Gordon in a small plot, all that she could afford on his penny policy from the Royal Liver, and had a tiny headstone with his name written on it. She put no mention of herself on it, there seemed little point in it. She had never been a wife to him, nor he a husband to her. And then she went back to work, a quiet woman. Almost as if she were biding her time.

Chapter 10

'In here with your mama, Alexander,' Edith Emmerson said as she ushered the young boy into the cool drawing room where Agnes sat in front of a small table laid with silver tea things. 'Sit down nicely, please.'

Alexander stared over the cakes at the pale woman who was sitting there, hardly looking at him.

'Are you really my new mummy?' he said curiously.

'I suppose I am,' Agnes returned, lifting up a stand of cream scones. 'Would you like one?'

'Ta.' Eyes wide open, Alexander grabbed one in each hand, squeezing out the cream through his fingers as he stuffed them both in his mouth at once.

'No!' Agnes slapped the scones from his mouth and they landed on the floor in a half-chewed lump.

'What?' Alexander tried to reach for the scones, but Agnes's thin fingers caught him.

'Emmerson!' she shouted at the top of her voice. 'Miss Emmerson, now!'

Edith Emmerson hastened into the room.

'What is wrong, ma'am?' she asked in a concerned voice.

'Take this thing away, and I'll see him when he's been taught some manners.' She put a hand to her brow. 'And send for Green. This really has been too much for me.'

Edith Emmerson dragged Alexander away.

'I want the cake!' he shouted, kicking at her.

'Come on, you little animal,' Miss Emmerson muttered under her breath. 'If you've made your mama ill, your father will not be best pleased.'

*

'How was tea with your mama?' Neil asked as he arrived in the nursery later that day.

Alexander just glowered into his chest.

'I want to go home,' he said mutinously.

Neil walked into Agnes's bedroom. A nurse was sitting with her.

'Oh Neil.' She looked up at him pathetically. 'I've had the most horrendous day.' She sighed. 'Where did you get that awful child? He behaves like an animal.'

'Did he hurt you?' Neil bent down till his face was level with hers.

'No.' She turned away from him, her eyes filling with tears. 'But it was just too shocking for words.'

'What did he do, Agnes?' Neil prompted with trepidation.

'I offered him something to eat, and he just attacked it like he was a wild animal. There was cream everywhere.'

'So he's eating something at last?' Neil said joyfully.

'He isn't fit to be at our table, Neil. I just couldn't stand it.' Agnes looked towards the nurse.

'Oh Agnes, he's been living in the most desperate circumstances,' Neil said through barely suppressed laughter.

'That doesn't excuse bad manners, Neil,' she replied. 'I really cannot abide him in my company until he learns to behave.'

Neil looked at his pale, drawn wife, her face set.

'All right, Agnes,' he said with resignation. 'I'll see Emmerson gives him instruction.'

Still laughing to himself, Neil went back downstairs to where his father was enjoying a malt.

'So you heard about Agnes's ordeal,' Richard said in amusement. 'You'd have thought he had bitten a lump out of her instead of a scone.'

'She has a point, though.' Neil poured himself a drink.

'He'll learn, and he'll learn well.' Richard smiled to

himself. 'He'll have tea with me, I can come over here and play chess with him. He's better than either you or Dick were.'

'And you never let us win.' Neil sat down heavily. 'Why can't Agnes give him a chance?'

'You did rather spring it on her, Neil.' Richard looked at his son. 'You knew about Alexander for years till you won him. It's all new to her. And women just aren't as strong as men.'

'That's ridiculous. Look at Alexander's mother. She's had a terrible life and still she won't give up. She's one of the bravest people I know.'

'She's working class, not like the rest of us. I'm talking about ladies, not women.' Richard took a long drink. 'Sometimes I wish all I had were their problems. Where to get enough money for drink, who to father a bastard child with next. They don't realize how lucky they are, these people.'

The summer came and went in a pile of work, most of the works were on short-time, and rumours were rife as to which one would close down next. Malise spent most of her time gathering figures about jute – what came in, what was needed, and what was being bought from the works that were based in India. But at least when she was thinking about imports and exports, she wasn't thinking about Alexander. Or Gordon. Or the quiet loneliness of the house at night.

Every Friday she went for a walk with Jessie, who still hoped to find a man on the Monkey Parade. But it was practically deserted, all the men had been killed, or were courting or married. And the Monkey Parade was slowly becoming a train of old maids, clinging on to the old ways, hoping that there might just be a chance for them.

September arrived, and with it the beginning of her university life. She would be a half-timer all over again, studying law in the mornings, while in the afternoons and evenings she would be working for the party.

She was up early, having slept little the night before. She hadn't been this nervous for years, not since the first time she had faced Richard Fraser at the factory, or had made her first speech in front of the suffragettes. But she wouldn't think of that, it was redolent of far too many memories. Eventually, Malise reached the discreet set of buildings that housed the Law School, feeling herself shrink to the size of a mouse as she walked over to a clerk who sat at a little desk.

'I'm here to see Professor Winkworth.' Her voice was quiet and with a definite wobble.

'First floor, name's on the door.' He gestured up the stairs.

Malise, gripping her handbag as if it were a shield, walked up the stairs to the first floor. She knocked on the door and it was opened by an elderly man with silver hair.

'I'm Professor Winkworth.' He smiled at the young woman standing in front of him. 'And you are the future of socialism, I presume.'

Over a cup of tea, Professor Winkworth explained exactly what the course would consist of.

'So you need to attend the lectures and the tutorials, and use them to practise your debating.'

She looked at him nervously.

'Oh don't worry, my dear.' He smiled almost fondly. 'You have far more experience in public speaking than most of your peers.'

'It seems like a dream,' she replied.

'Just don't lose your confidence, you're the only woman in your year and some of the others will relish the challenge of destroying your arguments.'

Malise stared at him, her words had deserted her. The other students actually wanted to beat her in an argument!

'One last thing.' Professor Winkworth reached into his wallet and pulled out a card. It was his membership to the

Labour Party, a card issued in Glasgow. 'You are amongst friends, my dear.'

'Thank you.' Malise gave an audible sigh of relief. 'I just need to get some books.'

'Have some of these.' Professor Winkworth handed over four large textbooks. 'I don't need them any more and they may come in useful for you.' He looked at his watch. 'Now I suggest you go downstairs to the lecture hall as one of my colleagues is about to begin his first lecture, and he's terribly boring, so you'll want a seat at the back, so he can't see you sleeping.'

Malise thanked him again and went down the stairs, following the signs to the lecture theatre. There she slipped into one of the polished wooden benches and took out the writing pad she had purchased the week before. The lecture was about the various kinds of law. Malise stared at some of the other students, many of them were paying little or no attention, lounging on the wooden benches. Why were they here if they didn't want to learn?

For the next three months, Malise devoured the law. She was good at it, her mathematical bent giving her an excellent grasp of the ability to construct arguments and put a principal into a theoretical argument. And she had no problems remembering citations, which proved useful in writing essays. But she made no friends amongst the students; they looked at her as if she were from another country. Which she might just as well have been, because in her country there were steamies and rent men, no tennis courts or trust funds. Even the few socialists she found on the course were idealistic young men who had no conception of what it was like to actually work. To need the money too much to strike, or to be too busy doing the ironing to march for revolution. But most importantly, when she was studying, she wasn't thinking about Alexander. About what he was doing, if he was growing, if he was happy. She couldn't think about that. For Alexander occupied her every dream, every moment's sleep was punctuated with his smile, and his laugh, and, on long cold nights, his screams as they took him away.

Jack, however, was proving to be very helpful. He was in Dundee every three weeks or so, and he spent as much time discussing law with her as he did discussing work.

'It's in my interests for you to succeed,' he said one day as they were discussing tort together. 'I was one of the ones pushing for women such as yourself to be given a chance. And if you fail, I'll look a proper fool!' He smiled.

'I won't fail, I promise,' she replied, and he hesitated for a moment.

'I don't believe it!' he said in mock amazement. 'You've actually smiled.'

Malise hesitated too.

'Now don't look guilty, everyone has to smile some time,' he reminded her gently. 'It's not a sign you have forgotten, it's just that you've able to move on.'

'Well, I do find myself thinking less about it these days,' she said with a certain amount of relief. 'But then I remember, and I feel terrible that I had forgotten for even a moment.'

'No one would want you to live your life in darkness, Malise,' Jack said softly. 'Come back into the light.'

She smiled again.

'And you look so pretty when you smile,' he said unexpectedly. 'There is something I want to ask you.'

'What?'

'Every so often I have a small gathering at my home, just a few like-minded friends.' His face was expressionless. 'Would you like to come on Friday?'

'I don't know.' Was he asking her out, Malise wondered?

'They will all be professionals, like you and I,' he continued. 'It would be good for you to get to know them.'

'All right, Jack,' she said quickly. 'I will.'

That Thursday she went to the baths, soaking in the water

and scrubbing her hair till it gleamed with the vinegar she had used on it. Then she rushed through her usual Friday till it was time to go home. She dressed in her second-best clothes, a simple round-necked blouse and a long blue serge skirt. Putting on her Sunday hat, Malise took a look at herself in the mirror, licked her finger, organized her eyebrows, and then left for the meeting.

'Come in, come in,' Jack said as he ushered her into the little house that sat detached, surrounded by its own land. Malise looked at him, but he was just the same Jack, in a knitted waistcoat and a collarless shirt. The tiny passageway led to a living room which was lined with books and large files. It was more of a study, and Malise felt herself sigh with relief that it was obviously the house of a man who lived alone.

'You know Gideon,' he said as he gestured to Professor Winkworth. 'And this is Bernard Hetherington.' Bernard, a small terrier of a man with wiry grey hair and twinkling eyes, came over with his hand outstretched.

'Pleased to meet you, Malise,' he said happily. 'I've heard so much about you from Gideon.' He nodded so enthusiastically that his head looked in danger of departing his shoulders.

'Pleased to meet you,' Malise said.

'I work at the university as well, but in the medical department.' He spoke in short, staccato sentences, as if he were in too much of a hurry to bother with stringing sentences together.

'What do you do?'

'Neurology, the study of the brain. Working on ways to help soldiers who have brain injuries which have resulted in their limbs not working properly.'

Jack handed her a glass of wine. Malise looked at it uncertainly; she'd never drunk wine before.

'Take a seat, Malise,' Jack said. 'We were just talking about the Russian situation.'

She sat down and as she heard the men talk, she found

herself unable to keep quiet. The night passed quickly and it was with real reluctance that she heard the clock turn ten and realized she had to leave.

Bernard and Gideon walked her to the tram stop, waiting with her till it arrived to take her back to the reality of her home: a cold house and empty rooms. But as Malise snuggled up in bed, she found herself thinking about Jack. He was so friendly, so charming. And, for the first time in months, she fell asleep thinking about someone other than Alexander.

'You could have spent Christmas with us,' Jessie said as she popped in to see Malise on Boxing Day the following year.

'I couldn't, Jessie,' Malise returned. 'Your family all think Alexander is dead. I couldn't face your mammy, knowing I had let her believe a lie.'

'Well, you couldn't have told her the truth.' Jessie squeezed her friend's hand. 'And you just said he was taken.' She stopped. 'Did you send the parcel?'

Malise nodded.

'I got a card, with a photograph. Fraser wrote it.' She went to the mantelpiece and took down the photograph. 'Isn't he handsome? It's been ten months already.'

'One day, Malise,' Jessie said gently. 'One day, you'll get him back.'

Neil sat and watched as Alexander opened his presents; they had been difficult to choose, he had so many toys already. There was practically the whole of the Army and Navy catalogue in the boy's stocking.

'Happy, Alexander?' he said as he watched the child touch everything over and over, as if he didn't know what to play with first. But then he chewed his lip.

'Are these all from you?' he asked suddenly.

Neil nodded.

'Did Mammy send me anything?' His eyes melted Neil's

soul. Malise had sent him something, something that was in his study. For it had been sent to the office.

'No, Alexander,' he said slowly. 'She didn't send anything. She told me to give you presents instead.'

Alexander walked over to the window, where it was snowing gently.

'Has she forgotten me?' he said uncertainly.

Neil walked out of the room and into the study. He picked up the package from under his desk and took it into the room, where Alexander was still at the window, fighting back the tears.

'There you are, I forgot, she gave it to me to give to you.'

Alexander ripped apart the brown paper. And out fell a jersey. Not a particularly well-knitted one.

'Father!' Alexander's face lit up and immediately he put it on. 'My best jersey.'

Neil picked a letter up from the package and held it out to his son.

'Dear Alexander,' Alexander read aloud. 'I love you and I'll see you soon. Love Mammy.' He threw himself into his father's arms. 'She hasn't forgotten me, Father,' he said joyfully. 'She is just waiting for her turn.' And with that he extricated himself from his father's embrace and ran off to play with his new toys.

Everyone was waiting for Hogmanay. Mrs Baker, like most of the rest of the inhabitants of the tenements in Dundee, threw an open house and there was dancing and singing all night as people moved from one house to another, first-footing each home to help the occupants celebrate. Malise joined in; for once, not minding that Keith, Jessie's brother, had appointed himself her main dance partner for the evening. But as the night turned into the small hours of the morning, Keith pulled her away from the dancing and she found herself outside in the frosty air, looking over the back green.

'Just like old times,' he said casually.

'Aye, Keith,' she giggled with the whisky inside her as she stretched her aching feet and jumped up on the low wall. 'Like when we were wee bairns.'

'New year, new start.' He scuffed his shoes on the stones beneath him. 'Perhaps a time to let go of the past.'

'The past we can forget,' she said wistfully.

Keith looked at the jumper, hand-knitted by his mother, the right arm sewn neatly up against the stump.

'We've known each other for a long time, Malise,' he said carefully. 'Since you were four. How old are you now?'

'Twenty-two next birthday,' she said, suddenly entranced by the little pulls of frosty cloud that each breath was making.

'Still a young woman,' he remarked. 'You'll be looking for someone else now. Now that Mr Scott's gone.' He cleared his throat.

Something clicked inside Malise.

'I think I might have found someone, Keith,' she said casually. 'He's a solicitor, same as what I'm studying.'

'You should keep to your own, Malise,' Keith said sharply. 'You've got ideas above your station.'

'Why is he better than I am, Keith?' She turned to him. 'Just because he's book-clever and has a posh voice. Just because he wears a suit to work?'

'Aye,' Keith returned. 'You need someone who understands you, not one of those kinds of people.'

'Perhaps I'm not interested in having anyone from round here,' Malise replied. 'Perhaps I want someone who thinks for himself, who knows there's a life beyond the pub.'

'I'm going to learn how to be a carpenter,' Keith said quickly. 'Going on a course. There's a charity for people like me . . .' He tailed off.

'That's good, Keith,' she said softly. 'It'll make it easier. And you can find a wife and start your own family.'

'Malise.' Keith took a step towards her.

'You deserve someone nice, Keith,' she interrupted him. 'And I'm sure once you start looking, you'll find the girl for you.' Hastily she jumped off the wall. 'Well, I'm going back in now.' And with that she fled upstairs to the party.

Once the holiday was over, Malise went back to work. After a hard morning's study, she arrived at the office just as the Steeple was showing noon. She walked in, and before she had even taken off her coat, lit the range. The office was cold and damp, the sea wind and high walls of the nearby tenements rendered the place permanently wet and dreary. As she waited for the kettle to boil, Malise began to leaf through the post till she came to the one letter she was looking for. Would Jack be having another one of his parties again that weekend? But it was a short note, handwritten, telling her that he had received information that the Elizabeth was closing. And she was to talk to Billy to get him to find out as much as possible. Sighing, she looked at her watch. She had time for a quick cup of tea before Billy left work, but he was never a good timekeeper. Perhaps it would be better if she just let the range heat up and wait a bit.

It was little more than half past the hour when she got to the road near the Elizabeth and to the public house that Billy frequented. He was just crossing the road to get to it.

'Billy.' She nodded to him politely.

'I'm just going round the corner.' Billy held out his arm for her. 'And there is something . . .' He gestured to the door of the pub.

'You know I'm Temperance League,' she muttered. Billy gave a snort and led her to the bar where, under an elaborately adorned mirror, he got her a port wine and a whisky for himself.

Malise squinted at the cheap grandeur through the thick tobacco smoke. It certainly looked like the kind of place that only a man could enjoy; why would a woman want to go there when she could sit in her cosy house and drink tea?

'Have you heard the news?' He took a large draught of his drink before saying any more. Malise shook her head. Unwilling to show her hand.

'The Elizabeth Works is cutting the rates.'

Malise gasped.

'But they can't do both of them. They're still on short-time. It's bad enough when one of them happens, but both at the same time!'

'Taylor himself told me, it's the second rate cut in as many years, and they don't need half the people any more.'

'So why don't they just close it?' Malise sipped at the port wine, then put it down, grimacing.

'Can't close the Elizabeth, can they? Apart from Cox's, it's one of the biggest in the town. What would it say to everyone? That the Frasers were finished.' He smiled grimly.

'So what can I do?' she said suspiciously.

'I'm calling for a strike, to show them they can't just push us around.'

'But Billy, a strike is playing into their hands. If they want to close it down then that gives them the excuse,' Malise insisted.

'I want you to come with me and talk to the women as they come off shift.' Billy drained his glass.

'Why don't I talk to the dock unions?' Malise began. 'I'm already working on some figures. I'll see if there is a ship booked to take the machinery to India. Then we'll know what the plans are.'

'Taylor says there's no market for Scots jute. It's too expensive. So there's no point messing about with the stevedores. It's got to be the women. They've got to come out.'

'You know women don't strike, Billy. We've got families to feed.'

'I remember seeing you on picket when you was just a wee bairn. And you've sat on others lines, with your own, God rest his soul.'

'That was different,' Malise insisted.

'Aye, you were fighting for your future then, weren't you? Bit different when you're getting paid by the party to go to university.' Billy's face screwed up bitterly.

232

'I know what it's like to go without, Billy,' she said softly. 'I don't know that I'd want someone else's wee ones to have to do the same, because I'd called it.'

'Got your feet a bit comfortable under that office table, haven't you?'

'Thank you for the drink, Billy.' She put it down on the bar. 'But I'd better be away.' She pushed her way out of the small room and into the crisp night air.

'Don't forget!' he shouted after her. 'I want you there.'

Work for Billy, they had said. But had they meant this? Be his rabble-rouser?

The next evening in the gathering darkness of the stormy autumn, as the weavers and spinners, sweepers and carders began to stream out of the works, Malise was standing next to Billy.

'You talk.' He turned and looked at her. 'You're one of them.'

For the next three evenings she was there, talking to the women, telling them how important it was to show the management that they could not just be thrown on the scrap heap. They had to fight, and use the only weapon they had.

'Here, eight o'clock tomorrow,' Billy said as she walked away at the end of the third night. 'Tomorrow we call them out.'

'What has Taylor said about the threat?' She looked up at Billy. 'You have negotiated with him, haven't you?'

'There will be no negotiation, Mrs Scott.' He waved to some of the men who were hovering outside the bar. 'Remember, eight o'clock,' shouted Billy as he crossed the street to the gleaming lights of the public house. 'And bring your whistle!'

That night, Malise went through the few things she had to remind her of her father. There were some photographs, of him and her on the Fife, sailing over to Tayport one summer's day. But there were none of her mother. Malise closed her eyes; she couldn't remember what her mother looked like, but she'd a kind face, and she'd smelled of lavender, she'd always remember the smell. What would Alexander remember of herself?

Then she picked it up, the one heirloom her father had left her. His whistle. And tomorrow, for the first time, Malise was finally going to call a strike.

She woke at seven, and by eight o'clock she was standing outside the works rubbing the whistle between her fingers.

'Ready?' Billy walked over to her. She nodded nervously as the blower went and the women all streamed into work. No sooner had the blower stopped, than Malise put the chain round her neck and picked up the whistle, blowing it heartily.

'Everybody out!' called Billy as the younger, unmarried women began to run out of the gate, past a bemused watchman. Malise began to walk in a quick march down the wynd as the younger, then the older, more reluctant women began to follow her.

'What the hell is going on?' Neil Fraser looked out of the window at his retreating workforce. 'Bloody Malise!'

'They're striking because they don't want a wage cut,' Archie Taylor said with a grin. 'And I'd advise a lockout, to make sure no one sneaks in to do some mischief-making.'

'And what makes you think that could happen?' he asked suspiciously. 'No, Archie. Just get our costs here reduced, we've little enough time left in this place anyway.'

'Well, we're not making anything now, so that's solved the problem.' Archie smiled, his lips ruby-red in his pasty white face.

'I'd rather not close the works until we have decided exactly what is happening.' Neil glared at his manager.

'But you said yourself, you cannot afford to keep it running the way it is now,' Archie wheedled

'Just sort it out, Archie. I really don't want to know the

details.' With that, Neil Fraser left the office to go to the other works they owned. They were working as usual. But why? He knew the rules, if there was going to be a strike, you had to make it hurt. And calling out the Elizabeth simply made life easier for him. So why had Billy and his union cronies done this? And why had Malise got involved?

Malise went back to the picket every night. Just thinking about Alexander. About the times she had demonstrated and he had been there. He'd loved the banners, the songs, the playing round the brazier. But now he'd never do that. How could she bring Neil Fraser's heir down to a line? As midnight came and went, they were now on the eighth day of the strike, a strike that was biting down hard on the workers. But Billy refused to budge, he was deaf to her reasoning. According to him, victory was in the air.

As the day shift of picketers arrived, Malise walked to the Labour Party offices, seeing a few of the men there, men from the docks and, more importantly, men who knew people who could get her facts. Solid weapons. She'd need them. She looked at the names and addresses in the little notebook. Time to go to work. By seven o'clock that night she had all the ships carrying Fraser's goods blacked by the dockers in Dundee.

She wrote letter after letter to the unions in Dundee, Glasgow, Liverpool and even London, asking for information about shipments of jute into the country. Then, if Fraser didn't move, and she didn't think he would, she would put her plan to the party. The docks would have to be stopped. More families would have to go. Because once she had started down the road of striking, there was nothing left to negotiate with.

Malise sat for hours looking at the figures she had from Customs. Now almost as much woven as unwoven jute came into the country. But it was even more worrying that it wasn't just the spinning they were losing. She took a fresh piece of paper, then she picked up the figure for raw flax imported into Dundee, and began to make some calculations.

It was late when she finished, and she rubbed her face as she put away the figures. This was not a job for the union, she'd have to take it to Jack.

She put away the last papers, then turned off the oil lamp and prepared to go home. She was just about to leave her office when she heard the front door open.

'Are you sure every one has left?'

Malise gave a start as she heard Archie Taylor's voice in the dank quiet of the offices. Instinctively, she crouched behind the door, shielding herself from anyone coming in.

'Of course, Mr Taylor,' Johnnie Turpin replied. 'Billy gave me the keys and told me it was the safest place to be. Only him and Jack Buchanan have a set, and he's in Glasgow.'

'It needs to be done tonight,' Archie Taylor growled. 'With this haar and the word I've had with the Fire Brigade, it has to be tonight. You got something to make it burn?'

'I know what I'm doing, Mr Taylor,' Johnnie insisted. 'I have done this before.'

'It has to be done at the right time, we don't want the machinery harmed, but the building has to go up. And it has to be done before anyone changes their mind.'

'Aye, Mr Taylor. And the money?'

'Half now and half when the job's completed.'

After a short interval, Malise heard first one, then another, heavier set of footsteps on the stair outside. It was only then that she dared breathe as she slumped down on the damp floorboards. So it was all a set-up. The Frasers were behind a strike in their own factory, an excuse to empty it. Billy's inflammatory rhetoric had been for more than the strikers. It had been an alibi for his brother. And a pay-off. The whole thing, the strike, the lockout, had been a set-up so that they could close the factory. And no doubt send the rest of the machinery to the Indian factories.

Malise listened intently as she heard both men leave the building. But how could she stop it? Who could help her? There was no way she would let Fraser burn down her works. She walked into Jack's room, he had a telephone so that he could contact Glasgow. She had never used it, although she had heard Jack on it a number of times. Nervously, she picked up the receiver. There was a voice at the other end, asking her who she wanted to talk to? Jack or Fraser?

'Neil Fraser, please,' she said clearly. 'He lives in the Ferry.'

There was a click and then a ringing noise, then someone picked it up.

'Fraser residence,' he said gravely.

'I need to speak to Neil Fraser,' Malise said urgently.

'I'm afraid he isn't in to callers at the moment. Would you like to leave a message, madam?'

Malise hesitated. She needed to say something that would tell him she was serious.

'Tell him Taylor cocked up on the burning tonight. And if the Elizabeth goes up the police will have all the evidence they need.' She put the telephone down with a satisfying click. And then put on her coat. There was something she had to do now.

Malise struggled along towards the works, the mist was deep and thick, muffling any sound except the rustle of the wind in the bare autumn trees. She pulled her coat closer to her; it was warm and thick and the soft scratch of the rabbit fur collar was oddly comforting. The Frasers weren't going to take anything else from her. She had almost reached Lochee Road, and from there it was only a few minutes to the Elizabeth. Neil Fraser was going to rue the day he tried to burn down her works. At least it was damp, she thought wearily as she began the climb. At least it wasn't dry.

There was no one at the gates, which were locked; the little watchroom at the front was also empty and locked up. Malise took a deep breath, then began to climb up, over the thick iron gates, newly returned after being handed over to make guns with during the war. At the top of the gates, she swung perilously, before clambering over the side and jumping down the seven feet, as her coat, caught on one of the spikes, ripped all the way down the back. Pulling it off and throwing it to one side, she ran over to the mill and began to try the doors.

It was dark inside the mill, the giant spinning machines stood naked and menacing. Malise walked quietly, listening out for a noise, but all she could hear were the small sounds made by the rats, the mice, and the cats which fought a losing battle against them. And the birds who lived high in the eaves of the building. But in the darkness she could see a figure moving loose piles of jute to a position by the carding room. He was there.

Neil stopped the car at the gates and got out, unlocking the gates and walking in. He could see that the door of the mill was open, and that someone had left an old rag lying on the ground. Why on earth would Archie believe that this was what he wanted? Bracing himself for a fight, Neil went over to the mill.

'You can't do this!' Malise was struggling with Johnnie, but he was bigger and stronger. 'It's wrong. You're putting three thousand people out of work!' She fell into the pile of jute that was sitting on the floor, near to some electrics.

'I'd get out of here, if I was you,' he said tightly as he slapped her hard across the face, sending her into the side of the machine. Malise kicked out at him, sending splashes from the open jerry can over the shoulder of his jacket.

'Why are you doing this, Johnnie?' She went to grab for him but he moved the jerry can menacingly, as if to douse her with petrol. Malise backed away as he poured it over the pile of jute, then began a trail. 'You'll be out of work yourself!'

'Billy said it's going, anyway. This way I make myself ten pounds and a job in Fraser's other works.'

'But what about everyone else?' She moved to put a hand on him but he was still throwing petrol around.

'What has everyone else ever done for me?' he shouted at her. 'I've worked hard all my life, served my bloody country and I live in a shit hole. One room, the same as my father did before me. My children don't have decent shoes on their feet, or warm clothes to wear, and I just think it's about time I looked after myself for a change.' He shook his fist at Malise with genuine anger. 'You can go and live in Russia with your comrades, but now I'm just helping myself.'

'But this way you're betraying the union,' she tried one last time.

'Don't be daft, lass, it's the union who have organized it, as a way for the Frasers to get out with some profit. Billy says—'

'Don't listen to him, Johnnie,' she said desperately. 'Please, do what you know is right in your heart.'

In reply, he simply picked up the other jerry can and trailed the petrol to the other, smaller piles, strewn at the entrance to the carding room.

'No, Johnnie. Please!' She began to run towards him but then there was a flash and her ears were stung with a numb ringing as she was thrown to the ground by a hot wind.

Neil heard the shouts, then the explosion as the backdraft dragged both of the figures into the carding room. Battling against his better judgement and the smoke, Neil made his way over to the room, to where the awful screaming was coming from.

A man, it had to be a man, was writhing on the ground inside a ring of fire, screaming and moaning, his face red raw, his eyes and nose gone. Neil stopped for a second, it was so like his time in the trenches, the horrifying truth of injury. He tore off his overcoat, but in those short seconds, the figure had become still.

He turned and saw Malise, standing next to him, shielding her face from the heat of the flames.

'Come on!' he shouted, and grabbed her, forcing her under his arm as he used his coat to shield them both from the burning embers which were falling. Neil didn't want to look up – if he did, he would see the fire chasing along the joists that Archie had just had painted. He felt Malise's hands holding on to him, and decided to make a dash for it out of the carding room. As he did so, he looked up to see a burning piece of wood falling from the roof. He pushed Malise out of the way, just before he felt it hit him.

'Neil! Neil!'

At the sound of her voice, Neil forced his eyes open.

'You're a ton weight, you know.'

Malise, her face streaked with smoke, sat on the ground in the courtyard next to him. She was smiling at him, smiling as if she was glad to be alive.

'For a minute there, I thought you were a goner.' She swept the hair from her face. 'You'll be fine, and the police are just coming through, so your little plan'll not come to fruition, after all.' She shook her head. 'And I'll have my day in court this time, Fraser. And send you and Taylor to prison for a very long time.'

Neil reached up for her hand, but a wave of dizziness came over him and he sank back down to the ground.

'Neil?' At the sound of his father's voice, Neil struggled to open his eyes. 'Hush now, son,' it said again. 'No need to push yourself.'

'The fire!' he croaked, and tried to move his head.

'I thought I'd lost you.' Richard's voice almost broke.

'Malise was there, she saved me.' He looked around. 'What happened?'

Richard took a deep breath as if he were about to tell him bad news.

'No, don't say she's dead. She got out, I saw her.' Neil was

240

forcing himself to sit up, feeling the smoke in his lungs slide, chafing them.

'She's in Bell Street. She and someone else started the fire. You must have managed to crawl out through the fire some way or other before it took hold. The factory isn't too badly damaged, but the mill's destroyed and the office roof has come down. All in all, not too bad.'

'We both know Malise didn't start the fire.' Neil reached for the pitcher of water sitting by his bed. 'Is she in hospital?'

'She's in a jail cell, which is the safest place for her to be until we know exactly what she plans to do.' Richard's mouth tightened.

'She dragged me out of the fire!' Neil said loudly, then began to cough.

'I have to meet with someone who will fix it all for us. And makes sure that she never tells anyone of your arrangement with the union.' Richard sat back in his seat. 'Good God, man, if you had died, can you imagine the trouble I would have had about the boy! It could have started all over again. And Taylor is taking a long holiday, he's going to work in India for the foreseeable future.'

'I opened my eyes and she was there, and . . .' Neil closed his eyes, reliving the memory.

'Don't forget who she is, Neil,' Richard warned.

'She's the woman I owe my life to.'

'What about my money?' Malise asked the custody sergeant who handed over her few belongings late the next afternoon.

'You didn't have any.' The sergeant pointed to where she had to sign.

'I had three shillings.'

The sergeant ignored her.

'I said I had three shillings.'

'I never saw it if you did.' He turned away and Malise felt the anger grow inside her. It just wasn't fair.

'Jack?' As she was walking up from the cells, she spotted him, standing there as if he owned the world.

'Come with me.' He put out his hand and ushered her away, as if she were a lady going into a theatre. 'Didn't treat you too badly, did they?'

'They accused me of something they had no proof of, then they stole all my money,' she said loudly, but no one paid any attention to her. 'Actually, all I want to do is go to the baths, then home to bed and to forget all about it.' She smiled up at Jack, a smile which, though embarrassing, she couldn't help. 'I know you probably want to talk about what happened, but all I can think of is how much I smell.'

'I've spent the occasional night in the cells myself,' Jack murmured as they got to his car. 'Three shillings.' He handed her three coins. 'Why should you lose them?'

'My thirty pieces of silver? I presume, since you are here, that you know?'

'They haven't identified the body as Johnnie, probably won't be able to.' Jack began to drive up towards Lochee.

'I tried to get him out, but he was on fire, his face, his hair, everything.'

'You did all that you could, Malise.' Jack looked keenly at her. 'And you saved Fraser, which will considerably help our position.'

'And Billy?'

'Well, we have no evidence.' Jack turned away as he said it.

'I heard Johnnie talking to Archie Taylor. Billy had arranged for the strike, he said so. Just like he had arranged for the burning.'

'As I said, Malise, we have no evidence. Only hearsay.'

'You can't just let Billy Turpin walk away from all this unscathed!' Malise returned angrily.

'Think, Malise.' Jack stopped the car and turned to her. 'What would all the weavers and spinners, all those people who believe in you, believe in Billy, believe in the union, say if they found out the union had taken money to close one of the biggest works in Dundee? How many supporters do you think you would have left at the end of it? How could the union hold its head up in the other works? The whole Labour movement in Dundee, perhaps even in Scotland, would be affected. And for what? To send a greedy man to jail? He will have to live with the knowledge his brother has died because of him.'

'So it's all being covered up? All our struggles are for nothing? We just let them load the machinery on to ships and take it to Calcutta?'

'It's a fight we can only lose,' Jack said gently. 'We're just trying to limit the damage.'

'Limit the damage? We're talking about a man who sold the futures of three thousand people down the river!' Malise looked at Jack in disgust.

'And if it becomes public knowledge, then we will lose our ability to fight for those who are left.' Jack moved to put a hand on her arm, but she flinched away. 'Don't, Malise, please. It's a difficult situation and I'm no happier than you are about it.'

'But you worked out the solution, Jack. Console yourself with that.' She got out and slammed the door, walking away from the car in the soft evening rain. It hadn't taken them long to work out a way to cover everything up and cover everyone's back.

As she walked away, she could feel Jack's eyes boring into her back. But she couldn't face him, not now. He was a man she admired, a man who believed in her, and he had disappointed her. She had reached the bottom of the High Street now, she could still see Jack's car, the only car in the street, but she kept on walking.

At the wash house, Malise paid her money to a small woman who was sitting in a cubicle at the entrance. In return, she was given a small sliver of coal tar soap and a short white towel that was as rough as sandpaper and she went into the bathhouse. She picked a cubicle, opening the rough wooden door that didn't reach the wet floor, and stripped off her smoke-stained clothing.

'Hot water in two!' she shouted, and, as the hot water began to gush into the tub, she stepped into it, shouting alternately for hot and cold till it was full and warm. As she lay there, trying to soak away her ordeal, Malise could hear the other women chatting, about nothing, and about everything. But mainly about the fire. She listened to their gossip, rubbing soap into her hair, watching as a few burned wisps came away in her hands, its acrid smell filling the air. What she wanted was some comfort, someone to tell her that it was all right. But there was no one, not Gordon Scott, not Jack Buchanan. No one to ease her conscience. She was just going to have to live with herself. Because she didn't know what else she could do.

The next day, before lectures, she went down into town. After some time she found Billy Turpin by the Pillars, talking to some councilmen. But he walked away from them as soon as he saw her.

'Mrs Scott.' Billy looked at her suspiciously. 'Heard they let you out.' He stopped near a pharmacy window.

'Sorry to hear about your Johnnie,' she said quietly, as she joined him, running her finger along the wooden surround.

'Too busy saving Neil Fraser to care about my brother,' Billy snapped.

'His face was burned off. He died in front of me.' She suppressed the memory.

'And what do you want to see me about?' Billy said belligerently.

Malise gathered herself together and looked him in the eye.

'There'll be a few changes from now on, Billy,' she said softly. 'I don't know if you can be trusted any more. Perhaps it's time you stepped down.'

He took a step closer.

'You ought to be scared of me.' His eyes narrowed.

'Well, I'm not,' she returned calmly. 'But you turn my stomach, and that's a start, isn't it?' She took a step back and considered him. 'Sime is a good man.'

'I am head of the union,' Billy blustered.

'Yes, but in order to be on the committee, don't you have to run a works?' She opened her hands. 'And didn't your brother just burn down the one you were convener of?' She walked away, then turned back to him. 'Think about it, I'm sure Sime has.' She smiled bitterly to herself. It was stupid and childish, scoring a point when three thousand people were out of work and a man had been killed. Despondent, but still spoiling for a fight, Malise made her way to the university where she was almost forty minutes late for her tutorial.

'Where were you, Mrs Scott?' Professor Winkworth stared at her as she walked in as if she owned the place.

'I've spent the past two days in prison, charged with attempted murder.' She nodded to the other students in the little office. 'But it all turned out to be a misunderstanding.'

'At least you know enough about habeas corpus to ensure you were treated fairly,' Martin, one of the students added.

'If they wanted to, they would just ignore it.' She looked at the young men, one at a time. Somehow, the difference between them was wider than ever.

But she had to go back to work, she knew she had. After her morning lecture on the history of law, she walked from the university to the little office in the Fishgate, and up the filthy stairs.

She saw the door to the other office was open, Jack was sitting at his desk, wearing a cardigan and reading some papers. He looked up, but he didn't smile.

Malise walked into her office, there was a pile of correspondence on the desk.

'How are you feeling?' Jack's voice floated over the air as he walked in behind her.

'Betrayed. Used.' She shrugged. 'Cheated.'

'This is the reality of politics, Malise. It's not a fight. It's about compromise. About sometimes doing something that you aren't happy about, because it is for the greater good.' He put a hand on her shoulder. 'If you can't stomach it, then you ought to leave.'

'So now you're throwing me out?' she said incredulously. 'For standing up for the people of the Elizabeth?'

'We need the union to be on our side, the owners would like nothing better than to watch the party and the unions tear themselves apart. Leaves them free to do whatever they want to.' He moved away from her, for a moment.

'So what you are saying is that I can't beat Billy? That he can walk away from all this and no one will say a word against him?' She gripped the edges of the desk.

'He is a powerful man, Malise, and we have to work with him.' Jack walked out of the office and she heard him, in the little kitchen, banging about with teacups.

She thought for a moment, then followed him through.

'I thought you had more principles.' She stared at the educated solicitor mercilessly.

'I'm not happy, but I know that we will need Billy for the next few years. After that, he will get his come-uppance.' He poured the boiling water into the teapot. 'He wouldn't get the candidature over you, but if he goes, you might have more problems.'

'So if I keep my mouth shut, you'll make sure that I get to fight the election?' She tried to swallow the distaste in her mouth.

'Put rather crudely, yes. Sime would be a real alternative to Billy and he is well-respected.' He opened the window and took the milk from the sill where it was kept cool.

She was still; for some reason, Gordon came to mind. It was the kind of thing he understood, that sometimes principles had to be bent. But could hers bend that far?

'Then there is no point in saying another word about it,' she said with mock brightness. 'Nice and strong for me, please.'

'I'm sorry, Malise,' he said as he poured tea into cups.

'Nothing personal, Jack, eh?' She wrinkled up her nose at him. 'Just politics.'

When she got home the house was cold, silent and bare. She needed to go to the steamie, but she hadn't the stomach for a blether. She hung up her coat and saw a note lying on the floor. She recognized the handwriting. What did Fraser want now?

It was a summons to his father's home in the Perth Road, that evening. Malise sighed, looked at the clock, then picked up her coat.

'Mrs Scott, follow me, please.' A man, dressed in black and with an expression of polite disdain, opened the door to her and gestured for her to come in. Malise hesitated. Although the hallway was lit, it looked like the walkway in a museum. There wasn't an ounce of life in the place. But as her shoes sounded over the tiled floor, Malise felt herself shrink under the portraits, the enormous vases that stood in recesses in the walls, and the clean, deserted smell of the place. Funny, she thought as she gazed at the rogues' gallery of family portraits, each glowering harder than the previous one, it always looked so inviting from the outside. Eventually they came to a door, but as the butler began to open it, Malise put her hand on his.

'Wait a moment.' She took a deep breath, then let it out slowly. She nodded. And the door opened.

'Mammy!' Alexander came rushing over to her, almost knocking her off her feet.

'Alexander, my Alexander.' She kissed and hugged him, as if she couldn't quite believe he was real. But he was, with strong and healthy bones and a clear-skinned smile.

'I've missed you so much, Mammy,' Alexander was crying as he wiped the tears that were falling from her eyes. 'Please, Father, can she come and live with us? Please?'

Malise looked up and there was Neil Fraser. They were in a sitting room, and he was standing by the fireplace, his elbow resting on the fine white marble.

'My, how you've grown,' she said as Alexander snuggled beside her. Then she closed her eyes, just breathing in his smell. It was different, but he still smelt like her Alexander.

'Don't upset yourself, Malise,' Neil said gently. 'Please don't cry.' He walked over and handed her a handkerchief. 'I thought that you and Alexander could spend some time together.' But Malise wasn't listening. All that mattered was Alexander.

Neil waited for a moment, he had worked out a small speech, but he could see he'd never give it. He left the room.

Alexander and Malise went over to the sofa, and they talked a little, but mostly he just burrowed himself into her lap and sat there.

Malise could feel the warmth of him, and the warmth of the large fire. She closed her eyes again. And felt the weight lift from her shoulders.

'Mammy?' Alexander awoke, rubbing his eyes as he pushed himself back up to a sitting position on her lap. 'I had a dream you were here and now it's come true.'

'Oh, Alexander,' she replied, stroking his face. 'It's just for tonight. And we both fell asleep.'

'I like it here, Mammy, but I miss you so much. Mama, that's what they make me call her, is scary, and she's horrible to me. It's so quiet, and no one ever laughs.' He jumped off the sofa. 'Let's run away. Please.'

'Alexander,' Malise took his hands in hers. 'I wish I could, but they'd throw me in jail if I tried. But no matter what happens, I love you, and I always will. And one day, when you are older, we'll be together again. You and me.'

'Why don't you go next door and have something to eat, Alexander?' Neil said softly as he appeared at the door. 'There's some food on the table, or tell the maid to serve you.'

The child nodded uncertainly, then left the room.

'Thank you,' she said humbly. 'For tonight.'

'You can see him four times a year, here. But you mustn't contact him any other time.'

'Why are you giving this to me?' she asked awkwardly. 'You don't have to. Your father and the party have already worked out a cover up.'

'You didn't have to drag me out of the mill now, did you?' He raised his eyebrow.

'I did,' she replied without thinking. 'I couldn't just let you die in there.'

'That's what I admire about you, Malise,' he said thoughtfully. 'You don't just pass by. This is a personal thanks from me to you.' Neil took a deep breath and walked over to the fire. 'And I want to say that I'm sorry. For everything.'

'You know the paper was a forgery,' she returned shakily. 'Just do the right thing. Give me back my son.'

'Malise, I can't,' Neil replied in frustration. 'He is settled at the High School and is a part of my family. I can't undo what has been done. You can see for yourself what I've given him already. A chance that he would never have, living with you. He'll never go hungry, he'll never have to worry about the illnesses that slum children suffer and his abilities will be recognized and tested. And I need him, as much as you do. He's my son and I love him.' He smiled uneasily.

Malise felt a wave of reality wash over her. She couldn't have Alexander, but Neil Fraser, the self-seeking, uncaring jute baron, loved him too. But she would get him back.

'Spend more time with him. He needs a father. And spend more time with your other son, he needs you even more.'

'Euan is well cared for,' Neil said quickly.

'Euan would make a man of you, Neil Fraser.' She took a step over to him. 'It's easy to love Alexander, it's harder to love someone who isn't perfect. Who isn't the child he is supposed to be. Because you feel guilty that you made him that way. You and your wife.'

Neil sighed, a deep sigh that came from his soul.

'Why do you make me think of things that I don't want to consider?'

'Then don't listen to me,' she replied. 'You never do anything about it anyway.'

Neil's chauffeur took her home, and as she walked into her lonely little house, she felt her heart lift. Only a few short months, and she would see Alexander again. Now she had someone in her life.

'It's out of the question!' Agnes put a hand to her chest as Neil informed his wife he wanted to bring Euan home to live with them. 'There are places for those kinds of creatures.'

'He's not a creature, Agnes,' he reminded her gently. 'He's our son.'

'Whatever made you think of such a thing?' She moved away, as she always did.

'Someone asked me why I was ashamed of my own flesh and blood,' he continued, 'and I didn't have an answer for them.'

'You awful man,' she replied. 'How can you bring such shame on me? Having that child in the house. It's bad enough that you bring your bastard here and make me his mother . . .'

'Since the only time you've spoken to Alexander is the one single occasion when you had tea with him, it's a wonder that you notice he's here at all. That any of us are here.'

'How dare you,' she said sharply.

'Oh, go upstairs and drink some laudanum,' he returned. 'At least when you are insensible I don't have to endure your company!'

'I should never have married you. You're an awful, boorish man!' Stifling a sob, Agnes fled from the room. Neil took a deep breath, it was the first time they had ever crossed words.

'You're absolutely right!' he said in relief. 'I should never have married you.'

*

'I've won a prize at school,' Alexander announced as Malise walked into the Fraser house on the Perth Road almost three long months later. 'I'm the best in mathematics.'

'You clever boy,' Malise said as she wrapped her arms around him, breathing in his lovely, clean smell. 'The cleverest boy in the class. I've missed you so much.'

'I'm getting my prize from the Rector, and I have to go up on stage for it. Will you come?'

'I'd love to,' she replied with shining eyes. 'I've waited so long for this.'

'For what?' Neil walked into the room; he liked to check what Malise was talking to Alexander about. For some reason, he didn't entirely trust her.

'Alexander was telling me about his prize-giving.'

Neil's face paled as he looked at the woman, sitting nervously on the chair as if she were frightened she might dirty it with her clothes.

'You surely aren't thinking of attending?'

'Why not? He is still my son. I haven't signed adoption papers, have I?'

'Malise, I cannot allow it. You cannot attend. My wife and I—'

'He's never won a prize before.' Malise's voice shook a little.

'I'm sorry. If there was any way . . .'

'There is never any way,' she said sharply. 'There is only your way.' She turned to Alexander. 'Now, let's see what you are doing in geography,' she said brightly, pointedly ignoring the man who was standing in the room. Neil bit his lip. But there was no other way.

It was almost eight o'clock the next evening when she arrived outside the gates of the High School. There were motor cars in the playground, the assembly had already started.

'He's done very well,' the Rector said to Neil as he patted Alexander on the head. 'And Alexander is generous in his praise of his mother's assistance.'

'Thank you.' Agnes smiled graciously.

They went back to the car. The chauffeur was waiting. But as they began to climb in, Neil caught sight of a figure standing at the gates.

'I have something to do,' he murmured. 'I'll see you back home.'

As he began to make his way to her, however, she moved away, heading up the side street to Euclid Crescent.

'Wait, Malise.' He caught up with her, catching her by the arm.

'I couldn't stay away,' she said softly.

'I understand.' He pulled her to face him and could see the tears in her eyes. 'Really, I understand, more than you think.'

'I just wanted to be proud of him.'

'You should be.' Neil touched a tear with his finger. 'You should be proud of yourself, too.' His hand was now stroking her cheek. 'Why do you always seem to end up weeping in my arms?' He had pulled her against him now but Malise pushed away.

'Because you hurt me, but I never cry over you, Mr Fraser. Remember that!' She bit her lip and strode away. He understood, he had said so. But if he understood, how could he have taken Alexander away?

And so Malise continued to live her little, fragmented life. On Mondays, she went to university and was a student, but in the evening, she went to the steamie and was a washer-woman. For the rest of the week, she studied and worked as the others played rugby or tennis or talked about philosophy, and then, on Thursday nights, she packed up her soap and little towel and went to the baths for a scrub and a gossip. The following evening she visited with Jack and his little groups of Fabians, as he liked to call them. And then on Sunday, she was the organizer of the marches, or the talks, and often afterwards she would find herself involved in a lively discussion with party speakers from Glasgow or

Edinburgh, or even from Manchester. All in all, she seemed to be different people; she was one person for Jessie and Mrs Baker, one for university, and yet another for her evenings with intellectuals. But she didn't fit into any of them, not comfortably. She was moving away from her old friends, from her family, and somehow she always felt as if no one really knew her.

Chapter 11

Malise stood in the tutor's lounge, a sherry in her hand, smiling at the other young men who were there.

'Congratulations on all your hard work.' Professor Winkworth raised his glass. 'And let's hope that you all have as successful a second year as you did the first.'

Malise smiled down at her hands. They looked different now; cleaner, softer. A year had passed already. More than a year without Alexander. If only he could have seen her, but that was impossible. If only he could hear her prayers.

'Jack is delighted with your progress,' Gideon said as she moved to collect the glasses. 'You don't need to do that, the maid will be in.'

'It feels as if I ought to,' Malise said awkwardly.

'Finding it difficult to fit in, aren't you?' He looked at her keenly. 'You come from a different world, Malise, and don't forget it. It's what made you the person you are.' He put down his empty glass on the little table. 'We can all learn a lot from you.' He came over and put his hand on her arm. 'Jack thinks a lot of you, you know. We all do.'

'I don't want to let him down,' she stumbled over the words.

'Let who down?' Jack walked in and she felt her heart lift. 'I was in the area, Gideon, thought I'd pop in.'

'I'm just leaving,' Malise replied.

'I'll walk you to your tram.' Jack smiled at her and offered her his arm.

They walked slowly along the Perth Road, towards her home, enjoying the late evening sunshine. For some reason, she felt happy and relaxed, just walking, with Jack. As her tram arrived and she sat down, she watched him, standing there. It made her feel as if she wasn't alone any more.

When Neil arrived home from work that night, Miss Emmerson met him at the door.

'You have to go to the drawing room, sir,' she said quietly. 'The doctor has paid us a visit.'

'Alexander?' he said immediately.

'No, sir,' she said shakily. 'Euan.'

Neil hurried into the drawing room. He saw the letter sitting on the mantelpiece. Pneumonia. Euan had died within a day of developing it. He read it again and again, a thousand different thoughts clouding his mind. Why hadn't he gone to see Euan that weekend? What had he been doing instead? Why hadn't he done as Malise had asked, and brought the child into his family? Why hadn't he done something with Euan when he had the chance to? He looked over at his wife, but Agnes was sitting there, only half aware of the world, as always.

'Agnes?' He crouched beside his wife and took a hold of her hands. They were warm and heavy, as if she were asleep. 'Our little Euan, he's been taken.'

Agnes let a sad smile creep over her face.

'Now we can forget what happened,' she said slowly, as if she were explaining it to a child. 'We can put all the unpleasantness behind us.'

Neil looked at her in horror. But as he walked away, into the dark garden, he knew that in some ways, Agnes was far more honest than he would ever be. They had put Euan behind them a long time ago. Agnes had simply put it into words.

There was no announcement in the paper; it wasn't seemly. Neil buried his son with only his father by his side. To invite those who had never met him would somehow have been disrespectful to Euan. Even Alexander wasn't told. But Alexander had never been told of the existence of Euan while Euan had been alive, so what was the point in him knowing now?

Neil buried his grief in bottles and dancers, in nights spent with women he hardly knew and cared nothing for. He shouted at the works manager of the new Elizabeth Electric Cable Company, which he had opened on the remains of the old works. At least when he was shouting, he was shouting at someone else, and not having to listen to the insidious voices in his head which kept asking questions about why he felt so guilty that a child he had ignored, whom he had hidden away, was now free of his prison and in a place where his family could no longer let him down.

'Winston sent this to my home,' Richard said as they sat having a late drink a few nights not long after the funeral. 'I met with him in London last month, and told him.' He handed the letter to Neil. 'He was most distressed to hear of Euan, he lost a daughter only last year. Marigold, her name was, just about Euan's age, too.'

Neil nodded and drained his glass.

'I'll read it later.' He made no attempt to pick it up.

'Don't you think you are drinking more than you ought?' Richard continued.

'I do a lot of things I'm not proud of, Father,' Neil replied. 'And keeping a few distilleries in business is not high on the list.' He put the glass down with a clatter.

It was with a light heart that Malise arrived at Jack's house the next evening. But as she knocked on the door, she was surprised when Jack answered it, wearing a suit and tie.

'Oh, I thought you said we were meeting up as usual,' she said nervously.

'Just you and me,' he said as he took her coat. 'I thought we could have a chat. There don't seem to be enough hours in the day. And since the incident about the Elizabeth, I know you feel awkward around me.'

'No, Jack.' She stopped. 'It's just that I want to look up to you, and it's difficult.'

Jack ushered her into the lounge, which was dimly lit.

'I know. But a part of politics is understanding that sometimes good doesn't always win. That there is a greater good which has to be served. I just wanted to apologize for letting you down.'

'You didn't let me down, it was Billy,' she said vehemently. 'He let the whole of Dundee down.'

'I'm glad you can see it that way.' He handed her a glass of fizzy wine. 'And I wanted to toast your exam results the only way they ought to be celebrated. With champagne.'

Their glasses clinked together and Malise took a sip. Champagne. This was what kings and queens drank. And now she was drinking it too.

With it, Jack went over to the gramophone and put on a large black disc.

'This is my favourite,' he said as the room filled with music. 'It's an Italian opera.'

As the music began to wash over them, he sat next to her, and unconsciously Malise found herself moving closer and closer towards him. She sat there, aware of the gentle pressure of his body against hers. It was perfect, the kind of evening that you spend with someone you care for, she thought. She smiled at Jack and he smiled back warmly. Then he stood up.

'Can I offer you a cup of tea? I think I've had enough champagne for the night,' he said with studied casualness.

'Of course,' Malise returned. What was he doing? Jack made the tea, turned down the music, sat in a armchair, and moved the conversation on to work. Malise gazed at him, and her mind began to wonder. He had sought her out for a reason, but he was too shy to make a move. By the end of the evening, as Jack saw her to the tram stop, she had decided. Jack was the one. That was what was missing in her life.

'And how are you, Malise?' Mrs Baker said cheerfully, as she opened the door that Saturday evening. 'Jessie's just getting the card table out.' As the older woman walked over to the range to pour the kettle, Malise sat down on the old, worn sofa.

'Guess what, Jessie,' she said in an undertone.

'You're running away to join the circus?' Jessie grinned as she wrestled with the skinny legs of the green baize table.

'I've got a young man,' Malise replied with a smile. 'He's a solicitor and he works with me.'

Jessie's face set. 'Oh.' Her features betrayed nothing. 'That's nice, Malise. You want a cup of tea now?'

'Jessie!' Mrs Baker said reproachfully. 'There's no need to be like that.'

'Just got to go,' Jessie mumbled, and went past them to the toilet on the landing.

'Take no heed of her, Malise,' Mrs Baker said comfortingly. 'She's just jealous, that's all.'

'But why would Jessie be jealous?' Malise said, confused.

'Because she's going to end up an old maid, and you've practically caught your second husband and you're a year younger than her.' She busied herself with the teapot.

Malise went out to the landing, Jessie was standing by the lavatory, arms crossed over her chest.

'Sorry, Jessie,' she said slowly.

'It's all right for you,' Jessie said sharply. 'You get to meet all those men and you get to talk to them about things they are interested in. All I meet is the butcher's boy and the postman, if I'm lucky.' She snorted. 'And you don't half get ideas above your station.'

'I'm going to be a solicitor too, Jessie,' Malise insisted.

'Yes, but you'll always be Malise, not like them over in Commercial Street. You'll always be different.' She slumped back against the toilet door. 'And I don't see why you can't just accept it. You might be a solicitor, but you'll only be a solicitor for the likes of us.'

'But that's what I want to be,' Malise replied.

'No, you don't,' Jessie returned. 'It was the same with Gordon Scott. You want to be posh, you want to spend your time with folk who read books. You pretend you're fighting them, but really, you just want to be one too.'

'Is that what you really think, Jessie Baker?' Malise said coldly. 'Do you think I married Gordon Scott because I wanted to be a schoolmaster's wife?' She rounded on her. 'I married him because the father of my child had left me with nothing and it was the only way of keeping myself off relief. He offered, and it never occurred to me until my wedding night that he had another motive. Every time he touched me, I felt sick to the stomach that he had the right to. And there was nothing I could do to stop him! And now, now that I actually have a chance with a decent man who works for the poor people of the city, not because he has to but because he wants to, you stand there and accuse me of being selfish! I have given up far, far more for this town than you could ever imagine!' She stormed off down the stairs.

'Malise, please,' Jessie shouted as she pelted down after her. 'Don't go. Please stay.' She put a hand out to Malise's shoulder. 'I didn't mean what I said.'

'Yes, you did, Jessie,' Malise returned. 'You meant every word.'

'Only because I want to be you!' Jessie stifled a sob. 'You're getting all educated and you talk almost as posh as they do now. And people like me, well, we work for people like you.' She took Malise's hand. 'And I'd hate to think that you'd be too ashamed to have a maid as your friend.'

'Away you go with yourself, Jessie Baker,' Malise said with a watery smile. 'Like that'd ever happen.'

'I'll still be able to beat you at whist,' Jessie said slightly shamefacedly.

'Aye, good job it's only buttons we're playing for, isn't it?' Malise linked arms with Jessie and they went back upstairs to the card game.

'So what do you think I should do?' Malise said as she sat playing cards with Jessie and Mrs Baker. 'Jack's fine, but he's terrible shy.'

'Well, shy's never been a problem with you, Malise,' Mrs Baker said mockingly. 'Och, the Jack of spades. That's me out.' She put down her cards and scooped up the buttons triumphantly.

'A wee stout to celebrate?' Jessie said hopefully.

'Why not?' As Mrs Baker went into the kitchen, Jessie bent over to Malise.

'Tell me about him,' she said conspiratorially.

'He talks to me,' Malise replied. 'And he invited me to his house, and we had champagne.'

'Doesn't sound that shy,' Jessie remarked. 'Did he have his wicked way with you?'

'No.'

'Would you like him to?'

Malise thought for a moment.

'He'd be a good husband,' she said resolutely. 'A good friend.'

'Then why don't you help him make up his mind?' Jessie giggled. 'Men need that.'

'All right,' Malise replied. 'I will.'

However, the next week, Jack wasn't in the office, or the week after that. Malise read each of his letters, looking for something personal for her. After all, he had invited her to his home, alone. But she couldn't find any. Till almost a month later, when, on the bottom of a report about the rates of unemployment of ex-soldiers, he had fastened a note: *See you on Friday at 8 p.m. in my home.* Malise held the note to her lips. He was coming back, to her.

'Hello, again.' Malise was dressed in her best summer dress and holding a cardigan. It was chilly for evening, but she wanted to look her best for him.

'Come in, Malise.' As soon as she walked into the room she realized why she'd been summoned. Gideon Winkworth and Bernard Hetherington were there, smiling broadly.

'I've had some interesting news from our comrades in

Russia,' Professor Winkworth began. And Malise's smile set into a grimace.

'This really is awfully kind of you,' Jack said as she brought in the glasses they had used. 'I have few domestic skills.'

'You need a woman,' Malise said clumsily, then bit her lip as her cheeks reddened. 'What I mean is . . .'

Jack looked at her face as he took the glasses from her.

'What are you trying to tell me, Malise?' he said gently.

'What I was wondering . . .' She tailed off. 'What I mean is, we're friends, aren't we?'

An inscrutable expression crossed Jack's features.

'Malise, I have many friends,' he said softly. 'Whereas you don't really have much time at the moment, do you?'

'What do you mean?' she said, confused.

'With your studying, and your work. And I'm sure you are finding it more difficult now. Your interests are changing and you might have less in common with the people that you love.'

'But we have a lot in common, don't we?' She could feel her stomach beginning to churn.

'It must get lonely, having lost your husband and son. You're only young. Be careful who you reach out to, Malise,' he said warningly. 'There are only too many men willing to take advantage of such a situation.'

'But I've got you, Jack.' She smiled up at him. He turned away.

'You are a valued colleague, Malise. I enjoy your company, you've made a lively addition to our group. But . . .'

'What I'm saying is,' Malise persisted, and took his hands. 'I like you, Jack. A lot.' Her fingers curled round his. Jack stared at them for a long time.

'No, Malise,' he said firmly. 'Don't ask me to explain why, but there will never be that kind of relationship between us. There is someone else.'

'But what kind of woman would let you spend so much time in other towns!' She said, confused.

'My friend – ' Jack stumbled over the words. 'Understands. And I couldn't take advantage of you in this fashion.' He looked up. 'It's getting late, perhaps I ought to see you to the tram stop.'

As they left the kitchen, Malise stared round the little sitting room. There wasn't a single photograph of a woman there, just a few snaps of Jack with some chums. Not a single woman in any of them. Had he just made an excuse?

'Come on, slowcoach,' Jack said mildly.

Malise looked at him, he smiled and ruffled her hair. And Malise knew that whatever she was to Jack, she'd never be his wife.

'Malise!' Jessie shouted as she opened the door the following evening. 'Well?' she asked, as her friend rushed into the living room.

'I made such a fool of myself,' Malise said shortly. 'He wasn't interested in that. He just wanted to be friends, and I thought he wanted something else.'

'We all get lonely, Malise,' Jessie replied as she sat down beside her. 'When my Arthur fell, I was live-in. I couldn't think of anything other than that I would die an old maid. I just wanted someone, anyone, to want me.' She took a deep breath. 'There was a police constable that used to come in on his way past, when he was walking his beat.' She picked at her fingernails. 'You know, I think I must have been sweating it, he could smell it on me. Because he knew. And before I knew it, he would be coming round every day, for a kiss or a cuddle, and quite often a lot more. I didn't love him, but I tried to convince myself that I did. Even though he never once offered to meet my family, the way a respectable man would. We hardly even talked. He would just put his hands on me and I would just let him. Because while he was there, for those moments, I wasn't on my own. And for a while anything was better than that.'

'Oh, Jessie, I wanted him to notice me, I wanted him to see me as a woman, not just someone from the office, someone from the party. And he did, he treated me like a lady, but also like an equal.' Malise put her hands to her mouth. 'I'll never be able to face him again.'

Luckily for her, Jack was nowhere to be seen that weekend at the speech, or the rest of the week in the office. He had left a note on her desk, however, saying he would be in Glasgow for a few weeks, and telling her what work needed to be done – letters which needed typing, and research needed on a particular landlord, as well as a report on drainage in the courts, which would mean a long meeting with various engineers from the university. Malise worked harder than she had before. She had to show Jack that she wouldn't let her feelings get the better of her. But she was also very glad that she wouldn't see him again till after Christmas.

Malise was now in her second year, and there was little time to wonder why Jack was avoiding her. So she buried herself in the library, reading books, writing essays and even looking up some points that helped her work. She never had time to think about the fact that she was growing away from Jessie and the Bakers, spending more and more time with students, in the refectory, talking about the law. Using words they wouldn't understand. Her clothes were now bought from a second-hand shop in the Ferry, and she noticed that when people came into the office, they treated her with more respect. Malise found herself wondering if Jessie was right. If she were trying to be something that she wasn't.

'I have your Christmas present here, Alexander,' she said as she handed him a parcel during her December visit to the Fraser house in the Perth Road.

'May I open it now?' Alexander said excitedly.

'No, you have to wait,' she replied. 'After all, a Christmas present wouldn't be a Christmas present if you opened it now.'

They both laughed uproariously. Neil, standing by the

window in the study, heard the unusual sound of laughter in the house, reminding him of a time when he was happy, when he wasn't burdened by the guilt of having abandoned his own son and having stolen Malise's with an affidavit she had been tricked into signing. This was a mistake, he should never have allowed her to come to the house, wearing clothes that suited her figure and pearl earrings that framed her pretty face, the happiness that she held just shining out of her. Drawing him to her, the way she had always drawn him. Whom had she found to buy her such things? Putting down his glass, he walked quickly to the door.

'Do you have to make such a lot of noise?' he demanded.

Malise turned. It was a shock seeing Neil for the first time in months. His strong handsome features were drawn, and he looked as if he hadn't slept properly in weeks.

'Mammy was just giving me my Christmas present.' Alexander rushed to her aid.

'I have a friend, a professor of neurology at the university. He has been researching ways of helping war-wounded people use their limbs again,' she said. She smiled, and her face lit up.

'I don't wish to hear about you,' he retorted. 'You are here for Alexander.'

'But Bernard's research might help Euan,' she returned. 'Exercises to train his limbs, perhaps he could teach him to sit up, maybe even to walk. Bernard says—'

'Euan died six months ago.' Neil slammed his hand down on the table. 'Even your wonderful Bernard can't help him now.'

'Alexander, go and get your things,' Malise said as she looked at the man tightening in front of her. Alexander fled from the room. 'I'm so sorry.' She pressed her hands to her lips. 'You poor man.'

'I'm not a poor man,' he shouted. 'I'm from one of the first families in Dundee. I have the perfect family and God help you if you don't fit in! Because I'll throw you away

and leave you to die somewhere, alone and frightened!'
He turned to the drinks table, but Malise was already at his
side.

'You did all that you could for Euan,' she said slowly.
'Some children just aren't meant to be.'

'I wanted to bring him home. But Agnes refused, and
I was weak. I didn't fight for him.' He put his hands over
his face. 'I didn't fight for him the way you fought for
Alexander. Even today, you hadn't forgotten about my son.
You still thought of him.'

'But you haven't forgotten him either,' she said gently.
'Don't torture yourself with guilt. You can't change the past.
But you can learn from it.'

'I kept telling myself there was no other way, but there
was. I was just too much of a coward to take it.' He grabbed
her hands almost violently. 'I'm a coward, Malise, and
you know that better than anyone. I try to do what's right,
but it doesn't take long for the Fraser blood to start showing.'

'Neil?' Malise said, shocked.

'You know, in a way I wish Euan had been your son,' he
said bitterly. 'Because you'd have seen the child, not the
cripple. You'd have loved him. He'd never have been alone
with you there.'

'I'm no saint,' she replied helplessly. 'Look at the way I
treated Gordon. That day will haunt me for the rest of my
life.'

'I made you do that,' he replied vehemently. 'It was
my fault. Everything I've ever done has turned out to be a
disaster.'

'No, Neil, you're a good man,' she didn't know why, but
she needed to comfort him, 'I know you are. If only you
could . . .'

'Could what?' He stared into her eyes, his own filled with
a longing for comfort, for the touch of someone who could
take away the pain.

'If only you could see another point of view. There is

always another way.' She held his gaze, sensing that his face was getting closer. Then he kissed her, so hard that she felt her lip push against her teeth as his arms crushed her to him.

'Neil!' But her mouth was muffled by his. Struggling, she wriggled out of his arms and stared at him, half horrified by what he had done. But half of her could feel how much she wanted him too. But it had been too much of a shock for her.

'I'm sorry.' He turned away and walked to the fire, resting his hands on the elaborate gilded mantelpiece. 'It's just that I'm so . . .'

Malise stood and looked at him, and her breathing evened. She wanted to touch him, to console him. But most of all, she wanted him to kiss her again. But her own cowardice took over and instead she ran from the room.

'Lonely,' he ended slowly. But it was too late. She had gone.

But for Malise, there was little time to brood over Neil. From breakfast, when she ate with a textbook propped up against the teapot, till midnight, she never seemed to stop. Jack was spending little or no time at the office in Dundee now, and she handled most of the work, often late into the night. There was a steady stream of people who came to the door. People who didn't have enough to eat, who were to be thrown out of their homes, or who, increasingly, owed more money than they could ever possibly pay to money-lenders. Suddenly, she found that all the work was bearing fruit, her practical experience of life complemented the legal knowledge she was gathering, and with it came confidence. Enough confidence to tell people what they ought to do. And to help them more than she had been able to before. Every question was logged down, and the party was gathering valuable information about the problems of Dundee. It came down to two things: there wasn't enough work, but, most of all, it was the slums.

Malise's year was split into the weeks before a visit to Alexander and then the weeks till the next visit. Now, each time she thought of Alexander, she thought also of Neil Fraser, with his eyes haunted by sadness. He wasn't the idealistic young man she had known. If only she could talk to him, make him realize that she understood him, make him smile again. But he wasn't at home for her spring visit, nor the summer one, when Alexander told her that he had been moved up two classes as he was so bright. As the watery summer faded into a chilly autumn, Malise was forced to admit that perhaps she had done the right thing. She didn't have enough time for herself, and Alexander needed Fraser money to get the education he deserved. But it didn't make the knowledge that he was moving away from her any easier. He no longer sounded like her Alexander, he sounded like a Fraser. But, despite asking her son about his father, she learned little of what he was doing. Except that he never smiled.

Her third year at university was now in full swing and with it came even more work. Malise saw little of Jessie; her world revolved around Jack, work and studying. How could she be so surrounded by people and still be lonely, she wondered, as she sat at the old table in the living room, writing an essay. Everyone needed her, but whom did she have? She looked at the mantelpiece. There was a photograph of herself, Gordon and Alexander. Gordon, the man who had always been there for her. The only person she had ever been able to tell her fears to, the only man who had helped her when she had no one. And how had she repaid him?

She walked over to the photograph and picked it up.

'I'm sorry, Gordon,' she said as she began to weep. 'I'm sorry, I never realized. I'm sorry that I was selfish and couldn't see you for who you were.' Tears were running freely down her face now. 'I'm so, so sorry.'

But even as she said the words, she found herself longing for someone else. Her soulmate, a man who had let down those he cared for as much as she had. The only man who had reached out to her. The one she had rejected.

As the New Year began, Malise found herself almost buried under her work, her studies and duties. Every Tuesday, she took her place in the Labour Party offices, to deal with problems, to organize marches she no longer bothered to go on, and to write speeches she never turned up to hear uttered.

But she was the backbone of the party, and she knew it.

As she spoke to the officers, she noticed that they were now treating her with a deference they hadn't displayed before. She wasn't sure why. Her clothes were smarter, but still second-hand and, increasingly, they would ask her opinion on a legal matter. She even smelt of flowers and fresh air, with shiny shoes and hands soft from liberal doses of hand cream. Whatever the reason, Malise accepted the respect she was now treated with. Because it had been a long time coming.

'Listen, everyone!' Billy walked into the office with some other union leaders just as Malise was putting on the kettle. 'All of you in here now.'

Malise followed him, bridling at the way he had commandeered Jack's office.

'I've just been over at the Chambers. Apparently the McPadden is closing, they're making the announcement tomorrow.'

'But that's seven hundred people,' Nobby Clarke replied in horror. 'All my family work at the McPadden, one of the best in the town.'

'Aye, which is why we have to be at all the works tomorrow for clocking in.' Billy gazed around. 'We have to get them all out, show Mr McPadden that we will not stand for it.'

'But a walkout, Billy?' Malise returned. 'How on earth will that help? Except to give some others a good reason for a lockout, or even more closures. You know—'

'Just because you made a mess of the one I trusted you to handle and which cost us the Elizabeth,' Billy snapped, 'don't think that the rest of us will do the same.'

'Please yourself, Billy.' She stood up. 'I'm going to see the people outside. You lot sit on your arses and work out what futile gesture you are going to make.' She left the room and pointed to the first man standing there, the smell of drink upon him.

'You, in there.' She opened the door to her little damp office. 'And if its money you're after, you've no chance, pal.'

She was just locking up at the end of the night when she heard footsteps coming up the stairs. It was Keith, Jessie's brother.

'What can I do for you, Keith?' she said as she closed the door behind her.

'It's Da,' he said thickly. 'He's died.'

It was a Catholic funeral, in St Mary's Church in Lochee. Malise sat at the front, next to Jessie and her mother, Keith and his fiancée sitting on Mrs Baker's other side. As she looked at the women, it was hard to see what they were thinking, as they were wearing thick black veils covering their faces. Even though she knew them, there was something frightening about the figures, the way they seemed to glide under the black. And it set her thinking.

'It was good of you to come, Malise,' Jessie said tearfully as they walked from Balgay cemetery, where Mr Baker had been interred. 'You being so busy an' all.'

'He was as much of a father to me as my own, Jessie.' Malise gripped her friend's hand tightly. 'And I'll never forget what you did for me.'

'I don't see you any more, not with this job,' Jessie replied. 'I miss you so much, Malise, life's not what I thought it would be.'

'No, Jessie,' she said sadly. 'Sometimes you just wonder if it's worth the fight.'

Instead of going home, Malise returned to the office and looked at the book of members. If she got the weavers and the communists involved too . . . She snapped the book shut purposefully. It was time for a visit to Mary Brockle-bank.

Mary lived not far from the Hilltown, where she was training as a maid on a government scheme to give the women of Dundee a new trade. She had never been a leader, but she had always been vociferous in her condemnation of the people who ran the works. And when it came to heckling, Mary could do it for Scotland.

'Aye.' The woman nodded as she heard Malise outline her plan over a cup of tea in the tiny parlour. 'I'll do it.'

'I don't want any trouble, Mary,' Malise warned. 'This is not a revolution. Just a way for Churchill and the rest to see what they are doing to the town.'

'My pleasure,' Mary replied. 'How many women do we need?'

'Between eight and ten, and tell each of them they need to find between four and ten. And everyone has to have someone they are able to mourn for, a brother or a husband, father or son. They need to be entitled to wear the black. And they must wear the veil.'

Mary frowned, her work-worn face creasing even more.

'But why don't I just get everyone?' She picked up the brown teapot and refilled both their cups.

'To stop us from being arrested for causing a disturbance. No one will want to touch a woman in mourning. Only we won't just be mourning our men, we will be mourning the death of Dundee's jute.'

'And where will we meet?' Mary said eagerly.

'Tell them there is a meeting to be held at the Con-federation of Jute Owners club two Sundays from now. Churchill will be speaking there. Let's show him that women can have armies too.'

*

That Sunday, as Neil went from church to the Con-
federation building for the garden party, he saw a large
amount of women walking the streets. All were dressed in
full black mourning. It was almost like a macabre costume
party.

Malise was itching to lift her veil and have a count of who
was there. But she couldn't. If she did, she might as well
have put a sign round her neck that said 'organizer'. All she
could see was women.

By the time Neil's car got to the gates of the building, he
was decidedly nervous. So many women, so many widows.
All silent, and all of them terrifying, like hovering vultures.
Waiting.

Malise and her party began to walk around the building.
She could see there were at least a hundred women, and the
police were looking on powerlessly, obviously unwilling to
touch a woman in mourning. A large black car drove up to
the gates and waited to be admitted. Suddenly, she raised
her hand, her black-gloved finger outstretched.

'Neil?' Agnes looked round in fear. 'What's happening?'

'I've no idea,' Neil replied.

'Think someone has just cursed you, sir,' Bruce replied
calmly. 'A widow's curse is terrible strong.'

Neil stared out of the car, but all he could see were black-
veiled figures. He could feel his heart tightening. This was
wrong, and it was unnerving. When he got inside, he could
see the worried expressions on the faces of the men. They
didn't like it.

'Gentlemen, Mr Churchill will be making his speech
now.' As the butler ushered them through, each man was
paying little attention to what was about to happen. All they
could think about were the women outside.

They went through to the garden, but as soon as Winston
began to speak, there came a low hum. There wasn't any
shouting, just a low hum.

'Gentlemen—'

'Father, forgive them, for they know not what they do.'

'I would like to thank you—'

'Father, forgive them, for they know not what they do.'

'For this opportunity—'

'Father, forgive them, for they know not what they do.'

'To speak to you—'

'Father, forgive them, for they know not what they do.'

Malise looked around; she hadn't intended for them to speak, it had just happened. Probably Mary or someone else in the crowd had started it, but it didn't matter. It was uttered like a prayer. Because what she had here were the widows of the Dundee jute. And they were making sure that the owners knew exactly what they thought of them.

'Father, forgive them, for they know not what they do.'

Churchill tried, but it was to no avail. Signalling to an aide, the men went inside, but the talk was not of international trade, it was of the black widows.

'Why are they demonstrating?' Churchill asked the assembled owners. The men all looked at each other.

'I think they are making a point about closures,' Neil spoke up clearly.

'And what are you doing to help these women, then?' The MP looked sternly at each of them in turn.

The men began to leave, each of the families getting into their cars and closing their eyes as they passed the now silent widows.

Malise watched them, praying that no one would get carried away and begin throwing stones. For this was just the beginning. Those who had closed down works were going to become very used to the sight of the black widows.

'Malise?' Jack said to her as soon as she walked into the office the next afternoon. 'The whole country is talking about what happened at the meeting.'

'What happened yesterday?' She brushed down her light-blue jumper. 'I must have missed it.'

'Two hundred widows marched on the Confederation, you should have informed me what you were going to do.'

'I didn't organize it,' she returned innocently. 'I mean, I went for a walk, it was a nice day. Didn't see anyone else, though.'

Jack threw down a copy of the *Glasgow Herald*.

'No one knows who is in charge,' she returned. 'In fact, some might say that it was just a coincidence. Just a gesture.'

'Well, you tell whoever it is that they can't stop now. In fact, going to each of the works in turn might be an idea,' Jack said, far too casually.

'I think you will find the owners' houses will be next,' she replied with a smile. 'Now why don't I put the kettle on?'

A few days later, Malise was sitting at home, working out where the women should demonstrate next. She had a list of the women she had talked to, and she would have to meet with Mary again and tell her where the next demonstration would be. But her preparations were interrupted by a persistent knocking on the door. She got up and opened it, to see Neil Fraser standing there, a look of fury on his face.

'What were you doing at the Confederation meeting?' he said as he pushed his way inside the hallway.

'Good evening, Mr Fraser,' she replied politely, hiding her pleasure at seeing him.

'You cannot accuse me of being the murderer of Dundee,' he continued. 'I've always been a fair employer.'

'You've always been the same as all the rest,' she returned mockingly. 'Don't give yourself credit for being better. You're despised in this city no less than the others.'

'You upset my family,' he continued.

'When you halved the Elizabeth's workforce, you upset a lot of families, Mr Fraser,' she answered quickly. 'So don't take it personally. It was only politics.'

Neil stopped dead in his tracks. He hadn't expected her to say that. He hadn't expected her to be so ambivalent about it. The way a politician would be.

'I want to meet those women,' he said eventually.

'Why?' Malise considered him. She had got to him, the way she had before. The way she always did.

'I don't know.' He stared at the lines of books that covered one of the walls, this wasn't the house of a mill lass, and it had an echo that was very like his own. 'But I do.'

She smiled softly, and for a second Neil was entranced by how alike the mother and son were.

'Trying to understand another point of view?' She laughed wryly. 'Nine o'clock tomorrow night,' She gestured to the door. 'But be careful, I'll make a man of you.'

As he left, Malise went back to her work. This was a chance to make a real difference, she had the ear of someone who mattered. She picked up her pen and chewed the lid. If he wanted to see some victims, she would let him. Victims hand-picked by her.

At nine o'clock precisely the next evening, there was a knock on Malise's door. Neil was standing there, wearing an overcoat, not new, but obviously expensive. He was trying to blend in, but there could be no mistaking his wealth. He sweated it.

'Good evening,' Neil said politely.

'Come on.' Malise smiled, and picked up her coat and hat. 'Time to begin your education, Mr Fraser. Been a long time coming.'

They walked out on to Lochee Road; it was mild for February and there was a soft persistent drizzle.

'My car is just outside,' he said as he pulled his collar against the wet air.

'Oh no, if you want to experience life in Dundee, Mr Fraser, you must use what most people here use. Shank's pony.' She gestured with her head. 'First stop not far from here.'

They walked round the side of the Law until they came to the Hilltown. There they headed down towards the Well-gate. The high buildings framing the slope were windowless, like a prison.

'This way.' She ducked her head and went into a small covered passageway, the cobbles slick with the waste of the hundreds of people who lived there. Neil put his handkerchief over his nose as the sharp smell of urine pierced his nostrils. They slid over the dark stone until they came to a courtyard. Around each side were open walkways, most with a few pieces of washing strung on lines.

'Up the stairs to the third floor,' she said cheerfully. 'And you know what that means.'

'Mr Fraser.' The elderly woman bowed her head as he arrived at the door. 'Please come in.'

Neil walked into the tiny room. There was an overwhelming smell of vinegar in the darkness, failing to conceal the sweet smell of the damp which seemed to pervade everything, including the woman.

'It's what we use for cleaning,' Malise whispered.

'Sit down.' The woman gestured to a single small wooden seat, the only furniture she had apart from a narrow pull-down bed that was stacked against the wall. 'A cup of tea?'

'No.' Neil shook his head.

'We'd love one.' Malise glared at Neil's impoliteness.

'So how are you, Mrs Briggs?' she said as the woman took the kettle from the stove and warmed a small metal teapot.

'Fine. My bones, you know, but it doesn't come alone, does it?' She smiled brightly.

'What doesn't?' Neil said curiously.

'Old age. Fifty, I am now.'

Neil looked at the woman, her small back hunched. She looked well into her sixties.

'Oh I know, Mr Fraser,' she replied mildly. 'You took me for someone much older. Used to work for you, in the Elizabeth. I was a spinner, one of the best. Started when I was thirteen as a half-timer and now, well, since it closed I've had to go on the parish.' She began to cough.

'Are you all right?' He started to stand up, conscious he was sitting on the only chair.

'Consumption.' The woman took out a rag and wiped her mouth, coughing into it. 'Same as everyone else.'

'Worked together for four years, didn't we?' Malise murmured.

Mrs Briggs nodded through her coughing.

'This lass was the best thing that ever happened to your works, Mr Fraser,' she said earnestly. 'Though she'll not thank me for saying it.'

'Peter not here?' Malise interrupted the testimony.

'My Peter lives with me.' Mrs Briggs waited for a moment. 'He's gone out, didn't want to see you. He hasn't worked since he was eighteen. You sack the men you know, when they come of age, as you have to pay them men's money. They turned him down for the Black Watch; he'd have been all right in that. But he couldn't pass the medical.'

'When you work in the mills, all the pieces of jute get into your lungs and congest them,' Malise added gently. 'That's why disease is so common in adults here. Our lungs have scratches on them, and that makes disease easy to get in.'

'And your husband?' Neil ventured.

'He died at Loos. Gassed. Didn't manage to escape like you.'

'Trying to shock me, Malise?' Neil said as they walked out and along the plettie till they were back at the stairwell.

'Actually, Neil,' she consciously used his first name. 'I was starting you off easy. The people who live higher up have better housing. It's the ones who live in the basement that have the worst time of it. That's where we're going now.'

'Hello, Jenny!' She craned into the dark of the room, as the front door swung open. 'Are they all asleep?'

The emaciated young woman nodded, but as they came closer, she shielded her face with her hands. But there was no mistaking the ulcerated sores on the sallow skin of her face, the redness of her nose, and the shaking of her hands, which were little more than skin-covered bones.

'This is Jenny, the sole breadwinner for her family.' Huddled like nesting rats under the fading light of a single dim lamp were the infested bodies of almost a dozen children.

'You have all these?' Neil said incredulously.

'They're my brother and sisters, those two on the end, they're mine and then some of the younger ones, they were my da's second family. After my ma died, he didn't want to make his own dinner, so he took up with Edie Smellie.'

'And where is she now?' Neil put his hand up to his face to stay away the stench of the bodies.

'She ran off.'

'Here, Jenny.' Malise sat down next to her and took out a small bottle from her bag. 'That shilling doctor is getting more expensive by the day.' She took out a few bruised apples, she had picked up at the market. 'And these still have a bit of life in them.'

'I went to school with Malise, we was friends.' Jenny turned to Neil and he saw the lesions on her face. 'She fell out with me over—'

'Johnnie Turpin.' Malise laughed to herself. 'Those were the days. I still see a lot of Jessie Baker, you know.'

'Wasn't her brother sweet on you?' Jenny looked her up and down. 'Till you got spoiled and—'

'Spoiled?' Neil looked at her.

'Difficult to hide being pregnant in a tenement.' She met his gaze and held it.

'Not here.' He glanced at the young woman.

'Jenny here knows the score. She got spoiled by Johnnie Turpin, his boy's the big one over there. Ended up on the streets, earning the way you have to earn.'

'Had a touch today,' Jenny said quietly. 'There's an orange boat in from Seville and the Spanish are a dirty lot.'

'You're a prostitute?' Neil looked at her in disgust. Who would want to sleep with someone who was so obviously syphilitic?

'How else am I supposed to feed all these? They'd be

taken away by the parish otherwise. My da sent me out to work, he got good money for me, but then I fell sick.' She was so matter-of-fact about it, that Neil was finding it difficult to believe what he was hearing.

'And where is your father now?' Neil said, trying to keep his voice calm.

'He died of the Spanish flu.' She took hold of Malise's hand and squeezed it. 'And I know you'll say why didn't I give up my wicked ways then.' She laughed shortly. 'I couldn't. By then I'd had a spell in Perth for it, and everyone knew what I was and even if there were jobs around here, no one would want me. Then I got sick and there's no point in stopping now, is there?'

'What will happen to the children when she dies?' Neil said as they walked out on to the plettie, trying to get some air into their lungs.

'They'll go to the parish; the girls will be taken to train as domestics and the boys sent to live on farms.'

'Better life than this,' he remarked.

'Of course they'll never see each other again, they'll be given new names, and if the boys are strong, they'll be sent to Australia to work.' She looked at him keenly. 'Still sound ideal?'

'At least their father isn't selling them into prostitution,' he replied.

'Yes.' Her voice became a little harder. 'I suppose I'm lucky that my da didn't force me to do the same, when some man spoiled me. I am so lucky that he just got himself killed.'

'You would never have done that!' Neil snapped.

'If he had made me, what choice would I have had?' She shook her head. 'You know, we have morals too. Ones we can afford. And once a girl has a bastard in her belly, no decent man will want to touch her. No decent place will employ her. And she has to earn her keep. Of course I would have done it, till I caught the pox and died.'

'I gave you money. You signed for it.'

'I never signed an affidavit, Taylor tricked me into that. And he took all my money and whatever you gave me. Moot point now, though; you won him, the way you always win. By being richer.' Her chin jutted out angrily. 'I'm wasting my time tonight. You just don't believe your eyes, do you?'

'Here.' He took out his wallet and handed her a note. 'Buy something for those children.'

She pushed it away with her hand.

'Oh no, Mr Fraser,' she said easily. 'This isn't something you can buy away with a pound.' She gestured with her head. 'Now we're going to see someone who remembers you as a child. A cheeky wee monkey, by all accounts. One of your old housemaids. Lives here now.'

It was almost midnight as they walked back to Malise's home.

'I don't think I'll ever forget what I saw tonight,' he said slowly.

'Och, away with yourself, you'll manage to put it behind you.' Her smile was caustic. 'You'll go back to that state of blindness that everyone born like you manages to have.'

'What do you mean?'

'Your fortune has been built on those people's graves, Neil Fraser.' She looked up at him from the light of the street lamp. 'That great house of yours is a mausoleum, a monument to workers dead from the diseases they caught in lungs weakened from your factories, and to dead children in that sewer of a tenement.'

'I have never exploited anyone in that way,' he said quickly. 'Never.'

'You own the land we went to, Mr Fraser,' she said shortly. 'That place, where you ruined your shoes on the dirt of the people, where you couldn't breathe because the air had already been used by a thousand other people, is owned by a holding company, owned by an investment company, owned by Richard and Neil Fraser!'

Neil staggered back, it couldn't be true. It just couldn't.
'You're lying.'

She reached into her bag and took out a document.

'The Land Registry entry,' she said simply. 'Think of
that, when you are looking at your dividend, your director's
salary. Remember whose mouths you have taken the food
out of and what you have given them in return.'

'What can I do?' He looked over at her, searching for a
lifeline.

'Pulling it down and building a better one did come
to mind,' Malise replied. 'But you're a businessman, not a
socialist. So you'll probably learn to live with the guilt. Ask
your father, he seems to thrive on it.' They had reached her
street.

Neil leaned back against the wall. He could still smell the
tenement; it clung to his clothes, to his money. To his name.

'Sleep well, Mr Fraser.'

'You know I won't.' He took a deep breath.

'That's what I'm hoping.'

Chapter 12

'Absolutely out of the question, Neil,' Richard said when he asked him about the tenement a few days later as they sat in Richard's great granite-tomb of a house. 'We have our investors to think about.'

'But if you had gone there, looked at what we make people live in, you'd understand that we cannot allow this situation to continue. We must do something about it.'

'You are measuring it against where you live, Neil,' Richard returned loftily. 'These people, if they are so unhappy, why don't they find someplace else? Because they are happy to live on charity handouts and to drink their lives away while you and I provide them with the bare minimum.'

'Father, I cannot allow myself to profit from that place!' Neil stood up.

'Are you turning into a socialist?' Richard asked testily. 'If it means that much to you, then go and speak to the City Engineers, see what they suggest.'

'That I will.' And with that, Neil stormed out. Where would he find an ally in all this?

'You have to help me.' He had arrived at her door as she was just about to go out for her weekly bath.

'Help you do what?' She put down her towel on the little table and turned up the oil lamp that lay next to it.

'Help me change things.' He put a hand on her arm. 'Please.'

Malise smiled in the darkness as she went to trim the lamp. It had worked.

She ushered him into the armchair, and got out the bottle of wine that Jack had bought her for Christmas. She had never had anyone to drink it with. Then she picked up her pen and notepad.

'Tell me what happened?'

She sat and listened as Neil went through the dilemma.

'I can't pull it down, I have a responsibility to my investors which I cannot discharge, and, according to the engineers, the drains in that area just cannot cope with the amount of people who live there.'

Malise sat back in her chair and pondered the problem. It seemed insurmountable, but there had to be a way they could do it. There had to be a way.

Neil savoured the wine, it was a good one, one that someone who knew these things would choose. Yet she hadn't bought it, and the knowledge disturbed him.

He considered her over the warm, soft lamplight. He could stare at her all night and not tire of her, the angles and planes of her face which was so like Alexander's. The way she chewed her lip and was playing with a curled strand of hair. But she seemed so quiet, so thoughtful, so unlike herself. He laughed.

'What's funny?' Malise looked round as an ember from the fire fell out of the grate, hissing on the slate.

'Something tickled me, that's all,' he said lightly.

'Are you suggesting I have fleas in my house?' she replied, outraged. 'I have candles to stop them. Regularly.'

'No, just the way you are sitting.' He shook his head to get rid of the laughter. 'You look so like Mackenzie, like that.'

'Mackenzie?'

'My solicitor.'

'This time next year I'll be one. The party are putting me through university.' She screwed up her face at him. 'That make you feel better?'

'Much better.' He grinned. 'More like my Malise.'

'But I'm not your Malise, Mr Fraser.'

'Yes, you are, Malise. And don't you think it's about time

you called me Neil?' There was something about her that was absolutely fascinating.

'I don't know about that,' she returned wryly. 'It's too short a name for when I'm angry at you.'

'Do you get angry a lot?'

'You could say, Neil Fraser, that you possess the capacity to rouse emotion in me.' She pressed her lips together to stop herself from saying more.

'As I am sure you are aware, you do the same to me.' He reached over and took her hand. 'Many, many emotions.'

Malise looked down at their hands, their fingers had become entwined.

'I don't know if I can solve your problem.' She kept her eyes on the fingers, his long, strong fingers. In their own way, they were so beautiful. It had been so many years since she had thought of Neil like this, but how quickly it came back to her. As soon as he had reached for her. 'I think you need something I can't give you.' She lifted her eyes to his, willing him to pull away, not to do this, not to complicate things with emotions she was frightened of feeling again. She couldn't let him use her again.

'Help me,' he murmured. She pulled her hand away and walked over to him, crouching at the side of his chair till their faces were level.

'I know you're a good man, Neil.' She put her hand on his forearm, forcing her fingers not to stroke the soft wool of his suit. 'Now be a great one. Change the way you do your business, it'll cost you, but you'll reap the benefits in the end.'

'I need you,' he said in her ear. 'You understand me.'

She looked up at him, his face was barely inches from hers and she could see it: the pain, the regret, everything that he had thought about himself had been torn down. He was telling her the truth.

He kissed her, in the half-light, in the silence. He kissed her desperately, as if she were the only one who could save him, and she kissed him back.

'I love you, Malise,' he said, and she was lost. Because she knew whatever happened, it happened because he loved her. As much as she loved him.

She felt his hand, on cotton then on skin. Then he took her hand, and led her to her bedroom. They lay in bed for hours, touching, talking, and making love. It was almost as if they had escaped who they were, what they were. And they were finally being given a chance to be themselves. Not the jute baron and the socialist, just Neil and Malise. Just two people who had waited for years to do this.

'I don't want to go,' he said as they lay together, wrapped in each other's arms. 'I just want to stay here with you. For ever.' He kissed her head. 'But—'

'Don't say it,' Malise whispered. 'Just go. And come back again.' She watched as he dressed, it was exquisite and painful at the same time. Like watching her husband getting ready to go off to work, already looking forward to his return.

'Tomorrow, after work.' He sat on the bed and stroked the soft skin on her face. 'I don't want to waste another moment.'

As he left, Malise lay back in bed. He loved her, someone loved her. Why had it taken so long for them to realize it?

He was waiting for her as she left the office that afternoon, and they drove out into the country. And talked. She told him of her life, and he told her of his. And over the weeks that followed, as they walked through windswept country lanes or sat in small tea shops together, Malise felt a contentment that she had never known. At last someone loved her for herself.

They slipped into a pattern – of visits to a quiet little restaurant in Arbroath or Barnhill, followed by nights spent in each other's arms in a boarding house. And Malise loved it; there were no politics, no visitors to intrude in the little world they shared. The only people in it were Neil and herself.

*

'Come on, you've worked hard enough,' Jack said as they filed away a list of papers detailing the medical complaints of ex-soldiers. 'Let me take you for a cup of tea.'

Malise sighed.

'That would be lovely.'

They walked up towards the town, past the Pillars.

'Looks like a Jute Owners dinner,' Jack said as they passed a car that stopped outside the Town Hall and some elderly men alighted. 'No doubt they will be congratulating themselves on another factory built in Calcutta.'

'Aye.' Malise shook her head sadly. 'And we can do nothing but watch.'

'Oh, don't be disheartened,' Jack consoled her and tucked her hand through the crook of his arm. 'Your time will come.'

Another car stopped and more suited men came out, the women dripping in furs against the harsh spring wind. Then another. Out of it stepped Neil Fraser and a woman who looked as if she had been freshly dug up from the Howff cemetery. Her skin was grey and her hair thin, and even through the coat, Malise could see the lack of flesh on her. Malise gasped and put her hand to her mouth. And he turned. He looked at her, his eyes full of longing. Then he turned back to the woman and ushered her into the hall.

'Come on, I've no appetite to stare at them,' Jack said quietly. 'Though with a wife like that, it's little wonder that Fraser has acquired the reputation he has.'

'Reputation?' Malise said faintly.

'I have it from reliable sources that the man falls in love every month with a different woman. Mainly dancers, but he's not too choosy. Generous, though.' He gently but firmly moved her away. But Malise couldn't think of anything except that one forgotten detail. Neil Fraser had a wife.

'Where is it?' Agnes rifled through the bottles and flasks on her dressing table, trying to find the bottle of laudanum that she now relied upon, every waking moment of the day. But as powder and lotions spilled like cake mixture over the fine finish, her fingers grew more desperate. She had to have some, but the bottle was nowhere to be found. He had taken it, her mind reached desperately for someone to blame, and came upon the usual suspect: Neil.

Leaving a trail of scent and make-up behind her, Agnes rushed into Neil's dressing room. The polished wood had few items on it, just a photograph of the family and the hair oil he used. She opened a drawer, but it was full of socks. The next simply had his underwear in it. Then her fingers found a box. A jeweller's box, the name in gold on the lid. Opening it, she stopped as she saw an ornate gold locket. He had bought her a gift!

Skilfully, Agnes took out the locket and tried it against her long thin neck and admired herself in the mirror. It had been so long since Neil had bought her anything, as he wasn't one for love tokens. She smiled. He must have known he had been neglecting her. As she fingered it, she felt the groove of engraving on the back. Curiously, she turned it over to see what was written. *My Malise.*

And Agnes felt the need for laudanum even greater.

'I have invited my father for dinner,' Neil said as he walked into the hallway that evening and took off his coat. 'Please try to make some conversation with him.'

'You ought to have invited your Malise,' Agnes returned shrewishly. 'Since you enjoy her company so much.'

'I have no idea who you are talking about, my dear,' Neil returned sharply.

Agnes took the box from her pocket and threw it at him with all her might. 'You are having a sordid liaison with that Malise!' she shrieked, just as Richard walked in.

'What the devil is going on?' he said as Agnes pushed past him and ran upstairs.

Both men walked through the hallway and into the drawing room where the fire burned merrily, all the lights lit in welcome. Neil walked over to the drinks table and stood, examining the decanters as he awaited his father's opinion.

'My wife thinks I am having an affair with someone called Malise.'

A stern expression came over Richard's face as father and son faced each other in the sumptuous room.

'And are you?' Richard said sternly.

'Yes.' Neil poured himself a drink.

Richard's face darkened.

'Have you any idea of the scandal this could cause? How much does she know about our business?' Suddenly, it was as if a curtain was lifted in Richard's mind. 'And I suppose she has nothing to do with your sudden conversion to socialist ideals?'

'She showed me where we made our money.' Neil downed his whisky in one gulp. 'And I'm going to divorce Agnes and marry her as soon as I possibly can.'

'I will not have the scandal of a divorce visited on my family!' Richard exploded. 'You will not let your family down in this way.'

'I don't love Agnes. I've never loved Agnes. What kind of a marriage is this?' Neil raised his hands. 'The woman is a drug addict, we haven't had any kind of relations for years. She refuses to sleep with me. And I want more.'

'Think what would come out in court, Neil,' Richard said suddenly. 'Alexander's parentage would be laid open for all. There is no way Briar would consider allowing his daughter to be divorced. And he holds great sway in this town. He knows where our skeletons are buried.'

'But what can I do?' Neil said in an exasperated voice.

'I think we need to construct a case, a watertight case, for your marriage being dissolved. Agnes's health and state of mind . . . we will have doctors' reports, then I will go to Briar. Tell him that he must agree to Agnes divorcing you, or you will have her committed.'

'Why should she be used like this?' Neil returned. 'I want free of her, but I don't want to destroy her.'

'I know Briar; there is no other way.' Richard looked at his son, and his face softened. 'I'm not blind, Neil. I know you are unhappy, but can't you just consider putting the girl up in a quiet house?'

'No, I want to marry her. Have more children. Be a family.'

Richard walked over to Neil, his manner bullish, but as he considered his son's quiet determination, something inside him changed.

'She's from the lowest folk in Dundee. She worked for us, for God's sake!' Richard exhaled heavily. 'She could have run the Elizabeth, she was a very trustworthy girl. Attractive girl. And you breed well together.' He was silent for a moment.

'I love her, and I'll be with her whether you want me to or not,' Neil warned.

'Then you have no option than have the doctor see Agnes. And in the meantime, I suggest you mend your bridges with Agnes. Deny, deny and deny again.'

'We don't even sleep in the same room.'

'Then start.' Richard turned on his heels and walked out.

'Agnes?' Neil walked into her bedroom that night. 'Agnes, I have to explain.'

'You've a mistress,' she said disdainfully. 'Have you any idea how disgusting that is?'

'No.' He sat down on her bed. 'I've been doing some work on one of our properties. Mrs Scott has connections in the socialist movement and she has been helping me.'

'You've been visiting her. You're never at home.'

'To look at ways I can improve the lot of the people who live in my property.' He put his hands on her skinny shoulders. 'Mrs Scott will confirm this.'

'You bought her presents.'

'Her husband is an invalid, it's from him for her birthday.' He laughed. 'I want you, Agnes. But you've been ill and I couldn't force my affections on you. You're too delicate.' He closed his eyes and kissed her cold, thin lips. 'You've no idea the self-control it takes to know you are lying next door and I can't touch you.'

Agnes looked up at him. He was so sincere, and the thought of him betraying his marriage vows was suddenly unthinkable.

'Perhaps I have been remiss in my wifely duties,' she said slowly. Then she took his hand and put it on her flat, boyish chest. 'Perhaps I shouldn't have avoided your advances.'

Neil closed his eyes as he moved on top of her. To do his duty.

Afterwards, Agnes scurried off to the bathroom to wash every last trace of him from her body. It had been so awful, she had closed her eyes and pretended that she was somewhere else. She shuddered. How could anyone possibly enjoy doing such a degrading thing?

'For you.' Neil was lying in bed with Malise after another snatched hour away from the world.

Malise took the slightly dented box.

'I don't want any gifts, Neil,' she said softly. 'I don't want you to buy me things. It makes me feel beholden to you.'

'I like buying you things.' He opened the box. 'Isn't it lovely?'

'It's beautiful,' she breathed. Then she turned it over.

'That's what you are,' he said his eyes twinkling. 'It's what you've always been.' He lay back in the bed. 'I want to buy you a home, somewhere we can be together. You can give up studying and just be there for me.' He looked around. 'Get you out of here.'

'What about what I want?' she said in disbelief.

'You want to be with me,' he answered mildly. 'If there was any other way—'

'Neil, there is never any other way, only the one that suits you.' She sat up.

'I've decided what to do about that horrible place in the Hilltown,' he added defensively. 'I'm making a charitable donation to the Corporation. I'm giving the building to the city.'

'And no doubt claiming a large amount of tax relief in the process,' she returned.

'Malise, you don't understand.' He put his hand on her shoulder.

'How could I? I don't know how to use people the way you do.' She scrambled out of bed and wrapped her dressing gown around her. 'I can't believe you expect me to give up everything and sit in a house you've bought, wondering when you'll visit me next.'

'Malise, if we were caught just now it would be disastrous. I'm not a free man.'

'Believe me, Neil, it would ruin every one of my ambitions too.' She stared at him incredulously. 'What we are doing will destroy everything I have worked for since I was a child. Everything my father wanted for me.'

'What do you mean?'

'Who do I work for, Neil? Your enemy. I'm a member of the Independent Labour Party and they're the ones who have paid for me to go to university. And when the election comes, I'm going to take the seat from Churchill. I can't have a bidey-in who is a jute baron!'

Neil was completely dumbstruck.

'But you'll never do that!' he said immediately. 'You can't beat Churchill.'

'Can't I?' She tied the cord around the candlewick dressing gown 'Who got the women of Dundee out when the McPadden was going to close? Who persuaded you to do something about your tenements?' Her voice tailed off.

Neil smiled fondly at her and held out his hands.

'All right, you've proved your point.' He tossed his head in the direction of the bed. 'We both need to be careful.'

'It's not just that.' She bit her lip.

'So what is it now?' he asked with more than a hint of impatience.

'You're married,' she answered simply. 'I disgust myself,

falling into your arms. You belong to someone else, and if anyone were to find out, you would go into your home, close your gates, and leave me to suffer the consequences.'

'You don't understand,' Neil tried.

'You did it before and you'd do it again.'

Neil looked down at the bed. Then he stood up and began to dress. As he put on his suit, his demeanour changed, he became more sombre as he moved back into his own world. And away from hers.

'I don't love her,' he said simply. 'But you're absolutely correct. I am duty-bound to protect my family name from scandal. Something you have been mercifully free from.'

Malise laughed bitterly.

'To protect my good name I had to marry a man old enough to be my grandfather, a man who could do anything he liked to me. And I had to let him. You might not love your wife, Mr Fraser, but when you have touched her, does she leave you feeling defiled? Because that's what Gordon Scott did to me – the man I had to marry when you left me alone and pregnant.'

Neil looked away. 'I love you.' He said the words in a flat tone, as if he were asking for something in a shop. 'I've thought about you for years. You're the only woman I've ever wanted. But I can't leave her. Not yet.'

'Well, it's ironic that I'm the one woman you can't have then, isn't it, Mr Fraser? The one thing that, despite your money, your esteemed status, you can't buy? That'll make you want me even more.'

They walked to the front door and she opened it.

'I want you because of the woman you are, Malise,' he said softly. 'This isn't the idle whim of a spoiled child.'

'Wish me luck for tomorrow,' she said suddenly. 'It's my graduation. I'm starting in a practice in Union Street next week. It's a new beginning for me.'

'Please, Malise,' he murmured urgently. 'I don't want to have to watch you rise and not be a part of it.'

'You've dragged me down so many times, and each time

I've gone willingly. Not any more. This time, if you want me, you sacrifice your name and marry me. Divorce Agnes and you and Alexander and I can be together. Have more children. Be a family. I'll give up my fight for election for you, but only if you will give up your respectability and endure the shame of a divorce.'

He started to speak, but she shook her head.

'That is my final offer. No negotiation. All or nothing now.' She closed the door behind him and left him to make his own way home in the dark night.

It was a bright, sunny day as Malise graduated with her degree in Law. Despite her best efforts, Jessie was unable to have the day off, so she went alone to her ceremony, with only Jack meeting her afterwards for a sherry in the grounds.

'So, you are a solicitor now,' Jack said as he proudly stood next to her. 'Well, almost.'

'But at least I have a partnership to work for. While I'm studying for my certificate.' She nodded a thanks to Gideon.

'A fine crop of people this year. Although not well inclined to rise for my nine o'clock tutorials,' Gideon added. 'I've heard the senior partner at your practice is an excellent chap.'

'Aren't you the senior partner, Gideon?' Jack said teasingly.

Malise turned and looked at the mists of people in cloaks and gowns, standing with their families. While she was alone. What would her father have said if he could only see her, she wondered. And Gordon? She would never have done it without his support. She would do well, for them. But most of all, she would do it for herself.

Neil sat in his office, reliving the events of the previous night. He wouldn't let her go, couldn't let her go. It would only take a few months, but now he had Malise, he didn't want to give up a single moment with her. If only he could explain to Malise that he would marry her, but that she would have to be patient. There was a risk that certain details about Alexander would come out, and that would ruin Malise's career – both as a solicitor and as a politician. He had a choice: he could explain the truth to her, or he could take his father's advice and pressurize the Briars into agreeing for a divorce. Then, once he was free, they would be together. He wouldn't burden her with his problems, he decided. He would sort this out on his own. It was only the solution that mattered.

'You're what!'. Neil said in horror as Agnes sat stiffly staring in front of her.

'I'm pregnant,' she said awkwardly, as if she was ashamed of the fact.

'You can't be,' he said in disbelief. 'When is it due?'

'March,' she said softly. 'When the doctor you insisted on me seeing examined me, he told me that I was with child.' She stared up at him accusingly. 'You insisted that we sleep together, Neil. And now look what's happened. I could die, you know, and what if the same thing happens again?'

Neil turned away. How could she have let it happen to her? They had slept together only a handful of times. How could he possibly divorce her now?

It was almost a month later that Malise attended the large house in Perth Road for her visit with Alexander. She had tried not to think of Neil, tried not to feel the bitter taste of disappointment that he hadn't given up Agnes for her. Hadn't even contacted her.

'Want to know a secret?' Alexander said as they attempted a crossword together. 'I'm going to have a brother. Or a sister. Father hasn't decided yet.'

'When?' Her voice was shaking, she could hear it.

'Next year,' he said. 'We can ask Father.'

'Let's leave it,' Malise said softly. 'And do our crossword.'

As Neil walked into the room to collect his son, Malise nodded to him.

'I believe congratulations are in order, Mr Fraser,' she said nervously. 'My son informs me that he is to have a sibling.'

Neil nodded silently.

'It's good to see such a devoted family.' She stood up and kissed Alexander. 'You take care of yourself till next time.'

'I miss you,' Neil said. He put a hand on her shoulder to stop her from going.

'You seem to have found a way to occupy yourself.' She pulled herself away from him and walked out, feeling his eyes boring into her back, but resolved not to look behind her. Ever again.

'She ought to stop using those sedatives,' Richard said to Neil as they enjoyed an evening brandy after the visit. 'It can't be good for the child.'

'I spoke to the doctor,' Neil replied. 'He won't renew her prescription until she has given birth.' He looked down for a moment. 'I've hidden the ones she still has, but she'll turn the house upside down to find them. She may have more hidden away.'

Richard gave a sigh.

'Let's hope the child takes after you and ends up like Alexander, rather than takes after her and ends up like Euan.'

'Don't say a word against Euan,' Neil sprang to his son's defence. 'He'd have done better if we'd tried to teach him.' But Richard's words had started his mind working. Could Agnes's powders harm the child?

Neil returned to the house; Agnes wasn't waiting for them.

'She is unwell, sir.' Adams helped him off with his coat.

'She's always unwell,' Neil snapped. 'Get me a whisky.'

As Agnes slept a sound, drug-induced sleep, Neil paced up and down in the drawing room. He would not be so weak as to go and see her. He would not . . .

*

'Stuck doing those awful land searches?' Anthony Baillie, who had just gained his certificate, came in and sat on her desk. 'I hated this office, I think it's just a broom cupboard with a desk in it.'

Malise laughed at the young man, his thick glasses glinting in the dusty sunlight.

'Well, you might be right.' She looked around; there wasn't enough room to move much in the office, the desk and obligatory case of legal books took up all the space. 'But I like the light.' She gestured to the large window that looked out on to the busy street. 'What are you working on, then?'

'Two brothers, fighting over a warehouse in Brown Constable Street. One of them has a signed affidavit, stating that the other relinquishes all rights to the property, but the other, the one we are representing, states that he never signed anything of the sort.'

Malise's heart skipped a beat. It was a familiar tale.

'So of course, we need to prove that it wasn't signed by our client. Luckily he had a ticket for a train to Aberdeen on that day, so we may be able to have it thrown out.'

'Because he couldn't get to a notary on the day!' she exclaimed triumphantly.

'It's not that complicated,' Anthony replied. But Malise was smiling to herself. Suddenly she had a way of getting Alexander back.

That night, she sat down and thought about how she could do it. She would begin her investigations, then after the election had been fought, she would put in papers. That way she wouldn't jeopardize her chances, but she would get her son back. Even if it meant having Jessie or Mrs Baker sign an affidavit. She would fight them with their own weapons.

'They've called the election!' It was a wet autumn Tuesday and a busy night for the party officers on duty. Malise turned to see Jack walking in with some of the other members, including a smirking Billy Turpin. Malise suppressed a smile. Billy was about to get his due. 'Everyone in the back office now, please.'

'So has the party decided who will stand for them?' Billy asked as he sat down in the chair and stretched his legs out confidently.

'Yes, Billy.' Jack scanned the faces of Billy, Eric, Manny and Malise. 'We need someone with the respect of the Dundee electorate.'

Billy's grin broadened.

'And as we know, this is the first election that will allow married women of a certain age to vote in it. The men of Dundee are not enthusiastic voters, but we now have a large population of females with no particular loyalty, no traditional allegiances.'

'Except to the union,' Billy prompted.

'Which is why Mrs Scott will be standing for us.' He looked at Malise out of the corner of his eye. 'She was a suffragette, a unionist, a weaver, is female, and now she's a solicitor. Well done, Malise.' He walked over and hugged her.

Malise could feel herself begin to shake. This was like a dream come true, the culmination of all her years' work. It was official.

'What!' Billy was outraged. 'But she's hardly a unionist now.'

'She's the key, Billy.' Jack put his arm around Malise proudly. 'Malise is the key to winning Dundee. Without her, the women won't know who to vote for, so they will go for the familiar. Winston Churchill.'

'Oh come on, Billy.' Malise moved away from Jack and walked towards him. 'We've got so much history. Fought together for years.' She held out her hand. Billy walked out.

'The fight has begun,' Jack intoned. 'Do you have the stomach for it?'

'Certainly do,' she said with quiet pride. 'Gabriel and Gordon taught me well.'

*

Every day, as Agnes sat at home, she seemed to grow larger, the baby enormous against her small frame. Every night she still went to sleep with her powders, waking dull and depressed the next day. But she continued to use them, the peace and contentment they gave her was such a relief from the life she lived in. There she hadn't failed, there she was cherished, there she never had to face the bored indifference that the Frasers showed her. But one day, as she lay in her half-life, Agnes became vaguely aware of a pulling in her stomach. It was too much effort to look, so she continued to lie on the chaise longue in her bedroom. She glanced spiritlessly in the mirror, but her sedated mind couldn't focus on the dark stain that was spreading all over her dress. She felt a pain, and through the warmth of her dream she felt her body push and push, as she reached for the bottle once more. Something was wrong, but she couldn't concentrate enough to understand. Agnes felt a give and then relief. She laid back her head and closed her eyes, drifting off into the warmth.

Almost an hour later, Anne, the senior housemaid, came in to ask her if she wished a cup of tea. But as she approached the woman and saw the blood on her dress, she began to scream.

As soon as he received the phone call, Neil felt his stomach churn. Agnes had been taken to hospital, and was about to die. There was no hope in the doctor's voice, she had lost too much blood. Neil arrived at the hospital just as the doctor walked from Agnes's room.

'Mr Fraser,' his expression was grim and set, 'I am sorry. There was nothing—'

'The child?'

'Far too young to survive; barely five months old.' He exhaled deeply, then looked at the man. 'She had been warned about using laudanum in her condition. This is a regretfully common occurrence.' He opened the door and Neil walked in.

Agnes was lying there; she looked peaceful. Almost content.

'Rest in peace, Agnes,' he murmured as he stroked her waxy skin. 'You're free from me now.'

He returned to his home, the cold, pale granite shining in the late evening sunlight. He walked through the carefully manicured gardens, the wind rustling through the tops of the trees. Agnes was gone, someone who only that morning had been a mere irritation. Now she was a victim. A victim of her suitability, a victim of his. He'd hardly talked to her, he'd been complicit in her laudanum use. And another child had died as a result.

'I'm sorry, Agnes,' he said aloud to the stars. 'You deserved better.'

Neil looked at the election notice posted on the wall in Barrack Street. It was an invitation to hear Malise Scott, Independent Labour Party candidate. His hand reached out and touched her name before he walked away and headed for his club. It was too late.

'Quite a surprise to see who Winston's up against,' Mackenzie said as he walked over to Neil and sat in his customary chair by the window.

'Not really,' Neil replied. 'Not if you knew her.'

'But what would our parsimonious electorate say, Neil,' Mackenzie continued. 'If they knew in what sense you knew her?'

Neil looked at the solicitor with barely concealed disgust.

'If I even suspected that a rumour had been started by someone betraying a professional confidence, Mackenzie,' he said coldly, 'then I would ensure that every business between Aberdeen and Hawick was made aware of it.'

'She's already got one vote, then,' Mackenzie returned as Neil put down his glass and walked out.

The grimy, sweat-stained man smiled grimly at the notice

pinned up outside the tenement. There was her name, bold as brass. Well, he'd have his revenge on that little piece. Show her where her disregard for rules got her.

'What?' Billy swung listlessly on the chair in the union offices as he tried to understand the latest jute figures. 'What the hell are you doing here, Archie? Thought you'd buggered off to India.'

'I came back.'

'Got your jotters, eh?'

'Some dirty wee whore made a few accusations, and when they investigated it, they found a few matters that weren't quite as they should be.' Archie shrugged. 'Thought it would be better to leave before anything else happened.' He shivered. 'So I see the bitch has got the nomination over you?' He gave a wheezy chuckle.

Billy grunted.

'You know, I was sorry about that brother of yours,' Archie said conversationally. 'And you never really got your chance, did yeh?' He sat down. 'What would you say if I was to help you get your chance?'

'She's a bloody saint in this town,' Billy said lazily. 'Untouchable.'

'Quite the reverse, actually.' Archie grinned, his stained teeth gleaming dirty yellow. 'You'd be amazed at exactly who touched her.'

Billy smiled, his brutish charm washing over him like an overflowing drain.

'Sit down and tell me.'

Once it was over, Billy watched the once proud works manager shuffle away. He was on his last legs; you could smell the scent of death on the man, but Billy didn't care. And he didn't care that Taylor was doing it to revenge himself on the Frasers either. Because he had just given Billy the one thing he needed. A last chance.

'If it's anything to go by, Malise,' Jack said as he arrived on yet another of his flying visits to the party offices, 'you'll be the new Member of Parliament for Dundee in a few weeks' time. That speech you gave last Sunday was a masterpiece.'

'I'm not counting my chickens until they are hatched, Jack. Cup of tea?' As she went into the other room to put the kettle on, Billy walked up to Jack.

'Malise is a fine young woman,' Billy said with unaccustomed quiet. 'And she was a real martyr with that husband of hers. Nursed him for years till he died, sudden like.'

'Yes.' Jack looked at him curiously. 'If you've something to say, Billy, now is the time.'

'You know that son of hers, the Alexander who tragically died? Turns out he's alive and well. Been adopted by Neil Fraser of the Elizabeth, and he's in his last year at the High School Primary. Saw him with my own eyes.'

'Billy,' Jack interrupted. 'That's a serious accusation to make.'

'I have a paper here, that she signed herself, admitting to Neil Fraser fathering her child. This paper was the prime evidence when there was a court case. She signed the child over to Fraser and got a pile of money for herself.'

'I've made everyone tea,' Malise said brightly as she walked back into the room. 'What are you two talking about? You're like a couple of fishwives huddling in that corner.'

'We were just talking about you and Neil Fraser,' Billy stated triumphantly as Malise put down the tray rather quickly.

'What about me and Neil Fraser?' she said.

'That Alexander is living with his father.'

She looked at the men, looked at the disgust on their faces. She had been caught with the one man to whom they could feel superior. Mumbling, she took to her heels and ran, down the slimy dark stairway until she reached the bottom. There she stood, against the tenement wall, taking in vast gulps of dirty, second-hand air, until her breathing began to slow.

'Your coat.' Jack stood there, next to her, holding her

coat and handbag, expensive items, both of them. 'And I think we could both do with some fresh air.' Carefully he wrapped her coat around her then leaned against the wall next to her.

'Well?' he said almost casually. 'Tell me everything.'

And she did. Everything. From the first moment she had set eyes on Neil Fraser to the moment she had walked away. She didn't hide anything, there was no point. She was finished as the candidate, she knew that.

'The weavers of Dundee will look upon you differently – they'll see you as a jute baron's mistress,' he reminded her.

'I know. Who will be the candidate now?' She bit her tongue.

'Who will take your seat, you mean?' He shrugged. 'Billy Turpin, probably.' He lit a cigarette. 'And it's a good thing you've finished your degree now, because you won't be able to work here any more.' He looked at her from the corner of his eye. 'But I think you'd had your fill of it, anyway.'

'I was fifteen years old, Jack,' she said softly. 'And I wasn't married when I gave birth. The paper is a forgery, but Alexander is with his father. Till I can get him back.'

'Malise,' Jack said thickly. 'I know what it's like, to love someone you can't be with.' He stopped for a moment. 'And if I can help in any way, my door is always open.'

'You're a good friend, Jack.' She reached up and kissed him on the cheek. 'But whatever I do, I'll do it myself.'

She returned to work at the practice, but despite working through the purchase of some land for a new factory making jam and marmalade, only one thing was on Malise's mind. Stopping Billy from getting the nomination. At lunch, she decided to go to the Pillars, to see if she could see some of the other party officers, to see if supporting Sime would be worthwhile. She was just walking in when a middle-aged man hailed her.

'Mrs Scott!' It was Neddie Scrymgeour, the blade-thin, maverick firebrand who was standing against her as an independent. 'Surprised to see you. You've fairly set the gossip mongers alight.'

Malise looked at him in amazement.

'I'm not standing any more, they're choosing someone more appropriate,' she said bitterly.

Neddie Scrymgeour laughed.

'Who pulled rank on you, then? Turpin? Always was a bad lot, but you know what they say. Scum rises to the top.'

'Did he force you out too?'

'No, I just didn't want to prostitute my politics any more,' Neddie returned. 'I started off with all these ideals about what a socialist state could be like, but the good intentions became diluted, till the point that I didn't recognize them.'

'Then why do you stand every time?' She leaned back against the wall. 'It isn't as if you'll ever get in.'

'Maybe, but I want to give the voters of Dundee a chance to vote for a socialist who won't do what his party wants him to do, but who will do what his electorate wants him to do.' He smiled gleefully. 'And that's a radical thought for you.' He took out his fob watch. 'Well, I'd better go. Want to catch lunchtime at the shipyard.' He nodded to her and disappeared in his usual rushed fashion. Malise watched him. There was a man who had never lost his principles. Despite being made a fool of. That took courage, courage that she hadn't had. He had courage to stand for what he believed in, and hang the personal cost.

Abandoning her quest, she walked back to the office. To think.

Malise awoke late the next day, to the sound of a thick letter hitting the rug. She got out of bed and picked it up, then opened it. It was formal notification which she had to sign, withdrawing her candidature in the election. And then she had to go to the offices and talk to the new candidate. Sighing, she got dressed and went to the Labour Party offices. Jack and Billy were there, frantically working out what to do.

'It's simple.'

She heard Billy's voice as she walked through the door.

'I'll get the wee whore to introduce me and publicly back me, so that all her followers do too. There's that big meeting on Sunday; it's the last before the polls, so we can do it then.'

As she heard the words, something stiffened inside her. She might have disgraced herself, but there was no way she would let a murderer like Billy Turpin take over the city.

'You're leaving it late, Billy,' Jack replied. 'And please do not refer to Malise in that way.'

'So you've got my leavings?' She leaned against the door jamb. 'And you want me to deliver the women for you, do you?'

'Aye, it's your duty.' Billy glared at her. 'You've let the party down with your shenanigans. Time to make amends.'

Malise laughed.

'Oh Billy, I just warmed his bed.' She walked past. 'Not like I burned down his factory, or anything.' She put her hands on the desk and looked at him. 'How is your brother? In Cardenden, I heard? Which is odd, because I know he is in Balgay cemetery.' She gave a deep sigh. 'Tell you what. You forget about my friends, and I'll forget about yours.'

'What do you mean?' Billy began.

'I don't want any unpleasantness, I have a standing in the town that I don't want damaged. She tossed her head in the direction of Jack. 'Be sure and come on Sunday, then, Jack Buchanan. Watch me hand over Dundee to a man who truly deserves it.'

Malise could feel her tongue sticking to the back of her throat as she stood on the hastily erected stage in Magdalen Green that Sunday morning, the last before the election. Everyone knew that she was out, everyone knew there were rumours, scandalous rumours about her and other men.

But no one knew the truth. This was what it had been like, all those years ago, when she had stood beside Miss Proctor and told her tale of being thrown out of the Elizabeth Works for being a female.

She looked at the candidates. Billy was standing in his good suit, waiting to give a mediocre speech since she had refused to write one for him, and, behind him, was Neddie Scrymgeour.

Malise walked to the front of the stage. She took out her father's whistle and rubbed it for luck, before putting it in her mouth and blowing as hard as she could. Within seconds, it seemed like the whole of the town was watching her. She took a deep breath, and then began.

'Ladies and Gentlemen, I am Malise Scott, and I am no longer able to stand as your Labour Party candidate in the election. But, as a woman who fought for universal suffrage, I realize how important it is that everyone uses their vote. This is why, gentlemen, and ladies in particular, I am standing here before you, not hiding away. Personal reasons have forced me to give up this fight, a fight I would have relished. So I can do no more than tell you that I will be voting for a man who is decent, and who is honest. A man who believes in equality, a man who believes in Dundee, and who is prepared to fight for it. Ladies and gentlemen, I will be voting for a uniquely talented man, and I urge you to do the same.' Her voice grew louder. 'Ladies and gentlemen, I will be voting for Edwin Scrymgeour!'

There was a shocked silence as the people realized she had damned the Labour Party candidate by not endorsing him. Then, as Neddie walked up to the front, the people began to clap, softly at first, then louder, then louder still. Neddie shook Malise by the hand, grinning broadly, before he turned to the crowd as she slipped away.

'How could you?' Billy hissed as she walked past him. 'This is *my* day, and you give it to that man.'

'That man is more honest and courageous than you could ever be, Billy,' she returned. 'And that man will be your

Member of Parliament, thanks to me.' She smiled triumphantly.

'I'll kill you for this,' he spluttered.

'I'm not scared of you, Billy.' She batted away his bad breath. 'Fight this election on your own. Fight it and lose it and then you'll be as finished as I am.' She walked away, carrying on until she was almost under the trees.

There was Jack, she could see him clapping, and he nodded to her.

'Well done, Malise. That took courage, and you'll need to do it every day between now and the election.'

'I know, Jack. But it's for the right cause.' She grinned broadly. 'I'm so glad you aren't unhappy with me. But I couldn't have Billy, and Neddie's a socialist anyway.'

'We all rebel at times,' Jack replied. 'It's your right.' He hesitated. 'But prepare yourself, Billy will probably get in despite even your efforts. Especially since Churchill's in hospital with appendicitis and can't canvass.'

'I know.' She took a deep breath. 'But at least this way I'm doing what I believe in.'

'I have as little appetite for Turpin as you have.' He tucked her arm through his. 'Now, why don't I walk you to the town centre and buy you a cup of tea and you can tell me how you are going to vote for Neddie Scrymgeour, seeing as you're under age?'

For the rest of the week, Malise rushed from one stand to another, drumming up support for the maverick Neddie. But as she did so, she could see the amount of people who were listening to Billy, or people who came up to her and told her they were voting for him. It would be a close-run thing. Jack seemed to have deserted her, another man who couldn't be seen with her in public in case she queered his pitch with the party. She missed his company, realizing how much she had grown to rely on him in the last few years. But at night there was another man on her mind. The way he had been for years.

*

The evening of polling day came at last. Malise stretched her feet – she had worn out her most comfortable pair of shoes walking the length of Dundee for Neddie. Sighing, she kicked off her shoes and put her feet up on a chair. Now there was nothing more she could do.

'Have you heard the news, Malise?' It was Jessie, barging into her house as if she hadn't a care in the world.

'Hello, stranger,' Malise said cheerfully. 'What news?'

'Apparently my brother saw some of the Labour men talking to a group of weavers outside the Claremont. Telling them to vote for Neddie Scrymgeour.'

'But why would they do that?' Malise moved her feet so that Jessie could sit down.

'They said that the vote has been split between Neddie and Billy and in order to get a socialist in, they ought to vote for Neddie. Damn right, too,' she said vehemently. 'And he said that as soon as he got back from the pub, he was going to vote for him. Don't think he realizes that Neddie wants to bring in prohibition!'

Malise laughed as she got up to make them a hot drink.

'D'you remember when we were bairns?' Jessie said as they drank their tea. 'Never thought life would turn out like this!'

'I miss the old days too,' Malise said softly. 'Remember the days when we used to jump off the low roof for a laugh?'

Jessie smiled.

'Now we do it because we have to.' She grasped Malise's hand. 'And we all think you're really brave to do it.'

It was late when Malise arrived outside the town hall and pushed her way inside. She saw Winston Churchill, standing statesmanlike at the side, talking to Richard Fraser. Did he have any idea what would happen, she wondered? He didn't seem unduly perturbed by events. Billy, however, was dancing about, his face hard and stressed. And then she saw Jack – he looked extremely concerned. The mood quietened as the announcement came for the candidates to take the stage, and they did, one at a time, all stern-faced as they waited for the final result.

Malise closed her eyes, her fingers rubbing on her father's little tin whistle.

'And thus I announce that the Member of Parliament for Dundee is Edwin Scrymgeour.'

Malise felt a bolt of triumph course through her. He had done it, she had done it. She had beaten Billy Turpin at his own game. The women of Dundee had spoken.

As Neddie gave his victory speech, she looked at the candidates. Churchill, despite being beaten, was taking it with far more dignity than Billy, who obviously wanted to storm off the stage. Sighing, Malise edged to the side, her fight was over.

She stood through Neddie's victory speech; he didn't mention her, but then again, she didn't want him to. She would go and congratulate him, and see to picking up what was left of her life.

'Don't,' a familiar voice said in her ear. She turned round. It was Jack.

'Don't what?' she returned, rather downheartedly.

'Don't think of what might have been,' he continued. 'Take pride in what you did. It took a great deal of courage to stand against everyone.' Jack shrugged. 'And maybe one day we will be able to rehabilitate you with the party.'

'What would be the point?' she said despondently. 'What is there left for me to do now?'

'You could still fight, as a solicitor.'

'Aye, the union will be beating a path to my door now, won't they? I've just destroyed their chances of getting their man into parliament.'

'Billy Turpin has used up all his lives,' Jack replied. 'You've done us all a favour. He's as finished in politics as . . .'

'As I am?' She looked up.

'Never say never, Malise.' He winked at her.

'You!' Billy Turpin's face was the colour of beetroot as he

strode angrily after her. 'You'll be sorry for this!' He grabbed her arm.

'No, Billy!' Jack shouted, but Billy had already slapped her hard across the face, sending her flying into the wall.

'I knew I should have got rid of you when I had the chance,' Billy shouted as he loomed over her, spitting the words into her face.

'But you couldn't, Billy!' she spat back, blood from her torn lip flying from her mouth. 'You couldn't get rid of the person who could put words into your mouth, thoughts in your head. You don't have the brains to think for yourself and you don't have the bollocks to do your own dirty work. I did it for the likes of Johnnie and the rest of the people you let down.'

'You, Fraser's whore, have the right to take *me* to task?' he snarled. 'You, who, for all your ideals, had warmed the bed of a jute baron!' His voice was cut off as someone hit him square on the chin, sending him sprawling on the ground.

'I presume you mean me, Turpin.' Neil was there, standing over him. 'Now perhaps you would care to repeat what you said. I missed some of it.' He flexed his hand menacingly.

'What did you catch off her, Fraser?' Billy growled as he staggered to his feet. Neil grabbed the man by his lapels and thrust him against the wall.

'Come on, then, Turpin,' Neil Fraser said furiously. 'You want a fight, you fight me.'

Suddenly silence reigned as everyone looked at the man standing over the union leader. Billy clenched his fists, then, as his finely honed instinct for self-preservation took over, he pushed past Neil and walked away.

'Go on, Turpin,' Neil said calmly. 'Give me the excuse I need to knock you into next week.'

'Might have known your fancy man would be rushing to your aid, Mrs Scott,' Billy said venomously. 'After all, his wife's been dead just a few months! All I could expect from someone like you.' He laughed in her face. 'Just think, what would all those working women think, if they only knew you were the mistress of Neil Fraser? Malise Scott, the weaver's champion?' He laughed harshly.

Malise looked at him, what was left of him. At the cheap suit, at the face that was a testament to a lifetime of drinking. At his wife, in her worn coat, at his mother, half dead from a life of never-ending drudgery. What did he have now? Leader of a union with fewer and fewer members, and the losing candidate in an election.

'Enjoyed your speech, Billy,' she said softly. 'Doubt we'll hear another.'

'Get rid of him, please,' Neil ordered the policemen. 'Your lip is bleeding,' he said gently as he took out his handkerchief and wiped away the blood.

Malise saw the looks of the people – they knew. Everyone knew. Everyone knew of her shame, of what she had done. She'd never be able to hold up her head in the city again.

'Why didn't you just put an announcement in the *Courier*?' she said as she pushed past him and ran off into the night, filled with crowds preoccupied with the shocking news that Neddie had actually made it.

'Malise!' Neil ran after her, grabbing her and pulling her round to face him. 'Don't you dare run away from me.'

'You've just confirmed the suspicions of the whole of Dundee,' she said desperately. 'Now I'll for ever be tarred as the woman who was your mistress.'

'Then let me make them forget,' he returned pugnaciously.

'How can you do that? You just publicly defended me in front of Turpin. In front of your friends, half the owners were there.'

'I don't give a damn what they think,' he replied. 'For once in my life I'm doing what I want to do.' He inhaled deeply. 'The only people who will never be able to forget the terrible treatment I have meted out to you are you and I.'

'I don't understand,' she said shakily.

'Marry me. Marry me and then let them talk. What could they say?'

Malise stared at him. Why was he doing this – out of some misplaced sense of honour?

'But your wife—' she began.

'She had a miscarriage and died. I was trying to hide the fact that I loved you. It seemed the most natural way. Unfortunately, it had consequences, and I couldn't divorce her when she was with child.' He took a deep breath. 'I'd even had talks with my solicitor. He'll vouch for me.'

'Why didn't you tell me?' she said in despair. 'I spent so many nights—'

'I wanted to wait till I was free, I couldn't ask you to give up your dreams and risk a public scandal.'

'I think they've got their story. I am now officially your whore.' She looked over at them. 'And anyway, they'll be far too busy with Neddie to bother with us. We're just not important enough.'

Neil put his hand on hers, the fine leather of his gloves shining in the moonlight.

'Then let me make an honest woman of you.' His voice shook as he said it. 'Let me do what I can to make amends.'

Malise gazed at his hands. And said nothing.

'Oh damn!' He ripped off his gloves. 'I'm not asking you because of the way I've treated you, Malise Monroe. I love you, and I want you to be my wife!'

Malise was silent. Then she bit her lip.

'I want to practise law.'

Neil smiled with relief.

'Well, I could hardly see you sitting at home embroidering cushions!' He grinned so hard Malise thought his face would split in two.

'And don't think I'll sit quietly if your father is doing something I don't approve of.'

'You wouldn't be my Malise if you did.' He took her in his arms.

'There you are, Neil,' Richard said as he walked up and glared at his son. 'That bloody MP has just called for the introduction of prohibition!'

'This is all your fault,' Neil said, laughing. 'You'll have to sort him out.'

'Sort out Neddie?' Malise shook her head. 'He dances to his own tune, not mine.'

'Neil!' Richard looked at his son, in a public embrace with a woman. 'You are still in mourning.' He gazed at Malise. 'Shouldn't you be with your communist cronies?'

'Father, Malise has consented to be my wife.' Neil faced his first test. 'I want you to be the first to know.'

'We've talked about this before. She's from the slums!' Richard said incredulously.

'I'm a solicitor, I work for a practice in Union Street. And you're in trade, aren't you?' Malise stared at Richard Fraser as if he were something rather unpleasant.

Neil watched his father. He saw the muscle in his cheek begin to tremble, then he let out a laugh.

'That bloody Monroe girl!' he said with something close to admiration. 'Only you would dare to say such a thing to me.'

'And don't you forget it.'

'My God, we'd better get a drink before Scrymgeour bans it completely, then.' He looked at Malise. Then he raised his arm. 'I don't think he should be walking with you until he is out of mourning, do you?'

Malise looked at Richard Fraser, one of the first sons of the city, offering his arm to her. And she took it.

'My dear Mrs Scott,' he said as he looked into her eyes. 'I know you will be a thorn in my flesh for the rest of my life. But at least you'll be on our side from now on.'

Neil and Malise just looked at each other.

'Of course, Father,' Neil replied. 'Of course. But her name will be Fraser.'

Richard Fraser actually laughed.

'Oh no, Neil,' he said loudly. 'She'll always be that bloody Monroe girl to Dundee.'

'Aye,' Neil said as he squeezed her hand. '*My* Monroe girl.'